SANGRE

Night Rebels Motorcycle Club

CHIAH WILDER

Editing by Lisa Cullian
Cover design by Cheeky Covers
Proofreading by Rose Holub

I love hearing from my readers. You can email me at chiahwilder@gmail.com.

Make sure you sign up for my newsletter so you can keep up with my new releases, special sales, free short stories, and other treats only available to newsletter readers. When you sign up, you will receive a FREE hot and steamy novella. Sign up at: http://eepurl.com/bACCL1.

Visit me on facebook at facebook.com/AuthorChiahWilder

Other Books by Chiah Wilder

Insurgent MC Series:

Hawk's Property

Jax's Dilemma

Chas's Fervor

Axe's Fall

Banger's Ride

Jerry's Passion

Throttle's Seduction

Rock's Redemption

An Insurgent's Wedding

Outlaw Xmas

Insurgents MC Romance Series: Insurgents Motorcycle Club Box Set (Books 1 – 4)

Insurgents MC Romance Series: Insurgents Motorcycle Club Box Set (Books 5 – 8)

Night Rebels MC Series:

STEEL

MUERTO

DIABLO

GOLDIE

PACO

Steamy Contemporary Romance:

My Sexy Boss

Chapter One

MAJOR MELTDOWN! Isla Rose collapses after sold-out show at the Troubadour in West Hollywood.
By Jen Kael, *Hot Radar*

Isla Rose, lead singer for Iris Blue, sang her heart out to a sold-out crowd at the Troubadour last Saturday night and then walked off stage and collapsed. As the crowd clamored and cheered, hoping for an encore, the other members of Iris Blue took the stage again and played two instrumental songs while paramedics rushed the crumpled singer to the nearest hospital.

The fans had no idea what was going on backstage. "I thought it was a little strange that Isla Rose didn't come back onstage with the rest of the band," one fan told *Hot Radar* after the show had ended.

"She gave a damn good performance. I hope she's okay. We love you Isla!" another fan gushed upon learning of the singer's frenzied rush to the hospital.

Isla Rose is the lead singer of Iris Blue—a band whose start began in Los Angeles. Just coming off of a sixteen-state tour with Hinder and Black Stone Cherry, exhaustion was the explanation for Isla Rose's breakdown in a statement given by the band's manager, Kent Sherwood.

Hot Radar has discovered that for several days prior to the show at the Troubadour, the band's drummer, Benz, and Isla Rose have been arguing nonstop. Just last Thursday, patrons at one of the couple's favorite hangouts, Burger Haven, overheard them shouting at each other to the point where Isla Rose jumped up and stormed out of the restaurant.

"Things have been very tense between Isla and Benz," an insider claimed.

Even though Kent Sherwood has downplayed the relationship between them, fans have been capturing pictures of the two kissing, holding hands, or simply embracing one another, then posting them to Instagram. Those who follow the band want nothing more than for Isla Rose and Benz to stay blissfully in love, but from the way things have been going as of late, it doesn't look like this couple is ready for their "happily ever after" any time soon. The question remains as to whether Isla Rose and Benz are, in fact, even still together. Benz, known as a notorious womanizer, seems like a hard man to tame. Could there be another woman behind this couple's trouble?

Since Isla's discharge from the hospital, Kent Sherwood has released a statement announcing that the band is taking a well-deserved break to record and get some much-needed rest. Iris Blue has been performing and touring nonstop for the past three years. No one's talking on where the band has gone to record or relax. Why is this such a secret?

Stay tuned as *Hot Radar* continues reporting on this story.

Sangre skimmed the six-month-old article again then looked at the photo of Iris Blue he had in the file. His gaze drifted to the woman in the middle surrounded by four men. She wore tight leather pants, a crop top, and a ton of makeup painted on her face. *What the hell did I get myself into? She looks like a fucking diva.*

"Having second thoughts?" Eagle asked as he sank into the chair in front of Sangre's desk.

Sangre ran his hands through his thick blond hair. "Yeah. I mean, the chick has high maintenance written all over her." He slid the photo toward Eagle, who picked it up and stared at it.

"She's hot," Eagle said.

"And I'm sure a major pain in the ass. What the hell do *we* know about rock stars?"

"That they have a lot of money. I can't believe how much the band's paying for this gig."

"I think it's Isla Rose who's shelling out the dough." He glanced at the article again. "Seems like she's got some emotional stuff going on with one of the dudes in the band."

"I'd think that's reasonably common when you're together so much. This should be a pretty easy gig. We just need to watch her until they go back to LA." Eagle leaned back into the chair, then he added, "Jon's a big fan of the band, so he's looking forward to it. I've never heard of them though, have you?"

He shook his head. "Nah, but then I don't do Instagram or Facebook or any of that other social media bullshit. Seems like that's how they got their start, and it's just been growing." He glanced down at the contract again: Bodyguard services needed while Isla Rose was in Alina.

Sangre had opened Precision Security over a year ago, bringing Eagle and Cueball into his company: Eagle as manager and Cueball as security supervisor. Since opening the business, he was busy as hell, providing security for businesses, parties, rallies, festivals, and concerts around the county. Normally, he passed on bodyguard services because they were rather time-consuming and spread out his employees too thin. He also had to balance his time overseeing Precision Security with his duties to the Night Rebels. As a club officer, he had certain responsibilities, and like every member, he was required to be available at all times. But Eagle was right about the money—it was damn good, so he'd taken the bodyguard gig while the singer was in town.

"Do you think she's in danger?" Eagle asked, crossing his legs, ankle over knee.

Sangre shook his head and tipped his chair back against the wall. "I think the whole 'crazed fan' scare is a ploy to garner more attention. These musicians, actors, and anyone else in the spotlight crave the attention and seemingly need to constantly be in the papers." He held his hands up. "But I'm not here to fuckin' analyze her. Like you said, the money's good, so we'll play bodyguard until she goes back to LA."

"Let me see the copies of the letters." After Sangre pushed the file toward him, Eagle opened it, pulled out some of the papers, and started scanning over them. "From the looks of it, I'd say they're becoming more obsessed and in a dangerous way." He scrubbed his face. "And they just started when the band got here a couple of weeks ago?"

"Seems that way. At least that's what their manager's saying, but I'm still thinking it's probably a publicity stunt. The diva got here about four or five months ago, and yeah, the rest of the band didn't come here until about two weeks ago."

"The postmarks are from Tula, Silverado, Durango, Cortez, and Alina."

"Yeah, I noticed that, but it's not hard to do. Those places aren't that far apart."

Eagle nodded. "True, but it could be legit." He pushed the file back toward Sangre.

"We'll find out soon enough. We'll give it our all and work it like Jack the fucking Ripper is after this chick."

Eagle grinned. "By the way, Army's offered help if we need it."

"I'm sure he did. He's been wanting to be a rock star for a long time." The men laughed. "Brutus and Skull are down too. We may have to use them because I don't wanna spread the guards out too thin on this gig. We need to be taking care of several other contracts too; she's not the only one."

"I'm working on that. I just hired the three guys you approved the other day. That should help. When do we start the babysitting?"

Sangre chuckled. "Tomorrow. The band has a show at Trailside tonight, so I'm gonna head over there and check them out. Do you wanna come?"

"I'll think about it. Why the hell are they playing if she's so scared?"

"Exactly. Maybe she knows she's not really in danger." A knock on the door stopped their conversation. "Come in."

A guy in his early twenties opened the door. His brown eyes darted between Sangre and Eagle. With shoulders slumped and a tentative look crossing his face, the young man stepped inside the room.

"What can I do for you, Jon?" Sangre asked. Jon was the son of one of his dad's friends who worked with him at Reland's Candies. Sangre hired him as a favor to his dad. One of the main problems with Jon was that he was timid around people, so he usually put the young guard on graveyard shifts or at posts where there wasn't any interaction with the public.

"I was just wondering if you need me to work the new gig." The guard lowered his eyes.

"The new gig?" Sangre said.

Redness crept over Jon's cheeks. "The Iris Blue one." He crossed his arms and leaned against the door frame.

"I haven't done the scheduling for the job yet. Eagle, Cueball, and I will handle the first few days until I assess the situation. I may need you to do a couple shifts, so I'll let you know." Sangre put his hands behind his head and smiled. "Eagle told me you're a fan of the band."

Jon bobbed his head. "Oh yeah, I love their music … they're awesome. Isla Rose is one of the best vocalists. She can do rock and blues like no one else. I've been following them on Instagram for the last few years. It's hard to believe they're in Alina. Man, I can't wait to check out their show tonight. I never thought I'd see them live."

Sangre ran his eyes over the guard. The way he gushed and rambled on meant he'd be ineffective for the job. He needed men who didn't give a shit who this Rose chick was or what band she was in. He couldn't tie up Eagle and Cueball with this twenty-four seven gig in case they were needed at the club, so he was dreading having to put some long hours in watching a woman who was probably making up the whole thing.

"I'd be honored to protect Isla Rose. I can't imagine anyone wanting to harm her. I'll make sure she's safe." Jon narrowed his eyes, and Sangre saw his body stiffen.

"I'll let you know. Anything else on your mind?"

Shaking his head, he stepped back. "I just wanted you to know I'm here to help any way I can."

"Good to know. Thanks, Jon. I'll probably see you at Trailside later on. I'm going to check out the band too. Close the door on your way out." Jon turned around and pulled the door shut behind him. Sangre breathed out through his mouth. "He's definitely not gonna help out with this job unless we're totally desperate."

Eagle laughed. "I'd say he's a rabid fan. I've decided I'll join you tonight to see what all the fuss is about. I love hard rock and the blues. Maybe they'll kick ass like AC/DC." Eagle stood up and jerked his head back. "What? Stop looking at me like that."

Fixing his gaze on Eagle, Sangre shook his head slightly. "To even hint that this chick and her band could remotely come close to AC/DC is fuckin' blasphemy."

"I'm not saying they are, I just meant they may give a good show. All right, I'm gonna check to make sure everyone's going to be where they need to be, then I'll see you at the clubhouse."

"Is Manuel handling the phones tonight?" Sangre asked, pushing his chair back and rising to his feet.

"Yup. If anything's fucked up, he'll call you. Later, bro." Eagle left the room.

Sangre grabbed Iris Blue's folder off the desk and placed it in the file cabinet, then grabbed his keys and headed out to the parking lot. Minutes later, he was speeding down the open road in the direction of the clubhouse. Like the majority of the single members, Sangre lived at the club. He had a room on the second floor since he was an officer; he'd been treasurer for the past four years, and he took his position very seriously. The previous treasurer, Rooster, practically had the club in bankruptcy, and it took a lot of effort and tightening of the reins to bring it back around. Because of his efforts, the Night Rebels MC had a strong cash flow, and Steel had been talking to him about opening another business in addition to their other dealings: Lust Strip Bar, Skid Marks Bike and Auto Shop, Get Inked Tattoo Shop, Balls and Holes Pool Hall, and New Leaf Dispensary.

The new prospect, Ink, opened the iron gates, and Sangre rode into the parking lot and parked his Harley. The savory and sweet aroma of hickory and apple wood, coupled with the piquant scent of chili pepper and smoky cumin, wafted around him when he entered the main room. He saw Army and Skull sitting at one of the tables with plates of ribs, mashed potatoes, and coleslaw in front of them. He went over to the table, pulled out a chair, and sat down, stretching his long legs in front of him.

"Hey, how's it going?" Sangre asked, glancing at their plates.

"Not bad. The ribs fuckin' rock." Army picked one up and bit into it, barbecue sauce slipping down his chin. Grabbing a napkin, he wiped his mouth. "Did you start the gig with that rock star chick?"

Sangre picked up the bottle of beer one of the prospects put in front of him. "Not yet." He took a long pull. "I'm going to check out the band tonight. You interested in meeting me at Trailside?"

"Hell yeah. What time are you gonna be there?" Army picked up another rib.

"Around nine."

"Sounds good."

"Count me in too. I haven't been to Trailside in a long time," Skull said. "My kid sister will kill me if I don't take her. She's in love with the guitarist in Iris Blue."

"I never heard of the band until their manager contacted me. I'm curious to see what all the fuss is about." Sangre jerked his chin at the prospect when he set a plate of ribs and all the fixings in front of him.

"How's their music?"

Skull gave a half shrug. "I never heard them. I just know about 'em because my sister won't shut the hell up about the damn guitarist. She'll probably want her best friend to come too."

"Anthony's cool. I know him real well, so he'll let them in. He'll just mark them so they can't booze it up." Army pushed his empty plate away from him. "Do you wanna ride over?" he asked Sangre.

"I can't. I'm going over to Skylar's first."

"Is she coming?" Skull put a toothpick in his mouth.

"Nope. I'm going over to talk with her."

Army guffawed and turned around toward the bar. "Brutus, Shotgun, Jigger, Chains—get over here. I'm ready to win some money." The four men sauntered over.

"What the hell are you talking about?" Sangre asked.

"What are you going to talk to Skylar about?" Army gave a lopsided grin.

Anger pricked his skin, and he wanted nothing more than to smack that infuriating look off Army's face. "How in the fuck is it your business?"

"Just answer the question." Army folded his arms and tipped his chair back.

Sangre pulled his leg in to avoid the temptation of kicking over the chair. "I have something I need to tell her."

"Like you're crazy in love with her?" Brutus said. The men laughed.

"Or you want to move in with her?" Chains added, winking at the other guys.

"Or—"

"Just shut the fuck up," Sangre gritted to Skull. "I'm breaking up with her, that's all. End of fuckin' story."

Army leapt out of the chair, his fist punching the air. "Yes! It's only been three months." He looked at each of the men crowded around the table. "Pay up." Laughing, he extended his hand.

"Fuck," Brutus muttered. "I thought you'd make it at least five months with this one."

Sangre watched as his brothers took out their wallets and turned over their money to Army. "You fuckin' bet on how long Skylar and I were gonna be together?"

"That's right, brother. You're making me a rich man with all your chicks." Army shoved the money in his pocket.

"I thought for sure you were gonna last four months. That's what I betted on," Chains said, picking up his beer.

"I can't believe you assholes are betting on this. At least I have relationships, not like you losers." The men burst out laughing, and Sangre pushed away from the table, knocking over a few beer bottles as he rose to his feet. "Fuck this." He walked away, his fists clenching at the sound of the loud guffaws behind him. Taking the steps two at a time, he arrived at his room in no time.

As he changed his clothes, he thought of Skylar and how he hated going over and breaking it off with her. He couldn't explain why he didn't want to see her anymore. Compared to all the other women he'd been involved with, she was, by far, one of the best girlfriends as of yet: She didn't nag him, liked her independence, was damn hot in bed, and mostly went along with what he wanted. *Then why the hell am I breaking up with her?* He couldn't say. He went over to the window and looked out at the San Juan Mountains silhouetted against the darkening sky. Running a hand through his hair, he leaned against the windowsill. *Fuck. It's always the same damn thing.*

He'd been through the upcoming scenario more times than he could remember, and it was always different forms of "I think we should see other people" or "It's not you, it's me." Shaking his head, he laughed dryly. The truth was—it usually *was* him and not the woman. The women he picked tended to be variations of the same model: pretty, smart, interested in motorcycles—or at least pretended to be, not clingy, understood the camaraderie with his brothers, and willing to have fun in bed. Sex was very important to him, but having a woman who respected his space and didn't try to change him was high on the list as well. Skylar checked all the boxes, yet he was going over to tell her they were done. He supposed she broke the one thing he didn't want from any of the women he'd dated: getting too serious about him.

When they went out to dinner a few nights before, he could see the look in her eyes, the way she gripped his arm and clung to him. It was the small things that night, that told him she'd taken what they had to a new level, and he knew he had to bail out. The way he figured it, he was doing her and all the other women a favor. If he ended it early enough, they wouldn't become that attached or hurt. Most of his relationships lasted three or four months, and a few times they'd go on for five or six months. It wasn't like he planned on ending them, they just always did. When he looked at his brother and sisters, who'd been married for years and had kids, he wondered why he couldn't be more like them. The reality was that he'd never been in love. After all the women he'd dated, the club girls he fucked, and the one-night stands he occasionally had between relationships, he'd never felt anything more than desire and lust. Sangre liked and respected the women he went out with, but the love thing just never happened. So, after a certain point—if what they had wasn't going anywhere—that'd be when he took a hike. *Yeah … it's definitely me and not them.* He pushed away from the window, picked up his keys, and headed out.

Two hours later he sat at the Trailside bar, a double shot of Jack in his hand and images of tears streaming down Skylar's anguished face flitting across his mind. Each time he went through one of those scenes, he swore it would be the last, and then he'd find another woman and have some hope, but it always ended the same. It was like his love life was on a never-ending reel of the same story.

"So how'd it go?" Chains asked, sidling up to him.

Sangre slammed the drink back then shrugged. "Okay, I guess." He motioned the bartender for another.

"It sucks, dude. That's why I prefer going with the club women. They know the score, we have fun, and no one gets hurt. It's a definite win-win."

"Yeah. Did you come with Army and Brutus?"

Chains picked up his beer bottle. "Just Army. Brutus was occupied with Ruby."

Sangre chuckled. "The band that's on now isn't bad. I've seen them before at Lion's Lair. They're local."

"I've seen them too. The drummer's the cousin of one of my friends. When does your band get on?"

"After this one."

"Did I miss anything?" Army said, squeezing between Chains and Sangre.

"Nope." Sangre scooted the barstool down a bit.

"Hey, dudes," Skull said as he came toward the trio, two teenage girls straggling behind him.

"This is so cool," the dark-haired girl said, snapping pictures with her phone.

"Go sit over there." Skull pointed to a table not too far from the bar.

"Aren't you going to introduce me to your friends?" she asked, her eyes scanning over Sangre's face.

"Guys, this is my sister, Ella, and her friend, Zoe. Now both of you go sit at the table. I'll bring you a couple of Cokes."

Ella came closer to Sangre and pointed at his arms. "Cool tats."

"Thanks." He brought the shot glass to his lips.

"Who's the one guarding Isla Rose?" she asked.

"Ella. Go over and sit down," Skull said, giving her a little push.

"My company's been hired to make sure she's safe. I heard you're a fan of the band," Sangre said.

"I love, love, LOVE them!"

"Me too," Zoe chirpped in, her curly hair bouncing around her shoulders as she moved in closer to Sangre.

"That's cool. They're coming on next," he said.

"They're headlining." Ella looked over her shoulder at the stage. "Have you met Arsen yet?" Her brown eyes widened.

"I haven't met any of them yet. I'm just checking out the music."

And seeing if anyone is acting weird or suspicious in the crowd.

"He's the lead guitarist, and he's so good. Way better than anyone out there."

"For sure," Zoe agreed.

"Better than Tony Iommi?" Sangre asked, a smile twitching on his lips.

"Who?" Ella asked.

"Is he in a local band?" Zoe said.

"Not only is he the Black Sabbath riff lord, he's the founder of metal music." Sangre turned to Skull. "How the fuck does your sister not know this?"

He held his hands up in front of him, laughing. "Don't blame me. I've been on my own since I was eighteen. My mom's favorite singer is Madonna. What can I say?" Sangre, Army, and Chains busted out laughing.

"Do you think you can introduce me—"

"Us," Zoe chimed in.

Ella nodded. "*Us* to Arsen or Isla Rose?"

"Enough. I told you guys to go sit over there. Now go. We got shit to talk about." Skull walked over to the table carrying two tall glasses in his hands.

"Please?" Ella whispered, her eyes darting from Sangre to Skull then back to Sangre.

"Sure. Why not? I'll let you know when I can arrange it."

Ella and Zoe squealed and grabbed each other's arms as they jumped in place. "That'd be so cool. Thanks!"

"Yeah, thanks," Zoe said as Ella tugged her toward the table.

Sangre chuckled and gestured the bartender for another shot.

"Thanks for making my sister and her goofy friend happy," Skull said, leaning against the bar. Sangre lifted his chin and picked up his drink.

After the local band finished their set, excited chatter filled the room. He watched as roadies made sure the equipment was in the right places, and then people started filling in the area in front of the stage, their faces bathed in strained anticipation.

A lanky man in long hair, jeans, and an AC/DC T-shirt grabbed the microphone and asked if everyone was having "a good fucking time." The crowd cheered, whistled, and clapped. He paused dramatically then stretched out his arm. "Let's give a big fucking hand to *IRIS BLUE!*" The crowd erupted, and Sangre saw Ella and Zoe right in front, pressing against the stage. The lights went off and a lone riff echoed through the venue, and then red, blue, and yellow lights flashed, revealing the band. The crowd went wild.

Sangre saw the back of a woman, who was bent over, microphone in hand, slowly straighten up while holding a note so strong and pure a hush fell over the audience. Then the lead and rhythm guitarists began playing, and she spun around, her long dark hair moving with her. Blue and red lights bounced off of her black sequined jeans as she swayed her hips in perfect rhythm to the beat of the song. He watched her, mesmerized by her movement and confidence. And then she sang. The sound of her voice was thick and sweet like warm honey dripping over him. It was intoxicating, and it captivated him completely. He couldn't turn away from her, even when Army handed him a drink. It was like she was pulling him in, and her voice was the magnet.

Damn. In that moment, he realized this wasn't going to be any ordinary job. There was something exhilarating, mysterious, sensuous, and … familiar about her. It was like he knew her, but he didn't.

All that in a matter of minutes.

Fuck.

Chapter Two

THERE WERE AT least four hundred people watching Isla Rose, bathed in blue and red lights, as she clutched the microphone and closed her eyes. Nerves were trying to take over her body, but instead, she focused on Arsen's killer riffs, her heart keeping time with Benz's drumming while she slowly lost herself in the music, in the performance.

It'd been almost seven months since Iris Blue performed live. The effervescence emanating from the fans breathed life into her; it was like liquid energy seeping right through her skin. *I fucking miss this!* Music pumped through her veins, and she dug deep down inside herself, seeking out the raw emotions needed for the song. The audience went wild. Their cheers, whistles, and screams were nourishment for not only her, but the other band members as well. She knew they'd missed performing just as much as she did. If she could only freeze-frame the enthusiasm, the love, the adulation during a performance, and live in it forever, her life would be perfect. For her, music was life and life was music, but it was all the other noise around her that played havoc with her nerves, her emotions—her soul.

Then Arsen was next to her, his fingers flying as he played scorching riffs and licks. Sweat streamed down his face as strands of his black, shaggy hair stuck to his forehead. The rhythm guitarist rushed over, and the two musicians made their instruments scream as they moved in perfect sync to the rhythm. Gage's long brown hair flew around as he head-banged to Benz's expert drumming. As Isla ramped her vocals up to blistering, the guitars blazed with fiery incandescence. Iris Blue was on fire, and Isla lost all sense of everything except for the music.

Two hours and three encores later, they stood together on the stage, arms linking around each other's shoulders like a chain, as they absorbed the tsunami of applause rolling forward. As Isla raised her head, the spotlights' bright glare blinded her. Breaking away from her bandmates, she placed her microphone on the stand then brought her hands together and bowed her head slightly. "Thank you all. You're the best," she breathed.

The stage went dark, and then the overhead lights came on as roadies scampered behind her, clearing off the equipment. She started to walk away when a female voice cried out, "We love you, Isla Rose. We love Iris Blue!" She turned around and saw two teenage girls pressed against the stage waving a CD at her.

"Do you have a pen?" she asked Benz as he stood at the back of the stage waiting for her.

"You don't want to start autographing shit. We'll be here all night."

"I didn't ask for your opinion, only a pen. Do you have one?"

He slowly walked over to her, the frown on his forehead deepening as several women squealed and clapped the closer he came to the front of the stage. "Here," he gritted as he shoved a pen in her hand.

"You should sign the CD as well." She smiled at the girls.

"Fuck that," he whispered in her ear, waved at the dying crowd, and walked away.

He can be such a jerk! "What's your name?" she asked one of the girls.

"Ella. I love your music so much. Arsen is the best guitarist ever. Is he still in the building?"

"I'm not sure." *He's probably got his tongue halfway down the mouth of the stacked redhead who was ogling him during the show.* She'd seen Kent, their manager, approach the woman before the end of their last song, and then she saw her walk with him through the crowd. "And what's your name?" she asked the other girl.

"Zoe. I love all of you. Are you dating Benz?"

"Zoe!" Ella elbowed her side.

"What?" Zoe rubbed her ribs.

Isla shook her head. "It's okay. The gossip rags love to talk about us.

We're just very close friends."

"I think it's so cool that you're from Alina," Ella's voice burst with excitement as she looked at the signed CD.

"I have good memories from growing up here. We'll probably do another show in town, so if you come, make sure you bring the CD, and I'll have the rest of the band sign it."

"Arsen too?" Isla nodded. A wide grin spread over Ella's face. "You're the best. That would be cool AF."

"If I bring my CD, will you all sign it too?" Zoe asked.

"Sure. I better get going. I hope to see you at the next show." She stepped back and turned to her right, and that's when she saw him standing to the side of the stage, a bottle of beer in his hand. Mysterious. Masculine. Sexual. A modern-day James Dean dressed in tight jeans, a leather vest over a black T-shirt, and arms covered in tattoos. Dark-blond stubble shaded his chiseled jawline, and a silver eyebrow ring glimmered over a rounded brow. He lifted the bottle to his full lips and drank. The movement mesmerized her. *Damn, he's hot.* He fixed his dazzling blue eyes on her, and she was breathless for a moment, unable to turn away from the intensity of his stare.

She should leave, go to the green room and pack up her things, but she couldn't move; she was rooted to that one spot, watching him as static charges jumped through her body. *What the hell's the matter with me?* It was insane, but this guy was putting her emotions in a twist. Enigmatic, rough around the edges, and hotter than hell, he was the type of man who would pull a woman in tight and most definitely end up breaking her heart. *No fucking doubt about that.*

"Isla?" Benz came over and grasped her elbow. "What the hell are you still doing out here?"

With her gaze still locked on the gorgeous man, she let Benz tug her to him, her back molding against his chest. Muscles deep inside her tightened as the sexy stranger leaned back on his boots, lit up a joint, and winked.

"Let's go," Benz said in her ear while he whirled her toward him then curled his arm around her shoulder.

Letting him lead her, she felt the hunk's stare boring into her back. Before she stepped behind the curtain, she glanced behind her and caught his penetrating gaze as heat burned between her legs. Benz pulled her backstage, ending the most intense and short-lived moment she'd ever shared with a stranger.

"That was a fucking great show," Benz said, wrapping both arms around her waist. "We need to get back on the circuit real fast. Rough Creek Records still wants us to sign on with them. I don't want to blow the chance to get with a label."

Rough Creek Records had been wooing them ever since the record company's rep had seen Iris Blue perform at the Ohana Festival in Dana Point, California, seven months before. The band had been more than excited, and then she'd crashed. "A breakdown from nerves and exhaustion," her doctor had said. Even though her bandmates hadn't said much, she'd sensed their disappointment, anger, and frustration bubbling beneath the surface. It was a huge compliment that the record label was still interested in them after so many months of non-performance and her publicized meltdown. Now, the last thing she wanted was to fuck up an opportunity to sign on with them.

"I don't want to miss the chance either. We're almost done recording, and I'm sure Rough Creek will be happy with our new album. I think it's our best one yet." Isla pulled away from Benz.

For a split second, his gaze flashed with anger then dissipated so quickly that she thought she might have imagined it. "I agree. I told the rep we'd be done with it in a month or less. You know, we need to get back on the road after that. If we sign with them, we'll be touring most of the year."

Panic tangled around her nerves. "I know," she said softly. "I just wish I'd stop getting those damn letters."

Benz came over and tugged her to him, holding her close. "That's why we need to blow this fucking town. You didn't have any of this shit before you got here. I told you I didn't trust small towns. There's a reason why most horror movies are set in them. And there's not a damn thing to do around here. How the fuck did you survive living here as long as you did?" He tilted her head back and leaned in, his gaze fixed on her mouth. She turned and pushed away from him. A frustrated sigh escaped his lips as he planted his fists on his hips and watched her, his brown eyes sparking. "What the fuck's your problem?"

"I'm just tired." An awkward pause ensued as Isla picked at the dry skin around her thumb, and Benz shifted from one foot to the other. She cleared her throat, crossing her arms over her chest. "It was great performing tonight."

"It kicked ass! It felt fucking awesome to be back on stage," Gage said, coming up to them.

Warmth spread through Isla. She loved how upbeat Gage was all the time—a direct opposite to Benz's brooding moods, Arsen's childish tantrums, and Jac's one-word conversations. The band had lucked out when Gage answered the ad they'd placed for a rhythm guitarist the year before. At twenty-four, he was the youngest member, but he acted more mature than the other three guys combined.

Relieved to have Gage as a buffer to soften the unspoken tension between herself and Benz, she laughed softly. "I can always count on your energy. Is Melody able to come for a visit next week? I know how bummed you were that she couldn't be here tonight."

Melody was Gage's girlfriend, and she'd moved to LA from Ames, Iowa, when Gage had joined the band. They'd known each other since high school. Isla loved seeing them together even though Benz thought they were "fucking nauseating," and Arsen couldn't comprehend "why a dude would want to settle for only one chick when there were so many who wanted to fuck a rock star." A part of her envied the love and connection Gage and Melody shared, wondering how it must feel. It was something that hadn't happened to her yet—falling in love—and she'd begun to give up hope it ever would.

"Yep. She's coming out next weekend. I told her I'd take a day off recording to hang with her. You guys are cool with that, right?"

Isla nodded at the same time Benz grunted and shook his head. "We're here to finish a fucking album. The band comes first, dude."

"One day isn't going to set us back," she said. Benz threw her a scathing look then took out a cigarette and lit it. She ignored him, knowing she'd overstepped an invisible line he'd drawn between him and the other band members whenever any of them contradicted him. Benz was super protective of Iris Blue since he'd started it right out of high school. The only one who could get away with arguing with him was Arsen; he'd been with Benz since the beginning.

Shoulders slumping, Gage quirked his lips. "I guess Melody can hang with us at the studio."

Isla gripped Gage's shoulder and took a deep breath, letting it out slowly. "Take the day off. We'll make it work." She met Benz's hard look without flinching. "I'm going to make sure the roadies got my microphone."

"They get fucking paid to make sure things are right." Benz blew a puff of smoke at her then smirked.

Real mature, asshole. "Yeah, well, we know that it doesn't always work that way. How many mikes have I lost? I'm not taking the chance on this one. I love it." Without waiting for his reply, she whirled around and walked to the stairs.

The first thing she did when she got on stage was look to the side, hoping the sexy guy would still be there. Disappointment wove through her when she realized that he wasn't. *Did you really think he'd be hanging around like a damn groupie? Anyway, so what if he's not here. Just because he's the hottest guy you've seen in a—*

"Good show," a voice said behind her.

She spun around and her gaze fell on *him*—with his masculine, square chin and eyes that burned as blue as the hottest part of a flame. His gaze raked over her body slowly, taking in every detail of her appearance before returning to her face. Suddenly, she was aware of herself in the most nerve-wracking way: tongue-tied and feeling like an idiot. Then he hopped up on stage and her mind went blank.

Standing close to her, he looked at her intently. "You really rocked it." His voice, low and gravelly, stroked her senses like velvet.

Say something! "Thanks. I just came out to check on my microphone. I wanted to make sure the roadies packed it. It's my favorite one, and I don't want to lose it. You'd be surprised on how often equipment gets overlooked. I've had that happen a few times with the microphone. It's my instrument, you know." *Stop rambling. Fuck.* She watched as he bit back a smile. She willed her breathing to slow down.

"Is that the only reason you came back out?" He leaned in closer.

"Yeah," she managed, breathless and blushing. "Why else?"

A sly smirk ghosted his face. "Well … you were checking me out after the show."

As he looked at her with a mischievous twinkle in his gaze, she sucked in her breath, crossed her arms, and took several steps away from him. In less time than it took her to exhale, her nervousness lifted. His cocky tone and easy manner pissed her off. *He thinks this is an amusing game. Asshole!* She tilted her head sideways. "As I remember it, *you* were the one checking *me* out.

"So, you did notice me." His smoldering eyes burned right through her, sending a wave of prickling heat along her limbs.

When she stepped farther away from him, it felt like he was undressing her in an appreciative yet animalistic way; his intense gaze left trails of burning embers across her skin. Pressing a hand against her chest, she tried to calm her pounding heart. Before she could reply, a tall, buffed guy with short hair walked toward the stage.

"Yo, Sangre!" he yelled.

The stranger turned around and jerked his chin up. "What's up?"

"Chains wants to know if you wanna go to Leroy's and get some food."

"Is Skull coming?"

"He's meeting us there. He left to drop off his kid sister and her friend at his mom's. Eagle's gonna join us too. You in?" His dark eyes skimmed over her quickly then flitted back to Sangre's. "Or do you have other plans?" Sangre laughed and glanced at her.

"In your fucking dreams," she said.

"Excuse me. Miss Isla Rose?" a timid voice said to the right of her.

She looked over and saw a lanky guy in his early twenties standing by the platform, staring everywhere but at her as he kept clearing his throat. For a split second, she wondered if this guy was the one who'd been sending her the love-obsessed fan letters. Something about him gave her the creeps, but she smiled and nodded. "That's me. Can I help you?"

"What the fuck, Jon?" Sangre said.

Turning slightly toward him, she relaxed a bit. "He's with you?"

"He works for me." Sangre went over to the edge of the stage, his muscular arm brushing against her as he walked past. "What gives?"

Jon grabbed the back of his neck with his hand and rubbed it over and over as he looked down on the ground. "I just wanted to see if I could get an autograph or something."

Sangre laughed. "That's right, you're a fan." He looked over his shoulder at her. "This dude loves your band, and he's crazy about you. Why don't you give him an autograph?"

"I didn't realize you moonlight as a PR man." She rolled her eyes then focused on the young man who acted like he was going to crumple down in a heap at any minute. "Did you bring a CD or something?" she said softly.

Bringing his hand to his pocket, he took out a cassette. "I brought this." He chewed his bottom lip.

She laughed, and it resounded through the nearly empty bar. "Excellent. I think you're one of the ten people who actually bought one of our cassettes. I was the one who wanted to make cassettes even though the other members tried to talk me out of it. You just made my night." Jon's face turned a deep red as she took it from his hand. "I wish the others were here so they could sign it too."

Crossing and uncrossing his arms, he fidgeted in place. "I don't care about the others. You're the only one who matters in the band," he said in a voice so low that she had to strain her ears to hear him.

"Don't let the others hear you say that." She whipped out a pen and signed her name. "But you're too sweet." Smiling, she handed the cassette back to him.

"Thank you. I'll always cherish this." He glanced briefly at her then averted his gaze elsewhere.

A single shiver rode up her spine. *I shouldn't be out here like this. How do I know if any one of these guys is the nut who's making me a nervous wreck?* She took a few steps backward and bumped into a wall of hardness. Looking behind her, she jumped away from Sangre's muscled body. "Oh ... sorry."

"No need to apologize. I didn't mind." He winked at her and she groaned inwardly. Jon still stood there staring at the signed cassette in his hands.

"Did you find your mike?" Benz asked, staring at Sangre. He came over and slinked his arm around her waist, yanking her close to him.

"No. I guess the roadies did their job. I was just signing autographs."

"I was getting worried about you. We're all packed up. Let's head out. The guys want some food. Is anything open at this hour in this godforsaken town?"

"Leroy's," Sangre said as she opened her mouth to reply. "It's a diner off of Ashwood and Cedar.

"Which reminds me. You never said if you wanted to join Skull, Eagle, Chains, and me." The tatted guy leaned against one of the freshly wiped tables.

"Yeah. I'm going." Sangre jumped off the stage, threw a lazy smile at her, and swaggered away. "Jon, stop gawking and get your ass over here." The young man shoved the cassette in his pocket and hurried to catch up with the two men as they walked out the door.

"He's got some attitude," Benz said, placing a kiss on the side of her mouth. "Did he come on to you?"

"We were just talking. I really don't want to go to Leroy's."

Benz narrowed his eyes. "Why? Because he's going to be there?"

She moved away from him. "No … because I'm tired, and I'm not hungry. You guys can drop me off at my place first."

Benz clenched his jaw as his brown eyes glinted in anger while he stood watching Isla. Not letting him intimidate her, she headed down the stairs and saw her other bandmates smoking pot as they sat on folding chairs.

"We're fucking starving," Jac said, his fingers curled around the neck of his bass guitar.

"Leroy's is a diner not too far from here, but I'm exhausted, so take me home first."

"That's cool," Gage said, and Arsen bobbed his head.

"Where's your redhead?" Isla asked.

"I finished with her," Arsen replied.

"She didn't even merit a bite to eat?" Gage said.

"I don't like eating with chicks I don't know. What the hell is there to talk about?" Arsen stood up. "Does this diner have good food?"

"It used to when I lived here. I'm sure it's still owned by the same people."

"Sure you don't wanna go?" Jac said.

"She said she didn't, so who the fuck cares? It's … whatever." Benz stormed past them and went out back to the alley.

"Why's he in such a dour mood?" Gage asked.

Isla shrugged. "Who knows? I'm too tired to care."

"Let's head out," Arsen said.

The rest of the band followed him out, and Isla noticed how Benz sat hunched in the front seat, staring straight ahead. They all piled into the van, which was a tight squeeze since it also held their equipment.

Twenty minutes later, she waved at them as Gage pulled away from the curb. During the drive, Benz didn't speak or look at her once, and that suited her just fine. She was so sorry that she'd allowed herself to get sexually and emotionally involved with him after a couple of years of vowing that she'd never give in to his advances.

Isla closed and locked the door then headed upstairs. Beyond tired, she was tempted to just peel off her clothes and fall into bed without taking off her makeup. Not wanting to wake up with a peppering of zits on her face, she shuffled to the bathroom and turned on the faucet.

After smoothing moisturizer on her face, she padded over to her bed, pulled back the covers, and slipped in. Her head sank into the fluffy pillow, and she reached over and turned off the small lamp on her nightstand. Sangre's face popped into her mind. *I've never heard that name before.* The man acted like some alpha asshole, but she had to admit that sex oozed out of all his pores. There was something brutish and exciting about him.

She turned on her side. *I have to stop thinking about him.* The band had to be at the studio early the following morning, and then Isla needed to meet with the security company in the afternoon. *I probably won't see him again. In another couple of months or so, we'll be headed back to LA.* Her stomach lurched with that thought. *What if I'm not ready?* The past year, she'd been run down by constant touring, the stress of dating Benz, the pressure of being in the spotlight, and the extra anxiety of being scrutinized every second because she was a woman. There never was a damn tweet about any of the guys either gaining an ounce of weight or eating a large bag of fries or not being tanned enough. They could do as they pleased and wear what they wanted without any repercussions, but it wasn't so for her: Isla was constantly being watched.

Isla began to pant as blood rushed through her ears; she sat upright and instantly felt a clammy sweat coating her face and back. *Dammit! I have to get a fucking grip. I love performing. I love singing. Why can't I just chill?*

Switching the lamp on, she reached for the bottle of prescription pills that would make her breathe normally and help her calm down and sleep. She unscrewed the top to a bottle of water she always kept on the nightstand and swallowed the two pills. Lying back down, she waited until the magic capsules took effect. Sangre entered her thoughts again, but this time he had his arms wrapped tightly around her, his handsome face close to hers as he leaned in and … her eyes shut and darkness erased all images from her mind.

Chapter Three

SANGRE STOOD AT the back of the room and watched his brothers leave the meeting. Steel and Paco had asked him to stay behind after church to go over some things. As he waited, he thought about the upcoming meeting with the hot little singer later that afternoon. He knew he should've told her who he was the night before, but he was having a bit too much fun with her. When the band had come into Leroy's, he'd been more disappointed than he'd liked when he didn't see her among the other musicians. There was something about her that piqued his curiosity, and there was something familiar about her that he just couldn't put his finger on.

"Why don't you come up here?" Steel said. The president sat at the head of a long table with Paco, the vice president, beside him.

He took a seat next to Paco then looked at Steel. "I got the figures for how much we'd need to lease a place for a restaurant. I looked at a ton of properties, but there's a lot of building going on in East Alina, and a slew of families and young couples are moving there. I think getting in on ground zero would be ideal, especially if we open a barbecue place or a steakhouse.

"Brianna thinks we should open a health food restaurant that would also have a lot of vegetarian and vegan items on the menu." Steel folded his hands on the table.

"Why the fuck would we do that?" Paco said at the same time Sangre said, "What the hell?"

Steel chuckled. "That's the reaction I had. She thinks there's a need for that here. There's so much going on about eating clean and healthy. She may have a point."

"No fucking way," Paco said, shaking his head.

"We could have some items on the menu that are health conscious and even vegetarian, but the whole damn restaurant? If we did that, most of the brothers wouldn't step a foot inside." Sangre leaned back and grabbed a beer from the mini fridge. "Want one?" he asked Steel and Paco. They nodded, and he took two more cans out. "This type of restaurant Brianna suggested may fly in Denver or Colorado Springs, but in a small town?" He took a large gulp then shook his head. "It's not gonna make it. We'd be wasting our money."

"When I told Chelsea the club's thinking about opening a restaurant, she immediately said it should either be Mexican or barbecue," Paco said as he popped the tab on the can.

"We got plenty of Mexican restaurants in town. I think we should do a home-style barbecue place and offer fried chicken too. Lena makes the best in town, and Rooster and Shotgun know how to fuckin' barbecue. The only other barbecue places around can't hold a candle to what we eat at the club," Sangre said.

"I agree. I think barbecue is the way to go. We make it simple with just a few kickass dishes, and I'm pretty sure we'll have a success on our hands." Steel lifted his beer to his mouth.

"We should think about building our own strip mall in East Alina. We'd have our restaurant there, and the other tenants would bring in a good stream of revenue. If we vote for that, then we could use Axe's woman, Baylee, to design it. He said she'd give us a good deal on her fees," Sangre said.

"That's a thought. How're Axe and the other Insurgents doing? I only talk to Hawk, Banger, and Throttle regularly," Paco replied.

"They're good. A lot of them are going to Sturgis. That'll be a kick-ass time. You dudes going?"

Steel nodded. "I'm going for about five days. I can't stay the whole time because Brianna's not going. She doesn't want to bring Aidan."

"Chelsea's been dying to go to Sturgis, so we'll be out there for the two weeks. Do some camping around the Black Hills before the main event starts. We could use some time together without any distractions. She's been so busy with school and work, so it'll do her good to have the time off. I'm also looking forward to seeing Hawk's new Harley. He's customized the whole damn thing."

"I can't wait to see that baby. I've been itching to get one of the new ones when they come out in the fall," Sangre said.

"Getting back to the strip mall, crunch some numbers and let's see if this can work for the club. You can present it to the membership at church when you have it ready." Steel stood up. "I've got to meet Brianna and Aidan. I promised I'd take them to the zoo in Durango."

"I should head out too. I told Chelsea we'd go for a ride," Paco said.

"And a fuck," Sangre added, a smile in his voice.

"What the hell's the point taking your woman on a ride if you're not gonna show her a good time?" Paco replied. The trio laughed as they left the meeting room.

"Sangre! Over here." Army waved his hand.

Sangre walked over to the bar and motioned the prospect to bring him a beer. "What do you got going on?"

"Skull, Chains, Jigger, and me are going for a ride. Wanna join us?"

"I wish I could. I gotta meet with this singer chick to go over some shit. My company begins the job tonight."

"You mean *you* begin the job tonight." Army threw back his shot of whiskey.

"I'll start it, but Eagle and I will figure out the schedule." Irritation pricked at his skin—he knew where Army was going with this.

"I saw the way you were checking that chick out last night. I don't blame you. She's fuckin' hot, and there's no damn way you're not gonna take advantage of this. I would."

"It doesn't matter what she looks like. This is strictly business." Sangre took a long pull on his beer.

"If you wanna believe that crock of shit, go ahead. We'll see," Army said.

"Yeah ... we will. This is just business." Annoyance laced his voice.

Army always had his mind on tits and asses. He was being ridiculous. Sangre grabbed another beer. *This is just a job. No fuckin' big deal. So what if this Isla Rose chick is hot as hell. A lot of women are hot. I'm not a goddamn teenager.*

"You coming with us?" Skull asked as he sidled up to the bar.

"Can't. I've gotta meet my new client," Sangre replied.

"Didn't you meet her last night? My sister was over the fuckin' moon that she got the chick's autograph, and then promised her the rest of the band would sign it. I'll admit I was blown away with the way she sang. Damn, that woman's got a great pair of vocal chords."

And tits. Fuck. Stop. Sangre pushed away from the bar. "The band was good. I wasn't really expecting to like their music. All right, I'm outta here." He lifted his fist in the air and added as he walked out, "Have a good ride. Next time, brothers." The last thing he wanted was Skull talking about her. She was his client, and he had to act like a professional, and he definitely had to stop thinking about her tits, her full lips, her heart-shaped face, and how soft she felt when she fell against him the night before. Nope … he was a businessman and needed to act like one, no matter how sexy his client was.

Sangre pulled up in front of the club's pool hall and went inside, jerking his head at Crow and Muerto as he sauntered over to the bar. Several groups of men played pool at the different tables. He was hoping to get in a game before meeting the singer, but it didn't look like that was going to happen.

"Hey," he said as he sat on a barstool. "You're crowded today."

"It's Sunday. The men come here while their women do the church thing," Crow said, wiping down the counter. "What'll you have?"

"A shot of Jack and whatever you got on tap. I have to meet a client in a bit, so I'm just killing some time."

Crow put the glass in front of him. "It's a fuckin' good day to go for a ride. I was planning to do just that, but one of the employees called in sick, so I'm stuck here instead of riding."

"I know what you mean." Sangre took a slug, loving the heat spreading around his mouth and throat. Being a biker meant that riding was *everything,* and every opportunity that came up to ride was taken. When riding was impossible, it was talked about. Motorcycles—Harleys in particular—were the favorite topic of conversation among bikers; it surpassed women by a long shot.

"I'm surprised you're meeting with a client on a Sunday," Muerto said as he came around the bar.

"It's not the usual gig. The job's for a bodyguard, and the client wants to start tonight." Sangre finished off his beer.

"Is it that rocker girl?" Muerto asked.

"Yeah. She thinks someone's out to get her." He glanced over at the pool tables. Still occupied.

"And you don't think so?" Crow said.

"With these drama divas, who knows? She's paying us, so I'll just do what she wants. But right now, I really want to play a game of pool."

"You should've stayed at the clubhouse. It'll be packed up until dinner time, then the dudes have to run home to their wives and kids. I'm so glad I'm single." Crow chuckled.

"Me too. I'd hate to make excuses about wanting to hang with the brothers and to have a ball and chain around me twenty-four seven. Not for me." Sangre took out a joint and lit it, inhaling deeply.

"It's not like that," Muerto said. "It's fun to be with your woman and do shit together. I guess it depends on how she is. Raven isn't clingy. She needs her time alone and gets that I need mine as well. It works good between us."

"I'll take your word for it, bro, but I don't want to experience it," Sangre replied.

For the next two hours, the brothers talked about motorcycles, Sturgis, and the possibility of building the strip mall. When the clock hit six, Sangre stretched out his legs then stood up. "I've gotta go."

He walked out of the pool hall, straddled his Harley, and took off with a roar.

When Isla Rose entered his office, her face fell, and he had to bite his inner cheek to keep from busting up. It was fucking priceless.

"What are you doing here?" she asked as she sat on the chair he pulled out for her. Her perfume was a smoky, warm amber scent with a sexy touch of spiciness that made it a bit dark. Smelling it made him think of warm summer evenings riding through Chaco Canyon at sunset with Halestorm's "I Get Off" swirling around him. *Fuck.*

"I asked you a question." She pulled down her crop top but not before he caught a glimpse of dark, burgundy roses curling up her right side.

He snapped his eyes away and went behind the desk. There was no way he was going to think about how far up her tattoo went, or how he wanted to see all of it and all of her. Clearing his throat, he took out a pen and pad and gazed at her. The way the sun caught the neon blue streaks in her hair, and cast a subdued rose glow over her face, was beautiful.

"I own the company."

She leaned forward, exposing more cleavage than he figured she was aware of, and pointed her finger at him. "You! Why the hell didn't you tell me that last night? You knew who I was."

"I thought about it but didn't think it would be professional to talk about it at the venue."

"And ogling me was supposed to be professional? Please."

"You're a pretty woman, and I'm a man. So there you have it."

A pink flush colored her cheeks and chin. "That's it?"

"I didn't mean to make you feel uncomfortable. Did I?"

She glanced at her hands in her lap, squirming a bit in the chair. Sangre liked that she was nervous and that he was most probably the cause of it. She looked up and captured his gaze. "No, you didn't. You should've just said something, that's all." Turning away, she dug through her large purse, took out a bunch of letters, and handed them to him. "These are what I've received just in the last week. I have to admit that I'm real spooked. I mean, I've received letters before from fans but never at this intensity or frequency. It's just damn scary. People are so nuts nowadays." As she chewed on the side of her thumb, all he wanted to do was to pull it away from her mouth and tug her to him, just to hold her close, stroke her hair, and tell her it'd be all right.

He looked at the letters. It seemed like they were all sent by the same person. Every one of them were written on notebook paper, and they all had a postmark of various towns in the surrounding area. Each of them had hearts next to the name, *Your Best Fan.*

"You never got these in LA?"

"I received a few in the last year that were very similar to these, but I didn't think anything of them. I get fan mail, emails, tweets, and Facebook posts from people telling me they love me, think I'm great, and other things. I never got any bad feelings about them … but these"—she waved her hand over the letters—"are in a category all of their own. I know it's the same person who wrote those few fan notes last year because the hearts are exactly the same."

"Do you have those?"

She shook her head. "I didn't bring them with me."

"That's convenient," he mumbled under his breath.

"What? You think I'm making this shit up? Why the fuck would I do that? I'm not in the habit of throwing away my money." She grabbed the letters and shoved them back into her purse. "I've made a mistake. I'll just go to the cops." As she stood up, he rushed over to her and placed his hand on her shoulder, gripping it.

"Calm the hell down. I didn't mean anything by it. You're overreacting."

Staring hard at him, she unloosened each of his fingers then pushed his hand away from her. "Didn't you know I'm a nut case? Yeah … I had a bona fide breakdown. So maybe I am imagining all of this. Oh … wait … maybe I'm the one writing the letters without knowing it. Yeah, a real wacko." She sank down in the chair and put her hands over her face.

Sangre stood there watching her. Regret left a bitter taste in his mouth. He ran his hand over her hair; it was soft and silky. *Why the fuck did I have to say that to her?* "Sorry. I didn't mean to upset you," he grumbled then went back behind the desk.

Isla Rose peeked through her fingers. "Do you think I'm imagining all this?"

He didn't know what to think. If he were being honest, at first he absolutely did; however, as he watched how upset she was, and after reading the content of the letters himself, he wasn't so sure anymore. Before he answered, she put her hands back in her lap.

"No." Of that he was certain. She didn't strike him as a nut job, and he'd seen his fair share of those over the years. "I really don't think you're *imagining* any of it." Now, whether she was just making the whole thing up for publicity … well, that was another story.

"I guess we got off on the wrong foot. I'm just really stressed today because recording didn't go so well."

"Are you recording at The Spots studio?"

She gave a weak smile. "Yeah. It's a killer studio, and Terry Z is beyond awesome, but he's a taskmaster, that's for sure."

"I've heard that," Sangre replied. Located at the foot of the San Juan Mountains, The Spots Recording Studio was opened by Terry Z, the lead guitarist from one of the biggest bands of the 1980s. Musicians from all over the world came to record at his studio. "It's cool that he agreed to record Iris Blue."

"It's actually a huge compliment, and we're eternally grateful for the chance to work with him. It's a major boost to our egos." She took out a pill bottle and shook some out into the palm of her hand. "Do you have any water?"

"Sure." He went over to the mini fridge and took out a bottle. "Here you go," he said, handing it to her. She put the pills in her mouth, took a gulp, and threw her head back as she swallowed.

"So, how does this work?"

Looking into her eyes, he paused. In the sunlight, the color of her blue eyes were too vivid. Her fingers tapping on the desk drew him back to her question. "We provide twenty-four seven bodyguard service. That means we're your shadow. When you're recording, if you feel safe there and don't want our man inside, then he'll wait in the lobby. At your house, we'll watch from outside unless you want us to be indoors with you. It's imperative that you get an alarm system—"

"I already had one installed. I bought the house about five months ago. The rest of the band came out a couple of weeks ago to start recording. The letters started up about that time. I feel safe in my home, but knowing that one of your men is watching the house makes me feel a lot safer."

"This guy may back way the hell off once he sees our presence. It happens like that a lot of the time. These jerks are bullies, and when they see someone challenging that, they ease off and move their attention to someone else."

"I hope that happens in my case. It's just a scary, vulnerable feeling to know someone is out there watching me, knowing my every move and making plans to strike, and I don't have a damn clue when or where. He has all the power."

"Now that you've hired us, his power has lessened."

"I do feel safer. Who is going to be watching me?"

"I'll do some of it, then it'll rotate between Eagle, Cueball, and some other guys we have working for us."

"Not that guy from last night I hope. What was his name?"

"Jon?" Sangre chuckled. "He's a good guy. A bit odd, but an okay dude. I didn't plan on using him for this job, so no worries."

"Thanks. He just kind of gave me the willies. I don't know. It's probably not fair for me to say that."

"You gotta go by your gut. I'll be the one working tonight. I want to go over to your house and check out the locks on your doors and windows and see if there are any vulnerable points of entry into your home … Check your alarm … You know, standard stuff."

"Okay. Will you be in the car all night?"

"Yeah. I'll be watching and doing some rounds to make sure you're good. Eagle will relieve me in the morning, at about eight."

"When do we start?" Her *too blue* eyes seemed a little out of focus.

What the fuck did she take? "Now. I can follow you home."

"Gage dropped me off. I told him I'd text him when I was ready."

"No need. I'll take you home since I'm going over there anyway."

"Okay."

Sangre walked around his desk and waited for her to stand. When she rose to her feet, she lost her balance, and he caught her. The scent of her perfume curled around him, and he was keenly aware of how soft her skin was since his hand rested on her rib cage. She was now steady on her feet, but he didn't let go. He didn't want to, and she didn't push his hand away either.

Isla Rose tilted her head up, her gaze catching his own. The thin silver nose ring in her nostril gleamed in the sun's rays, and the crystal silver bar in her eyebrow sparkled like a diamond. He dipped his head down, and the tip of her tongue darted out to wet her lips. How he wanted to capture it and suck it into his mouth.

Then the phone rang, playing out a heavy hitting tune, and shattered the moment. He let go of her, then she dug around in her purse, finally taking out a neon-yellow phone.

"I'm still at the security place. The guy wants to check out my house." She played with her purse strap, and it seemed like she didn't want to look at him. "I'm not hungry. You guys go on ahead. I'm going to crash tonight. I'll see you in the morning." Another pause. Now she had the purse strap so tightly wound around her finger that it was turning blood red. "Nothing's wrong. I don't want to talk about it right now. The guy's here." The strap wound tighter. "I'm not going to step out and talk. I have to go. I told you he's waiting to check out my house." The strap broke. She glanced down at it, a frown creasing her forehead. "I've gotta go. Bye." She put the phone in her purse and stared at the strap.

"You ready to go?"

Holding the satchel from the bottom, she nodded.

"Let's go then." He switched off the lights and opened the door, gesturing her to pass through.

When they came out into the sunlight, she groaned, again digging through her bag. Pulling out a pair of sunglasses, she looked around the parking lot. "Where's your car?"

Pointing to a metallic bronze Harley with a chrome skull emblazoned on the side, he held back his chuckle. "There."

"A motorcycle? This is going to be fucking awesome!" She rushed over to it, running her hands over the leather seat and slick handlebars. "I love it. Harleys are the best."

She's a biker chick? That surprises me. "You ride?"

Shaking her head, she knelt down and traced the skull's features. "No, but I've ridden on the back of motorcycles a lot. I used to date a biker in LA when I was still in college. He was badass, kind of like you. Now, your attitude makes sense." She stood up and lifted up her leg, falling against the Harley. "See," she said, pointing at her left ankle, "I've got a skull that looks a lot like your bike's skull."

He bent down and grasped her sandaled foot in his hands. A ghoulish watercolored skull surrounded by a half arch of red roses grinned at him. Running his thumb over it, he saw her skin pebble. "Nice tat." He gently placed her foot on the ground. "What club did your ex belong to?"

"Club? Oh you mean like the Mongols or the Insurgents?" He nodded. "He didn't belong to any club. Just a lone biker who loved to ride. He'd go to rallies and a bunch of motorcycle expos. You know, stuff like that. Do you belong to a club?"

"The Night Rebels," he said abruptly then added, "We better get going." He jumped on the bike, and she climbed on behind him; her arms wrapped around his waist, holding him tight. The Harley roared to life and they sped out of the parking lot. The feel of her warm body pressed against his back made his dick twitch, and he tried to focus on what he had to do to make sure her home was safe. It didn't work. The scent of her sensuous perfume, her arms around him, her silky tendrils sweeping across his cheeks in the wind, and her tits right against him made for an uncomfortable ride. Never had he wanted to get off his Harley as much as he did now.

When he pulled into her driveway, he killed the engine and straddled his bike. She got off like a pro and started toward the front porch. Looking over her shoulder, she placed her hand over her eyes as if to shield them from the sun. "Aren't you coming?"

"In a minute. I want to get the feel of the neighborhood. I'll meet you inside." He watched her enter her house. He'd be damned if he'd let her see him sporting a hard-on just from their short ride. She got him all worked up, and she hadn't even done anything. Not even an accidental slip of her hand on his crotch, yet his dick was as hard as a damn hammer.

I'm gonna have to keep my distance from her. This is just a job. Just a fucking job. She's got to stop wearing that damn perfume.

She came back out on the porch. "Did you want a beer or something?"

"No, I'm good." She went back inside. Alcohol and Isla Rose were a dangerous combination. He had to keep his head clear and level.

He got off his bike and walked up the brick sidewalk. *Remember. This is a job. She's a client.*

Opening the screen door, he went inside.

Chapter Four

ISLA SAT ON the tufted sofa watching Sangre as he checked the windows and sliding door in the family room. Each time he reached up, his T-shirt would rise, displaying seriously defined *V* lines, which slipped beneath his tight as hell jeans. She leaned back, enjoying the view of his hard butt. *So he's a sexy biker, who belongs to a motorcycle club. What did he say the name of his club was? Night something.*

"Your windows and doors are good. I'm gonna run down to the basement and make sure all is well there."

"Yeah, okay. What did you say the name of your biker club was again?"

"Night Rebels." He walked out of the room.

"Are you sure you don't want something to drink? I have coconut water and regular water. I could make fresh squeezed lemonade. It's my mom's recipe."

He popped his head through the doorway. "Lemonade? I haven't had fresh lemonade since I was in high school. A friend of mine's mom made the homemade stuff too. I'll go for that."

"Great. It'll give me something to do." *Besides watch your firm butt and fantasize a whole lot of dirty stuff I'd love to do with you.* She went into the kitchen and grabbed several lemons from the fruit bowl.

Gazing out the window, warmth spread through her as she admired her herb garden next to the weeping willow tree as its branches swayed gracefully in the breeze. The large backyard and the tree were what sold Isla on the house. Ever since she was a child, the weeping willow was her favorite. She'd loved sitting under it, mesmerized by the shimmering leaves and the sound of their rustle from the branches bending as the winds came through. The idea that the tree was weeping had always fascinated her. They were so different from the solid oak trees, which stood tall and rigid, fighting the elements. The oak trees always reminded her of her dad: unbending, hard, and stiff, while she was the willow tree: yielding, strong, and elegant. The cascading branches had hidden her more times than she could count when her father had been in one of his many foul moods. She picked up the knife and began slicing the lemons.

When she brought in two tall glasses and a pitcher of lemonade on a silver platter, which she'd picked up at a garage sale a few months before, Sangre was already sitting on the couch, leafing through the latest copy of *Rolling Stone*. He looked up when she came over to the coffee table.

"Everything secure?" She poured the pale yellow liquid into the glass and handed it to him.

"Yeah. You have a good house. Your alarm system is top-notch too. You just need to remember to always put it on. Most people who have the systems rarely use them." He brought the glass to his lips.

"I'm not one of them. I can be a bit paranoid, so I make sure it's on all the time. I even have it wired so I can open my windows a certain amount and it's still armed." She poured herself a glass.

"Damn. This is really good. It tastes just like the kind I used to drink a long time ago." He took another sip and ran his eyes over her face. "We haven't met before, have we? I mean you seem familiar to me, but I can't figure out why."

"You look sorta like a guy I used to know when I lived here."

Sangre's gaze widened. "You used to live in Alina?"

She nodded. "Yeah. You didn't know that?"

"No. When did you move?"

"Before my junior year in high school. My dad got transferred and we moved to California. I was bummed and so was my sister. She was going into her senior year."

He just stared at her, confusion creasing his forehead. "Where did you go to high school?"

"Jefferson High. Are you from here?" she asked him.

"Yeah. I went to Jefferson High."

"That's a coincidence. I'm not originally from Alina, but I moved here from Des Moines when I was about six years old. My dad works for an agriculture company, and they transferred him here."

"I think we know each other. Wait … I fuckin' know you, but your name wasn't Isla back then."

She laughed. "My legal name is Isla Rose."

"No, it's not."

"I think I know my name"—her mouth went dry. *Do we share memories of a joint past?*—"and I'm sure I didn't know anyone named *Sangre.* I would've remembered that."

He put his glass back on the tray, looking at her intently. "I can see some of your features are the same, but your eyes. Fuck, that's throwing me. They're fake, aren't they?"

"Fake eyes?" She chortled. "I don't think so."

"I meant the color. You've got that smart-ass way about you, just like Jordan did."

Everything stopped—and it seemed like the room was spinning away from her. Her ears pounded, making it hard to hear or understand what he was saying. She could see his mouth moving but couldn't hear anything coherent coming out of it. All sound was garbled. Then his cool hand on hers pulled her back in.

"Are you okay? The color just drained from your face, and I thought you were gonna pass out." He picked up her glass and handed it to her. "Here."

"What was your name in high school?" she whispered, running the cool glass over her face.

"Steve. Last name was Ansell."

"Fuck! I can't believe this!" *Is it possible that this hunk is my bestie from the old neighborhood? The one I fell in love with in high school? The one I spilled my guts out to whenever I needed to share, and who I told I loved him in a letter that he never responded to? The one who broke my heart?* "My name was Jordan Burnside," she said in a barely audible voice.

"Fuckin' hell! I knew there was something familiar about you." He leaned back, put his foot over his thigh and ran his gaze over her. "You filled out real good."

"I just can't believe this. How did I not know it was you? Now that I do, I can see it in your face, but this is too damn weird." She shook her head. "You didn't know I was in a band? Didn't you ever creep on the internet about me?"

"At first I did, but when I didn't hear from you, I moved on. So why'd you change your name?"

"You first."

"I'm a biker."

"That's it? Why did you choose Sangre? I mean, who calls themselves *Blood*?"

Pressing his lips together, he wiped his hands on his jean-clad thighs. "I just liked the name, let's leave it at that. So why did you pick Isla? It means *island* in Spanish."

"I know and that's exactly why I loved the name. I always wanted to run away to my own private island, especially when things got real shitty at home."

Reaching out, he grabbed her hand and squeezed it. "I remember that. You had it hard at home with your dad. Is he still the same?"

She slipped her hand away, and for a split second, she saw the look of surprise then disappointment in his gaze. "I'm sure he is. I don't really see my parents that much. I skipped out the minute I turned eighteen. I got a scholarship to UCLA, and I couldn't run away from home fast enough. Katherine married right out of high school to get the hell away. She's only thirty-four and has just divorced her third husband. Fiona is an overachiever and does nothing but work. Never had a real boyfriend once we moved to San Diego. She's thirty, lives in San Francisco, has a very high-paying corporate job, is anorexic, insecure, and a basic mess. And Jerry went all the way to the east coast to get away from the family.

He works for a bio-tech company, and he talks to me maybe once a year but hasn't talked to the rest of the family for over five years." She took a large gulp of lemonade. "Thanks, Dad," she said softly.

For the space of a held breath, there was silence. Then his gravelly voice banished it. "I don't know what to say."

"Nothing to say. It is what it is. I used to wish I had a normal family like yours. Your parents seemed to really love and care about each other. I bet your sisters and brothers are married with kids, and you all have big family gatherings and everything." She looked down, hating that her voice quivered, that the tears, hot behind her eyes, threatened to spill.

Then he was right next to her, drawing her into a big bear hug just like he used to do when they were in high school any time she was sad or freaked out about something. It felt so good, so natural. As Isla's body instantly molded into Sangre's, and her head tucked under his chin with the scent of him—spicy and fresh—cocooning her, she felt safe for the first time in a long while.

Sunlight flooded in through the window, making patterns on the Moroccan rug she'd purchased in a small shop off Ventura Boulevard the year before. She'd fallen in love with the colors and the geometric shapes that were unique to the Berbers. Beneath her cheek, she felt Sangre's heartbeat, and she nestled closer to him as he held her tighter.

I never want to leave his arms. This feels so right and so familiar. God, I've missed this. Him. A niggling in her brain reminded her that he never wrote to her after she'd left the letter professing her love for him. *He hasn't even bothered to look you up on the internet. He always just saw you as a friend.*

"Feeling better?" he asked, the vibration in his throat making her smile.

She pulled away. "Yeah. Thanks, I needed that. I still can't believe it's you. After all these years. I wondered if you still lived here."

"Why didn't you look me up when you got here?"

Because you broke my heart all those years ago. Doesn't he remember that he never wrote back or contacted me? Should I say something about it?

Not wanting to spoil the moment, she just shrugged. "I was so exhausted and such a bundle of nerves when I got here that I just wanted to lay low. I didn't look anyone up. I just spent days reading, sleeping, and watching movies. My brain and body needed that. The only people I saw were my neighbors and those at the grocery store. The mailman and I got real friendly." She took a breath and kept rambling on, "Oh … I'm also best friends with the two sweetest little girls who live next door to me. I've promised them that I'd make lemonade so they can sell it. Their dad is making the stand. He just dotes on those two, and so does Faith, his wife."

"Take out those blue contacts. You have the most amazing hazel eyes." He lightly brushed his fingertips over her brows.

"Benz loves my 'blue' eyes. I started wearing them because of the blue color I put in my hair and, the name of the band—Iris Blue."

"They look like shit."

She threw her head back and guffawed, her hands pressing against her belly. "You always told it like it was. Good to know you haven't changed."

"We're friends. Of course, I'm gonna tell you the truth. We were always honest with each other before, why would it be any different now?"

"Are we still friends?"

"Why not? Time doesn't stop friendships. We just lost touch, that's all."

"You were my best friend back then."

"Mine too. Damn. You know a lot of shit about me." He laughed.

"At least from back then I do. I don't know much about you now." She took another gulp of lemonade. "Are you married?"

"Nope. I'm leaving that to my brothers and sisters. They're all saddled down with kids, except for Connor, but he's been dating Kayla for a while, so you never know."

"Conner? Isn't he like nineteen or something?"

"Twenty-one. What about you? Ever been married?"

Shaking her head, she leaned over and put her glass on the table. "No. I've been so busy with the band. It's hard to find a guy who gets that you may be out of town for seven months out of the year. You don't have a girlfriend?"

"Not right now. I just broke up with someone."

"I'm sorry."

"Don't be," he said, his gaze fixed on her. "It ran its course."

The screams of the kids on the block, the whirr of lawn mowers, and the squeak of the occasional car driving past, filled in the nooks and crannies of the quiet space between them.

Sangre rose to his feet. "I should get going. I meant to tell you there was a change in plans—before I took a sip from the lemonade that opened the door to our past. I got some business at the clubhouse, so Mark's gonna be on for tonight. Eagle will relieve him in the morning, and I'll take over tomorrow night. Maybe we can get some dinner if you're up to it. Do you still like chili cheese fries?"

"More than ever."

"If you go out tonight, Mark will follow you. Don't feel like you have to chat with him or anything. He knows his duties. He's an ex-Marine, so you're in good hands. Give me your phone. I'll plug my number in, and you can call me if you need anything." He took her phone then handed her his. "Plug in your number."

She opened the front door and walked out with him. She saw a tall, built man with a crew cut, baseball hat, jeans, camouflage T-shirt, and black military boots getting out of an SUV. Sangre waved to him. "That's Mark. I'll see you tomorrow."

With her hands on the wrought iron bannister, she watched him go, admiring his corded legs and sexy butt. When he was halfway down, he turned around and threw her the most charming smile. "It's good to have you back in town, Jordan. I missed our friendship."

"It's Isla. I legally changed my name. And I missed it too." She watched him amble toward Mark, then talk with him for a few minutes before jumping on his Harley and riding away.

He just wants to be friends. I think I liked it better when he didn't know who I was and was hitting on me. Now he just sees me the way he used to for all those years. A buddy.

Waving at Faith next door, she opened the screen door and went back inside. Feelings she tried for years to suppress dug their way through her heart and her brain. After all this time, she still cared for him. A lot … Too much … and all he wanted was to be friends. She wasn't sure she could do it. It'd taken a long time for her to reconcile the fact that she'd made a fool of herself and had probably driven him away after he'd read her love letter.

Embarrassment strangled her, and she hid her face behind her hands. *I hope he doesn't remember about the letter. He didn't act funny or anything. I can't make a fool of myself again. I'm older, more mature now.* But why did she feel like she was fifteen and back in high school secretly crushing on her best friend?

Not wanting to sit around all night thinking about Sangre, she tapped in Gage's number.

"You guys going out to eat tonight?"

"Yup. Benz was just gonna call you to see if you wanted to join us. We're in carnivore mode, so the biggest, juiciest steaks are what we're seeking."

She laughed. "Count me in. Did you decide on a restaurant? I can meet you guys."

Some ruckus in the background and then Benz's deep voice came over the phone. "We'll pick you up. Maybe we can hit a bar afterwards. I've missed you."

"We'll have a good time tonight. Give me an hour to get ready."

She put her phone away and sighed. It'd be much easier if she loved Benz, but she didn't. Come to think of it, she'd never been in love with any man except for Sangre. *But that was when you were a teenager. The right man just hasn't come around. I refuse to settle like Katherine. She's already divorcing Dan, and they just got married ten months ago.*

Dashing up the stairs, she vowed that she'd have a good time that night and not think of Sangre once. She went into the bathroom and stepped into the shower, wondering if he was thinking of her.

She turned the knob and groaned as the warm water cascaded down her back.

Chapter Five

SHARLA DAVIDSON RUSHED to her dressing room, adrenaline pumping through her veins. The rehearsal was impeccable, and ever since she and Brad had started dating, their love scenes were spot-on. The director even told her that she had a glow about her whenever she'd kiss Brad onstage. Mr. Peery didn't know about her blossoming love affair with the handsome leading man. None of the cast or crew had any idea about it, and it was so hard for her to keep from gushing and telling everyone she knew. For reasons she still didn't understand, Brad wanted to keep their love affair secret.

A faint knock on the door made her heart pound in anticipation. "Come in." Expecting to see Brad walk in, she was disappointed to see Lexi enter. "Hey," she said weakly, turning back to the mirror on her dressing table. Taking another makeup tissue, she ran it over her face. "What do you want?"

Sharla wasn't too fond of Lexi ever since she'd heard her badmouthing her to the director after the auditions for the play. Sharla couldn't believe it because Lexi had acted like they were best friends for months before auditions took place. When she'd landed the lead role, Lexi distanced herself, acting like she barely knew her; to add insult to injury, Lexi was her understudy.

"I was wondering if you could go over some of the lines with me in case you get sick or something, and I have to go on in your place."

Sharla discarded the soiled tissue and pulled out a clean one, swiping it over her face. "That's not going to happen. I have no intention of getting sick for the next six weeks." She focused on cleansing her face, hoping Lexi got the hint and left.

"I guess I'll just have to ask Brad to help out. He's a very friendly guy."

Sharla could see Lexi's cruel smile in the reflection of the mirror. Her blood turned cold. There was no doubt that the bitch would swoop in and snatch Brad right from under her nose. Lexi had a reputation of liking everyone's boyfriend and husband—except her own. Sharla's sister, Dawn, had reminded her that Lexi was that way in high school too. Sharla had forgotten that, but then she hadn't hung around her very much.

Turning around, she clutched her throat when she saw Lexi opening the door. "All right. If you want to go over some of the lines, I can do it with you. No reason to bother Brad. He told me he's pretty beat, and I can see why—he works full-time and is the lead in the play."

"He needs the right woman to relieve some of the stress." A glint of competition shone in Lexi's eyes.

She knows about us. Dammit! How did she find out? Act cool. "Maybe he already has one."

Lexi gave a hollow laugh. "I'm positive he has a woman, but he needs the right one."

Wanting to shift the focus off Brad, Sharla smiled. "Did you hear that Jordan Burnside is back in town? She's here with that band, Iris Blue. She goes by Isla Rose. I had some friends go hear them play; they said they were awesome. I can't believe we have a bona fide rock star from Alina. Too cool. I remember when she got all the leads in the school musicals."

Lexi cocked her head. "Really? Isla Rose is Jordan Burnside? I didn't know that. I've been following them on Instagram for a while. Their drummer, Benz, is so hot. I'd love a night with him."

"Isn't he going out with her? I thought I read that somewhere."

"So what? If he's that much in love with her, no woman could take him away." She ran her long fingernail over her lips. "Let's just say, I wouldn't place any bets on him. That is, if I were a gambling woman, which I'm not. I always know exactly what I want."

All of a sudden the room got stuffy, and Sharla had to get out of there. She brought her slender fingers to her temples and massaged them, hoping that would stop the throbbing. Another knock on the door and her eyes flew open. Lexi rushed over and opened it, a wide smile filling up most of her face as she grabbed Brad's hands and tugged him inside.

"Brad, we were just beginning to rehearse some lines. Even though I'm just an understudy, I want to be ready if I have to."

Brad's gaze went to Sharla's and lingered there. "I get that. I thought you were tired," he said to her.

Sharla nodded. "I am, but I can go over a few scenes."

"That's ridiculous. Just do it tomorrow." Directing his attention to Lexi, he opened the door. "I need to talk to Sharla about one of our scenes. See you tomorrow night." His tone was casual, but there was an edge of finality to it that made her smile. Lexi threw her a mean look, smiled sweetly at Brad and slowly walked out, making sure she brushed her chest against Brad's arm before closing the door behind her.

"Thanks for that," Sharla whispered. In two long strides, he had her in his arms, kissing her feverishly, his hands roaming all over her body. Moaning, she threw her head back and let him devour her neck, knowing that the thick theater makeup would cover up any marks.

For the next two hours, he ravaged her until she couldn't take it any longer, the explosion of sensations was too much. She lay on top of him on the sofa, totally sated and buzzing with love. *I love him so much!* If only he didn't want to keep their affair secret. They could go to restaurants, the movies, dancing—*how I love to dance*, but their time together was confined to rooms: hotels, motels, her apartment, or backstage. How she longed to walk through the park with him, hand-in-hand, proclaiming to anyone who would see them that they were a couple in love.

"What're you thinking about?" he asked, making circular movements with his finger on her shoulder.

"That it would be nice to go out sometime. The two of us, and not care who sees us. I don't understand why we have to keep our love hidden."

The moment he withdrew his arms around her, she knew he was angry. She'd overstepped some arbitrary boundary he'd drawn. "Please don't be mad," she whispered, wanting his arms around her again. Sometimes the depth and magnitude of how much she loved him frightened her.

Brad pushed her off roughly. "I gotta go." He bent over and picked up his clothes then slipped his boxers on quickly.

"Don't. Please." She sounded pitiful, but she couldn't help it. If she had to beg she would. She wouldn't put it past Lexi to be waiting to pounce on Brad. She couldn't let that happen; if he ever left her, she'd shrivel up and the essence of who she was would die. "I'm sorry I said what I did."

"I hate like hell when you keep bringing it up. I told you from the beginning that we had to keep this secret."

"But why? That's all I want to know. Just tell me that."

He stared hard at her for what seemed like an eternity then he finished buttoning his shirt. Walking toward the door, he paused, then turned around and shook his head. "Because I'm getting married after the play closes. It doesn't have to stop with us if you don't want it to."

It would've been easier if he'd rushed up to her and stabbed her repeatedly in the heart. She was sure the pain wouldn't be as acute as his words were. Dumbfounded, she just gaped at him—her mouth open and limbs trembling.

"So there you have it. I understand if you want to stop. I have to go. Think on it." And then he was gone.

If I want to stop? How can I stop? Love isn't something you turn on and off like a faucet. How could he deceive me like that? Did he ever love me? She fell back on the sofa where she'd just spent the last two hours in blissful ecstasy and stared at the wall. She couldn't even cry. It was too unbelievable.

A soft knock and her heart leapt to her throat. *He's come back to tell me this was all a joke. He can be cruel sometimes.* She slipped her cotton robe on and rushed over to the dressing table and sat down. Sharla didn't want him to think she was brooding. She wanted to act casual and not let him know how deeply his cruel joke had hurt her.

"Come in," she said, closing her eyes while she rubbed the moistened tissue over her heavily made up eyes.

The door opened and closed quietly. She knew he was there. *He's probably waiting for me to say something. Well, two can play at his game. How dare he play around with my heart.* She kept rubbing the black mascara off her lashes. She heard the creak on the floorboard and smiled. He was coming to her, like he often did when she was taking off her makeup. He'd come over and pepper her neck with small kisses while he cupped her breasts.

He was behind her. She could hear his breathing, feel the light brush of his body against her upper back, smell—*Wait … that doesn't smell like Brad.* Her eyes flew open, and she stared at the figure behind her in the mirror. *That's not Brad!*

"What are you doing here?" Annoyance made the fine lines around her eyes crinkle. Each time that happened, she wished she wouldn't have baked in the sun since she was twelve years old. At twenty-five, she was too young to have any lines. "This is ridiculous," she mumbled under her breath.

The lamp on her dressing table fell down, breaking the light bulb and throwing the room into darkness. Then smooth, gloved fingers tightened around her throat, cutting off her airway. Frantically, she clawed at them, but they held on. Panic set in, and tears rolled down her freshly cleansed cheeks. By now, her eyes had adjusted to the dimness in the room, the only light coming from a large white sign lit-up from the church across the street. In the dimness something flashed, and she couldn't quite make it out. When it was brought close to her neck, she saw it was a knife. In that one moment of clarity, she realized that she would never perform her role on stage. She knew her next performance would be a cold, rigid corpse in a coffin at her own funeral.

The knife cut smoothly over her neck, and she stared at her fuzzy reflection in the mirror, watching the life seep out of her.

Chapter Six

"THAT'S FUCKIN' CLASSIC. Isla Rose used to be your best friend in high school. Ella's gonna flip over that one," Skull said before taking a big bite out of his bacon cheeseburger.

"It's fuckin' strange. I knew there was something I recognized in her, but I didn't figure it was Jordan. Damn weird." Sangre stirred cream into his coffee.

"You didn't know she was in a band?" Army asked.

"No. If I did, then I'd know the fuckin' name of the band and know it was her." He gripped his coffee cup and looked out the window. Sometimes Army asked the stupidest questions.

"It's actually kinda funny 'cause you were hitting on her at the club." Chains put a piece of banana cream pie in his mouth.

Sangre shook his head. "I wasn't hitting on her."

"Yeah, you were, dude," Skull said.

"Big time," Army added.

"For sure," Chains mumbled.

"Fuck you," Sangre replied as the men laughed and poked each other, him included.

"Admit it, bro," Chains said.

Scrubbing his face, Sangre looked at his brothers. "I may have been hitting on her, but I didn't know who the hell she was. What can I say? I like flirting with women."

"And now?" Army motioned the waitress over.

Sangre shrugged one shoulder. "Now, I know it's Jordan. She was my friend and still is, so it's different."

"I give this 'just friends' shit three weeks tops." Army turned to the waitress. "Hey, Tammy, what kind of cream pie do you have left?"

"Chocolate, coconut, and lemon meringue," she said while craning her neck.

"No more banana?" Army's eyes darted to the counter.

"If there was banana, she would've fuckin' said banana." Sangre splayed his hands out on the table.

"Just checking, dude. Chill, will you?" He quirked his lips and kept repeating the choices under his breath.

"While he decides, do you want me to freshen up your coffee?" she asked Sangre.

"Sure. Thanks."

Tammy came back with a fresh pot of coffee. She was the Night Rebels' favorite waitress, and they always asked for her section if she was working. In her mid-forties and raising two teenagers on her own had to be tough, so the guys tipped her very well, and her warming smile whenever she saw them showed that she appreciated it.

"Did you decide on the pie yet?" she asked.

When Army didn't respond, Sangre pushed the table toward him. "This isn't a fuckin' complicated algebra equation you have to figure out. It's a damn piece of pie. I'm sure Tammy's got other people to wait on."

"Chocolate," Army said.

"Coming right up." She chuckled and walked away.

Army shoved the table back at Sangre and glared. "What the fuck's your problem? Do you work for the goddamn union?"

"Maybe he's just pissed that he can't screw the rock star who is now his best friend," Skull said, straightening out the table.

"Maybe you should shut the fuck up or we can take it outside." Sangre's nostrils flared as anger licked at his nerves.

"Overreacting is a sure sign that Skull's onto something." Chains pushed his plate away from him.

Sangre glowered at him and lifted his fist. "You want some of this too?"

The three men chuckled, and Sangre scooted out of the booth and jumped to his feet. “I’m outta here. When you assholes grow the fuck up, let me know.” He threw a twenty on the table and stormed away, lifting his chin at Tammy as he passed the lunch counter.

The early summer breeze carried the light scent of jasmine. Sangre jumped on his Harley, craving a ride through the backroads so he could clear his head. He had a few hours before he had to relieve Eagle at Isla’s house. Leaving the main streets behind, he increased his speed and rode the mostly deserted roads leading to Chaco Canyon.

After thirteen years, she was back in his life. He remembered how she’d left without even so much as a goodbye. To say he’d been hurt was an understatement. He couldn’t figure out why she hadn’t told him her family was leaving. He’d been taken off guard by her actions. And now she was back in Alina, singing in a kickass band, looking hotter than hell, and wanting to be friends again. *What the hell am I gonna do?*

The Harley turned and twisted up the steep mountain until he arrived at the top of one of the smaller peaks. Birds swooped in the crisp air against the backdrop of a clear blue sky.

Crouching down on his haunches, he peered out at the horizon: Carpets of green blanketed the mountains; bursts of colorful wildflowers painted the sides of the canyon. The rushing of the river below echoed against the canyon walls. He was the only one there, and when things became tough, or he just needed to get away from everyone and everything, this was his go-to place.

He and Jordan—*Her name is Isla … remember that*—used to come to this spot a lot when they were in high school. She had a real tough time at home with her tyrannical dad, so he shared his place with her, taking her on the back of a motor scooter way before he even had his driver’s license. He chuckled at the memory of the two of them on the open road on a scooter that barely went forty miles per hour.

Sitting on the ground, he pulled a needle from a pine tree and chewed on it, a spray of freshness filling his mouth. As he sat there, memories of his childhood flooded his mind. Front and center was himself—a nine-year-old boy in a new neighborhood, kicking rocks alone until the eight-year-old girl next door came out and asked him what he was doing. She'd shown him her frog and then the bugs she'd caught that morning. He couldn't believe a girl wasn't afraid of bugs. All of his sisters were, and his mom would always call his dad to kill the stray spiders and other insects that crawled into the house. From that day on, he and Isla had become inseparable.

Back then she'd been a tomboy, wearing jeans all the time, baseball caps, hair in pigtails, and keeping up with him and all the other neighborhood boys as they climbed trees, explored culverts, picked up worms, and played touch football. Isla's curvy body, long hair, and heart-shaped face blurred the tomboy of the past. *I can't believe how fuckin' hot she looks.* But when he really thought about it, he knew she'd blossom into a real babe.

When she'd turned twelve, something happened: She grew breasts, and her straight lines were now round and curvy. Funny feelings had punched at his stomach whenever he'd look at her or see her in a bikini when they'd go swimming at the community pool. He'd changed too—he became taller with facial hair and muscles. He'd catch her looking hard at him when she didn't think he was watching. When he'd brush against her, instead of stickiness and grit, her skin felt soft and smooth. She didn't smell like dirt and fresh air but more like cotton candy and fruit punch.

Sangre ran a hand through his hair then glanced at his phone; he had less than an hour to get back to Alina and relieve Eagle. Pushing up, he took another look at the awe-inspiring vista and walked over to his bike.

The minute he pulled in front of Isla's house, Eagle got out of his car and came over. He bumped fists with him.

"Anything suspicious?" Sangre asked.

"Nah. Mark said it was quiet last night as well."

"Yeah, I talked to him."

"Cueball said that he'll be here at eight tomorrow morning. Do you need anything before I head out?"

"No. I know you're gonna hear this when you get back to the club, so before the story gets all fucked up, I want to tell you that I know Isla. She went by the name *Jordan* back when we hung out."

Eagle's eyes widened. "No shit? You guys dated?"

"No, not that. We were really good friends. Best friends, actually. When my dad got promoted at Reland's Candies, we moved out of our crappy-ass neighborhood and into the Sunnyside area. Isla lived next door to us. We hung out a lot and went to the same schools since I was nine."

"What happened?"

"Her family moved to California and we lost touch. That's how shit goes when you grow up."

Eagle glanced at the house then back at Sangre. "That's a small fuckin' world."

He pinched the bridge of his nose. "No shit. Anyway, it's good connecting again."

"Yeah. I never had a friend that was a chick. Wasn't it hard like when you were in high school?"

"We were friends. I respected that."

"You didn't answer my question, so I'm gonna guess it was hard as hell. She's a looker too. This is gonna be interesting." Eagle sniggered.

"What the hell does that mean?" Once again, anger pricked his skin.

"I'm just saying that she's hot, you guys have a past, and you just broke up with Skylar. You know?"

The muscle in his jaw tightened. "We're friends and she's a client, so no, I don't fuckin' know."

"Hey, Steve. Oops … I mean *Sangre*."

He looked at the porch and sucked in his breath. The early evening sun gave a rosy glow to Isla's skin and a sparkle to her hair like a rare tanzanite gem. Jean cut-offs revealed legs that went on for miles, and a form-fitting, low-scooped T-shirt molded perfectly over her breasts. *Damn.* Waving back, he said, "Hey."

"Come over here."

"I gotta go. See you tomorrow," he said.

Eagle clasped his shoulder. "Like I said, this is gonna be interesting. Later." Laughing softly, he went to his car.

As Sangre walked toward the front porch, he heard Eagle's car pull away from the curb. *I don't know why it's so hard to believe that a man and a woman can be friends.* "Hey," he said again as he walked up the porch steps. He glanced at the wicker table and saw two beer bottles, a plate of cheese and crackers, and bowl of green olives.

"I made us some refreshments. I figured you may want a little break."

"I just got here," guilt hit him when he saw her face fall, "but I'm always ready for a break."

Brightening up, she plopped down in one of the wicker chairs. "I slept so well last night. It was probably the first night I slept all the way through in a while. Not worrying about a psycho fan breaking in and hurting me goes a long way for a good night's sleep. How was your day?"

"Busy." He sat in the chair next to her and picked up the beer bottle. "Did you stay in contact with Madison?"

"Yes. She's come out to visit with me in LA many times over the years. She even thought of moving there, but then her mom had a stroke and she had to stay here to help out with that. Don't you ever see her?"

"Not really. I don't really hang out with citizens."

"What do you mean by that?"

"Non-bikers."

She leaned over and picked up a piece of cheese and nibbled at it, her gaze fixed on him. "How do your parents like you being in the Night Rebels? It's an outlaw club. I mean real badass like the Insurgents or the Mongols. I looked it up online last night. It's dangerous."

He laughed. "You're too funny. I know what it is. I'm a member."

She busted out laughing. "That's right."

Neither of them could stop laughing, and the more they tried, the harder it was. *This is good. Being with her, laughing about nothing. Just like we used to.*

"You're the only one I can laugh with like that, can you believe it? I'm going to tell you something." After a slight pause, she announced, "People think I'm kinda weird."

"Are you still telling people about haunted houses, trivial facts, and what strange combination of foods you like to eat?"

"But you never thought I was weird. Maybe your grownup side does now."

"I think your weirdness is what I liked. When I was younger, I never wanted to walk to the same beat everyone else did. I liked that you didn't either. It totally figures you're in a rock band, have beautiful blue hair, and hold up a middle finger to your dad and anyone else who doesn't get you."

Her hazel eyes sparkled. "That's what I liked the most about you—you *got* me. When I'd write dark songs, you knew where they were coming from."

Sangre nodded. "I'm glad you did something with your music. You were in every musical at Jefferson. It's cool to live your dream."

"Are you living yours? I remember you had a badass vibe about you, even when we were kids, but I never heard you mention you wanted to join a biker club."

"I was restless as fuck." She nodded in agreement. "I needed something different, and when I met some dudes who were in the club, I thought I'd check it out. I hung around the club for almost a year before I decided it was the life for me. I prospected and then patched in. I've never regretted it. There was no fuckin' way I was gonna end up like my old man, working for someone else, day in and day out. My brother Jim is at Reland's, Connor works there, and my sister Nicole's husband, Joe, works there. They're all at the same damn place. It wasn't for me. No. Fucking. Way."

"We're both unconventional. All I heard when I was growing up was that I had to go to college, get an education, and then get a good corporate job. My sisters and brother followed that road, but I ended up dropping out of UCLA my third year when I joined Iris Blue. Fiona and

Katherine kept telling me I was crazy, my mom worried I'd never be able to support myself, my dad called me a loser and a lot of other names, and when Jerry and I talk once a year, he always asks me when I'm going to get a real job. They just don't fucking get it."

"I remember you'd told me that you had to be able to express yourself. That you didn't care about money, just about respecting yourself and being proud of who you are. You did it, babe." Red stains painted her cheeks and she looked away. *What the hell? Did I embarrass her?*

"Are you still friends with Jay?"

"No." The mention of his old friend from high school pissed him off. Jay and Isla had dated, and it used to kill him every time he'd see them together, holding hands or kissing. The jealousy he'd felt surprised him, but back then it happened a lot whenever boys would gawk at her or ask her out. Shaking his head, he tried to dispel the memories.

"Does he still live here?"

"I don't know. I'm not the public census." He popped several olives in his mouth, chomping hard.

"I'm sorry. I didn't mean to upset you. Wait ... why are you mad because I asked about Jay?"

"Not mad. I just don't know anything about him. Does Madison know you're here?"

"Of course. She's the only one who did until just recently. I needed the peace and quiet like I told you last night."

"Right. You still wanna get those chili cheese fries?" The way her face lit up tugged at something deep down inside him. Pushing it away, he rose to his feet. "Let's get going."

Crazy shit twisted inside him, and he wanted no part of it. They'd go to Alfonso's for some killer Mexican food, and he'd stop at one beer only. There was no way he wanted to have too much to drink and do something stupid. He couldn't go there—didn't want to. *Not at all.* He would keep his focus on the conversation, keep his eyes above her neck, and not inhale her intoxicating scent too deeply. That had to be the plan. He couldn't afford to make any mistakes.

We're friends.

"Ready to go?" she asked as she came back outside. She'd changed her shorts to skinny jeans, and he couldn't help but look at her butt while she locked her front door.

"Above the neck. Above the neck," he muttered the phrase like a mantra.

"What?" She put on a pair of sunglasses and walked to his bike.

"Nothing. Just thinking aloud. You okay with going on the Harley?"

"Yeah. I loved the ride yesterday."

As they rode to the restaurant, she rested her cheek against his shoulder, her scent swirling around him. He saw Army and Goldie talking in front of the club's tattoo shop. Both of them lifted their chins at him as he passed. He saw the smirk on Army's face, but he didn't give a shit. Having Isla pressed against him on his bike felt damn good. A lightness danced through him. After thirteen years, it was good to have her back in his life. She was the only person he could tell everything to.

He'd missed their friendship.

He'd missed *her*.

Chapter Seven

"DO YOU REMEMBER Sharla Davidson?" Madison asked as she buttered a roll.

It'd been two days since she'd had dinner with Sangre, and Isla couldn't get him out of her mind. She looked up from the menu. "Vaguely. Refresh my memory."

"She was in our class at Jefferson. She's the one who got most of the leads in the plays."

Isla tilted her head back then snapped it forward. "I remember her now. I haven't thought about her since I moved to California. What about her?"

"She was murdered this past Sunday. She was the lead in the local play, and they had a dress rehearsal that night. The janitor found her sprawled on the floor." Madison took a bite of her roll and chewed while she darted her eyes all around before leaning over the table. "Her throat had been slit. Isn't that horrible?" she whispered.

Isla's hand clutched the top of her blouse. "How terrible. Do the police have any suspects yet?"

Shaking her head, she took another bite. "Nope. She's the third one to be killed like this." She shuddered. "It's too creepy and awful. A few months ago, Lizbeth Kelly was killed in the same way. She was coming back from choir practice and someone grabbed her. At least that's what the theory is. Then about eight months ago, Taylor Prentice was found in her apartment—throat slashed. It's all too horrible."

"Are the police saying it's the same person?"

"Not officially, but unofficially they think the same person did it. Do you want to know what's even freakier?" Madison paused for dramatic effect. "They all went to Jefferson and were in our class."

A shiver climbed up Isla's spine. "Are you sure?" The fan letters flashed in her mind. A sense of foreboding evil wrapped around her, squeezing her tightly as if to suffocate her. "Oh!" she cried out. A few patrons turned to look at her, and she grabbed her glass of white wine and took a big gulp.

"What's wrong?" Madison said, buttering her second roll.

"Nothing. I'm just a little freaked by what you said. How do you know all this?"

"My sister works in the sheriff's office. She'd kill me if she knew I told you. Don't say anything."

"I won't. I thought small towns were supposed to be safe."

"That's the irony of it. Most people think that, so they become laissez-faire about locking their doors, windows, and cars. In a big city, no one would think of leaving their door open, but it happens all the time here, especially during the day." She paused to look down at the menu. "What are you having?"

"I think I'll just have a Cobb salad. I'm not that hungry." Casually, Isla glanced over her shoulder and breathed out a sigh of relief when she spotted Mark. It made her feel so much safer knowing she had someone looking out for her.

"Now I'm going to feel like a pig if I have the pasta Alfredo. Do you want to split an appetizer with me? The potato skins are to die for."

"That's fine." Looking around the small eatery decorated in pastel colors and bright ceramic accents, Isla reclined in the white wrought iron chair. "It's so cheerful and cute in here. It's packed too. I'm glad we came earlier so we didn't have to wait in that long line."

Madison looked behind her. "It *is* a long line. That's why I said we had to come early. I don't know why they don't take reservations. I love it here. Vesta Grill opened about a year ago. They make killer cocktails. Are you sure you don't want one? I'm going to try an apple martini."

"I'm good with my wine. So how's it working out with Miguel?"

"Good. We should double date now that you're out of hiding. Maybe you could ask Steve."

Isla frowned. "You mean Sangre? I'm not sure he'd want to go, especially if it's labeled a 'date.'" She shook her head, "Anyway, we're just friends, and I'm going out with Benz."

"Maybe he'd want to go. I'd love to meet him up close, but, I thought you were going to break up with him."

"Me too. I caved in and am giving him another chance. It's so strange with some guys. Benz pursued me for four years, and I kept pushing him away because I thought it would fuck things up if we crossed that line in the band. Then I started to see a side of him he kept hidden from the other members. After a bottle of vodka and too much coke, we ended up screwing the crap out of each other. The next day, we were a couple. It went fine for a while, but then he started flirting with all the girls who'd hang in the front of the stage at our shows. I swore I'd never forgive him when he cheated on me, but after spending two months at the crazy house, his constant calling after I'd gotten here, and all the flowers and poems he'd sent me, I relented."

"Are you in love with him?"

Inhaling deeply, she blew out slowly. "No. Maybe. I don't know. It's complicated."

"If you don't know—then you're not, and love isn't complicated, it's wonderful."

"Are you ready to order?" the waiter asked.

After they placed their order, Isla leaned forward and propped her elbows on the table. "I've never really been in love"—*except with Sangre, but that was one-sided*—"so I don't know what it's supposed to feel like between two people. I mean Benz is an okay guy, but he wants too much from me. He's always pushing me, and I feel pressured. It pisses him off, and he used that as an excuse for straying with a groupie. Men …" She rolled her eyes.

"Not all guys are cheats." Madison put a potato skin on a small plate and handed it to her. "Are you glad you reconnected with Steve?"

A huge smile spread over her face. "*That* I didn't plan. I mean, I toyed with the idea of contacting him or his family when I first got here, but my head was in a different place, and I didn't want to deal with it." *He never tried to reach me after I left so I couldn't face him, but he seems cool... like nothing weird or anything ever happened between us.* "His name is Sangre now. The strange part is that he looks like Sangre and not like Steve anymore." She took a sip of her wine.

"I see him sometimes around town on his Harley. He looks mean and scary. Once I found out he joined the Night Rebels, I kept my distance any time I saw him. He looks so different from high school, but I can't say I'm shocked he hooked up with that biker gang. Remember how he used to get in so many fights? He came off as being angry a lot. I wonder why?"

"He's a rebel like me. We don't like to live in the world society dictates." She took a bite of the appetizer. "You're right about these potato skins. They are fabulous."

"I always thought you guys would've hooked up. You both seemed into each other back in high school. I used to tease you about it."

"We were only friends. Enough about me. Tell me more about Miguel."

Madison grinned, took a drink of her martini, leaned forward, and began to talk. Isla let the words fall around her, absorb into her brain, welcoming the respite from thinking and fantasizing about Sangre. He was dangerous territory, and she couldn't let her heart be broken by him again, but she also didn't want to lose his friendship. *I'm just going to have to focus on the band and not on* him. *Easier said than done.*

AFTER ENGAGING THE alarm, Isla kicked off her stilettos, sighing blissfully when her feet sank into the rug, and picked up the mail from the foyer table. For the past couple of days, she'd let the mail pile up without even glancing at it. Her psychiatrist in LA told her that she should take mental health days, times when she didn't deal with the everyday tasks that made her anxious, such as reading through volumes of emails, opening up mail, or listening obsessively to the news. Since she'd implemented his advice, life had been calmer, and her nerves were less frayed. Before settling in on the couch, she went upstairs to change and wash off her makeup.

Encased in a soft cotton night shirt and fuzzy socks, she poured a glass of wine, turned on "Caribbean Blue" by Enya, and stretched out on the couch. Enya was her go-to for grounding her, taking her out of the busyness of her head and letting peace flow through her.

Picking up the mail, she quickly perused it, her body freezing when she saw the now all too familiar handwriting on the envelope. With shaky fingers, she ripped it open, and a single notebook sheet of paper fell out. The printed words mocked her as the room spun around. Closing her eyes, she focused on taking steady, deep breaths while exhaling even more slowly. A friend of hers in LA had taught her that calming technique, and for the most part, it seemed to work on relaxing the whirlwind of anxiety that constantly threatened to overtake her. Opening her eyes again, she read the letter:

My sweet girl,
I fuckin' love you. My body is yours as yours is mine.

You seem to have a lot of men hanging around you. Are you trying to make me jealous? It's working. You know you belong only to me. I will love you for infinity. I'll never lose you, sweet, sweet girl.

You will always have my heart and my soul. Our day to come together is nearing. Soon it'll just be us and no one else.

I'm watching you, so you better fuckin' behave. Don't make me mad. I don't want to hurt you. Only love you. I can't wait to be inside you, fuckin' you the way you deserve. You know what I mean.

I'm coming for you.
♥♥♥*Your Best Fan*♥♥♥

A rush of blood filled her head as icy fear gripped her nerves, squeezing hard and strangling her. The letter dropped from her hands, and instinctively, she looked around the room, scared to death she'd see *him* lurking in the shadows. *What the hell am I going to do? He's watching me. I'm like a sitting duck waiting for the hunter to kill me. This is insane!*

Leaping up from the couch, she knocked into the table, spilling her glass of wine. "Shit!" she yelled out loud, rushing to the kitchen and grabbing a handful of paper towels. The lilting sounds of Enya's voice coupled with the swaying tune of her music that had relaxed her minutes before, now grated on her nerves. She cleaned the table then turned off the music. Her mind was racing a mile a minute. She ran around her house checking doors and windows, making sure the alarm system was engaged. Looking out on the quiet dark street, she saw Mark's vehicle and the outline of him in the driver's seat. *But wait … what if it isn't Mark? What if this fuckin' loon killed him and is pretending to be him. Oh my God. He's here. He's going to kill me.*

Without thinking, she grabbed her phone and tapped in Sangre's number.

"Hey, I'm glad you called," he said, voice low and deep.

"I think the psycho killed Mark and is pretending to be him in the SUV. He's going to kill me. I know it. I got a letter from him, and he said he's coming for me. He's here. He hurt—"

"Slow the fuck down. Mark's cool. I just talked to him. I'm coming over, so just calm down. I swear you're safe." She tried to muffle her sobs. "Damn, Isla. Please don't cry."

"I can't help it." Sobs escaped from her throat, and as hard as she tried, she couldn't stop the shaking, the tears, or the unraveling of her nerves.

"I'll call Mark and tell him to come inside until I get there. I'm walking out of the clubhouse right now."

"No! Don't tell him to come in. I know it's not him. Just please hurry."

"I just started my bike. Hang on, babe. Don't melt down on me. It's all okay."

"Just hurry," she whispered. She looked out the window again and the figure in Mark's car appeared to be watching her. She gasped and moved away, flattening her body against the wall. *A line of coke right now would really do the trick. I can't relapse. I just can't. Sangre's on the way. He said everything's okay.*

She stayed glued to the wall for what seemed like a lifetime until she heard the heavy footsteps on her porch, followed by a tentative knock then the doorbell. The chimes shot through her like jolts of electricity during a shock treatment.

"Isla? It's me. Sangre. Open up."

What if it's him*?*

"Look, I'll call you on the phone now."

Her phone buzzed and she stared at the screen, Sangre's name flashing over it. "Hello?"

"It's me outside your door. Open up. I checked on Mark and he's good. Said it's been super quiet."

"It's really you outside my door?"

"Yeah. Look out the peephole. You'll see my fuckin' good looks."

She laughed. *It is Sangre!* She turned off the alarm and swung open the door. Sangre stood on the porch, the red in his strawberry blond hair vibrant under the porch light. He walked in and she collapsed in his arms, relief coursing through her. *I'm safe.*

He held her tight, rubbing her back in circles as he told her she was okay. But she wasn't. She'd freaked out and imagined all sorts of crazy shit. *I thought I was getting better. If this made me almost go over the edge, how can I tour again?*

Sangre pushed back and held her at arm's length, his gaze fixed on hers. "Better now?"

She nodded sheepishly. "Sorry for making you come out here for nothing."

He placed his fingers on her lips. "Don't ever apologize for calling me or needing me." He looked at her clenched hand. "Is that the note?" She nodded and gave it to him, and his eyes scanned the crumpled piece of paper. "This shit is scary. This wacko's playing some serious mind games with you. I'm gonna have Mark come up to the porch so you can see that he's all right."

When she was convinced that all was good and her fears had simply gotten the best of her, she looked over at Sangre, who was at the door speaking with Mark. She overheard him tell the guard to go home, and she opened her mouth to protest but decided against it and settled back into the sofa's soft cushion. The truth was she didn't want him to leave, and the fact that he rushed over to her, concern etched on his face when she saw him, made butterflies flutter inside her.

After closing the door, he came over and sat on the other end of the couch. "I told Mark to head out. I'm taking over."

"I hope I didn't screw up a hot date for you." She laughed, but her stomach muscles tensed as she waited for his response.

"No date. Where did you come from? Mark said that you went out with a friend."

"Madison and I went to Vesta Grill for dinner. It was very good. Oh, by the way, she's scared of you since you joined your outlaw club."

He raised his eyebrows. "Really?"

"She should be."

"Why?"

"'Cause you're a badass." She poked him in the side, chuckling.

"Is that the way you want to play it?" he teased, snagging her around the waist. Then he started tickling her and she howled. Eyes watering, face red, words sputtering out of her mouth, she tried to push him away. One autumn afternoon when she was eleven, he'd found out that she was ticklish and had used it as a weapon whenever he wanted his way. That day, she'd help him rake the leaves in his backyard, and they'd both jumped in the big pile after they were done. He tried to stuff leaves around her, and she'd started laughing, telling him to stop. His eyes had sparkled with mischief when he'd found her weakness.

"Sangre! Stop!" Panting hard, she pushed her hands against his hard chest. He had her on her back and he hovered over her, his warm breath ghosting her face. Her hands dropped from his chest and she locked her gaze with the intensity of his own. Desire burned in them, and she held her breath as he lowered his head.

"You're so beautiful," he murmured, breaking eye contact to stare at her mouth. "So beautiful." She had to strain to hear him.

Closing her eyes, her lips tingled in anticipation of his kiss. Nothing. Her lids flew open just as he straightened out and slid down to the far end of the couch. *What the hell? I thought for sure he was going to kiss me.* Her body tightened in anger.

Smiling weakly, he wiped his hand on his jeans. "You're still ticklish. That's good to know."

"Yeah." Disappointment laced her response. "I'm exhausted. I think I'll go to bed. Are you staying inside?"

"If that's cool with you." He avoided looking at her.

"Sure. Are you going to stay down here?"

Nodding, he stood up. "I don't plan on sleeping. I'm doing a job."

I'm only a job. Just forget about it. I should be working on my relationship with Benz instead of lusting after my friend. I'm pathetic. "Okay, then. I'll see you in the morning. Help yourself to whatever you want in the fridge and cupboards. Night."

"Night."

Isla trudged up the stairs wishing like hell that Sangre was with her, but she knew he'd never cross that line. He'd always liked her just as a friend, so why was she surprised?

With a heavy heart, she pulled down the covers and crawled between the sheets.

Chapter Eight

THE SUN SET over the mountaintops as the blue sky merged with streaks of pink, orange, and gold. The MC members entered the main room, glancing around for their drinks and their club women. Both were waiting for them: glasses and bottles on the counter and scantily clad women smiling at them. Sangre went over to the counter, grabbed his shot, and threw it back. Church had been a bitch. Some of the members didn't think the club should get involved with buying real estate. They thought they may be spreading the club's money too thin, and the other half was all for it, thinking it was a great investment. In addition to the bickering about the club's financial goals, Diablo had given them the disconcerting information that the Deadly Demons MC had formed an alliance with the Satan's Pistons MC.

"You look bummed out," Kelly said as she brushed against him. Of all the club girls, Sangre felt the closest to her. When her younger brother had been beaten to death, Sangre asked the club to pay for his funeral. He'd also driven her to Minnesota for his services, and when she'd broken down at the gravesite, he'd held her tight. After that, a bond formed between them, and he'd tell her shit he'd never tell a dude. In a way, he was trying to replace the friendship he'd lost when Isla had left. It hadn't occurred to him before, but now that she was back in his life, he could see it clearly.

He shrugged. "Not much going on. I've just been pulling some long nights with this new job I have."

She pressed her tits against him. "I heard that your new gig involves a singer from a rock band."

Smiling, he nodded.

"And"—she ran her fingernail up his bare arm—"she's your long lost friend. True?" She pressed her lips on his cheek.

"Don't need the fuckin' tabloids around here with the way news travels. Yeah, Isla is my friend from years ago. I didn't know it when I took the job, but now that I do, it's cool to be back together again."

"So, she's just your friend?"

"Yeah. Why?"

"Because I wanted to have a bit of time with you before you do something stupid and get involved with another girl you're gonna break up with. You're good for a few months before you do that."

"You sound like Army, and that's not a fuckin' compliment."

She laughed. "Sorry. I didn't mean to." She took a sip of her drink. "Do you wanna go to your room and relax a bit? I can give you one of my massages that you love."

He ran his eyes over her full breasts, rounded hips, and toned legs, that made his dick twitch. Since breaking up with Skylar, he hadn't screwed anyone, but he had too much on his mind at the moment and knew all that shit would get in the way. "Another time. I've got too much going on."

"Okay. Just remember, I'm here when you need me, even if you just wanna talk." She walked away, and his gaze zeroed in on her swaying hips and firm ass as a thread of regret wound around his dick.

He spun around when a hand clapped him on the back. "Hey," he said to Paco. "It didn't go so well in there. I thought the membership would be down for a strip mall. Some of these bros don't know shit about business and making money."

Paco clutched his beer bottle. "It took me and Steel off guard too. Your job is showing the numbers and how they add up."

"I'm doing that. The reason I brought it up was just to get a feeling of where we stood as a club. I'll make sure to show them just how wrong we'd be *not* to invest."

"You guys talking about the fuckin' news Diablo shared with us about those damn Satan's Pistons?" Shotgun asked, joining in on the conversation.

"I was just getting ready to bring that up," Sangre said.

"We gotta be ready for some trouble at Sturgis if the Pistons go, which I'm sure they will."

"I say we need to crush those bastards once and for all," Muerto said, standing next to Sangre. "I talked with Jerry, and he said the Insurgents don't like it any more than we do. They don't think the fuckin' Demons will risk breaking the truce with the Insurgents, but he said they're concerned that some shit may go down at Sturgis between the damn Pistons and us. The word is they're vowing justice for what we did to their clubhouse. Fuck them. We'll be ready."

"Damn straight," Diablo said, his jaw jutted out.

"Hawk and Banger are worried that with the Demons watching their damn backs, they're gonna try to set up shop selling drugs in our neck of the woods." Muerto took a swig of beer.

"They better not try anything. After the shit we went through with the West Avenue assholes in Silverado, there's no fucking way *anyone* is getting near our county or the surrounding counties with any kind of dope. If we have to have an all-out war, we'll do it. I know the Insurgents are on board to help, and they'd bring in a lot of their chapters as backup," Paco said.

"Fuckin' right about that." Goldie raised his fist in the air. "Night Rebels forever, forever Night Rebels," he said, his voice loud and clear. Soon the whole room was on their feet, chanting, fists held in the air.

As Sangre looked around, a small lump formed in his throat. He was so damn proud to be part of the brotherhood. No matter what went down, business or personal, each member knew they could count on the club to come through. They were united through love, respect, and loyalty.

After several minutes, the din of voices died down, and Paco picked up the shot one of the prospects had put in from him and downed it. "I heard you're friends with the singer in Iris Blue," he said to Sangre.

"Everyone's heard that. Why're you asking?" He took out a joint and lit it, hoping it would calm the urge to go over to Army and punch him in the face. Many of the brothers gossiped way more than the club women, but Army was a million light years ahead of the pack. He was the club's version of *Entertainment Tonight.*

"Chelsea's really the one asking. I guess she's been following the band on social media for the past six months and loves their music."

"Oh yeah? That's cool. Maybe she'd like to meet Isla. We can go out to dinner sometime this week."

Paco's face broke into a full smile. "She'd love that. We were in Denver the night they had a show. She was so damn bummed."

"Isla told me they're having another one next week. I can get tickets for it."

"Awesome. I'll tell her."

"That should get you a long night of lovin'," Sangre said, nudging his elbow against Paco's arm. Nodding, the vice president laughed.

"I'll let you know what night works with Isla."

"Sounds good. I'm gonna head out. Later."

"Paco's not staying for the party?" Army asked, swinging his leg over the barstool before sitting on it.

"Doesn't look like it since he's walking out the door," Sangre replied, picking up his shot glass.

"You staying?"

"Maybe."

"What the fuck does that mean?"

Sangre shook his head and turned toward Chains. "Can you find out some information about property values in East Alina in the last five years? I want to know how much rent, land, and business values have increased."

"Just shoot me an email telling me what you want, and I can have it all compiled on spreadsheets. Hell, I can even put it together in pie charts with different colors and shit. When do you need it by?"

"In a couple of weeks. I'll send you all the details."

"So, you're gonna hang out with your *friend* tonight?" Army asked.

Sangre glanced at him. "Are you still on what the hell *I'm* gonna do?"

"What's the problem here?" Skull asked as he and Brutus came over.

Sangre's jaw tightened. "There's no problem. Army just isn't getting the answers he wants from me."

Army glared at him. "I just asked if you were staying for the party, and you're getting all butt hurt."

"I'm not getting anything except fed up with your stupid, fuckin' questions. I told you maybe. What the hell don't you understand about that?"

Skull laughed. "He's got a point, dude. *Maybe* is pretty easy to get."

Army turned his back to them, facing the bar. "You just wanna hang out with your friend who really isn't your friend. Just come clean, dude."

"Are you guys talking about that singer chick?" Brutus asked.

"I'm not, but Army seems to be," Sangre answered.

Army swiveled back around facing him. "What I can't figure out is how you can be just friends with a chick. I've never been friends with a woman, especially one built like Isla Rose. There's no way you aren't looking at her and wanting to get inside her pussy." He took a swig of beer.

Sangre finished his drink, leaned over and put the bottle on the bar, and then locked his gaze on Army's. "What I can't figure out is why anything I do is any of your fuckin' business, and why the hell you're obsessed with me and Isla."

"I'm not obsessed." Army scowled at him.

"Then quit talkin' about it."

"I'm with Army on this. I think it would be hard to be friends with a chick. I couldn't do it," Brutus said.

"Me neither," Shotgun added.

"Same here," Skull said, motioning Ruby to come over.

"I mean, how could you not think about her tits and pussy?" Chains replied.

"We've been friends since we were kids. We climbed trees together and caught daddy long-legs. You guys just don't get it."

"But didn't you ever think of her as a girl when she started growing tits? Or in high school?" Shotgun asked.

"Nope." Sangre lied. "I gotta make a few phone calls." He walked away, ignoring the kissy sounds the guys were making behind him. If he were to bet who they were, he'd say Army for sure, and Brutus and Skull a close second and third. *They don't know what the hell they're talking about.* They knew nothing of the friendship he'd shared with Isla ever since he was the new kid on the block and she befriended him.

Stepping out back, he took out a joint and lit it, inhaling deeply. The last remnants of the sun descended over the craggy peaks, turning the western sky a smoky purple as a few stars glimmered above. Leaning against a concrete column on the back porch, he smoked his joint and stared at a raccoon scampering across the yard. He smiled, the sight of the masked mammal brought back a memory of when he and Isla had snuck out of their houses one summer night to find a raccoon that she thought had been injured. She'd seen some blood by the trashcans one morning and was convinced a raccoon had been cut on the glass bottles inside the trash. Isla had been enamored with raccoons ever since she'd seen them, the first summer they went on a night walk through the brush and woods near their neighborhood.

The night they'd gone in search for the supposedly injured "raccoon," they'd ended up finding a skunk instead who was not happy about it. He'd told her it was a skunk and that she should stay back, but she'd been convinced it was the raccoon. When she'd gone after it, the frightened animal sprayed her and she cried out, stumbling backward. For almost a month, he had to pretend she didn't stink like hell. He laughed, remembering how many tomato juice and vinegar baths her mother made her take until old Mr. Haskell down the street told her mother about a concoction of hydrogen peroxide, baking soda, and dishwashing liquid. That had seemed to work the best out of all the others.

Too funny. I wonder if she remembers that.

"Hey," Goldie said as he stepped out on the porch. "Need some down time from the craziness that's starting inside?"

Nodding, he pulled out a joint and handed it to him. "Have any of the Fallen Slayers come yet?"

"Brick, Tats, Knuckles, Tequila, and Skeet just got here about fifteen minutes ago. Roughneck, Patriot, and the others couldn't make it. Steel's glad about that because Breanna wanted to go to the festival in town tonight. Hailey does too."

In the outlaw world, a president and vice president of the MC that's hosting a club party have to be in attendance if other MC officers come. Since the Fallen Slayers' president and vice president couldn't make it, Steel and Paco weren't obligated to be in attendance.

"I forgot that was going on. So you heading out?"

"Yeah. We're gonna meet up with Steel and Breanna. I'm pretty sure Muerto and Raven are gonna be there."

"Probably Paco and Chelsea. He took off a while ago. Do you miss the freedom of going to club parties whenever you want?"

Goldie stubbed out his joint. "Not really. I loved going to the parties and getting shit-faced and fucking different chicks all the time, but it started to get old and boring. I didn't enjoy it as much."

I know what you mean.

They stood in silence, listening to the sounds of the night: crickets' high-pitched melodic chirps, the low rumble of distant thunder, the clink of bottles in the clubhouse, the echo of the freight train's whistle, the hum of traffic.

"I better get going." Goldie took out his keys and walked toward the parking lot.

Without thinking, Sangre took out his phone.

Sangre: *Hey. Do u wanna check out the festival?*

He waited several minutes before his phone buzzed.

Isla: *Glad u texted. Feeling bored. Let's do it!*

Sangre: *B there in 1 hr.*

Isla: *Sounds good. See u then.*

Smiling, he put his phone back in his pocket then went back inside.

EACH WEEKEND DURING the summer, blinking white lights, a conglomeration of music, scents of buttery caramel corn and grilled onions, and the electric energy in the air transformed Main Square. Reminiscent of a Norman Rockwell painting, the tree-lined square and wooden bandstand beckoned locals and tourists alike. Rides and a small carousel that glimmered under the day's sunlight came to electrifying life at night.

Everywhere Sangre looked, the painted faces of children grinned at him while clutching neon green, red, yellow, and blue glow sticks in their hands. That night the place was packed, and people crowded before the bandstand, their faces shimmering in anticipation as the band set up their equipment.

"This would be a good gig," Isla said in his ear.

"You guys should do it."

"Maybe I'll talk to the band about it. I think I'd be a little freaked out with so many people around. I mean, I'd feel vulnerable. I still don't know who's sending me those letters."

"I'd be there to protect you," he said, her hand in his. "Have you received any more letters?"

"No. It seems to be working now that your guards are always around." She shivered and pressed her body against him. "I don't want to think about anything but having a good time. Deal?"

"Deal." She felt warm and soft against his arm, and he made a deal with himself right at that moment: Think of Isla only as his childhood friend, not as a sexy, beautiful woman.

They strolled around the area, checking out the booths, eating cheeseburgers and caramel corn, and laughing a hell of a lot. As they walked toward the bandstand, a woman bumped into them, her soda spilling all over Isla.

"Shit!" Isla yelled as she jumped backward.

"I'm so sorry," the woman said, handing her some napkins. "I didn't see you."

"Let me get you some paper towels," Sangre said before rushing to one of the food stalls. He came back in seconds and handed her the paper towels. The front of her camisole was soaked through and he could see her sheer bra. Knowing he should divert his attention, he tried, but he couldn't. He was mesmerized by her perfectly cupped breasts and their pebbled nipples. All he wanted to do at that moment was slip her soiled top over her head, release her round tits from the bra, and draw one of her nipples in his mouth as he pinched and flicked the other. "Fuck," he muttered under his breath.

"Does it look all right?" she asked him, throwing her shoulders back which pushed her chest out.

"They look great," he answered.

"I meant my top," she said softly.

Dragging his eyes away from her tits, he looked at her. "The top looks good too."

She shook her head, giggling. "You're too much."

"I'll pay for a new top if you can't get the stain out. I'm just so sorry," the woman said, bringing his and Isla's attention back to her.

"That's okay. Stuff like this happens when there are so many people."

"Jordan? Is that you? It's me, Lexi. Oh my God. I didn't recognize you at first. How've you been? It's been like forever."

Isla gave one of those smiles that said she was only being polite. "Lexi. Wow … it's been years."

"Are you here on vacay or did you move back?"

"I'm just visiting. It was nice seeing you." She gripped Sangre's arm and started to walk.

He could see she was not all that thrilled with this Lexi chick.

"Do you remember me, Steve? I know that's not your name ever since you joined that biker club."

He ran his gaze over her face. No spark of recognition lit inside his mind. "I don't. We gotta go."

She reached out and placed her hand on his. "Lexi Strobe. I was in Jordan's class."

A blank. "Nope." He pulled his hand away.

"Jordan?"

"Her name's Isla, and I don't think she wants to go down memory lane with you." Sangre gave her a hard look that seemed to dampen some of her enthusiasm.

"I know we weren't the best of friends in high school, but I didn't know you changed your name," she said to Isla.

"Now, you do," Sangre said at the same time Isla responded, "No worries."

They started to walk away when Lexi clasped Isla's arm. "I did hear you were in a band. Is that true?"

"Yes. Iris Blue."

"That's so awesome. I'd love to talk to you about it and just catch up. Are you open to going for lunch? It's on me."

"I'm not sure what my schedule is, but you can message me on Facebook. My name is Isla Rose."

Tired of Lexi's annoying prattle, Sangre pulled Isla away and guided her toward a booth that sold T-shirts.

"You didn't look like you were too thrilled to run into that chick."

"I'm surprised she was so friendly. When we were in high school together, she was a real witch. She went out of her way to try and make me feel insecure. I can't believe you don't remember her. I complained about her to you many times. Lexi belonged to the popular group."

"I sorta recall the bitch now. I'm surprised you told her to message you."

"That was a long time ago. I've so moved on from all the high school drama. Anyway, people change." Pointing at a couple next to the cotton candy stand, Isla smiled. "They're my next door neighbors. Do you want to meet them?"

Sangre jerked his head back. "No. Why would I?" She laughed as he tugged her in the opposite direction.

Later that night, as they sat on a bench watching the fireworks, the burst of lights in the sky brought him back to the summer before his senior year. It'd been a hot as hell summer that year. His family and Isla's had met up at the Fourth of July picnic in Liberty Park. For the first time in weeks, there'd been a light breeze rustling through the trees, delaying the firework display by over an hour.

Isla's mother had asked her to go to the car to bring the extra cooler, and he'd volunteered to help her. She'd had an open bottle of water in her hand, and as they walked to the car, he'd started teasing her about something—he couldn't quite remember what it was. For whatever reason it had irked her, or at least she'd pretended it did, and she poured the bottle of water on him and ran away. He'd run after her and snagged her around the waist, both of them toppling onto the soft grass. Hovering over her, he watched as she giggled and tried to get away.

He bent his head lower and kissed her glossy lips: feathery soft at first, then hard. She put her arms around his neck and kissed him back, and when she parted her lips, he slipped inside. Soon their tongues twisted together, darting in and out of their mouths. He placed a hand over her breast and squeezed it. It'd felt so soft and round, and he had to grind his hip into her to take some of the pressure off his hard dick.

She must've felt his hardness because she pushed him away and he fell on his back on the grass. She jumped up and headed toward the parking lot. He'd been ready to go after her, to apologize for touching her breast, but his friend, Jay, intercepted and said her mom wanted to know what was taking so long to get the cooler.

Without even a backward glance at him, she'd wrapped her arm around Jay and they sauntered away. Rising to his feet, he watched them fade into the shadows of the trees as the first burst of light lit up the sky. That was the summer she'd left without even saying goodbye to him.

"I know it sounds corny, but I love fireworks." Isla's voice brought him back to the present. She waved her hand outward. "I love all of this. The sense of community. I remember all the times we went to community events. LA is so big. So impersonal. You could die and your neighbors wouldn't know for months. It can be so lonely in a city of millions. Crazy."

With the memory fresh in his mind, the heat of her body pressing close against him, and the enticing scent of her perfume, he put his fingers under her chin and gently turned her face toward him. "Do you remember the Fourth of July in Liberty Park?"

She licked her lips and cleared her throat. "Yeah. They were all fun. The fireworks were always my favorite part."

Taking her hair in his hands, he moved it over her shoulder and leaned in close to her ear. "I'm talking about the summer you left." He felt her shiver against him, and it made him glad that he'd caused it.

She turned her head sideways and their lips almost touched. They were *that* close. "That time we kissed? I've never forgotten it."

"What the fuck!" a male voice boomed.

Isla jerked away from Sangre. His head snapped toward a tall man with angry eyes. He recognized him as one of the band members.

"I thought you told me you were going to stay in tonight. Not fuckin' cool, Isla." Glaring at Sangre, he pointed. "Who the hell is *he*?"

Sangre stood up and heat flushed through his body as it tensed. "You point your fuckin' finger at me again, and I'll break it."

Benz's eyes widened and he stepped back. Looking at Isla, he grabbed her hand. "Let's go."

She pulled out of his grip. "Hold on. Sangre's an old friend." She turned to him. "Sangre this is Benz. He's the drummer in the band."

"And her boyfriend," he said, his arm curling around her shoulders.

Sangre cracked his knuckles then flexed his arm muscles and stared at the asshole.

Isla slipped away from Benz and stood off to the side, her arms folded across her chest. "It's too damn loud to talk. Why don't we all finish watching the fireworks?" She sat back down on the bench, and Sangre sat to the left of her and Benz to the right.

All he could see was red. Crimson red. Blood red as in Benz's blood. And all he could think about was how he was going to hurt this jerk who thought he was hot shit because he played the damn drums. He had no idea what the hell Isla even saw in him. Out of the corner of his eye, he saw the wannabe rock star glancing at him on and off, and if Isla hadn't been there, Benz would be sprawled on his back with Sangre straddling him as he rearranged the asshole's face.

After the show was over, people started heading out of the square toward the large parking lot. Isla looked at both men and smiled. "That was good."

"Let's go," Benz said in a hard voice.

"I wanted to tell you about how Sangre and I got back in contact, but it was too loud before. Anyway, his company is the one watching over me. I had no idea, but it turns out that Sangre is Steve. I've mentioned him to you, remember? It's such a small world. So Sangre is on duty tonight."

"And you decided to hang out with your bodyguard at a public place where there are a ton of people and any wacko could off you? Smart." He tapped against her temple. "Real smart."

Sangre growled. "No one's gonna hurt her when I'm around."

"Isla. You forgot to mention that you have Superman guarding you. Bullets and shit can bounce off him."

In less than a second, Sangre had the front of Benz's T-shirt crumpled in his fist, as he shook the pale drummer hard. "I don't go for any fucker disrespecting me, especially sniveling pansy asses like you."

"Sangre! Let him go. He didn't mean anything, I promise. Benz has a caustic tongue sometimes."

"I don't like it, ass wipe. Next time, think before you fuckin' speak, or I'll rip that *caustic* tongue right outta your big mouth. Got it?" He threw Benz on the ground, and Isla bent down next to him, taking his hand and helping him up. "Keith will take over my shift." He whipped out his phone and called him, then looked at her. "I'll drive to your house and leave when Keith shows up."

Wiping off the dust from his jeans, Benz shook his head. "She's coming to the hotel with me. I'll watch her."

"What the hell did I just warn you about opening your mouth? I don't give a shit what you have to say." He turned to Isla. "This is your call."

Looking at the ground, she shrugged. "I'm going home."

Benz pulled her to him and wrapped his arms around her. "I'm going with you."

His pulse sped and he bared his teeth, but Benz avoided looking at him.

"Whatever," Isla muttered and began to walk toward his Harley.

"I have the rental car. You're going with me."

Sangre followed them as they drove to her house. When Isla opened the front door, she smiled at him, and he lifted his chin at her. For reasons he couldn't explain, he was madder than shit at her. He wanted nothing more than to drag the ass wipe out of her house and send him on his way. *I'm acting like a damn pussy. She's dated this asshole for a while. Why shouldn't he be with her? Why the fuck does it piss me off so much that he is? Grrr!* He pounded his fist on his handlebars, anxious for Keith to come and take over.

The living room curtains moved, and he saw Isla peeking out, her nose placed against the glass. Ignoring her, he looked up into the inky darkness covered in sparkling stars. The rumble of an engine focused his attention behind him, and he saw Keith's blue Suburban driving toward him.

Sangre shook hands with Keith then jumped on his bike. The roar of the engine garnered another peek from behind the curtain. Pulling away from the curb to make a U-turn, he glanced at the window, but she was gone.

Chapter Nine

SHERIFF WEXLER LOOKED at the crime scene photographs of Sharla Davidson, Lizbeth Kelly, and Taylor Prentice, a sick feeling coursing through his body. All three women had been viciously attacked—their throats slashed; and were former students from Jefferson High. *The same person did these killings.* "Dammit!" he said aloud. This was the last thing he needed, especially with the election coming up. There'd been an undercurrent of fear throughout the town when Taylor Prentice had been murdered and then Lizbeth Kelly, but with the recent killing of Sharla Davidson, full on terror had spread over Alina. The citizens clamored for news and were impatient with the time it was taking the sheriff's department to solve the crimes. Wexler and his staff understood the concern, and they assured the townsfolk that they were working hard to solve the killings, but the truth was—they didn't have a whole lot of forensics to go on. There was a clump of hair found in Sharla Davidson's fist, but DNA results came back showing it was her own hair. The sheriff surmised that she must've pulled out some of her hair when she'd fought for her life.

Hearing a soft knock on the door, he looked up and saw one of his deputies. "Come on in, Miles." The lanky twenty-eight-year old walked in and sat in the chair in front of his desk. "What can I do for you?"

"Not much. I was just checking in to see if there've been any new developments with the Davidson murder." The deputy had taken a leave for three days to attend the funeral of his grandmother in Durango.

The sheriff pushed the photos to Deputy Carmody then leaned back in his chair. "The results from the hair in Davidson's hand turned out to be hers. It was a damn blow to the investigation. I'd hoped it would've given us a suspect, but now, we got nothing. The few leads we have are drying up."

Glancing at the set of pictures, Miles shook his head. "The killer had to have known these women. This was definitely personal."

"We're on the same wavelength here. These women were murdered by the same person. He knew them or had some connection to them. If we don't find him soon, I'm afraid he'll kill again."

"Maybe he was just aiming for these three for some reason."

Shaking his head, he took the photos back. "He's not stopping. Someone who kills with this intensity enjoys it. There's a rage inside him that has to be sated. No way will the killings stop. We gotta put an end to him to make sure no one else is murdered."

"Are we sure it's a man? There was no sexual assault even though the women were nude from the waist down. Could've been a red herring, like the person wanted us to believe it was sexually motivated," Carmody said.

"True. It *could* be a woman, but it doesn't strike me that way. Even so, we have to keep all the possibilities open."

"I was just thinking that since there wasn't any sexual assault, and whoever did this went out of their way to make us believe these crimes may have been sexually motivated, that it could have been a woman or a younger person."

"We can't rule out anything." Wexler reached for his mug then took a sip of the strong, lukewarm coffee.

Deputy Jeffers walked in and sat on the chair next to Carmody. He glanced at the photos on the desk in front of Wexler then averted his gaze to the sheriff. Jeffers didn't say anything; he just sat and stared.

Sheriff Wexler had hired Nick Jeffers six months before, thinking he'd be a good fit with the department, but he'd been doubting that decision ever since. The biggest problem was that Jeffers was not a team player, which was essential in order to be effective in law enforcement. The deputy's probationary period was ending in a couple of months, and unless Wexler saw a change in the way he conducted himself, he'd have to let him go.

Frowning, he rubbed the back of his neck. "What do you want, Jeffers?"

"Just wanted to let you know I arrested the two teens who've been spraying shit on those buildings off Highway 57."

"The abandoned ones?" Carmody asked.

The deputy's nostrils flared, and he gave Carmody a cold hard stare. "It's still a fucking crime."

Miles put up his hands and laughed. "I didn't say it wasn't. It's just that we've got three murders on our hands."

The vein in Jeffers' temple pulsed. "So that makes it open season on crime?"

From the way the tension was building between his two deputies, Wexler was sure they'd be punching each other in a matter of seconds. "Good work, Jeffers. When kids start shit on abandoned buildings, it's just a matter of time before they move to other things." He saw Carmody roll his eyes. "And Carmody's right about focusing attention on the three murders. We gotta find this sicko before he strikes again, and my gut tells me he will."

"Didn't you go to Jefferson High?" Carmody asked Jeffers.

The deputy slammed his fist on the desk, knocking over the picture of Wexler's grandchildren. "What the fuck is *that* supposed to mean? What're you saying?"

Taken aback by the outburst, Wexler's muscles tightened in preparation of an altercation. "Calm the hell down, Jeffers. Carmody was asking a legit question. We're working to solve these damn murders. Now did you go to Jefferson High or not?"

Redness colored the deputy's face as he looked down at the ground. "I did. So what?"

"Did you know the three murder victims?"

"I recognized them. We were all in the same class, but I didn't hang with them if that's what you're asking."

A thread of adrenaline wove around Wexler's spine. "They were all in the same class? That's damn important. Do you remember if they were friends back then?"

Raising his gaze to Wexler's, he shrugged his shoulders. "I wasn't friends with any of them. They were part of the group who thought they were gonna be stars. You know the type—self-absorbed and stuck-up. There were a few of them in my class—like Jordan Burnside, who now goes by Isla Rose. Can you believe her? She thinks she's hot shit because she's in a rock band. Who the fuck cares? I don't. She was part of that arrogant theater group who never had the time to even acknowledge anyone else." He scrubbed his face with his open hands.

Wexler glanced at Carmody, who sat open-mouthed, then back at Jeffers. *Where the hell did that come from?* "It sounds like you didn't like Sharla Davidson, Lizbeth Kelly, or Taylor Prentice."

"I wouldn't say that exactly. In high school I wasn't crazy about them, but then, I didn't like most of the kids in my school. I actually hated high school, and after graduation, none of them ever really crossed my mind again. I never thought about or spoke to Sharla, Taylor, or Lizbeth. I had no reason to. Sometimes I'd see them in the store, but I run into a lot of people I went to school with. Alina's not that big. It's no big deal when you bump into people around here."

"Did anyone else feel the same way you did about the three women when they were in high school?"

"I dunno. I suppose there were kids who did. I know some of the girls were pretty pissed off that all the leads in the musicals, plays, and concert performances kept going to the same five."

Wexler's heart pounded. "And who were the 'same five'?"

"Sharla, Lizbeth, Taylor, Carrie, and Jordan. They kept getting the main parts all through high school. Jordan's the only one who left, and it seems that she's the only one who made it sorta big. She's in Iris Blue. I heard she's back in town."

Wexler jotted down everything Jeffers said, underlining the words "Isla Rose" and "Iris Blue." "What's Carrie's last name?"

"I can't remember, but she still lives in town."

"Do you know where?"

"I think at one of the music venues. She's a talent buyer. I bet she's even more insufferable now than she was in high school."

The sheriff closed his notebook. "Try and think of other people, men and women alike, who didn't care for these five ladies back in high school. I need your help."

A grin spread over the deputy's face as he stood up. "I'll get on it." With his chest thrust out, he hooked his thumbs into his belt loops.

"Go on and write up the report about the teens and the graffiti. I have to go over Carmody's cases now."

"Sure thing." He swaggered out and closed the door behind him.

Carmody cleared his throat. "What the hell just happened?"

"We got our first lead: Jefferson High, entertainment department, and our two victims both in the same class. Let's start with that. Also, find out who this Carrie is. Call all the music venues in the county, but start with Alina. I'll find"—Wexler looked down at his notes—"Jordan Burnside, a.k.a Isla Rose. I want to see if either woman can tell us anything that can help us. I also want to warn them because my instincts are telling me they're on this crazed person's hit list."

"I'm on top of it. I think we should also look at Jeffers. I mean the guy went loony when you asked if he knew the victims. Besides, why the hell *didn't* he mention that he knew them?"

Hating to think that anyone in law enforcement, let alone one of *his* deputies, could do something like that, he shook his head. "I admit the guy's odd, but I can't see him involved in this. We'll check his whereabouts and such, but let's not home in on him exclusively. If he felt that way about the victims back in the day, you can be pretty damn sure others did too. See if the theater, art, and music teachers are still at the school. If not, then find them. We've been looking in a totally different direction."

An adrenaline rush swept through Wexler's body as he watched Carmody rise to his feet and leave the office. For the first time since Sharla Davidson's murder, he felt that they had a bona fide lead in the investigation. Lightness spread through his chest as he swiveled in his chair. Facing the computer, he typed in *Iris Blue* and smiled broadly when the first link he saw read "Isla Rose Escapes to Hometown After Meltdown."

He clicked on it and began reading.

Chapter Ten

IT WAS EIGHT o'clock at night, and Isla stood by the window looking out at the street. She saw a dark blue SUV pull up to the curb, where a man of medium height got out and walked over to Mark. She watched while the two men talked to each other, but when Mark went into his car, started it, and drove away, her heart sank. She knew that the man who had just arrived was relieving Mark in watching over her.

For the past three days, she hadn't heard a word from Sangre and had a feeling that he was mad at her, but she wasn't quite sure why. He'd seemed more than annoyed when Benz had come over that night at the festival. It'd surprised her because she'd always thought that he didn't want anything more from her than just friendship. *But he was going to kiss me. I know it.* If Benz hadn't come by, she'd swear that Sangre would've kissed her. That thought made her stomach flutter and her head swim.

She'd kissed him only once, years ago, when they'd gone to the Fourth of July picnic in Liberty Park. After that, it'd been awkward between them, and they stopped hanging out as much. Sangre had ramped up his hours at Elmer's Shop and Go, and when she'd bring her car in for gas, he'd tell her that he needed all the money he could make because he wanted to buy a Harley.

When her dad had announced that he'd decided the whole family was moving with him to California, she'd been devastated. She wanted to stay and see if something would ever come out of their kiss. Not wanting to talk to Sangre about it, she wrote him a letter, left it on his door, and drove away, her heart breaking. The whole ride to California, she kept hoping to hear from him but never did. Her eyes stayed glued on the blurring landscapes as they changed from state to state. There was no way she'd wanted her dad to know she was crying; he wouldn't have been too sympathetic. For weeks, she'd rush home from school in anticipation of a letter, an email, or even a voice message from Sangre, but silence was all that had greeted her.

And now, he'd wanted to kiss her again. *Does he want something more than just friends, or does he want to be friends with benefits? Is that what I want?* The truth was that she still adored Sangre even after all these years and not hearing from him. When they hung out now, it seemed like old times, like a span of thirteen years never happened. *Won't everything fall apart if I*—we—*cross the line? And what about Benz?*

Isla wasn't the cheating type, and even when her friends dragged her to a nightclub and plied her with drinks, she didn't go home with the first good-looking man who came on to her. Amy, her bestie in LA, had been livid with Isla and had told her that she deserved a good "revenge fuck" after she'd found out Benz was screwing not just one but two groupies in their bed. But she hadn't wanted to get back at him by screwing a stranger; she'd just wanted to eat a pint of double chocolate ice cream with chocolate chips, wrap herself in a blanket, watch her favorite movie, and shed a few tears. The problem with the whole cheating bit that Benz had pulled was she hadn't been *that* hurt about it. Of course, her pride was bruised, and she'd been madder than hell at him for banging the women in *their bed*, but it hadn't been emotionally devastating to her the way she'd thought it should've been.

When Amy's two-timing boyfriend had been caught with his pants down, *literally*, Amy was inconsolable for weeks. She'd loved Jared so much, and she'd kept telling Isla over and over that she'd rather be dead than go on without him. Isla didn't feel even one-eighth of the heartbreak that Amy had. For her, the anger had always been directed at the way he disrespected her. *I wasn't and still am* not *in love with Benz. I'm not sure if I even know how to love as an adult. Sangre was teenage love. Right?*

She'd taken Benz back because he'd been moping around after she kicked him to the curb, and the band was suffering because of it. So she'd relented, and Benz was thrilled; the band was back on track with great music and performances. Did she believe he'd reformed? Not for a second. She suspected that he hooked up with a few women while they were on tour before her meltdown. When she'd confronted him about it in a hotel in San Francisco, he went ballistic on her, and they had one of their worst, most dragged-out fights ever. It made for great streaming on YouTube and random online sites; Instagram, Twitter, and Facebook blew up with all the tags, tweets, and shares. If only their concerts could garner such intense response in such a short time.

When they'd come back to LA, Benz kept pressuring Isla to forgive his outbursts—although he never did admit to his infidelity—as haters were saying awful things about her on social media. Kent was beyond pissed at the both of them, and reporters for online gossip magazines hounded her. It had all been overwhelming, and on top of that, the band had four shows to perform in Southern California before leaving on another four-month tour. The stress had been unbearable, and she'd turned to the only thing that made her feel empowered, euphoric, and energized: cocaine. By the time the band had performed the fourth show, she was so damn high, her brain on mega-alert even though her body was exhausted from lack of sleep, and she'd had a nosebleed for days. After she'd taken the last bow of the night, she walked off the stage and collapsed. Isla was a damn mess, crying and yelling at the same time as the staff tried to help her. She thought they were trying to kill her. The hallucinations had been severe.

Shivering, she folded her arms around herself. *God, I was so out of control. I never want to be that way again.* Being back in Alina brought her such a deep sense of peace, but now the stirrings of panic nipped at her nerves whenever she thought of touring, Benz, or going back to LA. Since Benz had come to Alina, she'd had to call her recovery coach a few times when the cravings for coke began to escalate.

Glancing at the street again, she saw the replacement sitting in his vehicle, his eyes fixed on her home. She turned away and took out her phone. Tapping her finger on the windowsill, she waited until Sangre picked up. *Maybe he doesn't want to be friends anymore.*

"Isla. What's up?"

His voice startled her and for a second she couldn't talk.

"Did Keith show up?"

"Yeah." She cleared her throat. "Yes, he's here. How've you've been?"

"Busy. How's the recording going?"

"Good. I was in the studio all day yesterday and today."

She waited for him to respond, but silence stretched between them.

"Are you mad at me or something?" she asked.

"No. Why would I be mad at you?"

"I don't know, but I have the vibe that you are. You seemed pissed about Benz."

"Benz? Oh ... the ass wipe you're dating. It doesn't make any difference to me who you go out with. I was pissed by his attitude and the way he acted toward me and you. Disrespect is something I don't tolerate. It's over. No big deal."

"We got in a big fight over you that night."

"No shit? Why?" She heard the satisfaction in his voice.

"Benz thinks I have a thing for you. I've told him many times that we were friends. He got pissed because we were sitting so close together when he came over."

He chuckled. "Do you have a thing for me?"

"As much as you do for me," she said casually.

Silence again. *Why the fuck did I have to say that?*

"Was the make-up sex good?" he asked.

"There wasn't any. I was so pissed and not in the mood, I told him to leave. He stormed out and has been giving me the 'talk only about music' treatment right now."

Silence again.

"I'm not all that into him, really. We broke up about eight months ago then got back together, and it's not working. At least I don't think it is. He wanted to stay with me at the house when he first came to Alina, but I wanted my space and told him so. He stays away when he gets mad at me, which has been for most of the time he's been here."

"He's a fuckin' jerk. You deserve better. You wanna go out for a drink?"

"That'd be wonderful. I could use one. Recording can be pretty long and grueling, so I definitely need to get out. Should I meet you?"

"I'll come by and pick you up. Can you be ready in a half hour?"

"Yes."

"See you then."

Happiness and excitement zigzagged through Isla as she put the phone down. She rushed upstairs and changed into a black, off-the-shoulder crop top that laced up and a pair of distressed jeans. Parts of her butterfly tattoo peeked out from under the front lacing of her top. The crystals from her navel piercing shimmered under the recessed lights in her bedroom. She fluffed her hair with her fingers and freshened up her makeup: brushed on another coat of black mascara, added a bit more rose-tinted blush, and applied a light mauve lipstick. Grabbing a slim wallet, she slid it into her small clutch bag along with her lipstick and gloss and left the room.

As Isla came down the stairs, her front doorbell rang. She looked out the peephole, her belly twisting when she saw Sangre standing on the porch. After disengaging the alarm, she flung open the door.

The light from the street cast a glow over Sangre, making the highlights in his hair a deeper copper. Dressed in a gray T-shirt that fit his body like a second skin, snug black jeans, killer black boots with silver buckles, and his black leather vest with patches on it, he exuded alpha masculinity and pure sex. *Damn, I'm drooling … but any woman would if he was standing on their porch. Close your mouth now and stop acting like you're back in high school.*

"Hey," she said a bit too cheerfully as she opened the screen door.

She heard his sharp intake of breath as his gaze slowly traveled over her body, examining every inch of it. Her skin tingled as if he were touching her.

"You look hot. I mean good," he said hoarsely.

"I like *hot* better." Their eyes locked as they stood staring at each other while the crickets serenaded them from the trees. Isla could feel his body heat and smell the night air on his skin. Her body hummed, and it took every ounce of control to not throw herself into his sculpted arms. Then her damn phone rang, breaking the intensity of the moment. Cursing under her breath, she looked down at the screen and grimaced when she saw *Benz* flashing across it.

Sangre nodded at her phone. "Aren't you going to answer that?"

"No." Regret wove through her as she saw him start down the steps. "I'm going to set the alarm. I'll catch up with you." She went back inside, activated the alarm, and then closed the door behind her. As she approached Sangre's car, she saw him talking to Keith. She leaned against Sangre's car and tilted her head back, loving the way the cool breeze felt against her skin.

"You ready?" his deep voice startled her.

Straightening out, she threw a smile at him and placed her hand on the passenger door. "Yes. I'm surprised you didn't bring your Harley."

"It's supposed to rain later tonight."

She settled on the seat. "It doesn't look like it."

"Have you forgotten the weather around here? It changes all the time. It can be sunny one minute then a hailstorm the next."

"I'd forgotten about that. I'd say riding on a Harley in a rainstorm isn't very fun."

"Nope, and it can be dangerous as fuck."

"Which bar are we going to?"

"Cuervos. Steel, our prez, is part owner. It's a decent place. If you're hungry, they have some kickass wings and great nachos."

"I may try the nachos. I have to admit I'm obsessed with them, but I rarely eat them because I'm always on a diet."

He looked at her sideways. "You're fuckin' kidding, right?"

"No. You have to look a certain way, especially in LA. Anyway, I was always a chubby kid."

"No, you weren't. Your dad kept telling you that, and I kept counteracting it. I'm telling you now that you don't have to be worrying yourself over dieting. A man likes to grab something when he's with a woman anyway."

Good ol' Sangre. He used to always build me up when Dad tore me down. She laughed. "I'm going to have to remember that when I get back to LA. My friend, Amy, is always dieting. I mean the girl eats nothing but salad and protein shakes. She's tried every diet around, and she's skinny as hell."

The touch of his fingers stroking her cheek made her quiver, but before she could grasp his hand, he placed it back on the steering wheel. "When are you going back?"

She inhaled deeply then let her breath out slowly. "I'm not sure. The band wanted to finish the album in a month, but it's taking us longer, so maybe a couple of more months."

"You looking forward to getting back?"

No. I don't want to leave you so soon now that we've reconnected. "I guess. I don't know. My life is pretty hectic, and I don't look forward to all the stress. Life is slower and simpler here. It's been great to just decompress."

"Stress will kill you."

"Thanks, doc." He laughed and she joined in, and before she knew it, he was pulling into the parking lot of the bar. "I keep forgetting how close everything is. In LA, or anywhere in Southern Cali, everything is so spread out, and the traffic is horrendous. I always plan on tacking an hour or two just for travel time whenever I go anywhere that isn't right around my condo. It's nice not to have to deal with all that congestion."

"I've heard LA can be a pain in the ass to get around."

"You've never been?"

"Nope." He switched off the engine.

"You'll have to come and visit me. I could show you all around. We'd have a good time."

"I'm sure we would," he said, tweaking the tip of her nose. He slid out of the car, and she followed suit.

Cuervos was bustling with people. Two large-screened televisions had a boxing match on as several of the men clad in leather vests and denim watched the screen. Sangre grabbed her hand and led her through the lines of people until they arrived at a table. Three couples sat there, all eyes falling on her as Sangre bumped fists with the three men who wore vests very similar to his. Placing both hands on her shoulders, he thrust her in front of him and pointed at a woman with dark hair. "This is Chelsea"—he pointed to the blonde next to her—"Breanna, and Raven. This is my friend, Isla."

Her heart twinged a tiny bit at the words *my friend*, but she was being silly. *I am his friend. We're just friends. He's made that clear since forever.*

"Come sit over here," Breanna said.

"Aren't you gonna introduce us?" asked a dark-haired man sitting next to Raven.

"You dudes don't matter." Sangre laughed and the other men joined him.

"I'm Isla Rose." Looking at the dark-haired man, she smiled. "Who are you?"

"Muerto."

Another one of them said, "Paco."

"Steel," said the man sitting next to Breanna.

"You're the president," she said.

Steel got up and motioned for her to come over. "Take my seat."

Sangre let go of her hand, and she instantly missed the warmth of his skin on top of hers. Muerto and Paco jumped up and joined Steel as he walked toward the bar. She sat down and Sangre bent down and whispered in her ear, "What do you want to drink? The nachos are a given." The heat of his breath on her neck made her quiver.

Her mind was foggy. She glanced around and saw a strawberry margarita in front of Chelsea. "A strawberry margarita." She watched him swagger over to the bar, threads of jealousy tangling around her as she saw different women checking him out, and a few others touching his arms and even his butt. It brought her back to the way she'd felt when they were in high school. He'd had so many girlfriends, and since they were best friends, he'd tell her about them when all she'd wished was that she was one of them.

"I love your voice and your band," Chelsea's voice pulled her from the past.

She dragged her eyes away from a curvy brunette who'd slinked an arm around his waist and leaned in close, whispering something in his ear that made him laugh. "Thanks. The band has a gig in a couple of weekends at The Rear End. I'll put you and your boyfriend on the guest list."

"That'd be great."

"Who had the strawberry margarita?" a waitress asked, lifting up a large glass.

"I did," Isla answered, tapping the space in front of her.

"Nachos are on their way," the waitress said before hurrying off.

As Chelsea, Breanna, and Raven asked her questions about living in LA and being in the band, she kept directing her gaze back at Sangre and the women who surrounded him as he leaned against the bar talking to the bartender.

I'm being ridiculous. Of course, women are attracted to him. He's damn sexy, and he's got that bad boy vibe down perfectly.

"Isla?"

She stared at Raven trying to remember what they were talking about. "Sorry, I zoned out for a second. What did you ask me?"

Raven glanced over at Sangre then back at her and smiled. "The Night Rebel men get a lot of attention from women. Don't sweat it."

Isla ran her fingertip along the rim of her sugar-coated glass. "No, it's not like that. I mean Sangre and I are just friends. We've been friends since we were in grade school. It's cool. I mean, I have a boyfriend—Benz. He's the drummer in the band. We've been on and off for almost a year, but he's trying to be a better boyfriend. Even though Sangre and I lost touch for all these years, we've picked up just where we left off. It's like that with friends."

Raven, Chelsea, and Breanna stared at her as she rambled on and on. Her English high school teacher's voice echoed in her brain, *"Methinks thou dost protest too much."* Mrs. Paulson would say that to her when Isla would make up excuses for not being prepared or for blowing a quiz.

Licking off the sugar from her finger, she looked at Raven. "Now what did you ask me?"

"How long you're staying in Alina."

"At least another couple of months. We're recording an album at a studio about thirty miles from here." As much as she wanted to see what Sangre was up to, she forced herself to not look over at him. A light sweat broke out at her hairline, and her skin pricked and itched, like a million ants were crawling over it. She jumped up, knocking over her nearly empty drink. "Oh shit. I'm sorry." Grabbing a napkin, she mopped up the spreading liquid.

"No worries," Breanna said. She motioned the waitress who came over and wiped the table clean.

"Where're the bathrooms?" Isla asked.

Pointing to a hallway right of the bar, Breanna's gaze fixed on her. "Are you okay? You look real flushed."

"I'm just hot all of a sudden. I'm good. I'll be back."

As Isla walked to the ladies' room, she glanced at Sangre and her heart skipped a beat as his gaze met hers. Isla lost herself in his eyes: They were the color of a perfect raindrop on a blue morning glory. They reminded her of the baby blue throw she wrapped herself in when it was chilly—cozy, warm, and familiar. When she was a child, she'd believed he had his own sky inside of him. At that moment, the noise around her faded away as she stood locked in his searing gaze. Desire flickered in them, ensnaring and captivating her, making her limbs tremble, her heart pound, and her mouth go dry.

And then a blonde with breasts spilling over a *way too snug* top came up to him and planted a big kiss on his lips.

Isla's stomach hardened.

She snapped her head away then walked to the restroom, refusing to give him a backward glance.

Chapter Eleven

SANGRE PUSHED THE blonde back. "What the fuck?" he growled as his gaze followed Isla until she disappeared down the hallway. For several seconds they'd been connected then the bitch had to come over and throw her tits in his face. The way Isla stalked away told him she was pissed, and that made him feel good even though he knew it shouldn't.

"I came over to say hi and to see if you're interested in having some fun. It's been a long time, Sangre. I heard you're in between bitches. Remember the last time you were like that? We had some good and dirty fun, baby." She leaned forward again, but he put his hands on her shoulders and held her at bay.

"Not tonight. I'm here with a friend of mine and some of my brothers." He pointed at Shotgun. "Hit him up. He's usually up for it."

"Are you sure you don't wanna play?" She stuck out her lower lip as she ran her fingers down his arm.

"Yeah." He fixed his eyes back at the hallway. Shaking her head, the blonde moved away and walked toward Shotgun.

I should be playing with blondie or hanging with my brothers, but instead, I'm sitting here, staring at the doorway and watching for Isla. Fuckin' lame. Since he'd started hanging around with her, he'd been acting like a damn pussy. Like the way he had acted a few nights before when that ass wipe drummer was hanging all over her. He'd been pissed as hell, and when the asshole went into the house with her, it was all he could do from breaking down the door and dragging his ass out of there. After that, he'd arranged for other guards to stand sentinel because he didn't want to be near her. He was madder than fuck that he'd been jealous.

That shit didn't happen to him with chicks, but for some damn reason it did with her.

Jay and Isla holding hands after school played through his mind. He'd been so damn pissed when his buddy started dating Isla. Of course, he'd never let on that it bothered him, but each time he saw them together, it was like an electric shock to his system. He'd even arranged to double date with them for his junior prom. *I was acting fucking lame even back then with her.*

Then he saw Isla come back into the bar, and the way several of the men checked her out made his blood boil, but he couldn't blame them. She was a walking wet dream with those luscious curves, firm, rounded ass, and tits that were begging him to touch. A guy in a leather jacket said something to her that made her stop. Then he dipped his head down and spoke into her ear. Her full lips curved into a smile, and in Sangre's mind, all he could see was that tempting mouth of hers wrapped around his hard cock. *Dammit!*

When the man's hand curled around her upper arm, tugging her closer to him, Sangre sprinted from the bar and was by her side in four long strides. Glaring at the dude, he drew her to him. "Back the fuck off," he gritted.

Puffing his chest out, the biker bared his teeth. "You want a problem?"

Swinging Isla behind him, Sangre's jaw tightened. "I already got one. You."

Isla tugged on his cut. "Forget about it. Let's go."

He turned his head sideways. "Go back to the table."

"No. I don't want you to get hurt."

Before he could answer, the guy's hand slammed into his jaw and patrons jumped away, standing to the side of them. Another blow came his way, but Sangre was prepared for it and ducked in time while throwing a punch low to the biker's belly. The scraping of chairs and the rush of footsteps gave room to the two men as they fought it out. Sangre hoped Isla had gone to the table.

Hands grabbed his arm as he raised it in the air ready to pummel his opponent. "What the fuck?" he screamed out, trying to jerk out of the viselike hold.

"Take it outside," a burly man with a ZZ-Top beard said as he pulled Sangre back.

"We don't want the place trashed, dude," Jorge, part owner of Cuervos, said.

Steel and another dude held the other guy, who glared at Sangre, his nostrils flaring. "Just chill the fuck out. Either move on, or I'll throw your ass out," Steel said.

The man shook his head. "This is bullshit."

The busty blonde ran up to him, her fingers running through his hair. "Oh, baby. You did good. Let me help you out." She wiped his sweaty brow with a damp towel. In his peripheral vision, he saw Isla's face contort as she stormed away.

Pulling away from the bearded guy, he shrugged off the blondie. "Enough. I'm good," he said to her.

Steel looked at Sangre and pointed at the guy. "You done with this shit or you wanna take it outside?"

Craning his neck, he tried to see if Isla had gone back to the old ladies. "Nah. I gotta find Isla." He spun around and stalked to the table. When he approached, he didn't see her.

"What happened to you?" Chelsea gasped.

"I got in a fight."

"Was all that ruckus you?" Raven said, handing him a bunch of napkins.

Nodding, he wiped the blood from the corner of his mouth. "Do you know where Isla is?"

"She told us she was going to the ladies' room," Breanna answered. Creases formed on her forehead. "But that was a while ago. She should be back by now."

"She was there when the fight broke out. She didn't come back to the table?" The old ladies shook their heads. "Fuck," he muttered in a low voice.

"Here," Chelsea handed him a glass of water. "Wet the napkins."

He quickly poured some water on them and scrubbed the dried blood off his face. "I've gotta find her." His insides tightened and he dashed away. He flung open the front door and stepped outside, his eyes scanning the area around him. In the distance he saw what looked like a woman walking, her back to him. From the way her body moved, he was positive it was Isla.

Cursing under his breath, he ran after her. When he was less than a block away, she spun around, terror etched on her face. When her gaze landed on his, she turned back around and started to run. He caught up to her, grabbed her arm, and yanked her to him.

"What the fuck do you think you're doing?" she said, twisting in his grip.

"Making sure your ass is safe. Why the hell did you take off? You got some crazy asshole after you, and you're walking alone at night down a dark street in a pair of fuck-me heels? What the hell were you thinking?"

"I didn't want to see you get your face smashed in. You acted like a damn Neanderthal back there. When you were in high school, I used to think you got in fights because everyone thought you were a tough badass and you wanted to show them you were, but … newsflash, Sangre—we're out of high school. You can stop trying to prove you're tough."

"I'm not trying to prove shit! The fucker gave me attitude. Anyway, what does that have to do with you running out and pulling a crazy ass stunt like this?"

Her face softened a bit. "Okay. You're right. I shouldn't have run out of the bar—it was a stupid thing to do. I was just so mad and upset. Why the hell did you come over and start all that up?"

"I didn't like the way he was touching you. He could be the sick wacko who's sending you those letters. You should've pulled away. You can't afford to be too friendly with strangers."

"Well, if you were so worried about it, why were you hanging at the bar with your bevy of girls instead of protecting me?"

The heat of anger bubbled beneath his skin as his eyes narrowed. "I was protecting you, that's why I pulled you away from him."

"Or did you do it because you were jealous? It didn't seem like you—"

"I wasn't jealous." He clenched his jaw.

"Are you sure?"

"Yeah. Why the fuck would I be jealous? We're not dating or anything. We're just friends."

She turned her face from him. "I know that. It just seemed that way."

"I don't want you pulling stupid shit like this again. You're damn lucky nothing happened to you. This nut could be anywhere." He was pissed at her but more at himself for letting his emotions claim him when he should've kept his distance and his eye on the situation. But when Sangre saw the asshole touch her, it was like the jerk had lanced a red-hot poker through him, and he acted without thinking. Isla was stirring up all kinds of shit inside him that he didn't want to feel.

An audible sigh came through her parted lips. "I know. I wasn't thinking. I don't know. It just freaked me out when I saw that guy hit you. It really scared me." She leaned into him and put her head on his shoulder.

All the fear and anger he had brewing inside him seeped away and he held her close. He inhaled, breathing in the fresh, citrus scent of her shampoo and the sultry fragrance of her perfume mixing together in a unique, warm, indefinable something that was only Isla. Her satin-soft skin glided under his fingers, making his dick stir. Tightening his jaw, he tried to clamp down his mounting desire.

"I didn't mean to scare you." His voice was hoarser than it should have been.

"What can I say? I'm fucked up." Her laugh was weak and dry. "It reminded me of my dad and how he'd throw punches at me and my sisters and brother. I just had to get away. I didn't want to see you hurt.

I wanted to stop it, but I felt helpless. Maybe that's the way my mom felt. I always blamed her for not doing anything when my dad would punish us, but maybe she just felt *helpless*."

A sudden coldness hit his gut. He'd known her dad was a strict disciplinarian and unreasonable, but she'd never told him that he'd hurt her or her siblings. "I didn't know your dad hit you."

"He knew where to leave the bruises so they wouldn't show," she said softly.

"You should've told me."

"I never told anyone. None of us did. He had a way of making you think you deserved it."

"Oh, Isla." He squeezed his arms tighter around her, hoping to block out the memories from her difficult past. It'd never occurred to him that her dad had been hitting her because he'd come from a home where corporal punishment had never been used. If he'd known, he would've done something that probably would've landed him in jail. The idea that she was being hurt while they were friends ate him up inside.

"I didn't mean to bring it up. It's just that the fight brought back all these memories. One time, I tried to stop him when he was beating on my brother. He stopped then came after me with such viciousness that I had to stay home from school for a couple of weeks until the bruises and swelling disappeared. After that, I learned not to interfere. So, whenever shit went down with one of my siblings, I'd just run to my room and cover my ears while my insides twisted and churned. I hated feeling helpless whenever my brother or sisters cried out."

Anger flowed through his veins. "Did he beat on your mother too?"

"Not with his hands—that privilege was reserved for us. He beat my mom up with his words and his cruel actions, like not giving her a gift on Valentine's Day because she'd gained some weight, and he couldn't reward that. Or he'd always tell her about the women he thought were sexy and attractive in our neighborhood or among her friends. It was terrible how he chipped away at her self-esteem. He did a great job of it with us too. I never could understand how he could do that to us. We loved him. Isn't your dad supposed to love you?" Her voice hitched.

He remembered when she'd been out of school for that time. When he'd called or gone over to her house, her mother had told him she had the measles and couldn't see anyone. There'd been no reason for him to have doubted it, and when Isla had come back to school, she'd acted like everything was all right. He ran his hands up and down her back. "It fuckin' sucks when you can't depend on your parents. They're supposed to be there for you no matter what, but it doesn't play out like that sometimes. Your dad had shit going on inside of him that he took out on you. Instead of dealing with it like a man, he made all of you miserable because he was. I'm sorry I didn't know." She sniffled, and he squeezed her. "Shh … it's all over now."

For a few minutes they held each other, a comfortable silence blanketing them. She lifted her head, tilted it back, and searched his face. "You have a cut by your mouth. Does it hurt?" She ran her finger over the wound then slowly across his lips, down his chin to his Adam's apple.

His breath quickened. "Nah. I'm good. You know, I used to look for fights, especially at bars, but I don't do that much anymore. Although, there're times when a man has to defend himself. I won't ever let a guy disrespect me or my brothers. That's what the brotherhood is all about—respect, loyalty, and love. That fucker threw the first punch, and there's no damn way I was gonna turn the other cheek."

"I know. I overreacted. The shadows from my past sometimes get in the way too much. I'm working on all that with my therapist."

"That's good. Are you sure that you weren't pissed at me for more than the fight?"

She stiffened under his touch. "What do mean?"

"I don't know. You seemed pretty annoyed when that blonde chick came over."

She pushed away from him and put her hand on her hip. "Are you saying I was jealous of her? How ridiculous is that?"

"Well, weren't you? I mean you seemed pissed when she came up and kissed me before you tossed your head and went to the bathroom earlier, and then she came over playing Florence Nightingale and pushed you away."

She blinked rapidly. "I don't know what you're talking about. I didn't really pay that much attention. Who kisses you and who you screw is your business."

Seeing she was getting all worked up, he tilted his head in the direction of the bar. "We should head back. We can grab a bite to eat at Leroy's. Are you up for that?"

She shrugged.

"I could go for something. And for the record, I don't have anything going on with that blonde chick or any woman right now."

Walking toward the bar, she tossed her hair over her shoulder. "I already told you that what you do is your business. Like you said, we're friends and friends don't get jealous of each other if they date or flirt or talk with the opposite sex. I'm about as jealous of you and your women as you are of me and Benz, or that guy talking to me in the bar."

Throwing his words back in his face felt like a bucket of ice water. There was something brewing between them, but there was no way he was going to admit it, and from what she'd just said, she wasn't going to either. The truth was, she was mad because the blonde was hanging all over him, and he was pissed beyond words when that dude touched her in the bar.

"Does Leroy's still have homemade pies?" her voice pulled him out of his brooding.

"Yeah."

"I could go for a piece of pie and coffee."

Twenty minutes later, they were sitting in a booth with menus in front of them. Leroy's was crowded, but Tammy made sure Sangre got the booth he and his brothers liked best: the last one in the corner next to the picture window.

"You seem to really like it here," she said as she picked up the menu.

"I do. They have real good home-cooked food and great coffee. The

Night Rebels come here a lot. We even have our favorite waitress—Tammy. She has the right amount of sass, knows when to leave us the hell alone, and treats us real good. Didn't you ever come here when you lived in Alina? My family came here at least once or twice a month for Saturday breakfast or dinner."

"I only came here a few times when I lived here. I'd always have pie. I remember it was so good. We came with our mom. My dad thought eating out was a total waste of money, so we rarely went out for meals."

"Hiya, Sangre," Tammy said as she poured a steaming cup of coffee for him. Glancing at Isla, she smiled. "What can I get you to drink?"

"A cup of coffee and a glass of water would be great, thanks."

Tammy poured coffee in another cup and put it in front of Isla. "I'll be back with your water in a sec." She ambled away.

"Is your favorite pie still apple?" she asked, stirring cream into her coffee.

He grinned. "I can't believe you remembered that. And it is. The one here is damn good, but it's not my mom's. Speaking of which, you're invited to dinner this Sunday. When I was at my parents, I told them you were back in town."

"So, the invitation is from your parents?"

"And me."

Her eyes quickly darted downward, and a delicate pink flush crept across her cheeks as she dipped her chin down. "Oh," she whispered.

His gaze drifted down to the snug top that clung to the soft swell of her tits, loving the way they rose and fell with her quickened breath. *Damn, she's beautiful.* A soft smile spread over her lips when she caught him looking at her, and it sent a bolt of white-hot lust right to his dick.

"Here's your water. Have you decided what you want?" Tammy asked, pen and pad in hand.

"I'll take a piece of chocolate cream pie," Isla said, her eyes never leaving his.

"What do you want, handsome?"

He tore his gaze away. "I'll have the breakfast burrito."

"Sriracha inside like usual?"

He laughed. "You know me too well."

"That's scary. It means I'm spending way too much time around here." She refreshed their coffee then scrambled away.

"She seems nice," Isla said, her gaze still on him.

"She is. She works hard. Single mom of two teenagers and no support from her loser ex."

"That sounds like lyrics from a country song." He guffawed. "Maybe you could help me out with the lyrics for a new song I'm writing." She ran her tongue over her top lip.

What I'd like that tongue to do to me. If she keeps flirting with me, I'm gonna bust. "So, do you wanna come over for dinner on Sunday?"

"I'd love to. It'll be nice to see your parents again. Will your brothers and sisters be there?"

"The whole damn clan." A grin broke over her face and her eyes shone like frost in the moonlight. Without thinking, he reached over and stroked her cheeks; they were soft and smooth. As he pulled away, she captured his fingers, holding them tight against her face while staring intently at him. He inhaled sharply. *Fuck.*

Plates hitting the table broke the connection between them. "Chocolate cream pie," Tammy said as she put the dish in front of Isla, "and breakfast burrito with sriracha. I don't know how you can eat that hot stuff."

"It's damn good." He winked at her and picked up his fork.

"Besides more coffee, are you all good for now?" They nodded and she scurried away.

"Best chocolate cream pie. Ever." Isla brought another bite up to her mouth. "Just so good."

"Glad you're enjoying it." He averted his gaze from her face because just watching her sweet lips open and close as she devoured the pie slice made him hard as hell. *How fuckin' lame is that?*

As he chewed, he looked over her shoulder, his gaze landing on Nick Jeffers as he made his way toward their table. Sangre had gone to high school with him, and he couldn't stand Nick back then, and now that he'd become a deputy sheriff, Sangre had no tolerance for him. He thought he was hot shit because he carried a gun and a baton.

"What the fuck does he want?" he muttered under his breath.

"What?" Isla asked, scraping the remaining crumbs on the plate with her fork.

"Do you remember Nick Jeffers?"

She shook her head. "Not really. The name sounds vaguely familiar."

"He was in my class at Jefferson. He joined the sheriff's department, and he thinks his shit doesn't stink. Never cared for him back in the day, and I can't stand him at all now. He's headed this way."

Isla looked over her shoulder then turned back around. "The way he's walking is like something out of an old seventies' cop show."

"Steve, how are you?" Deputy Jeffers asked as he came up to their table.

Instead of looking at him, Sangre took another bite of his burrito, chewing it slowly. From the corner of his eyes, he saw Nick's face turn red. He kept eating.

"I heard you were back in town, Jordan. How's LA?"

"Good, I guess. I'm sorry … but I don't think I know you," she said, pushing the plate away, "and my name isn't Jordan anymore—it's Isla."

Jeffers face grew redder and Sangre snorted. "You got something you want to say to me?" he said to Sangre, his hands gripping the side of the table.

"Nope."

"What the hell's with the attitude? I just stopped by to say hi to you and Jordan."

Sangre wiped his mouth, pushed the empty plate away, and rested his elbows on the table. "The first thing is that she just told you her name's Isla, not Jordan. It's not that hard to remember … Which brings me to the second thing—I'm not Steve, I'm Sangre. So, if some dude comes over and uses the wrong name, the fucker can't expect me to answer. Got it?"

"I refuse to call you Sangre. I won't recognize that outlaw club you're in." Jeffers looked at Isla. "And you think you're high-and-mighty because you live in LA and have a band. Do you know you're sitting with a damn criminal?"

"I wouldn't keep this up if I were you," Sangre's voice was low and hard.

Jeffers stepped back. "Are you threatening me? You can't be serious. I could run your ass in right now for threatening an officer."

Glancing at him, Sangre cracked his knuckles and held his chin high. "It's time you moved on. Maybe you can find an old lady who hasn't picked up her dog's shit in the park."

The veins in his forehead strained against the skin as Nick glared at him. "Stand up. I'm taking you in." His hand flew to his duty belt.

"This is ridiculous," Isla said.

Jeffers head snapped in her direction. "You shut the fuck up, *Jordan*. If you keep up with your haughty and snobbish attitude, something bad may happen to you like it did to Lizbeth Kelly and Sharla Davidson." Isla gasped, and he laughed dryly.

Sangre noticed that Isla's face had gone from a rosy hue to a gray pallor. "Get the fuck outta here."

"I'm not Wexler! I don't kiss the ass of scum. You think just 'cause you're in a biker gang that you can do whatever the hell you want? No fucking way. Now get your ass up, or I'll drag you up." Spittle gathered in the corners of his mouth.

"Go ahead and do it, but just note that'll it'll be the last thing you ever do in your fuckin' life." An edgy, twitchy feeling wrapped around his muscles and nerves. *If he lays one goddamn finger on me, he's a goner. It'll be worth the prison term.*

Jeffers stood with his hand on his belt, staring at Sangre. Neither of them moved a muscle; the tension crackled between them. It was as if Jeffers was waiting for him to make the first move, and he was waiting for the flunky cop to do the same. Nobody was giving an inch as each held their ground.

"What's going on?" Wexler asked behind Jeffers.

"Nothing," Sangre said to the sheriff.

"This asshole threatened me. I was ready to arrest him." Jeffers took out a pair of handcuffs.

"Now hold on and put those things away." Wexler looked at Sangre. "Did you threaten Deputy Jeffers?" Sangre clenched his teeth and stared. The sheriff cleared his throat and looked at Isla. "Did you hear Sangre threaten my deputy?"

"No, not at all. As a matter of fact, your officer threatened me. He said that if I didn't shut up, I'd end up like Sharla Davidson. How can he go around saying things like that to women? Something's off with him."

Wexler shoved his hands into his pockets and stepped back. Sangre could see a muscle in his jaw pulsing. "Did you say that to this young lady?" he asked in a low voice.

"I was just warning her to be careful. She's taking it out of context."

"Man the fuck up," Sangre gritted.

Jeffers slammed his fist on the table, making Isla jump. "See the way he talks to a police officer? We shouldn't have to put up with that bullshit."

The sheriff shook his head. "Let's go," he said to Jeffers.

"Aren't you going to arrest him? He threatened me." Nick followed Wexler out of the diner.

"What the hell was that all about? I'm glad the sheriff came. I was afraid that jerk was going to arrest you."

"I'd never let that asshole do anything to me."

"Wow, it was luck that the sheriff walked in."

Sangre glanced over at Tammy and nodded at her. Her smile widened then she spun around and went into the kitchen. "Who are Sharla Davidson and Lizbeth Kelly? When he mentioned their names you went white as a ghost."

Isla filled him in on the murders of the two women and how they'd both been in her class at Jefferson. As she spoke, a sick, gut-twisting feeling punched at him. The fact that the asshole deputy brought up both names meant the law thought the same person killed the two women. He didn't like it one bit that the women had been in Isla's class and seemed to both have careers in the entertainment industry. *Are the letters she's receiving from this sonofabitch?*

"Have you received any letters recently?"

"No. It seems having you buffed men around me is working."

"Anything else for you guys?" Tammy asked. Sangre shook his head and she handed him the bill. "See you soon."

When they arrived at Isla's house, he scanned the area to make sure no one was lurking around, then went over and opened the car door for her.

"Are you the one watching me tonight?" she asked, leaning against him as they walked up the front walk.

"Yeah. Keith will be here in the morning."

"Can you stay inside? I'm kinda creeped out by what that jerk said to me. It's made me wonder if he's the crazy one. I mean, he *really* went off on me. He acted like he hated my guts because I didn't remember him *and* that I'm in a band. What the hell?"

"That asshole's always been a douche. I can't believe Wexler hired him on."

"The sheriff seems to respect you. That's totally amazing."

He shrugged. The truth was that the Night Rebels and Sheriff Wexler had a tacit understanding: They stopped hard drugs from coming into the county, and he'd look the other way on their club's activities. It'd worked for the past eight years, but now that Deputy Fuckface was on the roster, things weren't as smooth as they should be. He made a mental note to talk to Steel and Paco about it in the morning.

After checking all the doors, windows, and resetting the alarm, he stood at the doorway to her bedroom. She'd run upstairs the minute they'd come in, and he wanted to let her know he was going to crash on the couch in the family room.

When she came out of the bathroom, she wore a short, white night shirt that barely covered her ass, showing off her curves and leaving very little to the imagination. Blood pounded in his ears, making a roaring sound as his breath grew quick and need clawed through him. *I have to get the fuck outta here.* He stepped back, and the floorboard creaked under his boots.

Isla cried out, her eyes darting to the door and then relief covering her face. "You scared the hell out of me."

"Sorry. I just came up to tell you I'll stay on the couch in the family room. I didn't mean to barge in on you." As she leaned over a chair to pick up her robe, her nightshirt rode up, exposing the underside of her butt cheeks. Unable to move, Sangre stared at her as his cock stiffened uncomfortably in his pants. Isla's enticing curves made him want to throw her up against the wall and kiss her with a hunger that refused to be satisfied while his dick thrust deep and hard into her until she screamed out his name. "I gotta go."

"Wait. I thought we could watch a movie or something."

Not wanting her to see what was going on in his jeans, he turned around and headed toward the stairs. "I'm pretty beat," he said loudly. "See you in the morning."

Sangre ran down the steps and went into the family room and flopped on the couch. He grabbed the remote and turned the TV on, decreasing the volume exponentially. There was no way he wanted her sexy ass coming in here to see what he was watching. She was his friend. Off-limits. He didn't want to screw this up.

As he watched the images flicker on the screen, his mind kept seeing Isla in that tight nightshirt that hugged her curves just right. *She's my friend. We grew up together. We're like family.* He repeated the mantra over and over in his head, hoping his aching dick would get the message.

It was going to be a long night.

Chapter Twelve

STARING AT THE flat tire, Isla groaned. "I so don't need this," she said under her breath. Looking around, she saw Keith's car and was just about ready to walk over there when her next-door neighbor started to come over. Faith's two daughters ran up to Isla and hugged her.

"Did you make the lemonade?" Carly asked.

"Daddy finished our lemonade stand and we're going with mommy to get some decorations for it," Letty gushed.

"That's great. I'll make the lemonade tonight, so you'll have it ready for tomorrow morning when you open for business," Isla said, waving at Faith as she approached them.

"What's going on there?" Faith asked, pointing at the flat tire.

"I have no idea. I must've picked up a nail or something. This is such a drag. I really don't want to fix a tire. Gah! I better go back inside and change out of these clothes." Isla glanced over again at Keith's car.

Keith opened the door and got out. "You having a problem?" he asked as he walked toward her.

"Don't bother him. Colt can fix it for you. He's still at home, so I'll just run over and get him," Faith said.

"That's okay. Keith can do it. You don't have to bother Colt."

"Nonsense. After all the things you do for the girls, he'd be more than happy to help." Faith looked at Carly. "Go get your dad and tell him that Isla has a flat tire." Carly skipped away.

"Thanks. I hope this isn't an omen for having 'one of those days.'" Isla looked at Keith. "I have a flat tire, but my neighbor's going to change it."

"Are you sure? I can do it."

"My husband's on his way," Faith said before Isla could reply.

"So you don't need me?"

Smiling, Isla shook her head. "Colt's going to take care of it. Thanks for the offer." She watched the guard amble back to the car then looked at Faith. "What are you and the girls up to today?"

"We're going to the store to buy some embellishments for the lemonade stand. Colt finished it up yesterday, and the girls are so excited to get started with their summer business. Where are you headed off to?"

"We're rehearsing today. I was hoping to get to the gym for an hour before heading over to the venue, but I guess that's not gonna happen."

"It shouldn't take too long to change a tire. I don't know if you've noticed, but there have been different cars parked in front of your house like all night. I called the sheriff's department about it, and they sent out a deputy, but they never followed through in telling me what was up. I still notice cars in front of your house. I don't want to freak you out or anything, but have you noticed it too?"

Isla smiled. "I guess I should've said something to you. It never occurred to me that neighbors would be paying any attention, but I hired a security company to watch over me."

Faith's eyes widened. "Really? It never dawned on me that they would be bodyguards. I guess that makes sense when you're a public figure. Did you have them in LA?"

"No. As bizarre as this sounds, I never felt like I needed to have any in LA. And even though Alina is a small town, I'm feeling very vulnerable here. I've been getting some wacko fan mail, so I just feel safer having somebody watch over me. Goes with the territory, I suppose. It seems that the more people who know about us, the more exposed I feel. I guess in time I'll get used to it though."

Letty tugged at the hem of her mother's shirt. "Mommy, when are we gonna go?"

Faith laughed and grasped her daughter's hands. "I guess we better get a move on it before she breaks a blood vessel."

Isla nodded. "I can't wait to see what you and Carly do to your lemonade stand. I bet you get a ton of cool stuff today with your mom." Shifting her eyes back to Faith's, she smiled. "Have fun shopping. I'll be by in the morning with the lemonade."

Carly ran up to her mom and pulled on her hand. "Come on, Mom. We gotta go."

Colt came up to Faith and wrapped his arm around her waist, kissing her cheek. He looked over at Isla. "Heard you have a flat tire."

Pointing at the front driver's side, Isla rolled her eyes. "Yeah. That's what greeted me this morning."

"You got a spare?" he asked.

"I do."

"We're gonna head out," Faith said.

Colt reached in his pocket. "Do you need my credit card?"

"I have our joint card. See you later." She walked over and gave her husband a quick peck on the lips, waved at Isla, and walked over to their SUV in the driveway. Letty and Carly hugged their dad quickly, yelled their goodbyes to Isla, and ran up to the car.

"I can't tell you how grateful I am that you're doing this for me," Isla said.

"No problem." Colt rolled the spare tire over to the front of the car and went down on his knees. "You didn't pick up a nail. Someone slashed your tire."

A cold chill wrapped around her as shivers ran up her spine. "You mean this was done on purpose?"

"Yeah. Looks like it was slashed by maybe a razor blade or a penknife. I wonder if any of the other neighbors had their tires slashed. Didn't have your car in your garage like me?"

"No, I was moving some of my belongings around and cleaning things out, so my garage is full of stuff that needs to go to charity. The truck's supposed to come by tomorrow morning to pick it up."

"That's bad luck. I should have it fixed in no time."

As he put on the spare tire, her thoughts were spinning a thousand miles a minute. *Whoever did this has been watching me. They knew Sangre was in the house with me last night.*

"When's your next show? Faith and I want to see you perform."

"Next Saturday. I'll let you know."

"Don't let this upset you. Got a couple of kids in the neighborhood who are a pain in the butt," he said, standing up. "Your tire is ruined. I can take it and throw it in the dumpster at my work. You should get a new one. You can't drive too much on a spare."

"Thanks a lot for all your help. I'll deal with getting a new tire tomorrow. I have a full day of rehearsal and recording, so I better get going. What's your favorite type of cookie?"

"I don't really eat cookies."

"Are you a beer drinker?"

Nodding, he smiled. "I like my Coors, but you don't have to get me anything. I'm just happy I could help you out."

"I'll give you two tickets to our next show and buy you both a round of drinks. Deal?"

"Sounds good. Faith will be excited because we don't get out very much. It's hard with the two kids."

"If you ever need a babysitter, just give me a call. If it works, I'd be more than happy to stay with Letty and Carly. They're great kids."

"Thanks. I'll let Faith know about your offer of babysitting. We may take you up on it sooner than you think. I better get going. See you."

Isla slid into the driver's seat and pulled away from the curb. After a quick glance in the rearview mirror, she saw Keith driving behind her and relaxed. *It probably was those two boys down the street who did this.* She made a mental note to ask a few of her neighbors who left their cars parked on the street or the driveway if their tires had been slashed.

Despite her tire incident, Isla still felt that since she'd employed Sangre's security services everything seemed to have stopped. She smiled like a schoolgirl when she thought of Sangre. *There was some intense, crazy ass connection going on between us last night.* A flush of heat spread through her when she remembered how he'd looked at her after she'd changed into her nightshirt. She had no idea that he'd be in her bedroom, otherwise she would've put on a robe before she came out. *His eyes almost popped out of his head ... and he definitely had a hard-on.* She giggled and turned on the radio, raising the volume when her favorite White Snake song, "Here We Go Again," came on.

Singing at the top of her lungs, she swung into the parking lot of the Fitness Gallery and stayed in the car until the song was over. Keith pulled in behind her, and she went up to his car.

"It's totally cool if you don't come inside because I know most of the people who work here. I should be about forty minutes or so if you wanna grab yourself a cup of coffee and come back."

He picked up a thermos. "I'm good. I gotta check with Sangre about not going in."

"Really, it's fine."

Keith shook his head. "Even so, I still gotta run this by the boss."

"Well, I'll give him a quick call then." Isla pulled out her phone.

"How are you?" she asked.

"Good. You?"

"Great. I'm at the gym for about forty minutes and then heading over to The Rear End for rehearsal. I just told Keith that he doesn't need to come inside the gym with me because I know a ton of people in there and feel totally comfortable and safe. Can you tell him to chill until I come out?"

"Let me speak to Keith." Isla passed the phone to him and then leaned against the car, straining her ears to hear their conversation. Keith had rolled the window practically all the way up, and since he was a low talker anyway, she couldn't really hear what he was saying. She did catch a few phrases, and they all related to her flat tire. Keith rolled the window down and handed her the phone.

"Sangre?"

"Keith said you had a flat tire?"

"Yeah. It turns out that some brats in the neighborhood slashed the tire. There're a couple of boys who live down the street from me, and they can be a pain in the ass."

"I didn't hear anything last night. Dammit."

"Relax. It's not your fault. My neighbor fixed it, and all's good. I'm going in tomorrow to get a new one."

"Was your neighbor's tire slashed?"

"No. Their cars were in the garage."

"Did you talk to any neighbors who parked on the street?"

Looking at the time, she tapped her foot on the asphalt. "Not yet. I was going to when I got home. I really have to go. I'm meeting the guys in an hour, and I want to work out before then."

"So, you don't really know if anyone else had their tires slashed, you're just assuming. I don't like it. Keith needs to go inside with you."

She groaned. "I need privacy, okay? I feel completely safe in there. I'm just going to work on the machines for twenty minutes and jump on the treadmill. No one followed us here. I'm sure you already asked Keith that."

"I did."

"Then …? It's all good. Tell him to be right in front in forty minutes. You can call him on his phone. I have to go, okay? I'll see you later tonight."

"I have club business tonight, so Jeff's on the schedule."

Disappointment weighed her down. "Oh. When will I see you?" *Don't sound desperate.*

"I'm not sure, but I'll call you. I'm calling Keith now."

As she put her phone into her tote, she heard Keith's ringing, and she walked away.

"Hey," Scott said as she entered.

"How's it going?" she answered, stopping at the front desk to swipe her card.

"Not too shabby. Going for a swim today?"

"I don't have the time. Just a quick workout," Isla replied as she walked into the machine area. Usually she incorporated a swim into her routine, loving the calming effects of the water. If her workout was too strenuous, she'd just float on her back and let the water soothe and cradle her. *If it hadn't been for those damn kids, I'd be able to get a swim in. And what's with Sangre? I thought for sure he'd be over tonight.* In fact, she'd been looking forward to it. *Probably has a date with that blonde. Who cares? I don't.* But she did, and that made her mad at herself and at him.

She went over to one of the elliptical machines and opened her duffel bag, taking out a towel, water bottle, and MP3 player loaded with metal and hard rock songs. After putting in the ear buds, she stepped onto the machine, turned it on, and started off at a slow pace to warm up. Lost in Anthrax's "Welcome to the Madhouse," a hand gripping her bicep startled her, making her stumble and lunge forward. She slowed the machine down and turned her head sideways. A man around her age, with killer abs and muscular legs and arms, gave her a wide, toothy grin. Her belly tightened as she pulled her arm away then wiped her face with her towel.

"What the hell? You know better than to do that when someone's on a machine," she said, her voice laced with irritation. The last person she wanted to run into at the gym was Devin, and here he was, as always, grinning at her like a damn Cheshire cat.

"I'm sorry. I just wanted to talk to you before you rushed out of here. I'm starting my workout, and after you finish yours, you're history." He laughed.

"I don't have much time to talk. I've already had to cut mine short this morning. What do you want?" She wished he'd go away. He seemed to be at the gym every time she was—no matter if it was morning, afternoon, or night. *Does he live at this damn place? Doesn't he have a damn job?*

"I have an extra ticket for a play this Thursday night. I was wondering if you wanted to go. We could have dinner before."

"I can't. I told you I have a boyfriend, and he wouldn't be too happy about me going out without him." *Why the hell can't he catch on that I'm not interested in him?*

Devin stared at her. "Is it that one guy with the long brown hair who's picked you up a few times?"

"You've asked me that before, and the answer is the same. Yes, it's him." Inserting one of her ear buds, she turned away. "I need to finish my workout."

"I thought you told me you like theater."

"I do, but it just isn't going to happen. I don't mean to be rude, but I only have limited time here." She put the other earphone in and cranked up the music. In her peripheral vision, she saw him still standing there scowling with his arms crossed. Unease filled her as she turned up the speed. After several minutes he stalked away, and she breathed a sigh of relief. The guy just didn't catch on. Ever since she'd joined Fitness Gallery, he'd been trying to get her to go out with him. There were a lot of nice, available women who exercised at the gym, and she'd even pointed out several to him, but he seemed hell bent on going out only with her. It had become annoying, and she'd decided if he didn't stop, she'd have to talk with the manager about it. Grabbing her arm while she was on a moving machine was stupid as hell, and she could've been seriously injured.

A half hour later, she was guzzling down water as she waited for her body to cool down. Ignoring Devin, she rushed off to the locker room, took a quick shower, changed, and was in the car hurrying to The Rear End to meet the band. Before getting out, she pulled down the visor, swiped a pink gloss over her lips, and smiled. "Thank God for waterproof makeup," she muttered as she opened the door and got out.

When she walked in the building, she noticed Benz leaning against the stage, cigarette hanging from his lips, and talking to a woman. Arsen gave her a high five, Jac jerked his head, and Gage jumped off the stage and came over to her.

"Jim said we can practice until three o'clock," Gage said.

Looking over his shoulder, she quirked her lips. "Who's Benz talking to?"

He looked behind him then shrugged. "Some chick that was here when we arrived. How's the new song coming?"

"Almost done. I think you're going to love it." She turned toward the bar and asked the bartender for a ginger ale with lots of ice.

"Hey, babe." Benz's deep voice washed over Isla, surrounding her with the scent of cigarettes, whiskey, and pine.

"Hi." She picked up her glass and put the straw in her mouth.

"You still pissed at me?" he asked, nuzzling her neck.

She put her drink on the counter. "As I remember it, you were the one mad at me and stormed out of the house."

Benz pushed her hair away from her neck with his nose. "That's 'cause you didn't want to fuck. It's been too long, baby. I've got needs and you do too. Why the hell are you putting us in the deep freeze?"

"I've been dealing with a lot of things, okay?" She inched away from him. "I just told Gage that I've finished the new song. I think it's amazing, and I'm sure you'll think so, too."

He narrowed his eyes. "Great news. Wow, I can see why that kept you busy. Tell me one thing, songbird. How in the *fuck* do you have time to hang with your asshole *friend* and write the goddamn song, but you have no time for your boyfriend? How the fuck does that work, Isla? I really want to know." He kicked over one of the chairs.

"Chill, dude," Gage said.

"Stay the fuck outta this!" Benz pointed his finger at the rhythm guitarist.

"Is there a problem?" the owner asked, coming around the bar.

Benz swatted the air with his hand. "Ask Ms. Fucking Songwriter!"

Jim bent over and picked up the chair. "Don't break shit in my place, or your asses are outta here."

"Sorry," Isla said.

Jim fixed his gaze on Benz. "Why're you apologizing? I wasn't talking to you."

Benz jerked his head back and met the owner's stare. Isla cleared her throat. "We better get rehearsing." She tugged on his sleeve. "Come on. All's good." Benz reluctantly let her pull him away, but he kept looking back at Jim, who maintained his stance.

"Don't fuckin' blow this, dude. We need to get the feel of the acoustics for our upcoming show," Arsen said.

Benz yanked his arm out of Isla's grasp. "Talk to *her* about all this. You never give her shit, and it's her fuckin' fault most of the time."

His words were like kerosene to an already burning fire in her. Benz never took responsibility for anything he ever did, even when he cheated on her. He had told her he was sorry when she'd caught him, but somehow, he'd managed to twist it around, making it her fault that she'd been so busy and hadn't given him the attention he needed as a man.

"That's not true," Gage said.

Benz brushed past him and jumped up on stage. "I don't listen to a fucking thing you say. I swear you've got the hots for my girl. You *always* take her side."

The muscle in Gage's jaw twitched. "I don't take anyone's side. You're usually out of line and *way* out there. If someone has to take responsibility for something, we can count on it *not* being you."

Benz threw his drumsticks at Gage and rushed over to the edge of the stage. "You want your ass thrown out of the band, dipshit? Iris Blue is *my band*. Believe me, I can find a rhythm guitarist just like that." He snapped his fingers.

"Benz, stop it," Isla said, holding her anger at bay. If they were alone, she'd let him have it good, but she didn't want things to escalate beyond repair with the band.

Pointing his finger at her, he glowered. "You shut the fuck up!"

Jac strummed his bass. "Forget the damn drama and let's get going. I have somewhere to be at three."

Benz shook his head. "What the fuck do you have to do in this stupid cow-town?"

"Raise it up a bit," Jac said to the sound man. He played the intro to "Let There Be Rock" by AC/DC and gave the thumbs up to the engineer. "You're up." He pointed to Arsen then looked at Benz, who stood staring at him, the microphone dangling from his hand. "By the way, it's none of your damn business what I do after rehearsal. Let's just get outta high school and get shit done."

Isla bit her inner cheek to keep from laughing. Jac didn't say much, but when he did, he nailed it. She jumped up on stage and took the mike from Benz then walked over to the stand. While she was adjusting it, waiting for her turn for sound check, she saw the woman who was talking with Benz when she came in approach the stage.

"Hi, Isla. I'm excited to see you guys rehearse."

She looked at her blankly. "Do I know you?"

Annoyance etched the woman's face. "Lexi Strobe. Remember we bumped into each other at the festival downtown?"

Oh yeah. The bitch from high school. What the hell's she doing here? "Sure. Up on stage, the lights can be blinding. What're you doing here?"

"Benz invited me."

More damn kerosene on the fire. "I didn't know you knew anyone in the band besides me."

"I met them at the festival, and then ran into Benz and Arsen at Beta the other night. You know … that nightclub on Fourth and Elm. I was surprised you weren't with Benz."

"I was busy working. I write most of the lyrics for the songs. Don't you have a job or something?"

She blinked. "Of course, I do. I just took the day off to come to the rehearsal." Her mouth turned downward. "Don't you want me here?"

"We normally have closed rehearsals, but it's cool with me as long as everyone else in the band is down with it."

"They are." Benz's voice had a hard edge to it.

She glanced over her shoulder and smiled sweetly at him. "Then all's good."

They took a break after a couple of hours, and Lexi made a beeline to Benz, who put his arm around her and showed her his drum kit. Jac came over to Isla. "He's an asshole. You know this, so don't let him get you down."

"I'm not, but thanks." Isla watched Jac saunter off, his head dipped down, cell phone in hand. The fact that he'd come over made her feel better. Jac was the one to get the least involved in all the drama between Benz and herself. Before they'd started dating, they had a whole lot less tension and antics, but after Parker had dumped her, citing the band as the reason, she'd been feeling so lonely and realized that no man would understand the dynamics of Iris Blue or the commitment it took to have a viable career in indie music. Benz had caught her in that weak moment in her life; she'd started a relationship with him, and it'd been an emotional roller coaster ever since.

Glancing back at Lexi and Benz, the anger she'd been fighting most of the day bubbled when she saw Lexi pressed close against his side. It wasn't so much that she was pissed because she was madly in love with him, because she wasn't, it was more a blow to her pride—especially since the woman was the one who'd made some of her time at Jefferson miserable.

She turned back around and pulled out her phone to call Madison. Whenever she needed picking up, Madison, with her cynical view about women and men, always came to the rescue.

"I was just thinking about you," Madison said. "I wanted to know if you were up for dinner tonight."

"I can't. I'm at rehearsal, and then I have to go to the studio to record a couple of songs. Maybe tomorrow."

"That won't work for me. My cousin's going through a crisis with her man *again*. I promised to listen *again*."

Isla chuckled. "Speaking of men who keep making us go through shit again and again, you won't believe who Benz is flirting up a storm with."

"Why the hell is he flirting at all?"

"He's an asshole, remember?"

"Isla you can do so much better. Who's the bitch?"

"Lexi Strobe."

"Ugh … the man's an asshole and an idiot. He's got you, and he's dissing you right now to play up to Lexi Strobe? I bet she's focused on him because you guys are dating."

"Well, sorta dating right now. He's so mad at me because I wouldn't fuck him a few nights ago, so I know he's trying to teach me a lesson. I guess I can kinda understand how he feels. I mean, I haven't been the best girlfriend to him for the past few weeks." *Not since Sangre and I resumed our friendship.* She didn't know what the deal was, but she had no interest in sleeping with Benz, and instead of yearning for him or fantasizing about them together, Sangre was the one who filled her thoughts. *But what would be the point even if we started something? I'm going back to LA soon. Maybe we could be friends with benefits? Would I like that?*

"Isla? Are you still there?" Madison's voice broke through her thoughts.

"I'm here. Sorry, I was just thinking about things. What were you saying?"

"I said Lexi's always after everyone's boyfriend. If you weren't with Benz she wouldn't even be there."

"You're right. I'd forgotten that about her. The other annoying thing is that she acts like we were best friends in high school. It's like she wants to be my buddy now. It's weird. Something's wrong with her. Seriously."

Madison sniggered. "Want to know another thing that's real weird? She's now the lead in "Mousetrap." It's playing at the Globe Theater. Sharla Davidson was the lead, but now that she's dead—enter Lexi."

Icy tingles skated across her skin. "Lexi was Sharla's understudy? That's not weird, that's just fuckin' freaky."

"I know, right? And …" Madison paused for dramatic effect.

"What?"

"She told everyone that she had the vibe she'd end up being the lead. She was so pissed when she didn't get the lead that she bad-mouthed poor Sharla all around the theater circuit. She's an evil person and would do anything to get ahead. She hasn't changed one iota from the bitch she was in high school, and she was so damn jealous of you when you'd landed all the leads. I can guarantee your success is eating her alive right now."

When Isla looked over her shoulder again and saw Benz hugging her gently, Lexi's gaze fixed on her. Isla shuddered: Lexi's eyes were cold, calculating, and hard. She faced the bar again. "Maybe she wants my life—you know … Benz … Iris Blue—all of it."

"This is a *Twilight Zone* episode," Madison said. When they were younger, they'd devour marathons of the show on the television.

Isla chuckled. "Totally. Oh, she can have my dad and my fucked-up family." Madison burst out laughing, which made Isla laugh hard. Soon Isla was sputtering and choking while she dabbed the tears from her eyes.

A warm arm snaked around her. "Who're you talking to?" Benz asked as he placed a kiss on her head.

His action was the antidote to her laughing, and she pushed him away. "Madison."

"It's Benz right? Is the bitch with him?"

"Yes and no."

"Where is she?"

"Not sure."

"Baby, the break's over," Benz said in a low voice, his hand making circles on her back.

"I gotta go. I'll call you later." She hung up the phone and slid off the barstool.

"After recording, I want to take you out for a nice dinner. We can have some wine, talk, and be like we used to before stuff happened."

"*Stuff* was you cheating on me. I'll be beat after recording, so maybe you can take Lexi. She seems to have captured your attention." *Filter. Damn, why did I say that?* She hated that the words slipped out of her mouth because she knew they'd make him satisfied. *I sound so petty and jealous, just what he wants me to be. Ugh. I gotta have a break from him. Since he's been here, my nerves have been in overdrive.*

"I can't help it if women find me attractive. You know I have to play the game for the fans, but you're my number one. I like that it bothers you. I was starting to think you didn't care about me anymore." He ran his fingers up and down her arm.

"Benz?" Lexi said as she came over. "What're you doing?"

Benz drew Isla close to him, and she felt him stiffen. "Talking to my girlfriend." His voice dripped ice.

If looks could kill, Isla would be dead on the spot. No question about that. She'd never had a person give her such a scathing and evil look before. She smiled. "We need to get back to rehearsal." She let Benz walk her to the stage but felt the daggers shooting from Lexi's eyes with each step she took. As he helped her up, the loud slam of a door startled her. When she looked out from the platform, Lexi was gone. Even though satisfaction coursed through her, apprehension pricked at her insides—but for the time being, she pushed it away, picked up the microphone, and belted out the song.

THE NIGHT HAD obliterated any lingering light when Isla came out of the recording studio. A cool wind from the mountains made her shiver and her skin pebble. A sprinkling of shimmering stars above illuminated the dark, moonless sky. She tugged her cardigan tighter and glanced around the small parking lot in front of the studio; her car was the only one there. *Where the hell is the security?* She rushed over to her car and slid in quickly, locking all the windows and doors. She started the engine and pulled onto the two-lane highway. As she approached Alina, silhouettes of cacti, brush, and rock formations turned into moving shadows and shapes, which made her insides twist and churn. There wasn't a car in sight, and she kept her gaze fixed on the road ahead, occasionally looking at the rearview mirror to make sure no one was following her.

When Isla saw the lights of the town, she let out a breath she didn't know she was holding. Relaxing her fingers a bit, she loosened her death-like grip on the steering wheel, shaking out one hand and then the other to get the blood flowing again. Isla took out her phone to call Sangre and ask where the hell the security was but cursed when she saw her battery was dead. She cursed even louder when she realized she'd forgotten to take out the charger from her other purse before she'd left that morning.

"I'll just stop in one of the restaurants and use their phone," she said out loud as she turned down Fifth Avenue. All of a sudden, a loud clanging sound echoed around her. *Is that my car?* She rolled down the window, and the sound was almost deafening. She stopped the car. No sound. She started it up again, and the noise began. "*Dammit!* This has been such a shitty day. First the flat tire and now this. *Shit!*" She pounded the steering wheel. If she could just get to Main Street, there'd be a lot of places still open, and she'd be okay.

The car bucked as she pressed her foot all the way down on the accelerator pedal, and the vehicle kept slowing down. It was like the gas wasn't getting to the engine. She glanced at the gas gauge, and it showed she had nearly half a tank full. "What the hell's wrong?" Then the car died. "*Fuck!*" Isla switched the key and all she heard were clicking and whirring sounds, but the engine didn't start. She waited a few minutes then tried again. Nothing. Looking around, she didn't see any one. *Where the hell is my bodyguard?* Mark had been there during the rehearsal and when she'd gone into the studio. *Who took the next shift?* She picked up her dead phone and stared at it like *that* would make it magically power up. *I can't just stay in the car. Main Street is only a few blocks away.* Sighing, she grabbed her tote and got out of the car.

The street was dark and deserted, the only light coming from sporadic streetlights that filtered through the overhanging branches of the trees on each side of the road. Isla moved quickly through the thin lights and shadows, her knuckles white from clutching the straps of her tote. Looking down the street, it appeared to just melt into the darkness. Isla picked up her pace and pushed onward, her soft footfalls absorbed by the pavement.

Then a gust of wind surged through the empty street, moaning like some horror movie opener. Trees creaked, bushes sighed, and cans and papers rumbled, bumping into walls and darkened corners. Isla bent her head down to avoid dust getting in her eyes, and then stopped to button up her cardigan. And that's when she heard it above the wind's groan: the clack of heels on the pavement behind her. Blood suddenly rushed to her head. She took a few steps then stopped, and the footsteps stopped as well. Swallowing hard, she walked faster and the steps matched her pace. Again, she stopped … Complete silence. No wind … No footfalls … Nothing but a deafening quiet.

With her body shaking, Isla started walking again, and even though everything inside her told her not to, she looked over her shoulder. Still nothing. No one—just eerie shadows from the trees crisscrossing over the sidewalk and grass. Fear ran through her. *Did I imagine it?* She didn't think so. There was someone out there. She *felt* it. Her eyes darted around trying to make sense of the sinister menace lurking in the shadows, and she picked up her pace while continuously looking back. She began to run, sweat pouring down her back as she turned the corner.

Sissss. Suddenly, a loud hiss and her high-pitched scream shattered the pervasive silence. She whirled around and tears poured down her face as she saw a bus pull up to the curb beside her. Several people alit as she ran over to the bus.

"Where're you going?" she said to the driver.

"The terminal on Main Street."

Putting her foot on the step, she began to climb into the bus when something pulled her back. She cried out, and the driver threw her a puzzling look.

"You okay, miss?" he asked.

"Where're you going?" a low voice said behind her.

She turned around and met the brown eyes of Jon. "What the hell are you doing? Leave me alone."

"Are you coming on, lady?" Impatience wove through the bus driver's voice.

"She's not," Jon said, pulling Isla away from the door.

"No!" She tried to break away from him, but his hands were like vices. "Please. No!" She watched the bus pull away, her heart sinking.

"What's the matter with you? Sangre wouldn't like it if I let you go on the bus."

"Sangre? *You're* the one who's supposed to be watching me?" When he nodded, fear, anger, and relief blended together to make a volatile mixture. "Where the fuck have you been? You weren't at the studio, and my car broke down a few blocks from here. I had to walk it alone in the dark. I'm not paying for that kind of service." People milling on the streets and coming out of restaurants looked at her as if she was a lunatic, and she supposed she was acting like one by cursing and yelling on the sidewalk at a young man who looked like he'd just lost his best friend. But she didn't give a damn. She'd been scared out of her wits, she was still pissed at Benz, and she was beyond exhausted. All she wanted was to go home and curl up under her comforter and forget about the day.

"I don't know why you're so mad. I've been following you the whole time."

"You're lying!"

For a second, his eyes flashed then they returned to normal. "I'm not."

"Then why didn't you help me when my car broke down?"

"I tried to, but you jumped out and ran away so fast."

She knew what she saw; there wasn't a car in sight on the street. *He's definitely lying. I know someone was out there.* A cold chill spread over her. *Why would Sangre have Jon on duty when I told him I didn't want him? Ever. The guy gives me the creeps. Something's wrong here.*

"I can take you home. All the mechanic shops are closed, so you can deal with your car in the morning."

There was no way she was getting in a car with him. Before she could answer, Carly and Letty came running up to her.

"Isla!" Carly shouted.

Startled, she just blinked at the two girls for a moment as nothing registered inside her head.

"We went to get hamburgers at Hamburger Hamlet. I got a cheeseburger. Did you go there too?" Letty asked.

"No, I didn't. So, it was good?" Her stomach growled, and she realized that she hadn't eaten since early that morning.

The girls rubbed their tummies and said, "Mmm." She laughed and looked around wondering where Colt and Faith were. She saw them walking toward her.

"We better get going," Jon said.

"Hi," she said, waving to Colt and Faith. "Your girls said you've been out for burgers."

"Yeah. I was so tired after shopping and decorating the lemonade stand that I told Colt the kitchen was closed tonight." She leaned against her husband.

"I don't blame you. Are you guys headed home right now?" Faith nodded. "Can I bum a ride with you? My car broke down a few blocks from here."

"You've had a bad day with car trouble," Colt said. "We'll take you home." "Sangre's not going to like this," Jon said in a low voice.

"These are my neighbors. It's fine." *I'm definitely safer with them than with you, you lying wacko.* "I'll deal with Sangre." *I'm going to blast him!* Without waiting for Jon to say another word, she grabbed each of the girls' hands and walked away.

After saying her goodbyes, she went inside and locked the door. *A real shitty day.* She set the alarm then climbed the stairs to her bedroom. She couldn't wait to wash off her makeup and put on her comfy pajamas. Her stomach growled, but she was so tired she didn't even feel like making the trek to the kitchen to make a sandwich.

A few minutes later, she had her cell phone charging, the night lamp switched off, and the covers pulled back. Happy the day was finally over, she slipped between the sheets, tucked the comforter under her chin, closed her eyes, and welcomed the refuge of sleep.

Chapter Thirteen

SANGRE TILTED BACK the folding chair until it hit the concrete wall. Church had been going on for over two hours, and he'd grown weary of all the yelling and pounding the brothers kept doing every time someone mentioned the Satan's Pistons or the Deadly Demons. He figured there would be trouble with the asshole clubs in Sturgis, but with the Insurgents and Fallen Slayers willing to help, he knew the Night Rebels could handle any shit they threw their way.

"The more immediate problem is with those damn 39th Street punks," Diablo said.

"They need to stay the hell in Durango," Goldie said, and the brothers whooped in agreement.

"You'd think the Los Malos fucks would be clamoring to do some shit seeing that we wiped out their strip bar in Silverado," Chains said.

"They're pussies now. We cut their balls off," Paco answered, and the whole brotherhood roared.

Steel leaned against the wall, laughing, then when the noise died down, he pushed off and looked each brother in the eye. "They think Silverado is open now that the West Avenue Bandits and Los Malos are outta business. They also think each of them double-crossed the other. The Pistons have been itching to establish a smack trade in the south for a long time. There's no fucking way I'm letting heroin anywhere in this area."

Silence descended on the room as an air of sadness fell over the members. Paco clasped Steel's shoulder, pulling him in a bear hug while the brothers lifted their fists in the air.

"We're all with you, bro," Sangre said.

"There's no way we're gonna let that shit get through," Shotgun added.

Each brother voiced his support until Steel stepped forward and raised his fist. "Thanks, brothers. I knew I could count on you. Each of us is strong, but together we're a fucking atomic bomb."

The members rose to their feet, their fists pumping in the air as they chanted, "Night Rebels forever, forever Night Rebels," over and over. After several minutes, they sat down, and Diablo came up to the front.

"Chains is monitoring the activities of these assholes." He looked at Chains. "We're in awe of your computer genius, bro." The members clapped and whistled. "Brick, Knuckles, Patriot, and me are feeling out some informants in Durango and Silverado. We've gotta crush them before they make a move, but right now it looks like they're not doing much but yapping."

"Satan's assholes haven't forgotten what we did to them. I don't think they're gonna want to butt heads with us any time soon," Muerto said.

"I agree, but we still gotta watch them. It's when we get cocky and too lax that shit happens." Diablo crossed his arms.

"Keep us informed," Paco said to Chains and Diablo. "I guess that covers it for now. We need to take the threat of this street gang seriously. I'd like to annihilate them and the damn Pistons."

"You may get your chance," Sangre said, standing up. "There's no way we're gonna let any shit happen, so I think we need to allocate some funds to building up our arsenal. We took a hit when helping the Fallen Slayers out a while back."

Steel nodded. "All those in favor of spending some of the club's money for weapons, say *Aye*."

"Aye!"

"Looks like you got the okay. Give Liam a call and arrange a date and time we can meet up with him in the next week." Steel brought the gavel down on the wood block. "Church is over. Go forth and booze, fuck, and get high."

The men guffawed as they pushed back their chairs and left the room. In the main area, Sangre went to the bar and picked up a bottle of beer and a shot of Jack. He walked over to an empty table and sat down.

"We got some major shit that's threatening to hit the fan," Army said as he joined him at the table.

"Tell me about it." Sangre threw back his shot.

"What's going on with the strip mall?" Jigger asked, pulling out a chair with his boot.

"Still getting the numbers together. I should have something concrete in the next couple of weeks. Chains is helping me gather the data."

"I don't know how the hell he can do all that computer shit." Army motioned to the club girls who were sitting on the couch next to the wall.

Angel pointed at herself and mouthed "Me?" Army nodded and held up three fingers. Kelly and Lucy jumped up and followed Angel to the table.

"You gonna play with all three of them?" Jigger asked as he watched the women approach.

"Maybe later, but right now, I want some damn food," Army said.

"What's going on?" Angel said softly, wrapping her arms around Army's neck from behind.

"Hey, Sangre." Kelly smiled and stood next to him.

"Hey. I think Army wants you ladies to drum up some food for us since tonight's Lena's night off."

"Is that all you can think about when you look at us?" Lucy folded her arms and pushed out her lips in a mock pout.

Army smacked her ass. "I see you as dessert, sweetie." The girls giggled and walked toward the kitchen. "How's your guarding going? Does your sexy friend still have her virtue?"

Jigger guffawed. "That's a good one." He gave Army a high five.

"Yup. Still intact." *Asshole.*

"Yo," Eagle greeted as he dragged a chair next to Sangre. "Seems like we had a problem last night with Isla's account."

Sangre's hand stopped in midair. "What problem?" He brought the beer bottle back down to the table.

"Some fuck up with Jon and Ron. She ripped me a new asshole. She was madder than hell she couldn't get a hold of you, so she took that out on me too. The chick's got a mouth on her."

He pulled out his phone and saw only one call from her during church. "I gotta get a new phone. Mine's been acting up big time." He stood up.

"What the fuck? The girls are bringing our food. You can call your friend after you eat. It's not like she's going anywhere." Army leaned back in his chair and jutted out his jaw.

"The *friend* shit is getting old, dude. And I don't need you to tell me what the hell to do. Get your own fuckin' life and stay outta mine." He stalked out of the room and bumped into Kelly coming out of the kitchen. "Sorry," he said as he looked at the sandwich and fries on the plate she carried. "Is that for me?"

"I made it just for you." She pressed her soft tits against him.

He took the plate. "Thanks. Eagle's at the table and he may want one too."

"That's it? Don't I even get a kiss for all my hard work?"

He kissed the top of her head then walked down the hall to the back porch. A wicker chair with a cushion covered in a bright tropical flower pattern stood near the window, and he sat on its arm. The club girls had been bothering the brothers for months about redecorating the screened-in porch, and they finally relented. He'd given them a few thousand dollars to redo the room with the proviso that they had to get a kickass grill for club barbecues. The women went all out, and the result was a bunch of furniture that looked like it belonged in a home décor magazine rather than in a biker clubhouse. He missed the comfortable, worn out couch and the overstuffed chairs they used to have. The only thing the girls got right was the stainless steel mega grill. Now, *that one* definitely kicked ass.

Sangre took a big bite out of his sandwich and tapped in Isla's number.

"It's about fuckin' time I heard from you!"

"Eagle wasn't kidding when he said you were pissed." He chuckled.

"I don't think anything about what happened last night is funny, nor do I think it's funny that you ignored me all day. I'm beyond pissed!"

"First off, I didn't ignore you. My phone's shit and I have to get a new one. Second of all, what the hell happened last night?"

"Eagle didn't tell you? Unbelievable."

"He said there was a mix up on who was on duty."

"No one was on duty. My car broke down and I had to walk to Main Street in the dark. I knew someone was following me. I could hear his footsteps. I could sense him. I'm not making it up. Someone was there, and if the bus hadn't come when it did, who knows what would've happened. And then, Jon pops up out of nowhere, insisting he was there all along. He was lying. I'm telling you that no one was on duty last night."

A sick feeling punched his gut. "Jon isn't supposed to be watching you at all. I told Eagle not to use him for your contract. Ron should've been there. I make it a point to know who's on. I'll call Ron and Jon and see what happened. What wrong with your car?"

"I don't know. It died on my last night. It's at the shop right now."

"How'd you get home?"

"I bumped into my next door neighbors, and they took me home."

"Why the hell didn't you call me when you noticed no one was watching you? I can't believe you didn't call me when you had car trouble."

"My phone was dead, and I forgot to take the charger out of my other purse. It just made me feel vulnerable. I've started feeling better the last few weeks, but then last night happened, and it let me know that he's still out there, watching me, waiting to pounce."

"Damn. I let you down. You shouldn't have gone through what you did last night. I'm sorry. I'll get to the bottom of it. I'm coming over."

"Okay," she said softly.

He smiled; she never could stay mad at him. "You can let me hear the new songs you've been working on."

"I'd like that."

"I'll be there soon." Sangre tucked the phone in the inside pocket of his cut and finished his sandwich and fries. He went back inside and came over to Eagle. "I had Ron on the schedule to watch Isla. What the hell happened?"

"After I talked with her, I called Ron. He said that Jon had called him and told him he was on the schedule and there was a mix-up. Ron balked at first, but he said the dude was practically crying about not having enough hours, and Ron's had over ninety this pay period, so he said okay to Jon. I was surprised when Isla said no one was there until a few hours later. I tried to call Jon to sort it out, but he's not answering his phone."

"I know where he lives. I'll swing by and try and make sense of what happened last night. And make it clear to Ron that unless it comes from us, he does the post he's given. I'll let him slide this one time, but next time, he's out on his ass."

As he turned to leave, Shotgun came up to him. "Are you gonna meet me at the pool hall?"

"I forgot about it, bro. Something came up, so we'll have to do it another time."

"Meeting your friend?" Army sniggered and the others joined him.

Ignoring them, he walked out of the club into the brilliant summer sunlight. After donning sunglasses, he straddled his Harley. Nearby, the faint buzzing of bees filled his ears while he breathed in the sweet scent of hay. It was a hot, still day. The trees stood mute in the summer air, the sun beat upon his back relentlessly, and wavy lines hovered over the road in front of him.

He rode over to Jon's apartment and banged on the door, but there was no answer. He checked out the parking lot and the streets around the complex, but he didn't see his car. After several calls to Jon went to his voicemail, Sangre climbed the metal steps once again to Jon's apartment and pounded several times on the doors and windows before he left.

By the time he arrived at Isla's two-story, brick house, beads of sweat poured down his neck, and the bandana he wore across his forehead was soaked. He took it off and threw it in a plastic bag then pulled out a towel from one of the saddlebags and mopped his face. He saw a colorful stand between Isla's house and the one next to it; two young girls sat behind the small counter. A man stood in front, his head tilted back and a cup to his lips. Sangre took off his sunglasses and saw the man wore a deputy sheriff's uniform. He ran the towel through his thick hair, tossed it in the plastic bag, and walked over to the stand.

"Would you like some lemonade, mister? It's homemade," a girl with brown pigtails said.

The deputy turned around and grimaced, and Sangre stiffened. *What the hell is Jeffers doing in front of Isla's house?* "Did you make it yourself?" He looked at the large pitcher filled with ice and lemon slices. His throat was parched, and a big glass of freshly squeezed lemonade sounded damn good.

"Our neighbor did. It's her own recipe," the other girl said, pointing to Isla's house.

"Then I'll take the largest glass you got." As the pigtailed girl poured, Sangre turned toward Jeffers who'd been staring at him since he'd arrived. "I thought you people go to donut houses."

The deputy's face grew taut. "What're you doing over here?"

"Same as you. Having a glass of lemonade on a hot as hell day." He looked over his shoulder and saw Mark approaching him.

"Here you go. It'll be one dollar for a large," the girl said.

He handed the money to her then drank it down all at once. "That was damn good, girls."

"Isla made it for us this morning. She gave the recipe to our mom."

"Isla?" Jeffers said. He glanced at Sangre.

He's such a bullshitter. There's no way he doesn't know Isla lives here.

He didn't just randomly come into this neighborhood for some damn lemonade.

"You know that, officer. You kept telling us her name was Jordan. Don't you remember?" one of the girls asked.

"No, I didn't. You must've misunderstood me. I said I knew a girl in high school who used to bring lemonade to some of the school functions that tasted just like the one you have. I said her name was Jordan."

The girl's pigtails flew back and forth as she shook her head. "That isn't what you told us. You said—"

"You girls have a crowd here," a blonde-haired woman in shorts and an oversized T-shirt said as she came over.

"We're doing real good, Mommy." The girl in pigtails showed her mother a big jar that had coins and dollar bills. The other girl beside her nodded vigorously.

She smiled and extended her hand to Deputy Jeffers. "I'm Faith—the entrepreneurs' mother."

"Nick Jeffers, ma'am."

She ran her eyes over Sangre, her gaze stopping on the tattoos coloring his arms. A look of concern spread across her face as she crossed her arms and stood closer to her daughters.

Mark came over and the girls giggled. "Didya want another one, mister?" one of them asked. Smiling, he nodded. "This is his fifth one," the girl whispered loudly to her mother.

"Carly, that's impolite," her mother said, giving a small smile to the security guard.

"No worries," he said as he took the cup from Carly. He dropped four quarters into the jar. "It's real hot today."

"Sangre!" Isla yelled from the porch.

He looked over and smiled as she stood on the threshold, holding the screen door open. Her shoulders in her lavender blouse turned slightly while the sun caught her hair and spun through it, threading it with golden honey and making the blue sheen sparkle like stars in the midnight sky. Suddenly, he couldn't move—he was mesmerized by her.

Then his whole body shuddered as he sucked a big breath into his lungs.

"How are the girls doing?" she asked.

"Great. Everyone loves your lemonade," Faith said.

He locked eyes with Isla and everyone drifted to the background. In the silence surrounding them, he could hear the hum of voices, the *whirr* of a lawn mower, and the call of a magpie somewhere behind him.

"You taking over the watch?" Mark's gruff voice broke through the spell Isla had cast over him.

Tearing his gaze away, he nodded. "Yeah. You can relieve Kevin over at the train depot. He's pulled a twelve-hour shift, so I'm sure he'll be happy to see you." Mark nodded then headed to his car.

Sangre threw his plastic cup in a small trashcan next to the stand and headed up the sidewalk to Isla's house. She'd stepped inside and when he entered, the scent of coconut and pineapple wafted around him. He heard some rustling in the living room. "It smells like the tropics or something," he said as he walked in. Sitting on the built-in shelves, the flames of brightly-colored candles danced.

"When I light these candles, it makes me feel like I'm in the Caribbean, lying on a white sandy beach, looking at the pristine blue water, and drinking a sweet, fancy drink," she said from the kitchen.

He glanced at the wet bar in the corner of the room. It had a large glass filled with small paper umbrellas, another glass brimming with maraschino cherries, and a platter of pineapple, lemon, orange, and lime slices. "Looks like you've taken the steps to having that fancy drink."

She laughed, and it sounded like chimes from a collection of small bells. "I have. I bought some shooters—white and dark rum, cherry brandy, and gin. I'll be there in a sec."

He sank down on the couch and glanced around the room. It was bright with the sunlight streaming in through the sheer curtains on the picture window. White, built-in shelves surrounded a sleek chrome fireplace. Books filled up the majority of the shelves, the rest had various music-inspired knickknacks, and the burning candles.

Isla walked in carrying a silver tray that had a couple of short and tall glasses on it along with an ice bucket. Throwing him a small, sly smile, she walked over to the wet bar, her hips swaying as he drank her in. She had the kind of ass made to wear a thong … or better yet, nothing at all. And then she bent over, her short skirt taut around her delectable butt.

"Whiskey, right?" she asked in a low, throaty voice.

"Yeah," he growled, growing tighter in his jeans, his eyes never leaving her backside. *The things I can do to that tempting ass.*

She stood up and pivoted slowly, glancing at him through half-lidded eyes. The swell of her breasts peeked out from her low-cut top and when she raised her arm up, running her hand through her hair, her top crept up, revealing a glimpse of color riding up the side of her toned body. He inhaled sharply, his gaze rolling over her narrow waist and breasts. Against the thin fabric of her top, her nipples pebbled as if waiting for his hands … his mouth. *Fuck.* He clasped his hands together to stop himself from grabbing her and tossing her on the couch. *What the hell am I thinking? She's my friend. I can't blow this just 'cause I'm hornier than shit.*

"Here you go," she said, handing him a glass and shooter of Jack. Her dark, sensual scent wrapped around him, making his dick jerk against his zipper. He groaned inwardly and took the glass and plastic bottle.

She sashayed back to the bar and poured some liquids in a glass as his gaze bored into her. Turning around, she held up the tall drink full of orange-y liquid, ice cubes, and a garnishment of pineapples, limes, and strawberries. A multi-colored paper umbrella floated next to the side of the glass. "Mai Tai. Paradise in a glass." She winked at him, and he thought he'd lose it right then and there; she was so damn cute and sexy.

Isla joined him on the couch and pushed a small bowl of bright red cherries toward him. "I know these are like total chemicals, but I love them. You want one?"

Chuckling, he shook his head. "We should use those in the club to get back at our rivals."

She smacked his thigh gently then popped one in her mouth. He brought the glass of whiskey to his lips, acutely aware of her sidelong glances at him as she munched on her corrupted cherries. That static was there again, that crackling in the air whenever they came within a foot of each other. He wondered if she felt it too.

"I'm guessing you're not mad at me anymore," he said, turning toward her.

"Not really. If you'd been here last night, I would've let you have it good, and then you'd probably never talk to me again."

He chuckled and brushed his hand against hers. "That would never happen."

"It did once," she whispered, curling one of her fingers around his.

"I was a fuckin' idiot for not trying to contact you," he said in a low voice.

"I won't argue with you about that." Dipping her chin slightly, she looked up at him from under her lashes.

The way the light hit her face made her eyes ignite with a glow that dazzled him. She slowly moved her gaze from his down to his mouth, staring at it for a few seconds and then looking back up to his eyes.

"Right now, it doesn't seem like all those years have gone by." Without breaking her gaze, she licked her lips with the tip of her tongue.

Fuck. He couldn't stop himself from gazing at her parted lips, imagining his hard as granite cock sliding between them, pushing in and out until he filled her. His eyes moved to the pulsing hollow at the base of her throat, the musky scent of arousal penetrating his nostrils.

"Did you ever think about me?" She stared at his mouth for a long moment.

"What?" A fog of lust had clouded his brain, making it hard to concentrate on what she was saying.

"I asked if you ever thought about me over the years. I know I've thought about you."

"Yeah," he said hoarsely. "I thought about you a lot. I wondered how you were, what you looked like, and other things."

"And how do I look?" Her gaze went back and forth from his eyes to his mouth, and it was driving him crazy. He wanted her.

"Damn hot."

She ran her fingernail over his lips, past his chin, and down his throat until resting it on his pecs. "You're pretty hot yourself. I bet you have a ton of women wanting you."

"You're fuckin' killing me," he rasped, his arm snagging her around the waist, yanking her to him.

Then they were kissing like crazy. Like their lives depended on it. Lips grinding. Teeth biting. Tongues tangling in a frenzied dance. She knotted her fists in his shirt, pulling him harder against her. He groaned softly, low in his throat as he wrapped his fingers through her hair, thrusting his tongue deeper into her warm mouth. She tasted like rum and pineapple, and the scent of her curled around and stroked him, and he want so much more.

Pushing her down, he pressed the weight of his body on top of her, letting her feel his hardness. Heat filled him as she writhed against him. The small sounds she made drove him wild, and he slid a hand up her thigh, pushing under her short skirt, touching skin he'd fantasized about ever since high school. The soft feel of her was incredible and more than he'd imagined it would be. But then, everything about her was irresistible. It always had been.

"Sangre," she rasped, digging her fingers into his shoulders.

He slipped his hand between her legs, resting it on the soft flesh of her inner thigh all the while his mouth was still fused with hers.

Door chimes resounded through the house, and she stiffened under his touch. "Forget about it," he said hoarsely as his fingers crept slowly over her silky skin, inching toward her panties. He was pretty sure that when he pushed them aside, her soft folds would be slick with need. He couldn't wait to taste her, to push inside her, first with his fingers then his tongue, and then his cock.

Bang! Bang! Bang!

Isla twisted under him as she placed her palms on his shoulders and pushed him gently away.

"What the fuck?"

"Someone's at the door."

"You can't be serious. Who the hell cares?" He drew her back to him, but she resisted.

"It could be important."

Frustration stabbed his body as he sat back on the couch watching her pull her skirt down and walk out of the room. For a second he just sat there, pissed as hell, waiting for his cock to calm down, but then he remembered that a wacko was stalking her and leapt up from the couch. When he got to the door, he saw a skinny guy with black hair, brown eyes, and a crooked nose staring at him. With the tats, the jean vest with a ton of band patches, and a spike cuff bracelet on his right wrist, he looked like a rocker.

"Who're you?" he asked.

The man jerked his head back as he stepped into the foyer. "I could ask you the same thing."

"This is Arsen – our lead guitarist." Isla kept smoothing down her hair, avoiding Arsen's gaze. "And this is Sangre. His company is the one who's protecting me. Remember I told you I hired a bodyguard service? It turns out that Sangre and I are old friends from back in the day when I lived here. A small world, isn't it?" She glanced at Sangre.

He grunted and stared at Arsen. The rocker flitted his eyes between them, and Sangre knew he wasn't buying Isla's bullshit for one minute. She looked like the musician had interrupted something: hair tangled, lips red and slightly swollen, cheeks flushed, and black smudges under her eyes. Satisfaction spread through Sangre as he watched realization spark in Arsen's gaze. *If he's anything like Army and some of the other brothers, he'll hightail it outta here as fast as he can to tell the fucker who doesn't deserve Isla.*

"Do you want a drink? I just bought a bunch of shooters. It's been so hot that I had the urge to make a bunch of tropical drinks."

"No thanks." An awkward silence filled the space between the trio.

"Then what do you want?" Sangre said, cutting through the quietness.

Arsen looked at Isla. "You asked me to come by and pick you up at four. We have to be at the studio at four thirty."

Her hands flew to her mouth. "Shit! I forgot."

The guitarist gave Sangre a sideways glance. "I can see that."

"Let me just get my purse. I'll be right down." She dashed up the stairs.

Arsen shifted from one foot to the other as he looked at his cell phone. Sangre looked at him fixedly, enjoying how nervous he was making him.

"So, that's cool AF that you and Isla grew up together."

Sangre nodded.

Arsen cleared his throat. "Do you know any good strip bars? We've seen a couple around here but they look sketchy."

"Lust is good. Tell them you know me."

"Oh yeah? Are the strippers there pretty hot?"

Sangre nodded.

"So … are you in a biker club? Your vest tells me you are."

"You're observant."

Arsen raked his fingers through his hair. "I see the one percent patch. Damn, that's savage as hell, dude. I bet that Harley on the street is yours."

"Nothing gets past you, does it?"

"Are you guys getting to know each other?" Isla asked as she came into the foyer.

"No," Sangre answered at the same time Arsen said, "Yes."

Looking at both of them, she gave an anxious laugh. "I guess we better be off," she said to Arsen. He walked out of the house and headed toward a white Impala parked in front. She closed the door to set the alarm, and Sanger pulled her back into him, bending down and nuzzling her neck.

"Call me when you're done recording and let me know where you'll be."

She stepped out of his hold. "That's okay. I'll probably go out to eat with the band, and I know they'll come over to go over some of the new music. A lot of times after recording, we listen to the scratch tracks and make changes and such. By the time we're done, one of the guards will be coming on duty."

Flames of anger licked up his every nerve. "I'll make sure someone is here at six in the morning."

"Will you pick up the shift tomorrow night?"

"No." His jaw tightened and he opened the door. "Set your alarm."

"Sangre. Don't be that way. I really do have to jam with the band tonight."

He put on his sunglasses, walked down the steps, and went over to his Harley. Arsen started to come up to him, but he started his bike and let his cams drown all the words coming out of his mouth as well as Isla's as she came over to him.

Pulling away from the curb, he pulled in the clutch and released the throttle; he wanted to put as much distance between him and Isla as fast as possible. As he sped toward the clubhouse, he cursed himself for being such a fucking idiot. *I never should've kissed her. I can't believe I let her tits and ass get to me.* He rode faster, harder, wanting nothing but to forget all about her. He didn't believe her about jamming with the guys after recording. *She wants to be with Benz. Go ahead, sweetheart, fuck your brains out.* He shifted gears making the Harley go faster as the landscape blurred by him and the wind cocooned him. It was hot just like the anger inside him. All of a sudden he was seventeen again, kissing a sixteen-year-old Isla in Liberty Park. After that kiss, it'd been tense and awkward between them, and then she left without even a goodbye. *Now she wants to do that same shit to me again.*

"Fuck!" he screamed into the wind.

He wasn't seventeen anymore, and Isla wasn't going to break his heart again.

That he was sure of.

Chapter Fourteen

THE CAFÉ SAT nestled between antique and craft stores, framed by several large maple trees that provided some shaded relief for customers seated on the patio. A large coffee cup with steam rising from it and a piece of cake on a small plate were etched in white upon the front glass window along with the name of the place—Sugar & Spice Café—written in a fancy font.

Inside, most of the round tables that sat two to three people were taken, and Isla glanced around, trying to determine which table would be empty soon. The scent of freshly baked muffins, scones, and sweet breads mingled with the dark aroma of roasted coffee beans, and Isla made her way through the throes of people to stand in front of the glass-fronted counter that held an array of cakes, pastries, and sandwiches.

"May I help you?" the barista asked.

"I'm waiting for a friend. Is there any seating out back?" Isla craned her neck toward the patio door, but the wooden shelves lined with prepackaged coffees and teas obstructed her view.

"Let me check," the woman said as she dashed away. From behind her, she heard the impatient sigh of a customer. A few seconds later, the barista came back. "There's a table out there. I put a reserved sign on it for you."

"Thank you so much," Isla said. "I'll have an iced cinnamon macchiato made with almond milk, please. And a mozzarella, tomato, and basil panini."

"Did you want your sandwich warmed up?"

"Yes, please."

With drink and panini in hand, Isla maneuvered her way to the patio and sat at the small wrought iron table near the fence. Multi-colored umbrellas adorned the tables, and boxes filled with an assortment of colorful flowers dotted the outside area. When she sat down, she took out her phone and glanced at the empty screen, her mouth set in a semi-pout. Even though it was bright and sunny on the patio, grayness clouded her mind. Sangre had yet to respond to her texts. She'd sent him two the night before, after recording, and one before she left her house to meet Madison at the café. Nothing. Her mood ricocheted between low and lower. *He's ghosting me. What if he never contacts me again? Like he did all those years ago after I left him that letter. I can't believe he's doing this to me.*

"There you are. Sorry I'm late." Madison flung her purse and several shopping bags on an empty chair. "I'm so glad that you got us a table outside. I love it here. It reminds me of being on vacation. What did you order?" Isla told her and she crinkled her nose. "I want real milk. I want all the calories and decadence they can shove into one cup."

Isla laughed. "Go for it."

"I plan to. I'll be right back." She walked back into the restaurant.

Isla nibbled on her panini, not really very hungry but knowing she had to have something considering she hadn't eaten since the morning before. When Colt came over earlier that morning to pick up the lemonade, she'd been sullen and had tried hard to be interested in what he was saying. If she hadn't promised Carly and Letty she'd make the lemonade, she wouldn't have answered the door. When Madison called proposing a coffee break, she'd almost said no but knew all she would do instead was check her phone a million times and brood.

"It's so crowded in there. I guess everyone had the same idea we did." Madison plopped down on the brightly-colored cushion on the black iron chair. "So what's new?" She stirred her coffee and licked off the foam from the small wooden stick.

"Sangre and I kissed yesterday."

Madison held the stirrer in mid-air, her eyes wide. "What the hell did you say?"

Isla pressed her lips together and leaned forward slightly. "Sangre kissed me, and it was so fuckin' incredible."

"Is that all that happened?"

"Yes, but that's because Arsen came over and interrupted us. I know if he didn't, things may have gotten out of control. I wanted to be with Sangre so bad. He was so ready."

Madison laughed. "Was he hard as hell?"

"Oh yeah. I kind of freaked when Arsen was there. I know he thought I fucked Sangre. I felt weird about that, and the whole way to the studio, I kept telling him how it's good to have a friend whom I've known for so long. I told him all we do is talk, talk, talk, but I knew he wasn't buying what I was saying. It would've been better if I had just kept my mouth shut."

"So he thinks you and Sangre *did it*?"

"I'm pretty sure he does. He would never tell me that. He doesn't get involved with stuff like that, but I know he was thinking about Benz." She groaned as Benz's anger-filled eyes flashed in her mind. "I don't know what's wrong with me. I've never cheated on Benz, and there I was, kissing Sangre like I was single or something."

"You're attracted to him. Face it, you always have been. I think you even liked him before high school."

It was true. As she got older, her first and only real love had been Sangre. When she'd turned twelve, she started to think of him as her boyfriend. Of course, she'd never told him that, but whenever her dad would rant and rave about all the time she was spending with *her boyfriend*, it had made her feel warm and fuzzy. Each and every time. "You're right, but he doesn't feel that way about me. Remember the letter and me pouring my heart out to him the summer I had to move? He hasn't even mentioned that letter. I think he's just looking at us as a 'friends with benefits' type of relationship. I'm sure he has a ton of women around him. He always has."

"Have you brought up the letter to him?" Isla shook her head. "Why not? I think it's real important you find out why he dissed you after you poured out your feelings."

"Maybe I don't want to hear him say that he never cared for me as more than a friend. The kiss was from a man who liked the way I looked. It had nothing to do with feelings."

"How's he acting now?" Madison took a bit of her sandwich.

"He's ghosting me, but I think he's pissed because I told him not to come over after recording. I told him the band was going to jam, and he didn't believe me."

"Why didn't you ask him to come over and watch you guys jam?"

"Because Benz was going to be there. The two of them don't mix."

"If Sangre's pissed about Benz, he must have feelings for you that go beyond friendship."

"I don't know. It's complicated. Anyway, just because he may be caveman-like and want to fuck me doesn't mean he has real feelings for me other than friendship. Haven't you slept with a guy that you weren't in love with?"

Nodding, Madison quirked her lips. "More times than I care to remember. I guess you need to figure out who you want in your life—Benz or Sangre. The answer may be neither, and that's okay too."

She sipped her macchiato. "I need to break it off for good with Benz. I've known that for a long while," she said in a soft voice.

"How do you feel about doing that?"

"If I were in LA, I wouldn't want to think about it. Not because I'm madly in love with him. Hell … I'm not even a little in love with him. I like Benz a lot. I admire his genius, his passion for music, his drive to succeed in a career that kicks your ass so much. But I've always been afraid of change even though I've had a lot of it in my life. Maybe that's why I cling onto things even when they are decaying or dead."

"To me, you're one of the strongest people I know. You left your family, all that was familiar to you when you were just out of high school, and went to LA. That took courage, and to pursue your dream takes guts."

"The weird thing is that I feel strong in some areas of my life and not so much in others. I guess the problem is that even though I live in a big city, sing in a band, and hang with friends, I feel lonely. It's weird, but I feel less alone in Alina than I do in LA. The year before I crashed was horrible. I'm not quite sure how to describe it other than to say that time felt thick and viscous, and I felt stuck." Isla propped her elbows on the table and shook her head. "I don't know, but I don't feel like my life in Alina is surreal. I know in my heart I have to break up with Benz. I don't love him, and it isn't fair to him. I also am still terribly attracted to Sangre, and even if nothing happens between us, my heart will be with him and not Benz."

"It sounds like you have the answer."

She breathed out slowly. "Yeah. The thing I've found the most surprising about change is that what was once fine for so long isn't anymore. It's amazing how suddenly that shifts."

Madison put her hand on Isla's, patting it. "I'm here if you need me. For what it's worth, you're doing the right thing. I always thought you shouldn't have taken Benz back after he cheated on you."

"And I think he's doing it again. I guess I can't blame him this time around. I haven't wanted to be intimate with him. Last night he was so mad at me when I told him I needed to be alone. Arsen just threw me one of those looks before he pulled Benz out the door. I've known Benz for a long time. He helped me through some of the shit I was going through with my fucked up family."

"Can't you still be friends with him?"

"I suppose. We'll just have to see. I'm good with it, but I'm not so sure about him."

"And Sangre?"

Isla gave a half shrug. "I guess the ball is in his court."

"It was the last time too, and you spent years trying to forget him. I'd go to his house and talk to him. Don't make the same mistake twice."

"He lives at his clubhouse."

"Then go there. Don't leave Alina without talking to him."

Isla glanced at her phone again. Nothing. "I'll have to think about it, but for now I've got to rework a few songs and write down another one that's in my head."

"A ballad?" Madison asked.

"Yeah. No surprise. Right?" Isla smiled. "Enough about me. Tell me about the fabulous trip you and Miguel are going on."

Madison's eyes sparkled. "We're going to Martinique. The resort is to die for. Let me pull it up," she said, taking out her phone.

"I'm so jealous. I want a tropical vacation in the worst way." While Isla watched Madison search for pictures of the place, warmth spread through her. She was so happy that one of her best friends had found the love of her life. Sitting with Madison and spilling her guts out to her felt right and real. She didn't have any friendships in LA that could even begin to compare to the one she shared with Madison. *I'm going to miss all this when I go back.*

"I found it." Madison passed her phone to Isla. "Isn't this the most spectacular place you've ever seen?"

Isla nodded, a thread of sadness wove through her when she saw the photo of a Mai Tai. *Just call me, Sangre.* "It looks beyond amazing."

For the next two hours, the women laughed, talked, and ordered another round of caffeine pumping drinks. By the time Isla arrived at her house, happiness filled her instead of melancholy.

She pulled into the garage then came back down the driveway, waving at Carly and Letty who sat behind the lemonade stand. Two neighbors from across the street were in front of the booth, waiting for their purchases.

As she walked toward the stand, she saw a police car pull in front of her house, and her heart sank. The last person she wanted to see or talk to was Deputy Jeffers. The guy was a creep and assumed an awful lot of untrue things about her. She'd noticed that he'd been driving by her house, stopping to buy lemonade and watching her.

"Let me know if you need me to make any more," she said to the girls as she rushed up her driveway, hoping to avoid bumping into

Jeffers.

"Ms. Rose?" a deep voice called out.

She turned around and saw Sheriff Wexler, and a sense of calm washed over her.

"I need to talk with you."

The calmness was short-lived as dread crept through her. "Is everything all right?"

"Let's go inside."

Did something happen to Sangre? Wait … if that were true why the hell would the sheriff be telling you about it? He'd go to his parents. Benz? Oh no. Please let everyone be okay. She opened the door, and Wexler followed her inside.

Gesturing for him to sit on the couch, she sat on the edge of one of the cushy chairs. "What's going on? Did something happen to one of my band members?"

A small smile whispered across his lips. "I'm not here about that. I wanted to talk to you about Sharla Davidson, Taylor Prentice, and Lizbeth Kelly."

Her muscles twitched, and she brought her hand to the base of her throat, fiddling with the silver necklace she'd bought in a small, eclectic shop on Melrose Avenue in West Hollywood. "Aren't those the women who were killed?"

"Yes. I understand they went to Jefferson High School."

"Yeah. They were all in the same grade as me. We used to be in a lot of the plays and musicals together."

"Do you know Carrie Nolan?"

"Let me see." She tapped her lips with her finger, mulling the name over and over in her head. *If I hadn't killed some of my brain cells with coke, my head would be a lot clearer.* She laughed dryly then looked up at him. "Sorta. Can you refresh my memory?"

"She was in your class too. My understanding is that she was in the school choir."

"I'm sorry, but I can't seem to remember her. Then again, I wasn't in choir, and she might not have been in any of my classes. I'm pretty sure she wasn't in any of the musicals or any of the other theater productions I was in."

"Did anyone in particular have a problem with you or the other women because you were in the plays?"

She tilted her head back. "Just the usual petty jealousy that's present in high school. Some of the girls were mad that I kept getting the leads in the musicals." Lexi's face popped into her mind. "I can't believe that all these years later one of them would do this because we were in the school plays. I mean how sick would *that* be?"

"Believe me, I've seen all kinds of sickos, and what doesn't make sense to the average adjusted person, makes perfect sense to them. Have you noticed anyone watching you? I know you have security. Some of your neighbors have called me about strange cars parked in front of your house all night and day. I checked it out and found you employed Precision Security."

"I did. I'd been getting crazy fan mail from someone, and it was persistent. It creeped me out, and I did feel like someone was watching me. I haven't received any more of the letters since the bodyguards came on board." Icy fear weaved through her. "Do you think the wacko who killed those women is the same one who's been sending me the fan letters?" Goosebumps broke out over her skin, and she trembled in spite of the heat.

"I'm investigating any leads. Right now it seems that the common denominator with all the murders is Jefferson High. I'm warning you to be very careful. Do you still have the fan mail?"

"Yes. I'll get them." She rose up and went to the small built-in desk in the kitchen. She opened the bottom drawer and took out a shoebox. "Do you want something to drink? Water, lemonade, or iced tea maybe?"

"Water would be great. Thanks."

She came back into the living room and handed Wexler the shoebox and a cold bottle of water.

He flashed a quick smile at her, took a gulp of water, and then opened the box. "I'd like to keep these."

"Go ahead. Hopefully you can get some DNA off of the envelope." She was going to tell him about the incident a few days before when her car broke down, but she didn't actually see anyone; she *sensed* someone was watching and following her. She got the idea the person meant to harm her, but the sheriff would probably think she was a loon, so she kept quiet.

"When did you start getting these letters?" he asked, flipping through them.

"About a three weeks ago. I received some similar ones when I was in LA, but I didn't get them as much as I have here. When I first got here, I stayed inside most of the time except to go to the grocery store. I sometimes even called and had my groceries delivered to me. I was totally incognito, but I'd emerged from my cave when my bandmates came to Alina. The letters started around then. The information that I'd returned to my hometown was shared on Instagram, so I was no longer invisible."

"Do your bandmates know about the letters?"

"Of course."

"I'll need their names and phone numbers and where they're staying while in town."

She shook her head. "They have nothing to do with this. Why would any of them do this?"

"I just need to talk with everyone."

"They weren't even here when those other two women were killed. I wasn't either."

"I'm not accusing them of anything. I just need to talk with them." He stared at her, the frown lines between his eyes deepening. She gave him the information, and after he jotted it down, he stood up. "Let me know if you receive any more letters or if anything out of the ordinary happens."

"Okay." She walked to the front door and opened it, watching him until he drove off. *I wonder if I should've told him how one of his deputies keeps coming around here. I can't believe this whole nightmare.* Fear curdled in her stomach as she contemplated the possibility that the person who murdered the three women could be the same one sending her the letters. It was too horrible. She glanced over and saw Mark sitting in his car looking at her, and it calmed down her fears a bit. Isla closed the door and went back to the living room to work on a new song that kept swirling in her mind.

After several hours of writing, she stretched her arms over her head to loosen up the kinks. The room had grown dark, and she switched on a floor lamp near the chair she sat in. Standing up, her legs screamed from stiffness; the time had escaped her. Glancing at her phone, she was surprised that it was almost nine o'clock. There were a few texts she'd received while working, but none of them were from Sangre. *He's ignoring me. Well … fuck him.*

She padded over to the hallway closet, took out her gym bag and terry cloth hoodie, and went to the garage. What she needed was to exercise her stiff muscles, and then take a relaxing swim in the pool to void her mind of all thoughts, especially the ones about Sangre.

After she pulled up in front of Fitness Gallery, she walked over to Mark's car. He stepped out and waited for her, his head moving as he looked all around.

"I'm just going in for a quick workout and a swim. I should be inside for about an hour. Do you want me to call you when I'm ready to come out?"

"I can wait inside."

"You don't have to. I need the space. Remember Sangre said it was okay when I was in the gym?"

"All right. You have my number if you need me. No reason to call otherwise. I'll be in front when you come out."

Mark was all business. He never chitchatted or even cracked a smile with her. He was efficient, reliable, and capable, but she thought it a bit odd that he never engaged in any conversation with her. Keith would ask about the band or how she was doing, but Mark never did.

Nodding her head, she walked away and went into the fitness center. When she entered, she saw Scott sitting at the front desk reading a textbook. He looked up when she came up to the counter to swipe her card.

"You're coming in late tonight," he said.

"I lost track of time. I've been working on songs that have been stuck in my head for too long. What're you studying?"

"Forensic Investigation. I'm getting a degree in Criminal Justice."

"That's cool. Where do you go to school?"

"I go to Fort Lewis College in Durango, but a lot of the upper division classes in my area are online. I'm taking a couple of summer school classes so I can graduate at the end of the year."

"That's awesome. I hope it all works out for you."

"Thanks." He threw her a wide smile, and she returned it then went into the weight room.

The first thing Isla did upon entering was glance around to make sure Devin wasn't around. The last person she wanted to see was him. He was so pushy and aggressive, and he definitely didn't catch on that she was flat out not interested in him at all. As she made her way over to the treadmill, several people looked at her, and a few of the women pointed at her, smiling. Not in the mood to engage in conversation, she opened her gym bag and rummaged for her ear buds and MP3 player.

"Did you just get here?"

Hearing Devin's voice froze her in motion. *Fuck. He's* always *here when I am. I'm beginning to wonder if it's planned rather than a coincidence.* Turning around, his dark eyes bored into hers. "Yeah. I needed to chill out. My brain is mush, and I just need to get lost in my zone."

His gaze roamed slowly over her body as though he was undressing her, and Isla cringed and clutched her duffel bag in front of her chest. "Your workouts are really paying off," he said, leering.

"I don't mean to be rude, but I'm not really in the mood to chat." She backed away.

"You are being rude." Hardness etched his voice.

She narrowed her eyes and shook her head. "No, you are. I told you I want to zone out and that I don't feel like talking, and you don't give a damn. You think you can bully or manipulate me to talk to you when I just told you I don't want to," her voice was loud and high pitched and a couple of men turned to look at her.

He pressed his lips together, his gaze raking over her body again, lingering on her breasts. "You're even prettier when you're mad. This is our first fight." He chuckled.

She threw her ear buds into the gym bag and turned away from him.

"Where're you going?" he asked.

"I've changed my mind about working out." She pushed through the doors and stormed past Scott as she made her way to the pool.

"Wait," Scott said.

She whirled around. "What is it?"

"The pool's closed."

"Seriously? I so need to decompress. I really need a swim."

"Sorry."

"Can I bribe you? I can give you two tickets to our show next week. Please?" She batted her eyelashes at him in an exaggerated way.

He laughed. "If you throw in an autographed CD by the band, I'll give you forty-five minutes."

"Deal." Laughing, she winked at him as she opened the door leading down to the pool.

The minute she slipped inside the water, her limbs began to relax. Isla lay on her back floating, the water softly lapping around her as the lights from inside the pool cast wavering shadows on the ceiling. Bobbing in the water, she felt a tingle between her legs as the memory of her kiss with Sangre filled her mind. She was totally enthralled by him. She wanted him, every part of him, and she desperately wanted him to feel the same way about her. But the fact that he'd been dissing her since their kiss didn't bode well. When she'd first seen him at the club after her band's show, she'd thought he looked like a heart breaker and that she needed to stay away from him. That was before she knew he was Sangre, but she should've taken her own advice and kept their encounters at a minimum. *He's the only one who can shatter my heart. He's done it before and now I'm letting it happen again.*

Then she heard it. The soft shuffle of footsteps like a threatening whisper. Isla's insides stiffened as she moved up, her legs treading water. Darting her eyes all around the room, she couldn't see anything. Her pulse ramped up. *It's nothing. I'm imagining things.*

But then footfalls clacked on the tiled floor. Louder.

The footsteps didn't seem to come from any direction. Just a sound enveloping her in dread.

"Hello. Is anyone there?" her voice resounded through the room.

Nothing except for the sound of water and her panting.

The overhead lights dimmed. It was so slight that she thought she'd imagined it, but then a metal scraping sound—like nails on a chalk board, bounced off the walls.

Isla froze—all her breath trapped. She was most definitely not alone. *Someone* was there. Continuing to tread water, she strained to hear, but her heart pounded loudly. Tendrils of terror curled into her stomach. The shadows that played on the walls and ceilings earlier now took on grotesque, eerie shapes lending to the rising panic inside her.

The scraping sound stopped.

Isla doggie paddled to the shallower part of the pool until her feet touch the bottom. She stayed perfectly still, her knees bent, water tucked in around her chin. Despite the warmth of the water, her teeth chattered and she shivered.

After what seemed like an eternity, she began to relax just a little bit. *I bet it was the pool's heater turning on and off. I'm such a fuckin' baby.* Looking toward the dressing room, she decided to get out of the pool. She waded over to the pool stairs, gripped the cool banister, and took a step, pushing herself upward.

Then she heard it. A clicking sound like some people do with their tongues. Very faint at first but then louder and faster. She pushed backward into the water and swam to the middle of the pool. Why she did that, she had no idea. She only knew that she couldn't get out and face whoever was tormenting her.

And *someone* was. Isla could *feel* eyes on her.

Water splashed around her as she spun around, checking out the entire room, a cry breaking from her lips.

That was when she saw the shadowy shape of someone against the wall.

Her pulse roared.

"Who are you? Leave me alone!" The echo of emptiness magnified her strained voice.

A rush of footsteps.

The lights went out plunging the room in darkness.

Isla screamed. *I'm going to die. The killer is here. I hear him. He's coming closer. Oh!*

Then a flood of illumination from the overhead lights.

"Miss Rose? Are you okay?" Scott asked, standing in the doorway.

Confusion flashed through her. "What?" she murmured.

"I heard you scream. I'm just making sure you're okay. Why were the lights out?"

Her limbs turned to jelly. "I don't know. I think someone was down here."

"You're the only one who came down. The circuit must've blown. We had some problems in the fitness area too. Are you sure you're okay?"

"I guess so."

"Okay, then." He turned around.

"Wait! Don't go." She swam to the pool steps. "I'm coming right out." Isla pulled herself out and walked toward the dressing room. "I'll just grab my stuff and walk out with you." She dashed in, scooped up her clothes, and shrugged on her robe.

"I'm sorry if I disturbed you, Miss Rose. I just wanted to make sure you were all right."

"I'm glad you came down. Something spooked me, that's all. Are you sure you didn't happen to see anyone coming down to the pool area?" She followed him upstairs.

Holding the door open for her, he shook his head. "Yup, but now that I think of it, someone could've slipped past me. I was pretty busy and had to leave the desk for a few minutes to help with one of the machines that was acting up. Was someone bothering you?"

"I don't know. I mean, I didn't see anyone. It was just a feeling I guess."

He smiled. "It can definitely be spooky when you're the only one in the pool. Sometimes when I go down there to lock up, all the noises and echoes give me the creeps, but that's just between you and me."

She laughed. "Your secret is safe. I'm sure that's all it was. I'll bring the tickets for next week's show when I come back in a couple of days to work out."

"Do you want me to walk you to your car?"

"Thanks, but I'm parked right in front." She pointed to a black Kia Soul, relief warming her when she saw Mark's vehicle. "I'll see you."

The whole drive home, she kept checking her rearview mirror, making sure Mark was behind her. The more she thought about what happened, the surer she was that someone had been trying to scare her. *I didn't imagine shit.*

After she pulled into the garage, she tapped in Mark's number.

"Is there a problem?" he said.

"No, not really. I'm just feeling kind of spooked. Can you come in and do a safety check?"

"Stay in your car. I'm coming now."

When she saw him enter the garage, she slid out of the car. Feeling foolish, she shook her head. "I know I'm being silly, but sometimes I just get nervous."

"No reason to explain anything to me. I'll make sure everything's secured." He went in and walked around the whole house while she stood in the foyer chewing the dry skin on her thumb. When he finished, he nodded at her then went out the front door. She watched him get into his car then she set the alarm. Isla went over to the wet bar and poured a double shot of vodka, downing it in one long gulp.

She glanced at her phone, the urge to talk to Sangre overwhelming, but he hadn't texted her back. Not even one sentence—he was ghosting her. Isla put the phone away and plunked down on the couch. What had happened that night reminded her of the night that her car had conked out. *This wacko is playing a cat and mouse game with me. What the hell does he want from me? When is the cat going to catch the mouse?*

She shuddered at the thought as she wrapped her arms around herself.

That night, sleep would not come easily.

Chapter Fifteen

SANGRE BENT DOWN low and made his shot, two of the striped balls rolling into the pockets in the far left corner of the pool table.

"Fuckin' lucky shot," Shotgun said, a joint dangling from his mouth.

"Bullshit. You already owe me three hundred for the last two games." Sangre picked up the shot glass Kelly had brought over and threw it back, its warmth coursing through him.

"You want another one, baby?" Kelly asked as she brushed against him. He nodded and watched her sway her hips sensuously as she went to the bar.

"She's so damn ripe, dude," Chains said.

"Why don't you put her outta her misery?" Cueball added.

"She's got you guys to do that, or aren't your cocks enough for her?" Sangre picked up the cue stick. "Ten ball in the right pocket." With one fluid movement, he made the shot.

"The way you've been staying away from her and the other club girls, I'd say your cock's gonna forget what the hell to do," Army said as the guys sniggered.

Sangre glanced at Army then back at the table. "Nine and twelve ball corner pocket left. And stop worrying about my dick, dude. It's fuckin' weird." He bent low and the clack of the stick against the balls was music to his ears. "That's another hundred and fifty you owe me."

Shotgun groaned and smacked Kelly's ass as she walked past him. Looking over her shoulder, she giggled at him then handed the drink to Sangre.

"Thanks." He took a sip and placed his cue stick on the rack.

"What the fuck? I gotta earn the money back," Shotgun said.

"I'm done. I have to go to the office."

"I thought Eagle was there." Shotgun put his arm around Kelly's waist.

"He is, but I have to go over the books."

"So, you're leaving now?" Kelly asked softly.

"Yeah. You been good?"

She half shrugged.

"I'm sorry I've been so busy and preoccupied."

"With that *friend's* pussy," Army said and the men laughed. Kelly's mouth turned downward.

"Shut the fuck up," Sangre said. He went over to the club girl. "We can go for a ride sometime next week."

Her eyes lit up. "I'd love that." She pulled away from Shotgun and threw her arms around Sangre. "I've missed being with you," she said softly in his ear.

"We'll just go for a ride. Maybe go to The Brass Plum for food."

"Don't forget," she said.

"I won't." He pushed her back gently. "I'm outta here."

"Are you going to Lust later on? Steel said you wanted to look at the books." Army drew Kelly to him, putting her on his lap.

"Shit, I forgot about that. I'll be over there in a few hours. Are you gonna be there?"

Army wrapped his arm around Kelly's small waist. "I start work at four, so if you come after that, I'll be there. Right now, I'm gonna relax a bit." He nuzzled her neck, and she giggled then kissed him.

"See ya." Sangre turned around and headed to the parking lot.

As he rode to the office, the only thing running through his mind was how much he missed Isla. It'd been several days since they'd kissed and she'd pushed him away, but he couldn't get her out of his mind. She smelled so good and felt so soft in his arms, and when they kissed, it was like electricity sizzled between them.

As he neared her street, he almost turned and made a beeline to her house, but he didn't. He rode past it, the raw anger from her brushoff still twisted inside him. The texts she'd sent to him that night and the following day just infuriated him more. It seemed like she didn't know what the hell she wanted. He knew she was with Benz, so he shouldn't have been surprised that she was sorry she let the kiss happen. No matter what, *he* was definitely not sorry it happened. The only thing he regretted was the guitarist interrupting them when he did. If he hadn't have come over, Sangre was sure she would've let him into her sweet pussy. *I bet she would've loved it.*

When Sangre entered the office, he saw Eagle by the file cabinet, rifling through folders. Eagle glanced over his shoulder then went back to the task at hand.

"Did Jon ever call you?" Sangre asked, throwing his set of keys on the desk.

"Nope. He didn't show up for his post either. I think he's history."

Sangre sank into his leather swivel chair. "The guy was weird anyway. I was just trying to help out my pops."

"Do you think he's the one who sent the letters to Isla?"

"Who the fuck knows? It seems funny that he lied to her about being on duty and then we never heard from him. I went over a few times to his apartment, but he was never there—or at least he didn't answer the door."

"How's Isla doing?"

"What the hell is that supposed to mean?" Sangre bristled.

Eagle rubbed his chin. "It's not a fuckin' trick question. Is she feeling okay?"

"How the hell do I know?"

He took out a file and slammed the drawer shut. "I thought you guys were friends."

"Well, that's what you think." Sangre turned on the computer and stared at the screen, looking at Eagle from the corner of his eye.

Tilting his head to the side, Eagle pursed his lips. "I guess you got some crazy shit going on between you two. We got a new contract today, so I'm gonna work on getting some guards together to train them on it tonight. Later." He sauntered out of the room, closing the door behind him.

Sangre picked up his phone and stared at it. "How are you, Isla?" he murmured under his breath. The ring tone startled him and a jolt of excitement shot through him in anticipation of talking with her, but when he looked at the name "Mom" flashing on the screen, the feeling seeped out of him.

"Hey, Mom," he said, trying to sound more cheerful than he felt.

"What's the matter?" she asked.

"Nothing. Why?"

"You sound like you're trying to be sunny." Her tone told him her "mom radar" was in overdrive.

"I've never been sunny in my life, so I'm not trying it out today. How's Pops?"

"Good. I can't talk too long because I'm watching Riley. Rachel kept him home from school, because he said his tummy was hurting, but the way he's running around the house, I think he played her so he didn't have to go today."

"He's in kindergarten. I think the 'staying-home-from-school' excuses will come in a few more years."

"I don't know. He can be awfully ornery and stubborn. Reminds me of you." She chuckled.

Sangre heard his five-year-old nephew's voice in the distance. "I want a cookie, Grandma."

"I thought your tummy hurt." The sound of ceramic on tile told Sangre his mom had just put the lid of the cookie jar on the kitchen counter. "Here you go. But just one. I'm talking to your Uncle Steve. Do you want to say hi?"

"Hi!" There was a lot of chortling until it faded away.

"Everything good with you?" he asked, reclining in the chair.

"Yes. I called to let you know that dinner on Sunday is at five. Let Jordan know. I mean Isla. What's up with you two using names that you weren't given?"

Not wanting to hear her lecture him again on what a horrible thing it was for him to go by Sangre when he had a beautiful name that she and his father had thought about for months, he cleared his throat. "Isla's not coming."

"Nonsense. Rachel saw her at the bakery yesterday, and she didn't say she wasn't coming. She just said she hadn't heard from you. Why haven't you called her?"

"I've been busy. I don't think she wants—"

"Of course, she does. Tell her to be at the house between four and four thirty. Nicole and Stephanie are bringing appetizers. It was Stephanie's idea. I think those things ruin people's appetites, but she said she found some recipes in one of her numerous cooking magazine subscriptions. Jim must be spending a fortune on all those magazines. They're expensive. I see them when I'm standing in line at the grocery store, and I'm appalled at how much they cost. When your father and I were first married ..."

Tuning her out, he turned to the computer and opened one of the company's newest contracts. He chuckled under his breath: In his mother's eyes, his brother Jim was perfect, and his wife, Stephanie, was flawed. A couple of minutes later, he heard a loud, frantic voice, "Steve? Are you there?"

"Sorry, Mom. The phone dropped. I'm at work so I gotta go."

"I do too. I just know Riley's into something. He's being too quiet. Make sure you tell Jor—I mean Isla to be at the house. Why don't you pick her up? That would be so nice and polite if you did. You two used to be tight when you were kids." A large gasp came over the phone. "I have to go. Riley's covered in glitter and paint. He must've gotten into my craft supplies. See you on Sunday."

Sangre put down the phone and scrubbed his face with his hand. *Isla said she's coming to Mom's?* He thought for sure she'd be pissed at him for dissing her, and a part of him wanted her to never want to see him. Something was going on inside of him that he didn't want to acknowledge. He kept telling the brothers and himself that they were only friends, but he didn't feel like a friend. When it came to Isla, he was one hundred percent male, wanting to touch her, taste her, and fuck her. All he could think about was how good it'd feel to be inside her as she screamed out his name until her throat was raw.

Those stirrings Sangre held inside were different than he'd had for any of the women with whom he'd been involved. There'd been lust with all of them, but nothing more than that. The lasting connection, the ease in conversation, the humor, and the need to be together were absent in all of his past relationships. His body, especially his damn dick, was in overdrive whenever he was with Isla or thought about her, which was all the time. She was turning his world upside down, and he didn't think he liked that one bit.

And now, Isla would be at Sunday dinner with his family, and he couldn't deny the rush of excitement at the idea of seeing her. Sangre pounded his fist on the desk, pissed at the way he was acting. *It's like I'm back in high school. Fuckin' shameful, man!*

The door opened and Eagle popped his head in. "Did you have a chance to go over the expenses for the new contract? I was thinking that we may want to put our new hires on it."

Sangre swiveled around to the computer. "I was just getting ready to review it. I got distracted. I'd like Ron to work on the gigs that require a lot more than sitting on your ass at a post. He's got the experience, and he'd be a good fit at the trucking company. The other two will probably work out okay at the new place."

"Sounds good. Cue Ball just came in. He's manning the phones tonight and making sure everyone is where they're supposed to be."

"Who's on for Isla today and tonight?" Sangre kept his gaze on the computer screen.

"Keith's on now, and Jeff is gonna relieve him for the graveyard shift. Mark has the day off. You good with that?"

He shrugged. "Sure. Why wouldn't I be?"

"I know you feel real protective with her since you guys go way back." Eagle walked over to the mini-fridge and took out a can of root beer. "Cueball said you're headed to Lust later on."

"I have to go over the books. It looks like we have a slight discrepancy, and I wanna make sure it's just an error and not intentional." His face grew tight. Anyone who tried to game the Night Rebels was playing with fire. A clerical error was understandable, but if he found out someone was cheating the club, there'd be hell to pay.

"When're you going? I may join you. I haven't been there in a few months."

"I'm leaving in a couple of hours."

"Count me in. Come get me when you're heading out." Eagle gulped down the drink, crushed the can, threw it in the waste paper basket, and walked out.

Pushing all thoughts of Isla from his mind, he squinted as he read the small numbers on the screen, hell bent on getting some work done before he headed over to the strip club.

When he and Eagle entered Lust, it took a few seconds to adjust to the dim lighting. Two women on stage wiggled and twirled on the poles while men sat transfixed by their movements. Army came over, smiling broadly.

"I didn't think you were gonna show," he said to Sangre.

"I had to finish up some things at the office. How's business?"

"Real good. Between four and six o'clock we're jammed during the week. It's the time when the husbands can slip in, watch a few hot dances, and be back home with the wife and kiddies before their dinner is on the table. Works out well for us."

The men laughed then Sangre headed to the office behind the stage. When he slipped behind the dark blue curtains, a few women milled around. A brunette wearing a tight-fitting short dress smiled at him.

"Where have you been hiding? It's been too long." She came over and gave him a hug. Her strong floral perfume made his nose stuff up.

"How've you been?" he asked, stepping back from her.

"Okay. Nothing too exciting going on with me. What about you?" She ran her eyes over his body, her gaze lingering on his crotch.

"I can't complain. I came here to get some work done, babe. I'll catch up with you later." He closed the office door behind him. Sangre hadn't seen Elise since he broke up with her the previous year. When she'd first taken the job at Lust, he'd been surprised that it hadn't bothered him when the guys leered at her. She'd blamed their break up on the fact that he was jealous and couldn't handle her taking her clothes off in front of a bunch of men, but that had nothing to do with it. The usual policy for club members was that they couldn't date or screw around with any of the employees at their businesses, so when Elise had been hired, Steel came to him and told him the policy didn't apply. The way the club had seen it, Sangre was already dating the dancer before she was hired. What the Night Rebels hadn't known was that he'd been on the verge of breaking up with her when she started working at Lust.

The fact that he'd never cared when she shook her tits and ass in front of the clientele told him he'd made the right decision in ending their four-month relationship; even seeing her just now, nothing stabbed at him. She still looked damn good, but his dick hadn't even twitched when she pressed close to him.

An hour later, he went back into the club and joined Eagle and Army at the bar. Soon Rooster and Shotgun walked in and headed toward them.

"What's going on?" Rooster asked as he plopped on a barstool.

"Not much. I just wanted to go over the books. It looks like the discrepancy was just an error, but I'm gonna keep an eye on it." Sangre curled his fingers around his beer bottle.

"I'm surprised your ol' lady let you out to play," Army said.

Rooster's pale blue eyes flashed. "Shannon doesn't tell me what the fuck to do." He swiveled around, his gaze focused on the stage.

"Shannon's gonna have your cock if she finds out you were here," Shotgun said while Sangre, Eagle, and Army chuckled.

"If she's lucky." Looking over his shoulder, he motioned to the bartender. "A double Jack."

"Shit hit the fan at home?" Eagle asked.

"My woman can be a real *bitch* sometimes. Right now, I got my phone turned off, and I'm gonna enjoy these pretty ladies showing their tits and asses." Occasionally, Rooster hooked up with the club girls, and his old lady was cool with it as long as he did it once in a while at parties. He respected that, and as far as Sangre knew, he never strayed with any other women but the club girls.

"All women can be real bitches. That's why I'm single." Army held his fist in the air as Brutus came over. "You can work the door later," he said to him. Brutus had just started filling-in at Lust a few weeks before. Steel wanted more members working the strip club, and Brutus had been the first one to volunteer when the topic had come up at church.

As the men talked and drank, Sangre noticed one of the waitresses pushing a guy away from her. He slid off his stool and walked over to see what the problem was. He came up behind her and gently tugged her away from the table.

"Are these guys giving you a hard time, Capri?"

"Only this one." She pointed to the back of a guy with collar-length brown hair.

Sangre moved in front of the table, his eyes narrowing when he recognized Benz. "The women aren't here for you to touch. Have some fuckin' respect."

Benz and Arsen stared at him, then recognition flickered over their faces. "Working in a strip joint and shoving tits in customers' faces for bigger tips is hardly respectable." Benz cocked his head and picked up his drink. "And why the fuck is this your business?"

Sangre knocked the drink out of his hand and the glass went flying, crashing against one of the pillars. He leaned over and grabbed Benz by the shirt. "What did I tell you about respect and keeping your fuckin' mouth shut around me? No one disrespects the women in our club. I'm giving you a choice to walk outta here or get your ass thrown out."

"Are you for real?" Benz yanked out of his grip.

Without a word, Sangre grabbed him and began to drag him out; Benz flailed his arms helplessly.

"You sonofabitch!" Benz yelled.

"You need some help with the fucker?" Eagle asked as Sangre dragged the drummer past the bar.

"I'm good." Sangre glanced at Arsen, who followed behind, his head turned toward the stage. When Sangre reached the front door, Brutus opened it wide, and Sangre threw Benz onto the sidewalk.

The musician jumped up and glared at him as he wiped the dust from his tight black jeans. "You're so fucking pissed that I'm in Isla's pussy and you're not."

Arsen yanked his friend to him. "Let's just go, dude. Keep your mouth shut."

But it was too late. His words were like red to an angry bull. Sangre rushed out and smashed his fist into Benz's face, knocking him down.

"Don't ever fuckin' talk about Isla like that, you goddamn asshole!" He kicked him hard in the stomach with his steel-toed boots, and the man groaned and writhed in pain on the ground, as drops of blood spotted the pavement.

Arsen bent down over his friend then looked up at Sangre. "Enough. Isla won't be cool if you beat the shit outta our drummer. We have a show next week."

Breathing heavily, Sangre stood off to the side, clenching and unclenching his fists. *The prick's right. Isla would be livid if I give this ass wipe the beating he deserves.* The way she'd acted when he got into a fight with a stranger at Cuervos told him she'd go ballistic over him kicking her fucking boyfriend's ass.

"Get the hell outta here before I change my mind," he said, gritting his teeth. Arsen helped Benz to his feet, and with his arm wrapped around the drummer's shoulder, he guided him to the car. Sangre watched as Benz fell into the passenger seat before Arsen took off.

"What the hell was that all about?" Brutus asked, standing in the doorway.

"The asshole was giving Capri a hard time. When I called him on it, he disrespected me."

Brutus chuckled. "These fuckers never learn. You staying for the Best Tits Contest?"

Since the club began the weeknight competition, the place was packed. He shook his head. "I think I'll head out." The altercation made him think about Isla and how her jerk boyfriend was at the club manhandling a waitress when he should've been with her. At that moment, the desire to see her overpowered him. It was like she'd gotten under his skin and made him crave her. It was a new experience for him, and it sent static charges jumping through his body. Just thinking about her made him feel a slight tug in his jeans. *The damn douchebag doesn't fucking deserve her.* He knew he should just go back to the clubhouse, but he didn't want to; he wanted to spend some time with Isla.

His Harley roared as he left the parking lot and headed to Isla's house. He wasn't sure if the ass wipe would be there licking his wounds while Isla smothered his bruised face with her kisses. Anger shot through him as images of her cradling the dirt bag's head in her lap whirled in his mind.

When he pulled up in front of Isla's house, he saw Keith parked in front, and he went over to his car. The bodyguard rolled down the window.

"How are things?" he asked his employee.

"Quiet."

"No one showed up to see her?"

"Nope. She's been inside since I got here. The only thing happening around here is that lemonade stand. The two girls are killin' it." He chuckled.

"Did a fuckin' badge show up to get some lemonade?"

Keith nodded slowly. "Come to think of it, a cop did come by and buy a glass. He kept looking at Ms. Rose's house even after he'd finished drinking. I didn't think anything about it. I just figured he was keeping an eye on her. Should I watch out for him?"

"Yeah. Let me know how often he comes by. If he ever starts to go up to her house, call me. I don't want him getting into the house with her."

"Noted. Are you taking over?"

"I'm not sure. I'll let you know in a bit." Sangre turned away and walked up the sidewalk. Ringing the doorbell several times, he grew concerned. *Keith didn't see her leave, so she must be inside. Why the hell isn't she answering?* The notion that she didn't want to see him crossed his mind, but he dismissed it and rang the bell again. He was ready to go around back and try and break in when he heard light footfalls approaching.

The door swung open and Isla, looking delectable in shorts and a tank top, stood staring at him.

"Hey," he said, opening the screen door. He brushed past her, and the wicked scent of her perfume made him want to throw her against the wall and kiss her hard as he shoved her shorts down and slipped his finger inside.

"What do you want?" She closed the door and followed him into the living room.

"My mom said you told Rachel you were coming for Sunday supper. I just wanted to confirm that with you."

"You couldn't just phone?"

"Why? Don't you want to see me?"

"You ghosted me, so I guess the answer is no." She went over to the window and stared out. Isla was in a funk, and he didn't think it was entirely because he'd disappeared from the radar for a few days.

Sangre went over to the wet bar and knelt down, taking out small bottles of booze and reading their labels.

"What do you want? Whiskey, vodka, rum, or gin?"

"A rum and Coke would be good. Wait, did I drink all of the Coke?"

"One left." He pulled it out and stopped when he heard the song that was playing. Looking over his shoulder, he saw her leaning against the window staring out. "What happened?"

She glanced sideways and gave him a questioning look.

He stood up holding four small bottles and a can of Coke in his large hands. "You used to only play Journey songs when something shitty was happening."

She faced him. "My life doesn't have to be in a state of chaos to listen to Journey."

He put the bottles down on the coffee table and walked toward her. "Yeah, it does. Do you wanna talk about it?"

Turning back around, she stared out the window again. "Maybe I'm just in a nostalgic mood." She pressed her head against the glass.

As Sangre watched her, "Don't Stop Believin'" filled the silence between them. He knew her too well. The summer between fifth and sixth grade, he'd talked her into climbing Mr. Wilson's oak tree as high as she could. He couldn't believe how well she'd done it and how brave she'd been when she lowered herself down the fire department's ladder an hour later. After that, his admiration for her grew tenfold.

He grabbed one of the glasses on the table. Isla turned her head slightly when the ice clinked in the glass. He unscrewed the bottle of rum, poured it, and then popped open the can of Coke. "I happen to remember that Journey is on your 'Life Can Really Suck' playlist." He walked over and handed her the drink.

Her shoulders slumped forward as she brought the glass to her lips and took a big gulp. Tilting her head back, she closed her eyes. "Okay. I found out Benz is fucking Lexi."

Sangre blew out. "That really sucks." *I should've beaten the shit outta the prick.*

"It's not that I care so much about it, it's more the satisfied look she had on her face when I walked in on them going at it in the studio's bathroom. I mean, lock the damn door at least, you know?" She took another sip of her drink. "The thing that sucks more than the humiliation of it all is that I don't seem to really care. What's wrong with me? I've known Benz for almost seven years, been his girlfriend for over a year, and I can't even cry about finding him screwing a woman I've despised since high school. I can't even get pissed about it the way I should."

He put his drink down and came over to her, placing his hands on her shoulders. "Nothing's wrong with you. The fucker never deserved you, and the inner *you* knows it."

"But you'd think I'd feel sad or mad or upset or something. I'm just nothing. Maybe it's because I was planning on breaking up with him. I don't know. How do you feel after a break up?"

"Kinda like you. I mean, I feel bad for the woman, but I don't think about it afterwards. I see it as just another blip on the timeline of my life. It's fun, and then it's not."

She groaned and tilted her head back. "What's wrong with us?"

"Nothing. We just haven't found the right person." A comfortable silence fell between them as they listened to the vocals of Steve Perry. When the song ended, Sangre stood up. "I'm taking you somewhere that'll get your mind off all this shit. Grab a sweater or hoodie. We're going for a ride."

"Where too?" A sparkle lit up her eyes.

"You'll see."

As she ran upstairs to change her clothes, Sangre went outside to talk with Keith.

"Hi, Sangre," the woman next door said while she helped a man fold down the lemonade stand.

"Hey." He'd forgotten her name and saw the man struggling with the booth. "Need some help?"

The guy looked up and shook his head. "Thanks, but I've got it." The two girls started doing cartwheels and somersaults on the grass.

"You have a beautiful motorcycle," the woman said walking toward him.

"Thanks." Not wanting to engage in chitchat, he turned around and headed over to Keith. Sangre, like most of the Night Rebels MC members, didn't like talking to citizens; doing so, just for the sake of talking, was definitely something he didn't do. The woman caught on and slowly walked back to her front yard.

"You can take off," Sangre told Keith. "I'll pay you for the three hours. Grab yourself a beer and relax for the rest of the night."

"Cool. Thanks, Sangre."

As he watched Keith drive off, he heard the clack of footsteps behind him. The scent of Isla surrounded him before he turned around, and he smiled. She'd changed into jeans and a floral tank top, but he averted his gaze from her because he didn't want his dick to get any ideas before they even pulled away from the curb.

"Are you going for a ride?" the woman next door asked.

"We are. It looks like Carly and Letty are closing up shop."

"Colt's trying to fold the stand, but it's not working. I don't know what's wrong with it."

"Why doesn't he just pick the fuckin' thing up without folding it? They put the damn stand up every day," Sangre said to Isla.

Isla smacked his arm lightly. "They'll hear you. Faith's real sensitive about stuff like that, even if someone's kidding."

"I'm not joking. The guy's a bonehead."

She giggled as she climbed on behind him. "You're so bad." She tugged his hair and pressed close to him, making his dick stir.

"Have fun," Faith said, waving.

"How the hell do you stand all that friendliness?" he asked, moving forward.

"Faith's really nice. I think she's desperate for adult conversation. Colt works a lot of hours, and I'd think being at home with the kids all the time would get a bit boring. I've volunteered to babysit, but they've only taken me up on it a couple of times."

"That's why I live at the club—No citizens around. *NO* nosy neighbors. *NO* fuckin' perkiness and … *NO* idiots who keep folding and unfolding a damn stand each day. The thing is cheaply made so no wonder it's starting to break."

She laughed. "This really pisses you off, doesn't it?"

"I don't have any patience with stupid people, dumb questions, or a million other things."

"Do you have patience with me?" Her breath was warm against his ear. The bike vibrated as they waited for the light to change green.

"You're in a class all of your own. Rules I have about other people never apply to you. You're different."

"I like hearing that." The light changed, and the bike jerked forward. "Oh! I didn't expect that," she said, squeezing her arms tighter around him.

I could get used to this. It felt good to have her soft body molding against his.

When they finally left civilization, he picked up speed, making wisps of her hair stroke his face. She planted her cheek on his upper back, and her scent swirled around him, driving him wild with desire. *She needs my friendship not my cock.* When he thought about it, it made sense, but his dick didn't think so. It was growing harder each time her hands slipped dangerously close, or she pressed tighter against him. It was killing him.

Concentrate on the scenery. The desert held a special calming effect over him. He loved it as much as the mountains and took every chance he could to ride through it. It was humbling to be surrounded by such beauty on such a large scale; it grounded him, pulling him away from the violent world in which he lived a lot of the time.

The road shimmered in the haze as the sun blazed down. Above, strands of gossamer clouds streaked the blue sky like spider webs. Parched ground, sagebrush, and telephone poles whirled past them. Lizards skittered across the sand seeking refuge under the shade of red-colored rocks. Up ahead, crows swarmed a roadkill; their sharp beaks tore at the flesh while above, more of them cawed, their iridescent black wings beating the air as they swooped down on the carcass.

In the distance, the San Juan Mountains pierced the sky, and after a long while, Sangre turned left and made his way up a steep road, leaving the desert behind them. When they reached the hilltop, he shut off the engine.

"Chaco Canyon!" Isla scrambled off the Harley and threw her arms around him. "Thank you. Thank you for remembering," she whispered in his ear, her warm breath tickling his neck.

He held her tight. "How could I forget all the times we spent here before you left me? This was our go-to place when life got to be too shitty. You *need* this."

"You're the best," she murmured against his shirt. She pulled away and put her hand over her eyes to shield them from the sun. "It's just stunning here. You don't know how I missed coming here and all our times together. I can't believe I'm back."

Sangre shrugged off his cut and laid it on the seat of the bike then opened one of the saddlebags and took out a blanket. Walking over to a cluster of pine trees, he felt happier than he had in a very long time. "Come over here in the shade," he said, spreading the blanket down on the ground.

"In a sec. I just want to take it all in." She went to the edge of the mountain and pointed. "Is that for real?"

He went over to her and looked down: A narrow bridge hung on seemingly translucent cables, curving over a frothing gorge below the steep rock walls. "You want to go down there and cross the bridge?"

"No way. It looks too scary. Have you ever been on it?"

"No. It was put up a few years ago."

"So, you come here often?"

"Not really. I love it here, but there are some other places I love too that are closer, so I usually go there."

"You'll have to show me your secret places. I'm sure the women are impressed when you bring them up here." She smiled.

"You're the only woman who has been here with me." She grasped his hand and squeezed it then let go and walked over to blanket. She patted the space next to her, and he went over and sat down. For several minutes they sat in silence, taking in the scenery and enjoying being there together.

"Do you want a beer or something?" he asked, breaking the stillness.

She laughed, and the softness of it mingled with the small breeze rustling the pine branches. "Do you always have beer with you?"

"Mostly. Water too. One of my saddlebags has a cooler liner. I had it custom made."

"That's awesome. Sitting here with you now seems like we're back in high school, like all this time didn't pass by. It's nice."

"Do you miss LA?"

"Yes and no. I miss the ocean for sure. I live right on the beach. I lucked out and found this amazing condo that didn't cost me a fortune to rent. It's tiny, but my front yard is the ocean, and I can never get enough of watching it. When I suck in the briny air, it's like an elixir to me. I can stand for hours on my balcony just gazing at the white-tipped waves roll in and spread like fine lace over the beach after they crash in their soft way." She pulled at a loose thread in the blanket. "But I don't miss anything else about LA. If I could just stay on that balcony, I'd be good, but I can't. The last few months have been wonderful in Alina. I like the slow-paced life, the congeniality of my neighbors, and the sense of community. All of that gets lost in the shuffle of a big city."

"Are you planning to go back?"

She shrugged, brushed her hair off her face, and stared at him. "Why didn't you ever contact me after I left Alina? I kept waiting and hoping to hear from you, but I never did."

"I was pissed as hell at you for cutting out without saying goodbye. I was shocked when I found out you moved. You didn't even call to tell me you were going."

She leaned back on her elbows. "After we kissed on that Fourth of July, things seemed awkward and tense between us. It felt like you pulled away. I guess I did too because I was mixed up about it. I loved that it happened, but I was dating your friend Jay, and you and I were best friends, so there was a lot of confusion inside me."

"There was for me too, but not even a fuckin' phone call to say goodbye?"

"My dad was such a bastard that summer. He kept telling me and my sister that we could finish out high school in Alina, and then, at the last minute, he told us we all had to move with him to California. He knew the entire time that we were all going to move, but he made us believe we could stay. And I *really* wanted to stay. I tried to call you, but you weren't home. I had literally a few hours to get my stuff together before we headed out. I didn't want to text you or leave a message on your phone, so I wrote you a letter and put it on the door."

Sangre cocked his head. "A letter? I never got it. There was nothing on the door. Believe me, my family would've given it to me if they saw it. I didn't see any letter when I got home that day."

"I left it on the screen door. I taped it really well so it wouldn't blow away or something. I can't believe you didn't get it."

"I didn't. I'll be damned. For all these years I thought you dissed me."

"Me too," she said softly.

"What did the letter say?"

"That I was leaving and would miss you. I told you to call me right when you finished reading it."

He moved closer to Isla and ran his fingers up her arm. "I'm sorry I didn't swallow my fuckin' pride and get in touch with you. I should've figured you wouldn't have just taken off. I guess I thought you didn't want anything to do with me after we'd kissed."

"I was scared because that kiss turned everything upside down for me. It was the best thing that had happened to me." The eyes gazing at him blazed with desire.

Slowly, he ran his fingertips along the side of her face. "Looking at me that way is gonna get you fucked," he said hoarsely. Isla glanced down at his crotch then back to his face, her eyes locked on his. He traced her bottom lip with his thumb, and she poked out her tongue and licked it. Lust pulsed through him as he pushed his thumb into her mouth. Her lips closed over it as she sucked it sensuously, making his cock strain painfully against his jeans.

Reaching up, Isla looped her arm around his neck and drew him to her, and he hovered over her, his gaze boring into hers. "You're so beautiful," he rasped, his dick aching to be inside her.

Pulling him closer, Isla teased his lips with soft sweeps of her tongue. He groaned and shuddered. *Fuck.* Sangre's willpower waned as he tangled his hand in Isla's hair and ground against her, wanting her to feel what she did to him. A small gasp escaped from her parted lips as she squirmed when his mouth hungrily covered hers.

She's mine. There's no turning back.

Chapter Sixteen

ISLA CLUNG TIGHTER to Sangre as his kiss intensified. Harder. Rougher. Deeper. His lips scorched hers, devouring them, and her body burned for him. She'd been craving him ever since their first kiss years ago, and now sensations crawled wild through her veins. She wanted his hands all over her, touching her, claiming her. The feel of his hard dick rubbing between her thighs, his fingers tangling in her hair, and his tongue thrusting past her lips and teeth—hot and probing, sent her nearly to the edge.

As Sangre ground harder against her, his callused hand slipped under her T-shirt, skimming up her rib cage as he moved his mouth from her lips and across her jaw to the sensitive spot under her ear. "I've been wanting to do this for a fuckin' long time," he whispered, his fingers undoing her bra.

Isla moaned then held her breath in anticipation as he eased up her shirt, exposing her soft rosy-tipped nipples. Sangre kissed a trail from her neck to her collar bone to the top swells of her breasts. "So pretty and tempting," he whispered against her skin, voice roughened by passion.

Then Sangre whistled softly, his gaze taking in her butterfly tattoo. Dotted borders went under each breast, wrapping around the butterfly, which was in the middle under her tits. Bright, purple ink accented the wings. "Fuck, that's sexy," he said, tracing the outline with his tongue.

Isla threaded her fingers through his hair, watching as he pulled one beaded nipple into his mouth and covered her other breast with his hand. As he squeezed and kneaded, he sucked, licked, and bit her other nipple all the while rubbing against her. Heat pulsed between her legs as tingles zinged through her all the way down to her clit. It felt so good and she never wanted him to stop.

He moved his mouth to her other needy, hard nipple while he slid a hand down the front of her pants and cupped her mound. She groaned. "Are you wet for me?" he growled.

"Yeah," she panted.

Sangre undid the button on her jeans and pulled the zipper down. Isla kicked off her shoes then pushed up a bit from the ground, and he tugged off her jeans. She grabbed the hem of his T-shirt and yanked it up, which made Sangre chuckle as he finished pulling it up over his head and threw it down next to her jeans. Isla sat up and he took her shirt off then tossed her pink lacy bra on the blanket, his gaze traveling over her nakedness.

"I love your tattoo," he said, his voice thick while running his fingers over dark Gothic roses on curly Q vines. The ink started at the tip of her right butt cheek and curled up the side of her body with the vine stopping right above her right breast. A musical score with notes wove around it. "It's fuckin' amazing. Did you design it?"

Isla nodded, keenly aware of his hands on her naked flesh. Sangre looked up at her; his eyes were molten, burning with lust. He stood up, and she propped up on her elbows, watching him as he discarded his boots, socks, jeans, and boxers. When Isla saw his dick, she gasped. It was thick and hard, and a vein throbbed down the side of it. Without thinking, she sat up, reached out, and curled her fingers around it; the skin was smooth and silky.

"Fuck, babe," he growled, dropping to his knees. He yanked her to him and kissed her deeply, and then pushed her back down with ease onto the blanket. He bent down and peppered kisses around her navel and across her stomach, then to her hips and thighs. He pressed his face against Isla's skin as if memorizing the feel of her. Looping his fingers on either side of her lace panties, he slowly pulled them down, and then kissed his way back up over her legs to her thighs, gently spreading her legs. He sat back on his knees and stared at her wetness; a heated flush spread over her and she dropped her head down. Sangre placed his hand under her chin, gently lifted her face, and closed his lips over hers.

"Don't be embarrassed. I never imagined you were this beautiful. I want to see all of you," he said against her mouth, his fingers slipping into her wet folds as he held her gaze.

"Oh, Sangre." She gasped.

"You like that, honey?"

A shudder of raw passion passed through her at the sound of his hoarse voice and the touch of his hot breath fanning over her face. Isla clutched his tatted bicep, loving the way his muscles flexed as his fingers moved closer to her slick and swollen clit, that was hot with need for him. He stroked her slowly before pushing one finger inside. She bucked against him as he added another. Her hips rocked with the movements of his fingers as she rode his hand. Isla arched into him, gripping his shoulders hard as the tension mounting in her threatened to explode. He bent down and flicked his tongue around her belly button.

"Fuck, I need you," he gritted.

"I need you too. By the way, I'm on the pill."

"You want this raw?"

"I want to feel all of you inside me."

"Me too," he whispered, dragging his lips across her stomach as his one hand glided over her breasts, down her waist, and across her inner thigh. The width of Sangre's shoulders kept her legs spread apart as he dipped his head low, his fingers still pushed far inside her.

The first brush of his tongue over her sensitive flesh had her clutching the blanket and thrusting her throbbing pussy into his face. "Sangre!"

While his fingers pumped in and out, he licked her heated sex up and down, using flat and steady strokes, but never touching her clit. She moaned in frustrated pleasure as he moved his mouth away and sought her nipples, biting and sucking them while he removed his fingers covered with her juices, reached around her and squeezed her ass cheeks before teasing her puckered opening. Isla's whole body trembled under his touch, and when he slid his knee up to meet her pussy, she rubbed against it desperately as his mouth left a few, parting, feather-light licks on her rock-hard nipples.

His lips seared down her body, nipping, kissing, and licking it until he buried his face between her legs. She groaned then cried out when his tongue flicked her sweet spot. "You drive me fuckin' crazy," he rasped. With his tongue, he made small circles over her nub, and the tension that had been building from the moment he kissed her, exploded. Isla cried out, frantically grabbing at him, until her hand found his neck and pulled him down to her. She kissed him between pants, tasting herself on his lips. She had never come so hard before with a man. It brought tears to her eyes, and her lids fluttered open, blinking them away.

Sangre kissed her gently and stroked her cheek. "Was it good?"

"The best," she breathed, her body calming down.

"There's more to come." He leaned back and raised her legs up, placing her feet on his upper chest. Isla's ass came up a bit, and he pushed inside her. Slowly and gently, his dick filled her up as her still tingling walls molded against him. Then he pulled out and an emptiness filled her; she craved him inside her again.

"You want me to be gentle?"

Isla swept her palms over his broad shoulders, her fingernails tracing the tattoos adorning them. She ran her fingers over the curves of his stomach and down his sculpted arms.

"Do you feel gentle?" she asked in a soft voice.

A knot of muscles at the side of his jaw pulsed. "I want to take all of you. Hard."

Catching his gaze, she threw him a wicked smile. "Then do it."

Pushing Isla's knees up and bending them toward her chest, he shoved his cock deep inside as she cried out from the sheer pleasure of it. He pulled out then began jack-hammering into her, withdrawing all the way and then driving his dick back in—deep and hard. Each time, she pushed up to meet his thrusts, over and over, shattering her to the point where she couldn't think. All she could do was feel and react.

Sangre bent over and kissed her, and she felt the passion flow between them. She kissed him back wildly, clutched him tightly, and moved with him as though they were one. The sound of their bodies slapping into each other only fueled her desire as Sangre pummeled faster, deeper—his eyes never leaving hers. "Isla," he growled as he brought his finger to her sweet spot.

"Sangre," she panted, her nails scratching down his chest.

He continued to pull out and plunge back in at the same time he stroked her hard nub, and a dazzling burst of fireworks exploded through her, coursing through her veins and carrying her away on a cloud of euphoria.

Sangre stiffened and groaned as he threw his head back, his hot come spurting deep inside her as he emptied his balls. "Fuck, Isla. What the hell are you doing to me?" She cinched his waist with her hands and pulled him close. He claimed her mouth hard and wet, and then he collapsed on top of her, her breasts pressed against his chest as her arms tightened around him. They lay panting and sated as his breath skated across her cheeks. Still connected, Sangre rolled onto his back, bringing Isla with him. Settled with her cheek pressed to his chest, she listened to his heart pounding, a loud thrumming, like a train speeding down the tracks.

She'd had some great sex before but never felt as she did right now with Sangre. Instead of feeling guilty or wicked, she felt alive for the first time in a long while. Sangre brought Isla to life, filling her with happiness and light—with passion and desire. She tilted her head back and looked up into his eyes, which were laced with tenderness and passion. He pulled her up, his softening cock slipping out of her, and kissed her on the mouth.

"That was fuckin' awesome," he said against her lips. "*You're* fuckin' awesome."

"So are you." *I love you. I have since high school. That's why I could never fall in love with anyone. You've always been in my heart.* She wanted to tell him how she'd poured her feelings out for him in the letter he'd never received, but she didn't dare. What if he didn't feel the same way about her? *What if this was just great sex, and now we've become friends with benefits.* A groan escaped from her throat.

"You okay?" he asked, stroking her hair.

"Yeah. It's a little chilly."

He laughed, easing her on her side, and then drew the blanket over them. "Better?" There was a smile in his voice.

Nodding, she snuggled deeper into him and closed her eyes.

The piercing ring of her phone startled her and she sat up, trying to figure out where it was. Sangre handed it to her, and she put it to her ears.

"Where the fuck are you?" Benz's angry voice sliced through her.

"In the mountains. I'm surprised I have reception up here."

"I've been calling you for the past three hours, for Christ's sake!"

Benz's anger didn't belong in the canyon. She didn't want to hear his noise or be sucked into his perpetual dark mood. This was her slice of peace, and she didn't want him to ruin it.

"Hello?" his voice crackled.

"I'm losing reception. I'll talk to you later."

"Wait! Is this your way of punishing me for screwing that bitch? It didn't mean shit—"

"I can't hear you." She lied.

"We have practice in an hour, or did you forget?" Panic replaced anger in his voice.

Shit. I did forget. "I'll be a little late, but I'll be there."

"What's up, honey?" Sangre asked.

"Who the fuck are you with? It's that goddamn biker, isn't it?"

She pictured him foaming at the mouth. The irony of the situation would be laughable if it wasn't so pathetic. "I have to go. See you at practice." She clicked off the phone then turned it to *Silent.*

"Do you have to get going?" Sangre tugged her to him, kissing the top of her head.

She leaned into him. "I forgot the band has practice tonight."

He stiffened. "Was that your ex?"

Isla smiled. "Yes." She pulled away and grabbed her clothes and began to dress. "Do you want to come with me?" She didn't want their time together to end.

"I have some stuff to do, but I'll pick you up afterwards, and we can grab some food."

The rush of adrenaline burst through her. "I'd love that. I think you can call off the bodyguard for tonight." She held her breath.

"That's what I was planning to do. I'll have someone spot me while you're rehearsing, but the rest of the night, I'm all yours." He gave her a lopsided grin.

Yessss! She stood up and tucked in her T-shirt, her gaze on Sangre as he dressed. *He's just perfect.* In the midst of her elation, a doubt niggled at the back of her mind. *But he's commitment-phobic. By his own admission, he can't stay in a relationship for more than a few months. Don't go overboard with your feelings.* "I already have," she said under her breath. *He's going to break my heart.*

"Ready?" he asked, reaching for her hand.

Nodding, she followed him then climbed on the Harley and wrapped her arms around his waist. As they rode back to Alina, she rested her face against his back, the scent of sex still lingering on him. Refusing to think of *what ifs* and determined to live in the moment for the rest of her time in Alina, she kissed the back of his neck, loving the way he looked behind him and winked.

The sun began to wane, and silhouettes of birds flew home across a sky that was now magenta. Isla wished they could keep riding, only stopping to make love. She pressed closer to him, closed her eyes, and let the feel of the wind and the scent of him dispel her fears, at least for the moment.

WHEN ISLA ENTERED The Rear End, she saw Benz on stage with the other band members. Waving at Jim, she walked toward the band and stopped when Benz turned toward her. Her hand flew to her neck when she saw his bruised and battered face. "What the hell happened to you?"

He glared at her. "Why the fuck are you so late?"

"I told you I was in the mountains. What happened to your face?"

"Do you really fucking care?"

"I wouldn't have asked if I didn't. Did you get in a fight?"

"No. I was drunk and had a bad fall."

She came closer to the stage and peered at his face: cheeks swollen, black eye, fat lip. "That was quite some fall. Are you sure you didn't get into a fight?"

"I told you I didn't. Quit nagging me."

"Did you go see a doctor?"

Benz shook his head, and Arsen coughed. "We better get started. Jim said we have to be outta here in two hours." Arsen picked up his guitar.

"Yeah. We're supposed to have four hours, but *she* decided to go to the mountains." Benz went over to the drums.

"I'm really sorry, guys, about being late. I totally forgot we were rehearsing today." Isla jumped up on the stage.

"No worries. Shit happens. In two hours we should get through our set," Gage said. Isla nodded, picked up the microphone, and waited for the first song to begin.

Almost two hours later, she placed the microphone back in the stand, sweat glistening on her face. "That was a damn good rehearsal, guys."

"Fuck, yeah," Arsen said. Jac mumbled in agreement, and Gage high fived her.

She jumped down and went over to the bar and picked up a stack of napkins, wiping them over her face. Jim set a bottle of beer in front of her, smiling. "You sounded damn good up there."

"Thanks." She picked up the bottle, tilted it toward him, and then took a long drink." Anxious to see Sangre again, she pulled out her phone and began to tap his number.

"We need to talk," Benz said from behind her.

"There isn't much to talk about. You're the type of guy who just can't be faithful. I knew that when I caught you with those two fans back in LA. We're better at being friends than we are at being in a relationship. The truth is, we shouldn't have gotten back together after we broke up the first time. I need so much more than what you can offer me, and you need so much more than what I can offer you. It's okay."

He jammed his hands into his pockets, and she saw a muscle jump in his jaw. "This is bullshit and you know it. You're not even going ballistic like you did the last time. You been fucking that asshole biker, haven't you?"

Isla rolled her eyes while shaking her head. "You're mad at me because I'm not flipping out about finding you screwing Lexi? Seriously? I gotta get going." She looked down at her phone again.

Benz grabbed her arm and shook her. "If I find out you were fucking behind my back, you're going to be more than sorry."

She jerked her arm out of his grasp. "So now you're threatening me? You really are an asshole, you know that? I'm out of here." She jumped off the stool and pushed past him. "See you all later," she said to the band members on stage, and then walked out the front door.

Mark's familiar car was parked in front, and she leaned against the brick wall and tapped in Sangre's number. As she waited for him to pick up, out of the corner of her eye she saw someone approaching her. Mark was out of the car in less than a second, walking around the front of it and coming over to her.

"Hi, Isla," Lexi said.

I can't believe this bitch has the nerve to say anything to me. Ignoring her, she turned away and smiled when she heard Sangre's voice.

"Are you finished?" he asked.

"Yes. Did you get everything done that you needed to?"

"Yep. I'm leaving now."

"I have to go home first because I need to jump in the shower. I always get so sweaty after a good hard practice."

"No problem. I should be there in about twenty minutes or so. See you then." Isla slipped the phone into her pocket.

"Is everything okay here?" Mark asked, his gaze fixed on Lexi.

"Yeah. It's just"—she waved her hand at Lexi—"this bitch wants to talk to me and I don't want to talk to her." She glared at the woman. "Why are you still here?"

Lexi shifted from one foot to the other as she tugged at her pearl necklace. "I just want to explain things."

Mark shoved himself between her and Isla. "Move on, lady."

Isla took a few steps forward and stared at her. "There's nothing to explain. You want Benz ... you can have him. I'm so over him."

Lexi's eyes widened. "Just like that? I thought you guys were tight."

She laughed dryly. "Sorry to spoil it for you, but you actually did me a favor. I don't have anything more to say to you."

"I didn't mean to do it. I'm really sorry."

"It's fine. It really is."

Before Lexi could reply, Mark stepped in front of her. "I told you to move it on outta here. I meant it. Go."

With slumped shoulders, Lexi turned away and went into the bar. Isla shook her head and smiled at Mark. "Thanks. Sorry to involve you in my drama."

He folded his massive arms against his chest. "It's my job."

"Sangre said he's coming soon. I can just wait in the bar if you want to take off."

"I don't leave until my boss says I can. I'll be in my car."

Isla went back into the bar, and when Benz saw her he wrapped his arm around Lexi while staring at her. She went over to the counter and slid on one of the barstools.

"You want another beer?" Jim asked.

"No, thanks. But a bottle of water would be awesome." As Jim knelt down and rummaged through the cooler, she placed her chin on her hand as she stared at Lexi and Benz's reflection in the mirror behind the bar. Benz was nuzzling her neck, but it seemed to Isla that Lexi wasn't all that into it. She had a strained look on her face, and her body looked stiff.

"Sorry that Benz is being such a jerk," Jac said, sidling up to her.

"We're through," she said softly.

"It's probably for the best. Even though Benz is my bandmate and friend, I never thought he deserved you."

Warmth spread through Isla when she heard his words. Jac rarely got involved with any of the band's drama. Other than being an awesome bass player, he rarely spoke and when he did, it was only a few words or grunts. She leaned over and kissed his cheek. "Thanks for that." He lifted his chin at her and sauntered away.

The roar of a motorcycle made her insides tighten as happiness and a huge dose of excitement zinged through her body. *Sangre!*

"Here you go," Jim said placing a bottle of water in front of her.

"Thanks." She brought the bottle to her lips and took a sip. The front door burst open, and Isla watched Sangre swagger—his tight jeans fit just right, and the tattoos danced on his flexing biceps. Her heartbeat increased the more she took him in, and delicious flashbacks of him pounding into her as he held her down with his powerful arms made her squirm on the stool as desire ribboned through her.

His smoldering gaze caught hers as he came toward her, and an intense heat sizzled between them. She met him in the middle, and he wrapped his tattooed muscles around her. "I love the way you feel," he whispered into her hair.

Acutely aware of Benz in the room, she gave Sangre a quick peck on the cheek and pulled away. "I need a shower." She didn't want to hurt Benz. She wasn't the vindictive type like he could be. Even if Sangre hadn't come back into her life, she and Benz wouldn't have made it. The fact was that Benz was a much better friend than he was a boyfriend. She walked into their relationship with eyes wide open, knowing that he'd never stayed faithful to any woman he'd ever been involved with. Somehow, she'd thought it would be different with her. He'd pursued her so ardently that she figured he'd be so happy they were finally together, that he wouldn't need to screw around. She'd been wrong, and it was okay. Breaking up with him was like a thousand pounds had been lifted from her heart and soul. It was liberating.

"Let's go."

"Let me grab my microphone." She whirled around and went back to the stage. Gage had wrapped up her mike neatly as he always did. *He's so thoughtful. What a sweetie. Melody has a keeper for sure.*

"Are you taking off with your new 'boyfriend'?" Benz's voice was hard and sharp like glass.

"I'm leaving with my *friend.* It looks like you won't be lonely. I'll see you at the studio tomorrow afternoon."

"Fuck, Isla. No one can hold a candle to you. Let's stop all this before we both have major regrets." Benz scrubbed his face.

"We're still friends. I've jumped off the roller coaster. I'll see you tomorrow, and I'll be on time. Promise." She yelled, "Goodbye" to the other band members and walked out of the bar.

"Isla, wait!" Lexi called after her. The clacking of her heels reverberated on the sidewalk.

Isla handed her microphone to Sangre who put it in one of the saddlebags. She turned to Lexi. "I'm done talking to you. I told you that."

"I just wanted to tell you that I'm done with Benz," she said, her eyes traveling up and down Sangre's body.

"Fuck off, Lexi." Isla settled down behind him and linked her arms around his waist. The engine fired up and the cams drowned out Lexi's reply. Turning her head away, she looked out at the street and the neatly mown grass banks surrounding the various storefronts bearing a façade of brick or stucco.

Sangre pulled away from the curb, and soon the warm air cocooned around her as they rushed past people, houses, and cars. Sangre veered the bike left, and they were soon in front of her house. Streetlights radiated pools of golden yellow on the sidewalks; here and there, illuminated windows cast slivers of paler light across the lawns, and glinting stars danced in the inky sky.

"Do you want to park inside the garage?" she said, pushing the button on the remote. He rode up the driveway and shut off the engine.

Soon they were wrapped in each other's arms kissing up a storm. Isla had taken a quick shower, and when she came into the living room, the sight of Sangre sitting on the couch—boots kicked off, feet propped on her coffee table, and folded arms adorned in tat sleeves—it was more than she could stand. She ran over and pounced on him like she used to do when they were kids, only now they weren't, and what once brought on a wrestling match now brought on a major kissing session.

As his hand slid under her top, her insides churned with burning desire for him. *I guess we'll be eating in.*

And that suited her just fine.

Chapter Seventeen

CARRIE NOLAN TAPPED her pink-tipped nail against the steering wheel as she glanced at the clock in her car: 10:00 p.m. *Why did I agree to meet at this hour?* Normally, she conducted business during the day, but when she got the call that the Deathriders wanted to book a show at the community center, she was beyond ecstatic. Having a big national band book a show in Alina was rare, and with a large concentration of heavy metal fans in the area, she knew landing the contract with the band would be a huge feather in her cap.

For the past eight years, she'd fought and scratched her way from working the ticket booth in a music venue to owning her own talent buying business. She was now the number one promoter in Alina, and the ones who used to turn their nose up at her when she started putting on local shows, now called *her* to book shows at their establishments.

She chewed on the cap of her pen. *I wished I would've booked Iris Blue. I screwed up on that one.* When she'd read about Isla Rose's breakdown and return to Alina, she'd thought the singer was just taking a break from the music scene until her band signed with a label and they headed back out to tour. When she'd heard they had booked a performance at Trailside, she called their manager right away, but Kent had told her he'd already committed to the two shows in town. *I can't believe I blew that one, and I knew Isla when she was Jordan.* Well, she didn't actually *know* the singer, but they were in the same grade in high school, and she saw her perform in all the musicals. She wished now she would've taken the time to get to know Isla. *Since she's out of seclusion now, maybe I should call her for lunch. It wouldn't hurt to befriend her for future contacts.* Carrie pulled out her notebook and scribbled—*Call Isla for lunch*—and stashed it back in her tote.

Outside the wind had picked up, shaking the trees and rattling along the warehouses' rooftops. *Why did I think this was a good idea?* She looked around the desolate area, cursing herself for agreeing to meet so late at night in the middle of nowhere. The message she'd received had told her the band wanted to find a warehouse and use it for the concert. She'd found the owner of the one she was parked in front of, and he agreed to rent it out for a low sum. When she'd relayed the message to the manager, they'd agreed to meet at the closed factory.

During the day, the area looked like any other, but under night's cover, it looked ominous—like one of those abandoned mental institutions that were so popular in horror films. She shuddered. *You're letting your imagination run away. Stop it.* She started tapping the steering wheel again and grew more and more agitated listening …

… for something. *Anything.*

The wind moaned loudly, and then a flurry of rain pattered against the car windows. She jumped and cried out when the clash of thunder roared as jagged lines of lightning lit up the sky momentarily. Inhaling and exhaling several deep breaths, she willed herself to stay calm.

Then she saw it.

The dark outline of a form fleetingly illuminated by lightning.

Someone's out there. Watching me.

Scared out of her mind, she slowly turned her head, but she couldn't see anything through the streaks of water running down her window. "I bet it was a deer or something," she said under her breath. There were lots of wild animals around the area, especially in desolate places.

Another boom made her cry out. Then a spectacular light show.

And the figure again.

But this time is was closer.

Her heart pounded in her chest; her hands curled in nervous energy.

There is someone … or something out there.

I have to get out of here.

More lightning streaks, but this time she didn't see anything. *Could it have been the trees?* It was so dark and rainy outside, she couldn't trust her eyes to see anything correctly.

Suddenly, bright headlights came toward her, and she covered her eyes with her hand. Then her phone beeped. She looked down and opened the text.

Manager: *Sorry I'm late.*

Carrie: *We'll have to meet another time. I'm already on my way home.*

Manager: *No, you're not. I'm here. My car is facing yours.*

Annoyed, Carrie pulled down her visor but it provided little relief from the blinding lights.

Carrie: *Is that you with the bright lights on?*

Manager: *Yes. Come to my car so we can go over the details and sign the contract.*

A shiver shot through Carrie. Suspicion niggled at the back of her mind. *Something feels off about this.* She turned on the ignition.

Carrie: *Let's meet another time. The weather is getting real bad.*

Manager: *If that's what you want. The band wanted a contract by the morning. I have been dealing with other promoters.*

She thrummed her fingers on the dashboard. *It won't hurt to meet now.*

Carrie: *I'll just take the contract and review it at home then we can meet up in the morning.*

Manager: *Perfect. I'm coming now.*

She turned on the windshield wipers and watched as the person got out of the car and ran over to her, an umbrella covering all features. She unlocked the door and the person slid in, the face still obscured.

"Here," the voice whispered. A hand gave her a yellow folder.

She turned on the overhead light and opened it. Confusion rushed through her as she frowned. Inside, there wasn't a contract; rather, there were clippings from Jefferson High when she went to school there. The articles were reviews of her performances in choir, and there were also photographs of her over the years, the most recent one from the day before. Icy fear wove through her, strangling her nerves.

"What is this?" she said in a barely audible voice.

"It's all about you." The voice sounded hoarse like the person had a cold or something, but it also sounded familiar.

Where have I heard that voice?

"I've been following you for a long time, Carrie Nolan. You always thought you were better than me. Remember how you laughed at me in high school? I wonder who's going to laugh tonight. I have a feeling it's going to be me." Again a low voice, but this time anger and cruelty laced it.

"I don't know what you're talking about. I don't even know who you are. Get out of my car."

The wind howled around them as hail beat down on the roof of the car sounding like gun fire. Carrie's mind whirled as she tried to figure out what to do. *If I run outside, the hail will get me, but it's my only chance.*

As if anticipating her move, the person grabbed her hands. The hood slid off, and under the overhead lights, she could now see the face more clearly.

"You!" she gasped.

Then the person broke the light and the car was plunged into darkness. Before she could react, the "manager" went into a frenzy: punching, scratching, stabbing. She screamed as she saw her own blood splattering across the windshield, the dashboard, and the steering wheel.

"No! Please no!" she cried, reaching forward to stop the knife.

But the sharp blade came down again, slicing through her, puncturing her dress and her flesh. The blade kept coming again and again, even after she stopped fighting.

I'm dying.

Then blackness descended over her.

Chapter Eighteen

"YOU'RE IN ANOTHER relationship," Army said, sitting down beside Sangre at the bar. "You always get that stupid look on your face in the beginning."

"Not in the mood, dude. Fuck off." Sangre turned away from him.

"Again, so soon? Man, you are a glutton for punishment," Crow added as he elbowed Army, who sniggered.

"Chains," Sangre called out, ignoring Army and Crow.

"Yo," Chains replied sauntering over.

"You got the real estate info?" Sangre asked.

"Yup. I got it in my room. Are you gonna be around for a while?"

"Nah. I'm going over to my parents' for dinner. I can get it from you in the morning."

"Are you staying the night at your *mommy* and *daddy's*?" Army said in a little boy's voice.

Sangre stood up and faced him. "I've had enough of your shit. You're fuckin' sick in the damn brain, dude. You should ask Breanna to recommend a good shrink. I'm trying to talk club business here, so either shut the fuck up, or I can do it for you."

"He's just joking around with you," Crow said.

"I'm not in a joking mood."

"I don't know what the fuck's your problem. You think it's funny when we all rib the other guys about chicks. You never had a problem before when we'd tease you about any of the women you went out with. What gives?" Army popped some peanuts in his mouth.

"Just not up for it today. I don't need to explain anything more to you."

"He's got a point. Some days you just want to smash anyone who even looks at you," Crow said. "Let's back off, dude."

Army shrugged and turned his attention to the big screen television. "Fuck, yeah! This dude is a major power puncher."

Sangre glanced at the TV and saw Anthony Joshua holding up his arms in the air while his opponent rolled on the boxing rink's floor. "I'll meet you in your room around noon to get the info," he said, turning back to Chains. He guzzled the rest of his beer and went up to his bedroom to freshen up before he picked up Isla.

Isla. Everything about her enthralled him. He'd finally stopped fighting his attraction and his feelings for her. For a long time, one side of his brain battled the other, and his heart battled them both in turn. He kept pretending that he didn't care, that they were just friends, that it was only lust, but after the last few days he'd spent with her, he knew that he *did* care for her in ways he never had for any other woman. Lust was there, of course, but it was more than that. The night before, he'd just held her close to him because she was so exhausted from recording. Just lying there and holding her had been more intimate than all the times he'd fucked his ex-girlfriends. Being with Isla showed him what he'd been missing all these years.

As he splashed on some cologne, he couldn't help but wonder what was going to happen when Isla went back to LA. He didn't like the idea that the asshole she used to date was still around, but he'd watched her with Benz before anything even happened between him and Isla, and she hadn't acted all that interested in the dude in *that* way.

Grabbing his keys from the dresser, he locked his door and went to the parking lot via the backyard. The last thing he wanted to hear was Army's smart-assed remarks on how he smelled, which would definitely encourage the rest of the brothers to join in on the ribbing.

In less than twenty minutes he was in front of Isla's house, having just told Mark that he was taking over. The two girls from next door waved at him and he nodded back. Their mother—*What the hell was her name again?*—yelled out a cheerful, "Hello," as he walked up the porch steps. Isla answered the door before he rang the bell, and she looked sexy as hell in her floral sundress and strappy sandals. He went in and snagged her around the waist, wrapping her long hair in his hands then yanking it hard before he claimed her mouth. Her lips were pillow soft and full, and he took the bottom one between his teeth and sucked it while he pressed close to her, wanting her to feel his bulge.

"See what you do to me, babe?" he mumbled, smothered against her mouth.

"You do a lot to me too," she said as her hands slipped under his muscle shirt, sliding along his taut ribcage to his back, her fingernails leaving marks on his skin.

"Oh yeah?" He glided his hand up her thigh underneath the short dress, twisting it between her legs until he cupped her mound. "Wet," he said, slipping a finger inside her. His mouth covered hers as he rubbed her knotted nub.

She groaned and arched her body toward him, and he swallowed all of her moans as their mouths pressed together fiercely, their tongues tangling as fire shot through him.

"So fuckin' wet, baby," he whispered as his hand molded over one of her breasts through the soft fabric. Dipping his head, he pulled her hardened nipple into his mouth and sucked it through the material.

"Sangre," she breathed as she clawed at his neck and pulled his hair. "Oh shit!" She shuddered as she fell against him, clinging to him.

He turned her around, and she automatically bent at the waist, put her hands against the ivory white wall, and spread her legs. He jerked up the dress to her waist and groaned when she moved her legs farther apart.

"You're so sexy and beautiful," he said raggedly. His black jeans pooled around the tops of his boots, and he sank his finger deep inside her. She bucked and pushed back, her ass rubbing against his stiff dick. He reached under the dress, his free hand skimming over her belly up to her tits. His fingers found her hard nipple straining against her bra, and he seized it and twisted it at the same time he spread her pussy lips with his free hand and plunged into her. The way her firm ass hit against him as she met his hard thrusts, and the noises she made while he fucked her, drove him over the edge, and he exploded, filling her with his warm seed.

She quickly followed as her forehead pressed against the wall and her body quivered. He held her close, sinking down to the floor like crumbling sand. The only sound was their heavy breathing and the scent of sex permeated the air. She curled next to him, and he entwined his fingers in her hair as he tried to regain his energy. Placing a finger under her chin, he tilted her head back and kissed her deeply.

"Fuck, honey. Just … *fuck*." Smiling, he brushed away an eyelash from her cheek.

"Not bad." Mischief danced in her hazel eyes.

"Oh yeah?" He started tickling her and she tried to push his hands, but he had her pinned down on her back, her face red as tears streamed down her cheeks. He'd never seen her more beautiful than at that moment. He seized her lips and kissed her passionately, and she looped her arms around his neck and returned the gesture. They stayed like that, kissing and touching each other, until a familiar ring tone broke through their sexual haze.

Pulling up his jeans a bit, he rummaged through the pockets and glanced at the screen. "Shit. It's my mom. I bet we're late." He winked at her. "We're on our way, Mom," he said.

"Do you have car trouble?"

"No. I just lost track of the time. Sorry. We'll be there soon."

"I wanted you to have some time to mingle before dinner."

"I know. See you soon." He hung up and swatted her ass playfully. "We better get going, or my mom's liable to send over the militia."

"I have to freshen up," Isla said as he helped her up. "You can use the bathroom off the second bedroom to clean up. I can't believe I let you fuck me before going over to your parents' house."

"You gotta watch out for me. I'm a bad influence." He followed her up the stairs and went into the bathroom.

Thirty minutes later, they pulled up in front of his parents' house. He drove Isla's car over, knowing that his mom wouldn't let up on him for the whole night if he'd taken Isla on his bike. Anyway, her dress was too short, and he didn't want to fight anyone who said something crude to her. If that had happened, they never would've made it for dinner.

Before they went inside, Isla stood on the sidewalk staring at the house next door. "It's like I never left," she murmured.

"Not much changes around here," he said, clasping her hand in his.

"It's about time," his mother said, opening the screen door wide.

He bent down and kissed her on the cheek. "I thought we were eating at five thirty."

"I told you that I wanted you to have time to mingle," she said in a soft voice. Turning her attention to Isla, she smiled. "Jordan. It's been a long time. I don't think I would've recognized you. Your hair is blue now."

"Mom," he said, pretending to be exasperated.

"Only in the sunlight and under bright lights. It's nice seeing you, Mrs. Ansell."

His mother looped her arm through Isla's. "Call me, Diana. Mrs. Ansell makes me feel too old." She laughed and led the singer into the house with Sangre following behind.

For the next hour, he watched as Isla held her own with his boisterous clan. Family gatherings got to be a bit much for him, so he was glad to see that she was having a good time.

"Steve, can you come into the kitchen, please."

He jumped up and went to see what his mother wanted. "Need some help?"

"I would like you to take the prime rib out of the oven. It's too heavy for me." She handed him the pot holders. "Jordan's grown into a very pretty girl. She seems to fit in nicely with the family."

"Where do you want this?" He held the large roasting pan.

"Over there," Diana pointed to the counter behind him. "Don't you think Jordan's a pretty woman?"

"Yeah. Did you want me to take the roast out of the pan?"

She handed a large platter and cutting board to him. "Put it on the cutting board then put the slices on the platter. I noticed you were holding her hand when you came up to the house."

"Did you move the carving knife?" He stared at the empty space where the knife block used to be.

"It's on the other counter. Do you like Jordan?"

He smiled at the deep frown crossing his mother's brow. "Of course, I like her. We're friends."

"The way you were holding hands and looking at each didn't appear like any friendship I ever had."

Sangre put the knife down and looked at his mom. "Don't try to marry us, okay? You do this all the time."

"No, I don't. You've only brought two girls over here and that includes when you were in high school. I just want you to be happy like your brother and sister. I'm pretty sure Connor's going to ask Kayla to marry him. Don't you want a family?"

"Someday, just not today. Don't worry about me, Mom. I'm cool."

"Are you going to live at that clubhouse your whole life? Don't you want your own home?"

"I thought I'd come in and save you," Nicole said as she walked into the kitchen. "You've been in here too long, and I saw the way Mom looked at Jordan."

He winked at his sister. "I owe you."

"You two." Diana shook her head and handed a large bowl piled with mashed potatoes to Nicole. "Put this on the table. I don't see Steve very often."

"She changed her name to Isla," he said to Nicole as she walked toward the kitchen door. "She really doesn't want people calling her Jordan anymore." Nicole nodded then left the room. "And that goes for you too, Mom."

"If I can remember. Anyway, don't you want your own place?"

"Someday." He picked up the platter and went into the dining room.

During dinner, the chatter of adults and children filled the room, and Sangre kept darting his eyes to Isla, making sure she wasn't overwhelmed. She wasn't. Her face glowed under the lights and candles, and her hands waved around as she spoke about her music and the band. One of the things he always thought was endearing about Isla was how animated she'd become whenever she referred to anything that she felt passionate about. *Music's her life. She could never give it up.* He didn't know why that thought pushed into his brain, but he knew the music scene wasn't in Alina.

"The food is so good, Diana," Isla said, and his mother beamed.

"How did you like Stephanie's appetizers?" Sangre asked, inwardly smiling when his mother threw him a scolding look.

"They were really good." Isla speared another piece of roast beef with her fork.

"Did you hear about Carrie Nolan?" Rachel asked.

Sangre put his utensils down. "What about her?"

"She was found murdered in her car by that remote warehouse off the old highway near Gilmore. The police think it happened last night."

Sangre heard Isla gasp then she sputtered and began coughing. He handed her a glass of water and rubbed her back. "Are you all right?" he said in a low voice.

"Rachel! Why would you bring something like that up at dinner? That's not a good topic of conversation, especially with the children."

"Your mother's right," Martin Ansell said.

"I'm sorry. I just thought Isla might know her since they were in the same grade at Jefferson." Rachel looked down at her plate.

Isla, pale as a winter's moon, dabbed her face with her napkin. "I didn't know her. I remember seeing her in the halls, but we weren't friends. This is awful. Horrible. Do they have any idea who did it?"

Rachel flitted her eyes from Diana to Martin, and then looked right at Isla. "No clue, or at least they're not saying. She's the fourth woman to die in less than a year. I'd say there's a serial killer in Alina."

"For Christ's sake, Rachel," Nicole said.

"Enough of this conversation. Can't you see how upset Isla is?" Diana pressed her lips together.

"It does seem like the same person is doing these killings," Tom said.

"Now, don't you start," Diana chided her eldest son.

Sangre slipped his hand under the table and placed it on Isla's thigh, massaging it gently. "Are you sure you're okay? Do you want to go out for some fresh air?"

She placed her hand on top of his. "I'm okay. It's just shocking and kind of freaky."

It's more than freaky. The fuckin' psycho is killing women on some arbitrary list he made, and I know Isla's on it. Who's this fucker?

For the rest of the dinner, the conversation centered on lighthearted topics, and everyone had a lot of questions for Isla about LA, spotting movie stars, and touring with four men in a van for months.

After the women cleared the table and washed the dishes, Sangre stood up and went over to his parents. "We're gonna take off. I have to be at the office early in the morning."

"She looks so pale. I could kill your sister for bringing up what happened to that poor woman. She frightened Jordan half to death."

"She'll be all right. She's just tired from recording and practicing." *She* is *scared to death. I have to make sure she stays safe. I gotta find out who this fucker is.*

Isla came over and leaned against him. He bent down and kissed the top of her head, and from his peripheral vision he saw his mother beam and Nicole and Rachel whisper to each other. "I'll come by during the week to help you with the deck, Dad."

"I almost forgot," Diana said, wiping her hands on her apron. "I have a box for you to take home. It's the stuff that was in the corner of the closet in your old room."

"You still had all that shit?" Sangre said.

"Yes. I still had all that *stuff.* I'm turning it into a craft and design room." Diana and Rachel were co-owners of the Sweet Spot Bakery, and

Diana was the one who designed most of the cakes and cupcakes.

"My old room's gonna be a craft room? What are your plans for Tom's room?"

"Pool table and wet bar," Martin said, coming over to the door.

"Here you go," Tom said, handing a large box to Sangre.

On the way back to Isla's house, she sat mute, staring out the passenger window. Sangre stroked the side of her face. "I know you're freaked out."

"Whoever this madman is, he's coming for me. I *feel* it. The sheriff told me that I'm one of the five girls from Jefferson that the killer seems to want to hurt." She rubbed the back of her neck. "Four are dead. I'm the last one still alive," she said softly.

"There's no fuckin' way I'm gonna let anything happen to you."

"If I go back to LA, I'll be safe. I didn't have this shit in LA. Some damn psycho wants to kill me, and I don't even know why."

"If he's intent on doing it, he'll find you in LA. I'm gonna try and figure this out. I'll ask my club to help. In the meantime, you're with me."

"You can't be with me twenty-four seven. That's not realistic."

"I have the top guards watching you. They'll be going everywhere with you even if you don't want them to: like at the gym, the recording studio, practice, every fuckin' place. Do you have any idea who'd want to hurt you from high school?"

"No. I've wracked my brain over and over, but I just can't come up with anyone. So much has happened to me that high school seems like a lifetime ago."

"Is your band trustworthy?"

"You mean my bandmates? Of course. Definitely. Absolutely. Anyway, they don't even know the women who were killed."

"Maybe the women were just decoys to get to you."

"Don't say that. I'd feel awful if I was responsible for their deaths. I just can't believe this is happening," she said, her voice hitching.

"I'll keep you safe. I've got your back, honey. There's no way I'm letting *anyone* hurt you." He brought her hand to his lips and kissed it.

When he pulled into the driveway, his senses were on high alert as his eyes scanned the area. He closed the garage door while they were still in the car. "Make sure you close the door while you still have the car in gear. It's just a precaution."

They went into the house, and she disarmed the alarm then set it again right away.

"I'm gonna check around the house. You hang in the living room." He slipped his hand inside his cut and took out a gun.

"You carry a gun?" she asked, her eyes wide.

"Yeah. I left it in the trunk when I was at my parents'. In my world, you can never be too sure about what's going to happen from one minute to the next. I'll be back."

After a thorough check of the whole house, he climbed the basement stairs then froze when he heard Isla scream. Adrenaline pumped through his veins as he raced up the rest of the way and dashed into the living room, gun in hand.

She sat on the couch, her face a mask of fear, a piece of paper on the rug by her feet.

"What the fuck's wrong?" he asked, sprinting to her. He bent down and picked up the paper. He saw an envelope on the coffee table addressed to her.

"I found it on the floor under my mail box. He's going to kill me. I'm going to die," she muttered.

He pulled her to him and wound his arms around her trembling body. "I'm never gonna let that happen. You have to trust and believe in me. Okay? Do you trust me that I've got your back? Look at me." He pushed her away slightly and cupped her face between his hands. "Do you trust me?"

"Yes. I do," she whispered. "Oh, Sangre." Isla smiled weakly and put her hands on his thighs, and he crushed her to him, rocking her back and forth until she stopped shaking and relaxed in his arms.

As she sat pressed to his side, her head resting on his chest, he looked at the letter.

I see you. I watch your every move.

I know your daily routine. Where you go.

I stalk from behind the trees, the rocks.

I lurk in the darkness. Face hidden. Knife gripped tight.

I'm your shadow … your constant companion.

No one can save you.

I creep closer and closer. Waiting for the kill.

If I can't have you, nobody will.

♥♥♥*Your Best Fan*♥♥♥

Anger seared his nerves, curled tightly around his muscles, and bubbled under his skin; it was like acid—burning, slicing, potent. *I've got to find this psycho and give him everything he's given to Isla and the other women. I need to talk to Steel, Paco, and Diablo tomorrow.*

"Isn't that creepy? This is the worst one yet." Isla said in a hushed voice.

"He's a fuckin' bully who gets off on scaring you."

"But he's killed four other women."

"You don't know if it's the same person. It could be someone obsessed with you who wants you to believe he's the killer." *I don't believe that shit one bit, but I've got to ease her mind.*

She sat upright. "I never thought of that. That actually makes sense. Should I show the letter to the sheriff?"

"No harm in doing it. I'll go with you in the morning." He brushed his lips across hers. "We should get some sleep."

After turning the lights off on the main floor, they went up to her room. As she washed up, Sangre stood by the window looking out at the street. The neighborhood was quiet, and all the houses were dark. *Are you out there, motherfucker*? He stared at the trees in front of her house and the ones in front of the neighbors', but he couldn't see anything. It was quiet as a graveyard.

"See anything?" Isla asked.

Giving the street one last look, he closed the shutters and moved away from the window. "You live in a quiet neighborhood." He went over to the bed and stripped off everything except his boxers then slid between the sheets.

"That's why I love it here." She joined him under the covers.

He tugged her to him and held her close. She snuggled deeper into him, and he lightly ran his hand up and down her arm, smiling when he felt her skin pebble underneath his fingertips.

"I feel so safe in your arms," she whispered.

He squeezed her tight and kissed her hair. Her breathing deepened as she fell asleep. Staring up at the ceiling, he knew sleep wouldn't come as easily for him. Thoughts whirled around in his mind: Isla, Carrie Nolan's murder, the threatening letter, Jefferson High, the killer. He couldn't let her get hurt. They'd finally found each other after all those years apart. He couldn't lose her.

All at once, she had become someone very special to him.

And he meant to keep it that way.

Chapter Nineteen

ISLA WATCHED AS Sheriff Wexler stared at the note she'd just handed him while Sangre sat next to her, holding her hand. It meant a lot to Isla to have him with her. The night before, Sangre told her to trust him, and she did. It was a new feeling for her—complete trust in a man. For a long time, she'd thought Sangre hadn't cared about her, but after he informed her that he never received the letter she'd left on his door, it suddenly made sense as to why he never contacted her.

"Last night, was anyone from your company watching Ms. Rose?" Wexler asked Sangre.

"No. Last night we were at my parents' having dinner, so I didn't have any of my guards watching the house."

"I heard about Carrie Nolan," Isla said softly. "How terribly sad." The muscles in the sheriff's jaw twitched. "Do you think the person sending me the letters is the same one who killed Carrie?"

"We can't rule anything out. You need to be extra careful." He grabbed a cup on the desk and took a sip. Looking at Sangre, he leaned forward. "You need to let me and my deputies do our job. We'll catch the one responsible."

Sangre pressed his lips together, his chin jutted out and arms folded across his chest, and stared at Wexler, not uttering a word. Tension crackled between the two men.

"I guess we're done, right?" she said, hoping to slice through the discomfort.

Before Wexler could answer, the door burst open and Deputy Jeffers rushed in. He glanced over at her and his mouth turned down in contempt.

"What the hell's going on?" The sheriff's facial features were pinched and sharp.

"I got a lead on the car thefts over in the Sunnydale neighborhood." Then, Jeffers looked over at Isla. "What are *they* doing here? Did you get some more fan mail?"

"I'll talk to you about the thefts in a few minutes," Wexler said.

Jeffers sank down in one of the chairs, and Sangre stood up, pulling Isla up with him. "We're going."

"I'll need to keep this," the sheriff said, placing the note in a large folder.

"Go ahead. Please let me know if you find out anything," she said, her hand in Sangre's.

"I will. And remember what I said, Sangre. We've got this."

He tugged her out the door and didn't say a word until they were out on the street. "Do you want to grab some lunch?"

She put her hand on the back of his neck and drew him to her, kissing him passionately. "Thanks for coming with me. I know this was a big deal for you. I've picked up that you're not a fan of the sheriff's department."

"I don't trust badges, or anyone else associated with the government."

"You have no intention of stepping back, do you?"

"No fuckin' way. Leroy's for lunch?"

"Sure, but it'll have to be a quick one. I'm meeting the band at the recording studio in a couple of hours."

He straddled the bike and she swung her leg over it. Sensing someone staring at her, she looked up and saw Deputy Jeffers' intense gaze fixed on her. An unpleasant, tingly chill crawled up her spine, and she quickly turned away. *What's up with that jerk?* She tightened her hold on Sangre as he rode toward Leroy's.

Two hours later she walked into the recording studio and made sure the door locked behind her. Gage sat in one of the rooms, tuning his guitar.

"You're early," he grinned then focused back his guitar. "I need to change one of the strings. Can you throw me the pack? It's on top of my duffel bag."

Isla tossed it to him and went over to the microphone stand. "Are we the only two here?"

"Jac and Benz are smoking weed out back, and Arsen is running a bit late. According to him, the chick he hooked up with last night kinda threw a scene when he tried to leave this morning. She's going to work, so he's making his escape." He chuckled.

"Sounds kind of fishy to me. He probably wanted some more time with her but doesn't want to admit it."

Gage lifted one of his shoulders. "Maybe. He's always with a different chick, so who knows. Are you excited about playing on Saturday? You've seemed a bit tense."

Isla went over to the small refrigerator in the corner and took out a Coke. "I am. How's Benz? Is he still super pissed at me?" She popped open the can.

"He's usually super pissed at something. I haven't noticed him madder than usual. Are you guys finished?"

"Yeah. We never should've started. We're much better as friends."

"Me and the other guys agree with you on that. It was a lot of drama last year."

"Wasn't Melody supposed to fly out to see you? Is she coming for the show this Saturday?"

He shook his head as he threaded the third string into the tuning peg. "She can't take too much time off work, so she wants to save it for Sturgis."

"I didn't know you like motorcycles." She placed her mike on the stand.

"I didn't know *you* did. I've see you on the back of that dude's bike. I'm not really into them, but his is wicked-looking."

"It's a Harley, and I love riding on them. It's so freeing, and with the wind all around me, it feels like I'm one with nature. It's exhilarating."

She turned her microphone on.

"Is that dude the friend Benz is bent out of shape about?" She nodded. "No offense, but he doesn't look like anyone I'd want to meet in a dark alley."

She giggled. "He does look badass with his swagger and tats, but he's a nice guy. He's super cute with his nieces and nephews, and he's got a big heart even though he doesn't want anyone to know that. He's just awesome."

Gage looked up from his task, locking gazes with her. "Sounds like he may be more than a friend."

"We've known each other a long time. I've always had a crush on him."

"So, you're with him now?"

"Yes. I am." The admission made her stomach flutter and a rush of warmth spread through her. *I'm dating Sangre. We're together, having the most amazing sex. He wants me.*

Before Gage could comment, Benz and Jac strolled into the room. "Glad you decided to show up," Benz said, walking past her and going over to the drums. She bit the inside of her cheek to keep from snipping at him. "Where the fuck's Arsen? I'm really getting sick of this unprofessional bullshit from all of you." He adjusted the drum heads.

No one responded. They'd all been around Benz long enough to know that when he was in one of his moods the best thing was to let him get it out of his system, but sometimes he was too much and she'd end up getting into a fight with him, or Jac would tell him to shut the fuck up. Even Gage, who was normally calm, would go off on him if Benz kept goading them. Arsen seemed to be the only one who knew how to handle him, but then they went back since high school.

"Are you guys ready to go?" Terry Z asked as he came into the room.

"Our lead guitarist isn't here yet, but he's on his way," Isla said.

Benz glared at her. "Did he personally tell you that, or are you just talking outta your ass?"

"That's what he told me, dude," Gage said.

Still scowling at Isla, he picked up the drumsticks. "Then why the fuck are you acting like you talked to Arsen? Are you trying to show us how important you are?"

Anger pricked at her skin. "Give it a fuckin' break. This is petty shit and you know it. If you're going to be a major asshole the whole time, I'm leaving."

"So you can fuck your friend?" The drumsticks slamming on the cymbals clashed deafeningly.

Arsen walked in at that moment. "Sorry I'm late."

Isla turned around, her back to Benz, and smiled at him. "We're just getting ready to start. Why don't you tune up, and I can lay down the vocals?"

"The drums go first. You should know this. You're supposedly a musician," Benz said.

Terry Z folded his arms across his chest and stared at Benz. "I don't know what the fuck's going on with you, but this shit stops now, or you can take your pain in the ass attitude outta here. I don't have time for juvenile bullshit. I told Isla we're laying down her vocal tracks for 'Before I Ever Leave You' then we'll lay drums for the new song. I'm the one calling the fuckin' shots." He glanced at Isla. "Ready?" She nodded. "Let's get going."

As Terry Z went into the soundproof booth and settled in front of his sound board, she picked up the microphone and put on headphones. She could feel the intensity of Benz's stare burning through her back, but she ignored him and watched Terry Z for her cue to start singing. Soon Benz faded away as she lost herself in the music.

Two hours later she sat in the lobby, drinking a bottle of water when Arsen joined her.

"You sounded great. You nailed that song." He pulled out a joint and offered it to her.

Isla stared at it for a few seconds, the craving for it tearing through her body. She shook her head then brought the water bottle to her mouth.

"It's only pot." Arsen lit up his joint.

"I can't take the chance." She was afraid that if she smoked, it'd trigger something in her that was always just beneath the surface—calling to her, making her sweat, enticing her to just take one last hit. It'd been seven months since she snorted a line or smoked a joint. *I can't risk it. I can't go back to using.*

"Did anyone tell you we got a gig at Sturgis?" He took a pull off of his joint and blew out. The familiar sweet scent spread around the area as spirals of smoke wisped upwards and vanished above his head.

"No. Gage mentioned he and Melody were going to Sturgis, but he didn't say the band was going to perform there." Excitement shot through her. "We've been trying to play there for the last five years. This is so cool."

"So you told her?" Jac asked as he flopped down on the cushy armchair next to the loveseat she sat on. "Benz wanted to be the one to tell her."

"So, the fuck what? He's in a mood, and we need to be on the same page for the gig." Arsen handed a joint to Jac.

"When do we leave? We have to practice our asses off." The water bottle, slick with chilled condensation, began to slide through her fingers, and she tightened her grip around it before it fell to the floor. "Which venue are we playing at?" She leaned over and put the bottle on the small oval table.

"Buffalo Chip," Arsen replied.

"Rough Creek Label is gonna be there." Jac leaned his head back against the leather chair.

"They wanna see if we sound as good live as we do in our recent recordings," Gage added, sinking into an overstuffed chair. He snapped his fingers, and Arsen looked up at him. "Gimme a joint." Arsen handed him one.

Isla's insides quivered and she pressed a hand on her churning stomach. *If we get signed on that means months of touring. Can I do it without falling back into my old lifestyle?* All of a sudden the room began to spin, and she closed her eyes and reclined against the cool black leather cushion. *How will I see Sangre if I'm touring? Is this what I* really *want? Damn. Get a hold of yourself.*

"Are you okay?" Gage's voice pulled her back to the conversation.

"Yeah. It's just hot in here."

"Terry Z worked you pretty hard," Arsen said, craning his neck. "Here he comes. I must be on." He pushed up from the chair and disappeared down the hallway.

"How'd it go?" Jac asked as Benz took Arsen's seat.

"Good." He looked over at Isla. "We got a gig at Sturgis." Knowing he'd be pissed as hell that she already knew, she feigned surprise and delight. "It's going to be such a good time. And the exposure's fantastic. After the gig we'll head back to LA, so you'll have to bring your shit on the tour."

"I have to come back here to close up the house and all that," she said softly.

Benz narrowed his eyes. "You've got almost a month to do that. We gotta start touring and playing festivals and shows around California." He crossed his leg over his thigh. "We take off for LA after Sturgis. And that means you, too."

Of course, he was right. They'd been out of commission for too long, and they had to get back to performing. *The band would've already played several festivals if it wasn't for me. I can't hold them back. It's not fair. I just have to grow the fuck up and step up to the plate. Vacation is over.* Sadness descended over her. "Okay. I'll get everything together."

Benz nodded, smugness creeping over his face. "Are you going to sell your place?"

She jerked her head back. "No, I'm going to keep it."

"When we're on tour, you can't be running off every fuckin' minute you have to come back to this dump of a town." Benz got up and went into the small kitchen down the hall. When he came back, he had two beer bottles in his hands. He twisted off the top, took a long pull then sank back down in the chair.

"I'm keeping my house and will come back here when I need to get away. I like it here, and since you don't ever have to come back, there's no reason to get bent out of shape."

"The band comes first—just remember that." He took another gulp.

She nodded and glanced down at her phone. *It's going to be a long night.*

Later that night, around ten o'clock, her phone woke her up. She'd fallen asleep on a cot in one of the back rooms that had been set up for artists who worked through the night.

"Hello?" she said groggily.

"Hey. Are you still at the studio?" Sangre asked.

"Oh … yeah. I'm sorry. I should've let you know that we're going to be here for a long time."

"No worries. I was just making sure you're good. Are the doors locked?"

"Yep. Terry Z always keeps them locked. He's got millions of dollars in equipment." She yawned and continued, "I can't believe I fell asleep. I'm not sure how much longer I can be here. I'll do one more song since we have the show this weekend, but I don't want to blow out my voice, you know?"

"I'll come over and hang with you. I've never been in a recording studio, so it should be interesting."

She smiled. Just hearing his voice made her weak in the knees and breathless. "I'd love for you to see my world."

"Leaving now. I'll give you a buzz when I get there."

She stared at the blank screen for a long time. *How am I going to live without him?* Putting her hands on the back of her neck, she kneaded the sore muscles. *I don't want to think about that. I'll just enjoy the time I have before I have to leave.*

By the time Sangre arrived, Isla had at least two energy drinks and was raring to go. She sang her heart out, happy that the man she loved was in the booth with Terry Z watching her. The lyrics she'd written about finding each other again and letting go of all the hurt from the past held special meaning now, and she sang them to him, knowing that each time she'd perform the song she'd think of him. He was engraved in her mind, her soul, and her heart.

By the time the recording session ended, the sun had risen and cars dotted the highway past the studio as people made their way into town. Isla jokingly called that time of day "Alina's rush hour." In LA, it took her over an hour just to go fifteen miles, and when she told Sangre that, he thought she was exaggerating.

"I'm going to have to drag you to LA for a visit, so you can judge for yourself. I also want to walk on the beach with you at sunset and feel the spray of the ocean air across my face as you hold me close." *How can I go?* She shook her head in a vain attempt to rid any sad thoughts.

"That'd be nice," he said, squeezing her close and kissing her deeply.

When they arrived at her house, bone-weary tiredness curled around all of her limbs, and she didn't think she'd make it to the back door. The morning air was already warm, indicating that the day would be a scorcher. The whole neighborhood smelled of roses, and the sunlight brought back the greenish hues to all the leaves, plants, and grasses as it ushered in the new day.

"Hi, Isla!" Carly's cheery voice sounded tinny amid the chirping birds, the shrill droning of cicadas, and the low hum of distant traffic.

"Hey." She waved at her and the little girl skipped up the driveway. "Getting ready to set up your stand?"

"Daddy's taking it out of the garage now. I put some more decals on it." She gripped Isla's wrist. "Come see."

Isla turned to Sangre as Carly tugged her along. "Come and see it with me." She laughed brightly when she saw his are-you-fucking-kidding-me face, but gestured him to follow her nevertheless. Stone-faced, he walked behind, stopping next to her as Colt came over with the folded booth.

"You're up early," he said, opening out the stand.

"I'm just coming back from a long recording session."

"Hi, Isla," Faith said, coming over to her with Letty in tow.

"Hi. You know Sangre, right?" Faith nodded. "I've been at the studio all night, and I'm pretty beat." She turned to Colt. "Do you know Sangre?"

"Not really." He glanced at him. "I've seen you on your Harley Davidson. Awesome bike."

Sangre gave him a chin lift.

"Here are the new decals," Carly said pointing to several lemons making funny faces.

"They're so cute." Isla turned to Sangre. "Don't you think they're adorable?" She laughed inwardly, knowing how much he hated every minute of mingling with the neighbors.

"We should get back." He tugged at her upper arm.

"Okay." As she started to say goodbye, she dug in her purse and took out two orange tickets. "I almost forgot. Here are two VIP vouchers for the band's show this Saturday at The Rear End." Carly and Letty giggled and clasped their small hands over their mouths.

"Thank you," Faith said, her eyes shining. "It's been forever since Colt and I went out alone."

"The tickets get you in the door and give you a reserved table. It'll be a good show. Iris Blue is headlining, but there's an awesome band from Denver—Immortal Sÿnn—that is direct support, and a local band that's opening. Oh, the food is pretty decent there too."

"What do they have?" Colt said, taking the vouchers from his wife.

"Burgers, wings, nachos, soups, salads … stuff like that. The menu is fairly big." She glanced at Sangre. "You've eaten there before and like the food, right?" Jutting out his jaw, he nodded.

"Sounds like a good time. I'll call around and get a babysitter," Faith said.

"We've gotta go," Sangre said, pulling Isla away.

"Okay. Thanks again, Isla," Faith said.

"You're welcome," she answered, rushing to keep up with Sangre's long strides. "What the hell?" she said softly.

"The conversation was done, two minutes after we went over. You need to get some sleep."

She smiled at his concern and let him lead her into the house. In the kitchen, she poured two glasses of orange juice and put them on the granite breakfast bar. "Did you want something to eat?"

He gulped down the juice. "Nah. We need to get some sleep. How often do you pull all-nighters?"

"Not very often. Terry Z is a taskmaster, so we've done more with him than all the other recording studios combined. He's the best, so it's worth it."

"You're pretty friendly with your neighbors."

"I tend to be that way." She poked him lightly in the ribs. "Remember when you moved into our neighborhood?"

"Best move ever." He winked at her. "Are your neighbors from here?"

She put her glass down. "Faith and Colt aren't. They moved here from Omaha. I think she told me it was about five or six years ago. The Elderberrys, on the other side of me, are from here. They're an older couple, and Eleanor will come over and water my plants and flowers if she thinks they need some loving care. I'm grateful that she does that, because when I get busy, I tend to forget about everything. The Farrells, from across the street, have the cutest baby and dog. I think they're from Denver." She went to the fridge and came back with the carton of orange juice and poured another glass for her and Sangre. "Having neighbors I actually talk to beyond 'hi' is an anomaly for me. In LA, I'd be lucky to even see my neighbors, let alone talk to them."

"I guess. For now, you need to put the brakes on being too friendly since everyone is a suspect."

"And I thought *I* was paranoid." She laughed and put the empty glasses in the dishwasher.

"You just never know. Even the old lady is a suspect."

"Eleanor? No way." Standing behind him, she wrapped her arms around him and kissed his neck. "I think the lack of sleep has made you delusional. Let's go upstairs," she murmured against his skin.

When they went into her bedroom, Sangre walked over to the window and stared out for a few minutes before closing the shutters. After shrugging off his clothes, he went into the bathroom. Isla pulled out a short nightshirt from her dresser, peeled off her clothes, and slipped it on. She shuffled to the bed and slipped between the cool cotton sheets.

"You smell fresh," she said to Sangre as he approached the bed. "I should probably take a quick shower too."

He slid in behind her, his arm looping around her waist, and pulled her to him, so her butt was against his stomach. "You smell sexy and wicked. Just the way I like it."

She placed her hand on his, and an overwhelming sense of comfort filled her. "You make me happy," she whispered.

He scattered feathery kisses on the side of her face. "I'm glad. You do all kinds of shit to me." His strong arm pressed her closer, fusing them together, and his warm breath on her shoulder brought goosebumps to her skin.

This is so perfect. I never want it to stop. Feeling protected and cherished, her eyelids grew heavy and her breathing became slower and deeper as she dropped off to sleep.

Chapter Twenty

SANGRE SAT WATCHING Steel and Paco as they mulled over what Sangre had just proposed: finding the serial killer who'd taken the lives of four women in their small town.

"You want us to become badges?" Steel asked.

"I'm just asking for some backup. Got a gut feeling that Isla is on this crazy asshole's hit list. I'm gonna look into it because I think the connection is Jefferson High School. I just want to make sure that if I need some help with it I've got your okay to involve the other brothers."

Paco pressed his lips together. "I don't see why not. I know when all that shit went down with Chelsea, and I needed the club's support, they were right there for me. We'll stand behind you." He glanced over at Steel. "I think I'm speaking for you, too."

Steel nodded. "Just let us know what you want us to do, and we're there for you, bro."

Sangre stood up, walked over to Steel and clasped his hand on his shoulder, then he did the same to Paco. He walked out of the room and made his way to the bar. When he entered the main room, he saw Crow, Shotgun, Skull, Diablo, and Muerto sitting at a table playing cards. He dragged a chair over and joined them.

"What's going on, bro?" Diablo asked, placing a card down on the table. "Did you talk to Steel and Paco?" Sangre nodded. "They said it's cool, right?" Again Sangre nodded. "Just let me know if you need my help, and I'll be there for you. You know it."

"Same goes for me," Crow said.

"You know I'm in," Muerto added as Shotgun and Skull bobbed their heads in agreement.

Pride swelled inside Sangre and he lifted his chin at his brothers. "I'm gonna get this fucker. There's no damn way I'm letting him hurt Isla."

"We hear you, dude." Muerto waved over one of the prospects. Ink came over carrying a tray with a fresh round of drinks for all of them.

"Would Isla be cool about getting the band to sign my sister's CD? She's been bugging the hell out of me ever since the show a few weeks ago. I wanna give her the signed CD so she'll shut the fuck up," Skull said.

Sangre sniggered. "Sure. Give me one and I'll make sure Isla does it."

"Of course Ella and Zoe want to go to the show on Saturday." Skull took out a joint and lit it.

"That sucks for picking up chicks." Sangre looked at Diablo's cards and nudged him. "Great hand," he said in a low voice.

"Raise fifty bucks." Diablo looked stoically at the other players.

"Fold." Skull put his cards face down on the table then placed them onto the discard pile.

"So soon?" Crow shook his head.

"I gotta pick up some stuff for my mom." He pushed away from the table. "I wanna talk to you for a sec," he said to Sangre.

The two men stepped outside and the hot air circled around them.

"What's on your mind?" Sangre asked.

"What you said about not being able to do the Skull magic with the chicks is absolutely right. Ella and Zoe are definitely cock blockers. Since you're not looking for a chick, I was wondering if you could keep an eye on them for me while I hit on some women."

"How do you know I don't wanna hit on anyone?"

"I figure you're there with Isla, and I know the friend talk is bullshit. Actually, we all know, so Army wasn't able to get anyone to bet on it."

"That fucker. I oughta beat his ass." Sangre chuckled.

Skull laughed. "He's always got an angle to pick up some extra cash. Anyway, can you help me out? I like hunting for new pussy."

"I hear ya. I'll keep an eye on them, even if you want a quick fuck in the back."

"Cool. I owe you." Skull stubbed out his joint on the pavement. "Are you going to the party tomorrow night?"

"I was thinking about it. We got a lot of brothers coming from different clubs."

"I heard most of the Fallen Slayers will be here. It'll be a good time. Maybe you can get them to go to Iris Blue's show on Saturday."

"I think it's sold out. I'll ask Isla."

Skull jingled the keys in his hand. "I better get going. I'll see you later." He ambled over to a canary yellow Harley.

Sangre watched him until he disappeared, then he took out his phone and called Isla.

"Hi, sexy." She laughed softly. The sound of her voice—light, breathy, smooth—gave him a rush that made his pants tight and his imagination work overtime.

"Hey, hot stuff. What're you up to?"

"Writing lyrics. The guys are coming over to jam later on. We want to record two of the new songs. I like you calling me 'hot stuff.' Makes me tingle all over."

"I wish I was there to make you do more than that. I fuckin' need to be with you. I'm hard just hearing your voice."

A breathy laugh. "Just from hearing my voice? Poor boy."

His cock strained against the denim fabric. "Everything you do makes me hard."

"I can fix that." He heard her smack her lips, then a low chuckle. "Come over here."

His dick groaned. "You don't know how bad I want to, but I'm meeting with two clients who want security, then later I've got an appointment with Chains to go over club business. I'll come over after that."

A loud sigh. "The guys will be here until real late. We have to get the songs perfect before we go into the studio tomorrow."

"Fuck, babe. I miss you." If Army, Crow, Chains, Shotgun, or some of the other brothers had been standing there, they would've had a field day with that one. But he *did* miss her, and it wasn't just the sex, although being inside her was incredibly hot. He missed holding her, talking with her, listening to her sing as she wrote lyrics. What he missed was *everything* about her. *Yeah, the brothers would be outta control over this.*

"Me too. Let's go out to dinner tomorrow night. I should be home from recording around six. Does that sound like a plan?"

"The club's having a party here tomorrow night. A lot of officers from other clubs will be there. I want you to go with me."

"That'd be great." Her voice squeaked with excitement, making her sound adorable.

"Don't be so eager. Biker parties aren't like the average citizen's party."

"I'm sure they're not any wilder than rock parties or Hollywood parties with the too-much-money set. Believe me, I've seen it all."

"I forgot you live in LA and are jaded." He smiled when he heard her crack up on the other end. "Even though you're experienced with all kinds of debauchery, I'll have to go over the rules with you before you step inside the club. The way you look, you'll be deer to the hungry lions that'll be here tomorrow."

"Definitely sounds like a Hollywood party at around midnight. I'm looking forward to it. Thanks for asking me. I've been reading up on biker clubs, and women who aren't there to put out are usually not included in the club's activities. Reeks of chauvinism, but hey, it's your club."

"It's more than my club. It's my world … my life, and I wanted to show it to you. I saw a glimpse of yours at the studio the other night, and it's time you get a look at mine."

"Did all your old girlfriends get to party with you?"

"Nah."

"How come?"

"I didn't want them to." And that was true. He kept his relationships at arm's length from his world. Some of them would ask him to take them to the club or the parties, but he never felt like sharing that part of him with any woman until Isla came back into his life. Now he wanted her to be a part of everything, and he wanted to know her world as well.

Silence fell between them, and he wanted to tell her that he never cared or wanted a woman to be part of his life like he did with her, but instead, he glanced at the time then cleared his throat. "I gotta meet the first client. Mark is on duty tonight, and your band mates will be with you. If anything spooks you, or you need to talk, call me. Do you want me to come by to take you to the studio in the morning?"

"No. The guys will probably crash over tonight, so I'll just go with them."

His stomach hardened and he clenched his jaw. "I don't like that fuckin' drummer staying over without me there."

"It'll be fine. By the time we're done, everyone's so damn tired that they usually crash on the sofa and floor even though I have three guest rooms. Don't worry about Benz—I'm in control, not him. You trust me, don't you?"

"Yeah, I do. I just don't like that asshole."

"He's really okay. You just don't know him. It's all good."

"I'll call you later."

Sangre went over to his Harley, bitterness punching at his gut. The idea of the ass wipe spending the night at Isla's burned deep inside him. The reaction took him by surprise since he wasn't the type to be jealous, but when it came to Isla, everything was upside down; she got to him in ways no other woman ever had. He pulled over hard to the left lane and hammered it, moving through traffic like a falcon through the trees.

Upon arrival at the office, Sangre had reached a decision: he wouldn't go over to Isla's that night. Every fiber in his body wanted to, but he wasn't sure what he'd do to Benz, and he didn't want Isla to think he didn't trust her. She told him she'd be working late, so he'd call her a few times, but he wouldn't go over. Sangre switched off the engine and headed inside to meet with the company's new client.

★ ★ ★

"REMEMBER TO STAY close to me. If you have to go to the bathroom, I'll go with you and stand outside the door. You're not wearing my patch, so the men who don't know you will think you're fair game, and there'll be a lot of brothers here, and the way you look right now, there'll be a lot of trouble if one of them messes with you," Sangre said when they arrived at the clubhouse.

When he'd gone over to pick up Isla earlier that night, she'd greeted him in a short black skirt and a tight-fitting top that showed off her cleavage. Without missing a beat, he had her in his arms, kissing and touching her all over. His lust had been palpable; it'd filled the room. He'd taken her right there, on the floor, her legs wrapped around his waist as he pounded in and out of her until she cried out as she rode the wave of ecstasy. After a few more pumps, he followed her orgasm then rolled onto his back, tucking her close to him as they'd lain sated on the cold tile floor. Just remembering it now made him tilt her head back and crush his mouth on hers.

"Wow," she said against his lips.

He pulled away. "Just stay close to me."

"If you're trying to scare me, it's not working." She looped her arm around his waist.

"I'm just telling you like it is." He draped his arm over her shoulder and held her close.

As they approached the club, she slowed down a bit. "There're a helluva lot of men outside."

"There're a helluva lot of men period. At parties it's usually ten men to every woman."

"Damn. Are all the women here willing to sleep around?"

"Yeah. The women who come to biker parties usually know the score. If she doesn't respect the brothers it can be a problem."

Isla stopped and looked at him. "What does that mean? You guys don't *force* women, do you?"

Sangre shook his head. "We don't do that shit. If a woman doesn't want to put out, that's her decision, but if she mouths off or shows disrespect, she gets her ass thrown out. The problems start when brothers from other MCs come. They have different rules and ideas at their clubs, so sometimes things heat up. We try and maintain order, but it doesn't always work out. You know, no two motorcycle clubs are the same, just like no two bikers are the same. Attitude, image, and actions of all MCs shift over time, but what never changes is the basic glue that holds all clubs together—brotherhood, trust, and security."

"Does trouble happen a lot?"

"Not a lot, but sometimes. Almost all the women who come to the parties know the score and want to have a night of wild sex, booze, and weed. Sometimes the trouble comes from brothers fighting each other. It's the way it goes."

"With all that testosterone and megawatts of badass attitude, I'm not surprised the guys duke it out."

As they passed the men milling about in front, Sangre tightened his grip on her hand, pride mixed with anger rising inside him when he saw the way they looked at her. Several of them called out to him, and he raised his free arm in the air and waved his fist.

Inside, red lights lit the main room, which was thick with smoke. A greenish glow lit the bar area that was packed with men in black leather, and Sangre chuckled as he watched the prospects hustling their asses to accommodate the burgeoning crowd. It reminded him of his prospecting days and how glad he was that they were over. Music blasted and it seemed like the walls shook. Women ran their gazes over him, smiling seductively, and men blatantly assessed Isla, lust and hunger glinting in their eyes.

"Let's go out back," he yelled near her ear, leading her through the labyrinth of bodies.

The fresh air was a welcome relief from the scent of sweat, weed, and cigarettes of the main room. He guided Isla over to a picnic table and pulled out the bench for her.

"This is so much better," she said, looking around the yard. "Something smells delicious."

"Lena's our cook and she makes the best damn food in the county. The club girls help, but she's the one calling all the shots. We can get a plate. The table's in the far corner of the yard."

"Lead the way. I'm starving." As they approached the long line, the men and women made room for him to go in front of them since he was an officer of the club. He picked up a plate and handed it to her.

"I like the special treatment you get around here." She poked him in the stomach then leaned in close, placing her hand on the back of his neck and tugging him toward her. "You'll have to show me around after we eat. I want to see where you live," she said, her warm breath fanning over his neck.

He wrapped his arm around her, letting his hand drift to her ass. "I can't wait to get you to my room." He pinched her butt lightly then nudged her forward.

As they sat at the table, his plate piled high with tacos, enchiladas, and Spanish rice, and Isla dancing in place while she ate her burrito, Patriot came over with Kelly plastered to his side.

"Hey," he said to Sangre, his gaze fixed on Isla.

"How's it goin'?" he answered, slinking his arm around Isla's waist.

The vice president of the Fallen Slayers MC snapped his eyes to Sangre, a quizzical look spreading over his face. "Not bad. What've you been up to?" His gaze darted to Isla then back to Sangre.

"Surviving." Sangre picked up the beer one of the prospects had put on the table.

"I love your hair," Kelly said to Isla. "It's so pretty."

"Thanks."

"Do you strip it to get it that color?"

"No. I just put it over my black hair and it gives it this sheen. It pops in the sun or under lights, but if it's night, it just looks super black."

"It's really cool."

Sangre saw Kelly checking Isla out, and detected a hint of resignation flickering in her eyes. She turned her gaze to him and smiled weakly.

"I see you've picked up a real hottie to have dinner with." Patriot leered.

"Isla's my woman," he replied, body stiffening.

Patriot's demeanor changed immediately, and he averted his gaze from her. "Sorry, dude. I didn't know." For the rest of their conversation, he didn't even glance at Isla, and Kelly stood next to him, her eyes cast downward.

Why the fuck did I tell Patriot that Isla's my woman? He took another swig of beer. *Because she is. I feel something real for her.* He popped a chip dipped in guacamole in his mouth, and groaned low when he saw Army approaching with Shotgun and Crow following behind.

"What wrong?" Isla asked.

"Nothing. Just some of my brothers coming over. The one with the short hair can be a real asshole. Just warning you."

"I can handle anything he wants to bring on."

"He won't be rude to you because he knows I'd bash his face in. It's just that he can be too much at times."

"Hey, bro," Army said, slapping Sangre on the back while he looked at Isla. "You gonna introduce me to your lady here?"

Before he could answer, Crow and Shotgun came up to the table, beers and joints in hand.

Shaking his head, Sangre knew he wouldn't get any peace until he let his brothers meet Isla. "This is Isla," he said. "And this is Army, Crow, and Shotgun."

She smiled. "Hi."

"Aren't you Sangre's *friend*?" Army asked.

"Yeah," she said.

"You better fuckin' stop there," Sangre said in a low voice.

"I just asked a damn question." Army glared at him.

Isla tugged on Sangre's arm. "Do you mind getting me a cheese enchilada? These beautiful shoes that I spent way too much money on are killing me."

He laughed and tweaked the tip of her nose. "Sure, hun." He got up from the table then pulled Army away from it.

"I was gonna talk to your friend," he said to Sangre.

"There's no reason to. I'm telling you to back the fuck off."

"Chill, dude," Crow said as he followed them to the buffet table.

"Don't you start." Sangre picked up a dish.

"We're just ribbing you because it's so fuckin' obvious that you're more than friends with her," Crow replied.

"So the fuck what? How's this any brother's damn business?" He placed a cheese enchilada on the plate.

Army busted out loud. "Fuck! This isn't a friends with benefits, you're hooked on this chick."

The dish broke in several pieces when it hit the concrete as Sangre's fists sunk into Army's gut. Crow intervened and Sangre drove a fist hard into his jaw; pain screamed through his hand. Crow punched back, and from his peripheral vision, he saw Army coming for him. Sangre catapulted, putting Army beneath him, hitting him in the face.

"I told you to back the fuck off," he said between short breaths.

Soon a circled formed around the fighting men. Crow had come up from the side and pulled Sangre off Army. Crow then swung a punch at him, but he deflected it, grabbed Crow's arm and flipped him on his back.

Strong hands yanked Sangre back and he cursed and yelled.

"That's enough, bro." Diablo's terse voice washed over him.

Crow jumped up, wiped the trickle of blood from his mouth with the back of his hand, and took a beer Lucy handed him. "Fuckin' good move, dude," he said, tipping the bottle in Sangre's direction.

Cleaning off the dirt from his jeans, Army looked at Sangre. "You're hopeless. You're so fuckin' hooked, bro." He guffawed and went over to the buffet table and grabbed a plate. "Your woman said a cheese enchilada, right?"

Every muscle in Sangre's body was tight. *I lost my fuckin' cool over a woman. Over Isla. And in front of all the brothers.* He gave a slight nod and took the ice pack Kelly handed him.

"You don't wanna have that swell up," she said, her hand lingering a little too long on his.

"Thanks." He put it against his jaw and narrowed his eyes when Army came over to him with the plate for Isla. He spun around and stomped back to the table.

"What the hell happened to you?" she asked when he sat down. "Were you involved in that ruckus?"

"Here." He pushed the dish toward her. "I had to set some things straight with a couple of the guys."

Shaking her head, she picked up her fork. "It's unbelievable how testosterone-driven your club is." She took a bite of her food.

"I don't take shit from anyone." He watched her wiggle in her seat and a jolt of heat went through his body. *I'm so outta control when it comes to her.*

"This is so good," she said, taking another bite.

He swept the hair back from her neck. "You're fuckin' turning me on, babe."

Her eyes widened. "Just by eating?"

She knows exactly *what she's doing.* "I can think of something I'd like to be eating." Slipping his hand under her skirt, he caressed the skin of her inner thighs. "So soft," he whispered against her ear before pulling her earlobe between his teeth, sucking it gently. A low moan escaped from her parted lips and went straight to his dick. Then his fingers grazed at the edge of her panties, and she squirmed.

"What're you doing?" She glanced up from under her lashes, her lips curving into a sexy smile.

Staring at her glossy lips, desire burned through his veins, and he lowered his gaze to the swell of her tits. "Nothing." Burying his face in her neck, he left a trail of tiny kisses there down to the sensitive hollow at the base of her throat as her soft moans egged him on. His finger slipped under her panties and skimmed over her slick folds before pushing inside her.

"Fuck," she murmured, parting her legs a bit.

"That's a good girl," he said in a low voice as he slowly moved his finger in and out of her.

She gasped. "There're so many people here," she rasped as she opened her legs wider.

"Do you want me to stop?" He kept pushing in and out. She shook her head and he smiled then thrust in and out of her with speed again and again until her face muscles tightened and her eyes closed.

"Oh, Sangre," she said in a barely audible voice, and at that moment, he knew she was ready to explode. He dipped his head and covered her mouth with his as she came, swallowing her moans and cries. Isla leaned into him, and he held her close as the ultimate pleasure overtook her.

"I heard you let Army and Crow have it," Skull said, scooting on the bench across from Sangre.

With one more thrust, he removed his finger from Isla while nodding. "They had it coming to them, especially Army." Isla nestled closer to him, and he slinked an arm around her shoulders.

"Did you ask her about the CD?" Skull took a big bite out of his taco.

Sangre looked down at her and smiled when her eyelids fluttered open. "What CD?" she asked.

"The one for Skull's sister."

"I don't know if you remember two goofy teenagers shoving CDs in your face at Trailside." Skull picked up his beer. "One of them was my sister and she's fuckin' nuts about your band, especially the guitarist."

She straightened up. "Yes, I remember her and her friend. I don't remember their names."

"Ella—my sis, and Zoe's her friend."

"That's right. They both have the hots for Arsen. Did you want me to get the band to sign a CD for them?"

"If you don't mind." Skull glanced at Sangre. "You were supposed to have asked her."

"I was gonna." The truth was he'd forgotten, and that seemed to be the norm for him since Isla came back into his life. All that mattered was her and, of course, the club, but she was always forefront in his mind.

"It's fine," Isla said, picking up her drink. "I'll have the band sign one for Ella and Zoe. Are they coming to the show tomorrow night?"

"Yeah."

"I'll give the CDs to them at the show." She cocked her head and paused. "Is that Ozzy playing? I'm pretty sure it is, but it's loud out here."

"Yup. It's 'I Don't Wanna Stop,'" Sangre said.

"I thought so. Let's dance. I love this song." She scrambled out of her seat and swayed her hips in rhythm to the song until he grabbed her hand and led her into the main room to a makeshift dance floor. She spun around, her head bobbing in beat to the music, her hips moving so damn seductively. There was a sheen on her flushed skin and her hazel eyes were bright, and he wanted nothing more than to pin her against the wall and fuck her good and hard.

The song ended and the slow strains from Bon Jovi's "I'll Be There For You" filled the room. Sangre yanked her to him and she curled her arms around his neck and leaned into him, tucking her head against his chest. His arms were around her waist and his hands rested on her ass. Flexing his hips against hers, he ground his hard cock against her. She lifted her head and he crushed his mouth on hers. Kissing, they swayed to the song, and Isla rubbed her tits against his chest.

"Fuck, baby," he growled against her lips. Cupping her ass, he lifted her inches from the floor.

The song ended and they broke their kiss. Sangre slid Isla down his body, planting her feet on the linoleum floor. The hard-hitting beats of AC/DC rocked the room, and Isla spun away from him and shook her sweet ass in time to the music. She shimmied up to him, her tits jiggling in erotic motion, her mouth moving to the lyrics of the song. He reached for her, but she pulled back, tossing her head back in laughter.

After several more fast songs, the pace slowed down again with another ballad and she moved toward him, her arms outstretched as if to curl around his neck again, but he gripped her hand and pulled her away from the dance floor and up the flight of stairs to his room. His cock was so hard it was painful, and he couldn't wait to pump it inside her.

Before he opened his door, he pinned Isla against it, kissed her throat, and squeezed her tits. "You were teasing me on the dance floor with these," he said, dragging his mouth to the swell of her breasts and biting them.

"Let's go inside," she murmured, her hand grabbing his hair and yanking his head up. She kissed him, and his tongue pushed against her teeth, urging her mouth to let him in. Parting her lips, her tongue delved inside, and she moaned as he twisted her hair in his fingers and drew her lips even closer to his until there was no space between them. The key jingled in the lock as he tried to open the door. Holding her tight, he pushed it open then kicked it shut.

He skimmed his hands over her curves then reached under her skirt and slid his hand inside her panties and grabbed her ass cheek.

"I gotta have that sweet ass, babe," he said. With his free hand, he put her hand on his throbbing cock. "See what you do to me?" She squeezed hard and he thought he was going to lose it.

Then she took his hand and placed it on her crotch; the sheer fabric covering it was wet. Desire burned in her eyes. "See what you do to me?" she whispered before running her tongue up the length of his throat.

"Get on the bed," he ordered.

"Not yet," she said, tugging his zipper down. His cock sprang out and she curled her hand around it, her thumb caressing its head.

He sucked in his breath. "Fuck, babe." He tangled his fingers in her long hair.

Isla opened his pants and tugged his jeans and boxers down then dropped to her knees. He watched as she stroked his cock's head with the tip of her tongue, running it on the underside before she took him in her warm mouth, pushing him deeper and deeper until his balls hit against her chin. "Damn, woman," he rasped as he yanked her hair. His dick slid in and out of her mouth, each thrust harder than the last, and he relished the fire she lit in his cock and balls.

"I love fucking your mouth, but I'm gonna blow, and I don't want to, babe." Placing his hands on the sides of her face, he gently pushed her back. She looked up at him, her lips glistening. He yanked her up and covered her mouth with his, kissing her hard and deep. He kicked off his boots, then threw off his clothes before he watched Isla undress in front of him. Her hard nipples beckoned him, and he came up to her as she shimmied out of her panties, and sucked one of the buds in his mouth while he grazed the other with his thumb.

She buried her fingers in his hair, moaning and squirming under his touch. "So good," she mumbled.

"Get on all fours on the bed." He watched her ass sway as she planted her knees on the mattress. "Ass in the air." She looked over her shoulder and threw him a sly smile then pressed her upper body into the sheets and spread her legs. He was riveted by the firm flesh of her butt. Under the overhead light, he could see her juices glistening between the engorged folds. He licked his lips and climbed on the bed. Taking his index finger, he flicked her clit over and over.

"Fuck me, Sangre," she moaned.

He chuckled. "You're impatient, hun." Flipping on his back, he scooted under her dripping pussy and, with his hands on her hips, he eased her down until she was right above his mouth. He slid a finger inside her then ran his tongue from her wet slit to her swollen clit. Back and forth with his tongue; in and out with his finger. Isla's guttural groans filled the room.

"I want to fuck your ass, baby," he said as he kept up his pace on her sex. "Have you ever done it?"

"No," she panted. "I never trusted anyone enough to do it with."

"Do you trust me enough?" His free hand squeezed one of her firm globes.

"Yeah, but it better not hurt."

He chuckled. "It'll hurt a little, but I'll go real slow until your ass adjusts to my cock."

"I hope you have a lot of lubricant."

"I do, babe. I love knowing I'm your first." He slid out from under her, and smeared her juices over her ass cheeks then bent down and licked, kissed, and bit them. Running one hand over her smooth globes, he cupped her wet mound with the other. "So fuckin' tempting," he said, smacking one of her cheeks with his hand.

She yelped.

"Too hard?"

"No. Harder."

"That's what I like to hear, babe." He smacked again, that time harder. Then his other hand spanked her, and soon he was delivering firm slaps on each cheek in rhythmic order as she moaned and pushed her ass closer to him. With each smack, she got wetter and his dick ached more. Bending over, he soothed the stings to her ass with his tongue while admiring the redness that colored her rounded cheeks.

Leaning back on his knees, he reached over and opened the nightstand drawer and took out a large tube of lubricant. He dipped down and kissed her on the lips then ran his hands down her back.

"You're sure about this?"

"Yeah," she whispered. "I'm so hot right now that all I want is you inside me."

Sangre leaned over her. "I'm gonna fuck your ass and pussy, baby. I'll have you tearing out your hair," he whispered. He felt Isla shiver under him.

Dipping his fingers into her wetness, he smeared her own juices as lubricant then slowly inserted his finger into her. She moaned and he pushed in a little farther then pulled out. Opening the lubricant, he smeared it over his dick, and then adding a bit more to his finger, he covered her rosy entrance with it, pushing it inside little by little, making her very wet and slippery. She moaned and wiggled her sweet ass back into his hardness.

He chuckled. "You can't wait for my cock to come in. And you're so fuckin' wet."

Bending down, he lightly bit her rounded globes then smacked each one a few times until a pale red colored her soft flesh again. He kissed her tenderly then spread her ass cheeks open, and gently pushed in his dick's head.

She bucked and cried out.

"How're you doing, honey? Everything okay?" He rubbed his hand over her back in circles.

"It's burning."

"Just relax and push down with your sweet ass. If it's too much, we can try another time. I can get you a butt plug to stretch you."

"No it's not bad. Just different. It feels full, but I like it. Keep going."

He dipped his head down and kissed the back of her neck. "I'll take it slow."

He reached his hand under her and stuck two fingers inside her sopping heat, pushing them in and out. He brought his thumb to Isla's hardened nub and started stroking the side of it as he inched deeper into her tight entry until he was buried up to his balls. Isla moaned between pants, her butt pushing back against him as if she were trying to take more of him inside her. Her muscles were so tight as they molded around him that he thought he was going to blow his load without even moving.

"It feels so fuckin' good," he rasped as he pulled back then pushed back in, his two fingers inside her heated wetness moving in slow rhythm with his dick while his thumb stroked her sweet spot.

A long, breathless gasp from Isla punctuated the sex-filled haze around them. "What the hell are you doing to me?" She wriggled her ass, moving forward a bit then back into his erection. "It feels incredible," she panted.

His breathing became more and more labored as he slowly pushed in and out, her moans and gasps driving him crazier by the second. He'd never experienced sex the way he did with Isla. "You're fuckin' amazing," he said in a low voice as his free hand grabbed onto her luscious cheek and he rocked his hips forward, pumping in and out of her with steady back and forth thrusts, his fingers and thumb matching his pace.

She pushed up slightly on her elbows, and looked over her shoulder. "You're killing me." Her voice was throaty, earthy, and so fucking sexy.

Their gazes locked on each other, their breath ragged and uneven. With her tangled hair, her face contorted and scrunched up, and her forehead dripping in sweat, she looked more beautiful than he'd ever seen her. Sex with her was raw and primitive, and he knew he'd never have enough of her. She was so real, and the way her tight ass squeezed him was more than he could stand. He flicked her sweet nub a few times, then she turned away and buried her face in the sheets.

"Sangre, I'm coming. Oh, it feels so damn good," she said, her voice muffled. He hooked his fingers and hit her G-spot, and she turned her head sideways, her eyes fixed on his as she screamed out her release, shuddering and gasping.

Sangre growled deep in his throat. "Fuck, Isla," he grunted as he released in three long body-quaking spasms. He stayed, panting, the musky scent of sex filling his nostrils. He caressed her soft cheeks and slowly pulled out then lay down on the bed, drawing her to him. Their legs intertwined on top of the crumpled, damp sheets.

Isla burrowed her head in the crook of his arm. "I've never experienced anything like that." She ran her nails over his chest.

"You mix me all up, woman. The things you do to me blow me the fuck away." He threaded his fingers through her hair.

"I think I like that," she said, a smile in her voice.

They lay sated and spent, the slight rustling of branches scraping against the open window as a breeze blew in, cooling their bodies. As she slept in his arms, he looked at the silhouette of the trees in the moonlight and realized that he was in deep with Isla. He'd never been this consumed by a woman before. It was like she'd cast a spell on him. He had a constant, burning desire for every inch of her all the time. He needed her hot breath on his lips, the taste of her, the touch of her soft skin molding into his, and the sound of her voice running through his veins. What he felt for her was deep and raw, and it was new for him. He wanted to be buried in her all the time, entering her gently then riding her rough and deep. He was like an addict and she was his fix.

But she's going back to LA. She has a life there. I have a life here.

If he were with another woman, he'd be thinking about moving on about now, but with Isla he couldn't think about not having her in his life. He wanted and needed her.

As he thought about all the women he'd been involved with, he snorted. He was always the one to leave and never look back, but with Isla, he couldn't imagine letting her go.

But he knew the time would come when he'd have to.

Chapter Twenty-One

ISLA PEEKED OUT from the curtains backstage, scanning the throngs of people as they filled in the venue, packed together like sardines. The electric atmosphere sparking through the room was intoxicating, and that feeling of conquering the world pumped through her as it usually did before she took the stage.

She saw Keith and Jeff standing with security around the stage, and Mark was her constant companion backstage. Sangre had spoken to Jim about beefing up the guards, so their presence was visible. Metal detectors were also installed at the front doors, making her feel safer.

Sangre thought of everything. A hot flush crept up her neck when she remembered the hot sex they'd had the night before. It had been incredible, and he'd been so caring and loving as well as sexy and rough. In the past month since she and Sangre had crossed the line and became lovers, she'd come to know him as a rough around the edges sweetheart. She suspected that she was the only one who saw his soft and playful side and that made what they had even more special.

The night before when he'd told the men at the club party that she was his woman, her insides had turned to mush when she'd heard his words. Even though they spent a lot of time together they hadn't had "the talk" yet. She wasn't sure if they were in an official relationship, but when she'd heard him say "my woman" her heart had soared. *I also went to his parents' house for dinner, have met his friends, and went to his club's party.* To her, it meant they were boyfriend and girlfriend—and it thrilled her. Just thinking about it made her tingle from her head down to her toes.

"You doing good?" Sangre's gravelly voice caressed her. He slinked an arm around her waist and drew her back into him.

"Yeah. Just checking out the crowd. The opening band was good and I know Immortal Sÿnn's going to rock it. It's great when a direct support band gets the crowd all fired up. Benz wants them to tour with us in the fall."

"When did the tour thing happen?" Sangre held her tight.

"I just found out about it at sound check. We leave after Labor Day weekend. We're touring the coast of California, Oregon, and Washington."

"For how long?"

He sounds kinda sad or am I imagining it? "A little over a month. I have mixed feelings about it."

"Why?" He nuzzled her neck.

"Because I'm really going to miss you."

A pause. "There's texting and phone calls."

Texting and phone calls? I thought I was 'your woman.' "Yeah, you're right."

"You've got a sold out show tonight. Good job, honey." He spun her around and kissed her hard.

I should be thrilled. We're so close to signing a record deal, our fan base is growing every day, and we're going on a kickass tour. This is everything I've ever wanted, but I'm sad and anxious as hell. If only Sangre could come on tour with me. Would he?

Sangre pulled back and gripped her shoulders as he scanned her face. "What's going on in that pretty head of yours?"

"Nothing."

"Aren't you happy about the show? Don't lie to me because I know when you're down and trying to pretend that you're not."

She shook her head. "I'm excited for the show. It's just that everything seems to be happening so fast with the band. If we end up signing on with a label, it's a big deal and involves a huge commitment. I mean, my whole life would be taken up with touring and recording."

"Don't think about that tonight. Just take it one day at a time.

You're getting all worked up before you even know if the band has a label contract. You guys may decide the terms are shit and not sign with the company. Just enjoy tonight."

"You're right." He always knew how to cheer her up when she was low. *He knows me so well.*

"Madison is here with some dude. Did you see her?"

"There're too many people. Did she actually come up to you?"

"Yeah, but she looked scared as shit." He chuckled. "The brothers are here with their women too."

"Oh yeah … I have the two CDs for Ella and Zoe. Make sure you bring them backstage after the show."

The crowd grew quiet as Immortal Sÿnn opened their set with hard pounding, double bass drum beats. Isla stepped away from the curtain. "I need to have some time alone before we hit the stage."

"Sure, babe."

"I'll be in the green room area. There are two security guys who are making sure no one goes down there except for Iris Blue. I'll see you after the show." She hugged and kissed him then headed downstairs.

"You want a vodka shot?" Arsen asked as she entered the green room. Benz, Jac, and Gage were sprawled on the two couches, smoking weed and drinking beer. She shook her head.

"You ready for this?" Gage asked.

"For sure. The place is sold out," she replied as she grabbed a bottled water from the fridge.

"It feels fuckin' awesome," Jac said, gesturing her to bring him another beer.

"I can't wait for Sturgis, then the tour." Arsen pulled out a cigarette and lit it.

Benz stared straight ahead. He hadn't acknowledged her since they'd finished with the sound check earlier that afternoon. *How the hell are we gonna tour together if he can't stand the sight of me?* She gave Jac a can of Coors then picked up her tote. "I'll see you guys on stage." Isla walked out and headed to one of the rooms to do her warm up exercises and meditate—her ritual before every show.

The whistles and cheers from the crowd an hour later meant that Immortal Sÿnn had finished their set, and Iris Blue would take the stage in twenty minutes. Isla went into the green room and smiled at the guys as they pushed themselves up from the couches. As they milled around backstage waiting for the roadies to clear off the equipment of the last band, Isla looked out at the crowd as the background music played.

Isla saw Madison and her boyfriend talking in front of the stage, and spotted Faith and Colt sitting at one of the VIP tables. The crowd kept pushing toward the front stage and she noticed Ella and Zoe shoving their way through the throng. Then Isla noticed Devin standing off to the side, his legs apart, his muscular arms crossed. *What the hell is he doing here?* She'd seen him a couple of days before at the gym, but he hadn't spoken to her. He only stared at her, making her so uncomfortable that she cut down her workout just so she could get away from him. Isla felt weird about seeing him in her space. Never once had he mentioned liking Iris Blue's music or really anything about the band.

"We're almost ready to go on," Arsen said behind her. "You feeling the energy?"

Isla nodded. She felt a massive wave of anticipation sweeping across the crowd as people filled in all the spaces on the floor, their eyes focused on the stage, waiting and watching for that first view of Iris Blue walking onstage. Adrenaline pumped through her as her heart raced a mile a minute. She shook out her arms and jumped in place. Then she saw Jon, standing in the middle of the crowd, his dark eyes fixed on the stage. The last thing she'd heard about him from Sangre was that he'd quit his job. She turned around to find Sangre, but saw Mark instead. Before she could tell him about Jon, the stage manager came up to them and held up his hand.

"Get ready. Five, four, three, two, one," he said.

The background music faded down, and suddenly all the lights went out and there was total blackness. Isla and her band mates scrambled on stage and took their places. Arsen played the first few notes of their opening song and the audience erupted into screams and applause as colored lights lit up the stage and the musicians. Isla picked up the mike and belted out the lyrics, loving how the crowd sang along while they jumped, danced, and swayed. The connection she had with all these strangers was euphoric, and she forgot where she was as she absorbed the music, letting it consume her. When everything worked, performing was better than any drug.

For the next two hours, Iris Blue gave the crowd exactly what they wanted: escape, hard hitting notes, showmanship, and favorite tunes. When they finished their final song, the roar from the crowd was deafening; it'd been a kickass show. The overhead lights went on, and the roadies dashed on stage and began to break down the equipment. Isla followed Jac off the stage and down to the green room. They were on a natural high, pumped with energy, talking nonstop.

Benz grabbed Isla and hugged her tight. "You were fuckin' incredible, babe." She hugged him back, and for that moment, they were united in music and camaraderie.

"We all kicked fuckin' ass out there!" Arsen plopped down on the couch, a bottle of whiskey in his hands. "I've got a couple of chicks I'm taking back to the hotel, but first let's toast the band. We're on our fuckin' way." He poured the amber liquid in five glasses handing them to each member. "To Iris Blue," he said then downed his shot.

"To Iris Blue," they repeated in unison.

Benz leaned down. "To you, babe," he whispered in Isla's ear before she threw back her shot. "Let's go back to the hotel and celebrate."

A low growl from behind her tickled up her spine. She smiled, spun around, and met Sangre's smoldering eyes. "You did good, honey." Isla walked over to him and he folded her in his arms. "Let's you and me celebrate," he murmured.

Isla gave him a sly smile. "Let me pack up my mike." She went out and approached one of the roadies and asked him for her microphone. As she wound the cable around it, Skull came over to her with Ella and Zoe in tow.

"Great show," he said.

"Totally rad," the two girls gushed.

"Thanks," Isla said. "Follow me." She led them to the green room, laughing when the teenagers almost fainted upon seeing Arsen. "Here are some diehard fans of yours—Ella and Zoe."

Arsen patted the space next to him. "Why don't you pretty girls come on over?" Isla rolled her eyes. Arsen was the charmer of the group, and women ate it up each and every time. He grabbed a couple of the band's T-shirts and handed them to the girls. "Compliments of Iris Blue."

After a while, Arsen, Benz, Jac, and Gage headed to the van. "You sure you don't wanna celebrate with us?" Benz asked.

"Next time," she said softly. "I need to talk to some of my friends who've been waiting for me at the bar. I'll see you guys on Monday."

By the time Isla finished talking with everyone, it was well past one in the morning. When Sangre pulled into her garage, she was relieved that they were home, and all she wanted to do was make love to her man and fall asleep in his arms. They went up to her bedroom and she went over to the window and looked out at the quiet street. Moonlight shone over the trees, lawns, and sidewalks. Isla looked up at the full moon and smiled. *Tonight was perfect.*

As she stood by the window, she heard Sangre come up behind her, then felt his arms around her hugging her close to him. He bit and kissed her neck, whispering in her ear, "Mine." She leaned her head back against his chest welcoming the rush of happiness and love as it spread inside her. He cupped her breasts and squeezed them gently.

"Do you have something on your mind?" she said softly.

"When it comes to you, I always have the same thing on my mind. I can't get enough of you, babe."

Isla whirled around and snaked her arms around his neck drawing his face close to hers. She pressed her lips to his and kissed him passionately. He slid his hands down her back and cupped her buttocks and lifted her up in his arms. With long strides he took her over to the bed and lay her on the mattress.

"Don't move. I want to undress you." He shrugged off his clothes and boots and climbed on the bed, hovering over her. He covered her mouth with his and kissed her hungrily, his tongue pushing past her teeth delving deeper inside. As he kissed her, he undid the buttons on her tight leather top. Sangre's fingers played with her nipples, teasing them into hard peaks. His mouth left hers then trailed down past her throat, landing on the swells of her breasts. He sucked the soft flesh, and she knew he was leaving his mark on her. She wanted him to cover her body in love bites claiming every inch of her bare skin.

Sangre slowly took her clothes off, piece by piece, kissing and caressing her skin as he revealed it. His gentle yet arousing movement stole her breath. Isla reached out and ran her fingers through his hair as his fingers slipped between her legs to tease the slick, puffy folds of her sex.

A throaty moan fell from her lips. "The sounds you make get to me," he rasped.

A ball of fire rushed down her spine to right between her thighs. "I need you inside me." She pulled his hair.

"Not yet, honey. We've got all night."

Isla sank deeper into the mattress and let all sensations overtake her.

THE FOLLOWING AFTERNOON Isla sat on the couch, a book in hand and face scrunched up, writing lyrics for a new song that had come to her that morning. Her phone vibrated and she leaned over and picked it up.

Sangre: *Dinner at 6?*

Isla smiled. Sangre had gone into the office early that morning to help Eagle figure out the scheduling. He had told her that Saturday nights and Sunday mornings were when people called off work the most. She'd wanted to make him her famous pancakes, but she overslept and he was gone before she woke up.

Isla: *Sounds good.*

Sangre: *Whatcha doing?*

Isla: *Writing a new song. U inspire me.*

Sangre: *And u fucking slay me. Later, babe.*

Isla: *xoxo*

A large smile spread over her face and she picked up her pen and went back to writing. The chime of the doorbell broke her concentration, and she jumped up from the couch and went over to the door. Looking through the peephole, she chuckled when she saw Colt standing there. She swung open the door.

"Those girls of yours are killing it. Are they out of lemonade already?" She opened the screen door, motioning him to come in.

"What can I say? The customers love your lemonade." Colt closed the door behind him. "Am I bothering you?"

"No. I was just writing a new song, but you actually gave me an excuse to take a break." She went into the living room. "Have a seat. It won't take me long to whip up another batch. Do you want something to drink while you wait?"

"I'm good. What's your song about?"

"Love. Isn't that what most songs are about?" Isla laughed. She bent down to pick up her notebook, and for some inexplicable reason, a finger of nausea poked her stomach. The room was perfectly quiet. She straightened up and turned around startled that Colt was right behind her. The hairs on the back of her neck stood up. A dark thread of unexplained fear wove through her consciousness.

"I'll make that lemonade now." Colt took a step closer to her, pulled out an envelope from his shirt's pocket, and handed it to her. "What's this?" she asked, taking the envelope.

"It was delivered to our house by mistake." His voice was strange and ominous.

Something told her she needed to get away from him. She tossed the envelope on the coffee table. "Wait here. I'll be right back with a fresh batch of lemonade." She turned to leave but he blocked her way.

Colt bent down and picked up the envelope handing it to her again. "Read it."

Isla took the envelope in her shaking hands, her eyes widening when she saw the all too familiar handwriting on it. She looked at Colt and his gaze was cold. She ripped it open and took out the piece of notebook paper from inside. She read it: "Got you." Isla's hand flew to her mouth, suppressing a cry from her lips. Her heart hammered against her rib cage, and she jumped away from him.

Then he came for her.

Chapter Twenty-Two

"THE NEW UNIFORMS have come in," Eagle said, carrying a big box. "Where do you want me to put them?"

Sangre went over to the corner of the room and picked up the box his mother had given him. "You can put it here."

Eagle but the container down. "What do you have in there?"

"Some old shit my mom gave me. I don't even know what it is." Sangre took the lid off and shook his head. "It's just a bunch of old yearbooks and junk from when I was in high school."

"Oh yeah?" Eagle came over and picked up one of the yearbooks. "I wanna see what a nerd you were in high school." He laughed.

Sangre grabbed the book from him. "I haven't looked at this in years." He thumbed through the pages and found Isla's class picture. The sixteen-year-old's bright eyes and small smile stared at him. He brushed his thumb over her photo, memories flooding his mind.

"From the look on your face, I figure you're looking at Isla." Eagle came next to him. "Damn. She was even hot in high school."

She was all I thought about back then ... and now. Isla. "She was in all the musicals. I'm pretty sure there are some pictures of her in those productions." As he flipped the pages, people he hadn't seen or thought about in years rushed past him. His eyes landed on several photographs of Isla in different costumes for different musicals. "I saw every one of these pansy ass plays." He chuckled.

"*Grease*? *Cats*? You must've really had it bad for her back then, dude." Eagle smacked him on the shoulder.

I did. But I've got it worse now. Sangre stared at the picture: it was like he'd been transported to the past. He was just ready to flip to another page when someone in the background caught his eye. "What the fuck?" he muttered.

"What's wrong?" Eagle asked.

"This kid looks familiar," he said, tapping his finger on the face.

"He should. You went to the same damn high school." Eagle moved away.

"No. Like I've seen him now. You know all grown up, but I don't know where." His chest tightened as he put the yearbook down and started rummaging through the things in the box. "Here it is," he said out loud, taking out the program for *Grease*. He scanned the names, and his eyes fell on the name *Justin Colt Varner, Crew*. He jerked his head back. "Fuck." He picked up the yearbook again and went through all the pictures in Isla's class. He saw Madison Cartwright, Sharla Davidson, Lizbeth Kelly, Carrie Nolan, Taylor Prentice, Lexi Strobe, and Justin Colt Varner. "He's her neighbor. He told her he wasn't from Alina. He's the fucker." Sangre threw the book down and grabbed his phone.

"What's going on, dude?"

"Isla's neighbor lied to her. Said he was from Omaha. Why the fuck would he do that unless he's the sonofabitch who's been sending her the letters." Sangre rubbed the back of his neck. "Pick up, Isla," he said under his breath.

"Let's bring the asshole in for questioning," Eagle said, his hands clenching.

"My thoughts exactly, bro." He tapped in Mark's number. "Did Isla go out?"

"No. She's still inside. Something wrong?"

"She's not picking up."

"The neighbor from next door is with her. Maybe that's why."

White, icy cold fire flowed through his veins and he picked up the yearbook and hauled it across the room. "Is it that bastard with the girls selling Isla's lemonade?"

"Yeah. Their dad. What's going on? Did I fuck up?"

"No. I did. Shit!" He pounded his fist on the desk. "Isla's in danger.

Do you have a gun on you?"

"No. Do you want me to call the cops?"

"No fuckin' badges. I'm on my way. Get inside that house, but be careful. The fucker carries a knife and is dangerous. Go now." Before Mark could answer, Sangre had the phone in his pocket as he raced out of the building, Eagle at his heels.

"I called the brothers. They're on their way," Eagle said. He grasped Sangre's arm. "We'll get to her in time."

Tension choked his nerves. "We fucking have to."

The motorcycles sped out of the parking lot.

Chapter Twenty-Three

COLT'S BEEN SENDING me the letters? Isla's mind couldn't comprehend it. She scrambled over the couch and ran into the kitchen heading for the back door. Cold hands pulled her back and she screamed.

"Shut the fuck up, Jordan." She pushed away but he quickly pinned her against the granite counter. "You scream again, and I'm going to cut your fucking throat."

Isla raised her hands. "Okay … okay … just relax." Colt stepped back a little and stared at her. "Why did you call me *Jordan*?"

Colt shook his head. "You don't even remember me."

"How could I? I've never been to Omaha."

"Does *Justin Varner* ring a bell in that stupid head of yours?" His eyes flashed angrily.

He wants to hurt me or kill me. I have to stay calm. Do I know him? I don't.

"Do you know the name or not?" Spittle formed in the corners of his mouth.

"No," Isla said in a voice barely above a whisper.

"You fucking bitch!" he screamed, his face mere inches from hers.

Anger shot through her. "Just fucking tell me." A loud crack bounced off the walls as the sting of his hand across her cheek shot through her.

"You're the same as you were in high school—an arrogant, diva bitch."

High school? "I thought you were from Omaha."

"I'm from here, Jordan. I was in your goddamn class at Jefferson, but you were so busy thinking you were hot shit because you were the lead in all the musicals that you didn't pay attention to anyone who wasn't in your circle."

"What are you talking about? I didn't belong to a circle. I just loved to sing. And why didn't you tell me you went to Jefferson? Why the lies? Why did you send me those letters?"

His nostrils flared as he jabbed a finger in her face. "You thought you were so damn clever hiring bodyguards, but they weren't around when I slashed your tires, or when your car broke down, or at the gym."

"That was all you? Even when I was in the pool?"

"The inept guy at the front desk believed my lie about one of the machines not working. He left his post. It was so easy."

"Why? I still don't understand." *How am I going to get away from this nut? I have to buy time. Wait … what the fuck am I buying time for? No one knows I'm in danger.* Her chin tremored and she bit the inside of her mouth to stop it. *I can't just let him hurt me. I have to figure out a way out of this craziness.*

"Remember a chubby guy who everyone bullied at school? That was me. The only time I had any peace and felt like I was a part of anything was when I worked on sets for the theater and music department. I fucking asked you out and you said yes, but you never showed. I sat at the counter in Bartell's Drugstore for two fucking hours! You made a fool out of me. You all did." He leaned in close again. "Now who's the fool?"

Isla could smell the musky sweat rolling off him as she felt the color drain from her face upon the realization that the man responsible for cutting short the lives of Sharla, Taylor, Carrie, and Lizabeth was in front of her. She had no doubt in her mind that he planned the same fate for her. *If only I could contact Sangre.*

"Do you remember me now, Jordan?"

Think. My damn life depends on it. "I'm sorry if I hurt you. I didn't mean to."

"Bullshit! That's what Taylor said before I drained the life out of her. Sharla, Carrie, and Lizabeth always looked at me with disdain. Did you know I volunteered to do the sets for the play Sharla was in? She wouldn't even talk to me during rehearsals. Acted like I was a fucking untouchable. What a bitch! They all were. They knew who I was and they acted like they were better than me when I'd say hi to them on the street or see them in social situations. They didn't change one fucking iota from high school. They got what they deserved."

"I never treated you like that. I've always been friendly to you, Colt."

"I'm Justin." He rubbed his temples. "Don't fucking mix me up. You're the same bitch as you were in high school. You don't even remember me."

"Did my moving back to Alina trigger all this with you?"

"No. It was just luck that you moved in next door. I was planning to go to LA and pay you a visit. I even told Faith I had to go to Southern California on a business trip, but then you came to me. At last."

From the recesses of her mind, a shy, pudgy boy crawled out. *I remember him. He used to stare at my breasts all the time. He creeped me out. There's no way I would've made a date with him.* "I do remember you, Justin. Just now. You worked behind the scenes, and I was nice to you."

"You fucking teased me. Just like you do now with your shorts and tits."

"I never made a date with you. I was going out with Jay."

"You're a whore. You dated him and now are screwing Steve."

Think back. Then the fog cleared. *I remember. I bumped into him in the hall and he asked me if I wanted to go and get a milkshake with him the next day after school. I said yes, but that night Dad beat the shit out of me. I didn't go to school for two weeks.* "I remember now," Isla said softly. "I didn't stand you up to be mean or because I was teasing you. I couldn't go because my dad … well … I got in trouble and was grounded for two weeks." *You can't even tell the truth about what Dad did to save your own life.*

"I don't believe you. You always flirted with me. You were like my girlfriend."

Isla knew it was hopeless to explain things to him; he was in too deep. His delusions made him remember things that never happened. She put her hands behind her on the counter, and that's when she felt the cable. *My microphone.* Slowly, she inched her fingers toward it.

The front doorbell rang. "Open up, Isla." Mark's voice soothed her, connecting her to the real world and giving her hope.

Colt turned around and that's when she grabbed her mike and slammed it with all her might against his head.

"Ow! Fuck!" Blood streamed down the side of his face as he brought his hands to his head.

Isla bolted from the room and dashed toward the front door, but Colt recovered faster than she'd anticipated, and he came running out of the kitchen. She took the stairs two at a time and went into her bedroom and locked the door behind her. Her pulse raced, and the sound of her heartbeat thrashed in her ears. Breathing heavily, she sprinted over to the French doors, flung them open, and stepped out onto the balcony.

"Mark! Help me. Break the windows. He's coming for me." Isla looked down, but the drop was too far. The door groaned as Colt slammed his body weight against it over and over. She ran into her walk-in closet, closed the door, and hid in the corner, praying that he'd think she'd climbed down the balcony. She took out her phone and called Sangre. No answer. She called 911, but hung up when she heard the door splinter. Her heart leapt in her throat as she sat in the dark waiting to see if she would live or die.

Chapter Twenty-Four

When Sangre arrived at Isla's house, he saw Mark on the porch throwing a chair through the window. He jumped off his bike and ran over. Eagle was behind him, and in the distance, he heard the low rumble of motorcycles.

"Isla's in trouble," Mark said as glass shattered everywhere.

Sangre grabbed the other chair and threw it, breaking a second window, then climbed in, the glass ripping his jeans and cutting him. Ignoring the blood dripping down his arm, he heard noise coming from Isla's bedroom. He took his Glock 9 mm out and carefully walked up the stairs. From the sound of glass dropping on the floor, he knew that Eagle had followed him. Sangre looked over the banister and saw Eagle turn the lock on the front door. The house walls shook as the roar of bikes permeated the neighborhood.

"Where the fuck are you, bitch?" a deep voice screamed.

Eagle was behind him as they plastered themselves against the wall, inching toward the doorway. Heavy footsteps thudded in the foyer, and Sangre saw Diablo, Goldie, Crow, Shotgun, Army, Skull, and Rooster standing at the bottom of the stairs. Sangre held up his hand indicating for them to stay where they were; they nodded their heads, their bodies poised for action.

Sangre heard a bang in the bedroom then Isla's scream. He and Eagle ran in, and he found Colt in the closet with his arm in the air and a knife in his hand. In the distance, the wail of sirens pierced the air. Not sure where Isla was, Sangre didn't want to fire into the closet, so he stormed in, knocking Colt down on his face.

"What the hell?" Colt cried out. "Ughh … I'm hurt."

Sangre kicked him hard in the side with his steel-toed boots, the sound of splintering bones bringing him a modicum of satisfaction. "Isla?" he said.

"Sangre." She came out of the corner of the closet and threw herself into his arms. Eagle had the fucker pinned down on the floor. Behind him, he heard the rush of footfalls.

"Everything okay here?" Diablo asked.

"Yeah. The badges are on their way. Go ahead and take off. We don't need this to be more complicated than it already is."

"You sure you don't want us to take the fucker?" Goldie said from the doorway.

"I'm pretty sure he's a goner," Eagle said as he switched on the light. Colt's body lay still on the blood-soaked carpet.

"Asshole fell on his own knife." Sangre kicked him again and a low grunt emitted from the listless man.

"Poetic justice," Isla whispered. "You came. How did you know?" She buried her face into his chest.

Sangre stroked her hair. "I told you I wouldn't let anything happen to you, honey." He kissed the top of her head and walked out of the closet with her tucked by his side. Eagle handed him a towel, and Sangre wrapped it around his bleeding arm.

By the time Wexler, Jeffers, and Carmody arrived, the only Night Rebel in the house was Sangre. The sheriff called the paramedics then asked Isla what had happened. As she told her rendition of the events, Wexler locked eyes with Sangre then tilted his chin slightly. Stone-faced, Sangre stared back at him, but he knew the sheriff was grateful that the reign of a madman had come to an end.

"You should go to the ER and take care of those cuts," Wexler said as he walked to the front door.

"I'm good."

The sheriff stood aside as crime scene investigators came in. "You should find somewhere else to stay for the next few days," he said to Isla then ambled out.

Sangre pulled her close to him. "You're staying with me."

With a dazed look, she nodded slightly. "The sheriff's right. You need to check out your arm. The blood has soaked through the towel."

"DR will take care of it."

"Who's that?"

"He's a doc who loves Harleys. He helps us out when we need it. You'll have to drive. I won't be able to ride."

"Okay. Let me get you a second towel to add another layer."

As she climbed the stairs, more law enforcement personnel filed into the house. He saw Wexler talking with Faith on the sidewalk. Neighbors had come out and stood on their porches and lawns watching.

Isla came over with a yellow towel. "Here, let me put it on the other one." As she wrapped it around his forearm, he watched her. "Does it hurt?"

Like hell. "Not too bad."

"You need to call that doctor right now."

"I need to get you back to the clubhouse. Go grab some clothes and let's get outta here." Isla brushed her lips across his then went upstairs. He took out his phone and called DR. He knew he was cut bad and the pain seared through him. The doctor told Sangre he'd meet him at the clubhouse, and he ended the call just as Isla came over to him, wheeling a small suitcase.

When they walked outside, Faith sat hunched over on a folding chair, staring at Isla. "Should I say something?" Isla said.

"I'd leave it alone. I saw Wexler talking to her. She's gotta be in shock, Finding out someone you trusted betrayed you like that is damn hard."

Isla sniffled. "Poor Faith. And Carly and Letty. How could he destroy his family that way?" She leaned against him as they walked up the driveway.

He glanced over again and saw Faith holding her face between her hands. "It'll drive you crazy if you try and find some reason to the fucker's madness. He didn't give a shit about his family or anyone. Just himself."

"He said he was going to come to LA and kill me." Sangre felt her shudder and he tightened his grasp around her. "He was after me because I didn't show up thirteen years ago to have a milkshake with him. How fuckin' sick is that? He killed all those women because he thought they made fun of him. He seemed so normal when he was my neighbor."

"*Seemed* is the operative word. He's a sick sonofabitch, but it's done and you don't have to be afraid anymore."

"I can't keep the house. Not after all that happened here today. I don't want to spend any more nights in it. How could I?" She opened the passenger door and looked at him. "I'm driving. I'll help you in."

Sangre let her play nurse as she helped him slide into the seat. His arm throbbed like hell and he was glad she'd offered to drive. He wanted to ask her to stay in Alina with him, but after what she'd just gone through, it wasn't the right time.

Later that night, after ten stitches and a long shower, Sangre stood by the window looking at raccoons as they scurried across the yard in search of food.

"How's your arm?" Isla said as she wrapped hers around his waist.

The scent of her wisped around him. "Fine. How're you doing?" He placed a kiss on her forehead.

"Better. A hot shower does it for me all the time. I still can't believe all of this. It's so damn surreal. It's like it didn't happen but then I remember that it did. Too crazy."

"It'll take time. Now you can breathe. It's over."

"I know. I feel so free. I don't have to be scared by every noise or strange look someone gives me."

"Are you going to take a break from recording?"

"No way. We have to be in the studio tomorrow morning. It's going to feel so strange not having Mark, Keith, or Jeff tailing me. Anyway, we have to finish our album before we head out to Sturgis."

Sangre jerked his head back. "You're going there?"

Isla's eyes widened. "I forgot to tell you about it. I meant to, but then all the craziness happened. Anyway, we're playing two shows in Sturgis at the Buffalo Chip. We've been trying to get a gig there for five years. It finally happened, and it's exciting. I bet you've been to Sturgis."

"I try to go every year or so. The club's going this summer. That's cool. You can ride with me."

She moved over to the bed and sat on the edge of it. "I should go with the band. We can definitely hook up once you get there."

Hook up? What the fuck? "Sure. How long are you gonna be there?"

"A few days. What about you?"

"A week or so. Some of the brothers will stay the two weeks, but I have to get back. We don't like leaving the club shut down for too long."

"I love that we'll be there at the same time. Do you stay in a RV or tent?"

"RV. Eagle, Shotgun, and I went together on one. Where're you staying?"

"Kent booked a hotel for us. I have my own room. I want you to stay with me while I'm there."

"Damn straight. Are you coming back to Alina afterward?"

Isla broke eye contact and lowered her head, and he knew the answer was no. A sharp pain socked him in the gut. "Very soon after our show, we start a five week tour in California, Oregon, and Washington. The label's most probably going to sign the band on."

I should tell her I want her to stay. That I love her, but I don't wanna fuck up her dreams. "That's what you wanted."

"Yeah." She wrung her hands over and over in her lap. "Would you like to go on the tour with me? I'd love for you to be with me."

"I can't leave the business or the club for that long. Maybe I can come out and see you in LA when you get back from touring."

"That'd be great," she mumbled.

A silence stretched between them.

Sturgis was a few weeks away and he planned to make the most of their time together. He went over to the bed and sat down next to her.

"Take a day off recording and let's spend it at Crystal Lake."

She wiped her nose with the back of her hand. "I'll see if I can get away."

His chest constricted, and he curled his arm around her. "It'll be fun."

She raised her head and fixed her eyes on him. "Are we still just friends? I mean is what we have a friends with benefits type of deal? Because I don't really know how you feel about me."

He sucked in a deep breath then slowly let it out. "We passed the friends stage the minute I realized it was you."

"So what does that mean? Tell me how you *feel*, dammit."

Sangre scrubbed his face: He didn't talk about his feelings. All he knew was that she was the only woman who moved him in a way no other woman ever had or could. She was all he thought about, and he wanted her always in his life. When he was in high school, he spent most of his time wanting her and the rest of the time telling himself that he'd blow their friendship. He didn't want to do anything that would take her away from him, so he held back.

"By you not answering me, you spoke volumes." She rose to her feet, but he grabbed her wrist and pulled her back down.

"I don't want you to leave, but I don't wanna fuck up your music career and your dreams." He pushed her down on the mattress and leaned over her, his fingers gently caressing her bruised cheek. "I've had you buried so deep in my heart that no woman could ever capture it. I just didn't realize it until you came back into my life."

She blinked rapidly. "Are you telling me you love me?"

He pressed his lips to hers. "That's what I'm saying, babe. I love you. I've never said that to any woman. When I thought I was gonna lose you today, that was the worst feeling in the world."

Tears streaked down her face as she pushed him down next to her. "DR said you're supposed to keep pressure off your arm."

He guffawed and, with his good arm, drew her close to him. "That's classic. I never say shit about my feelings and I just told you I love you, and your response is about my arm. I fuckin' love it."

She giggled. "I just didn't want the stiches to break or something."

"And dirty your robe?" He burst out laughing and she joined in, their guffaws filling the room.

When they'd calmed down, she tilted her head back and looked up at him. "In the letter I wrote you the day my family moved, I told you how much I loved you. But when I didn't hear from you, I was crushed and felt like a fool for telling you about my feelings. I've loved you for a very long time. No one *ever* compared to you. You've always been in my heart."

Sangre crushed his mouth on hers and kissed her as though it would be their last kiss. After a long while, he pulled back and held her gaze. "You told me you loved me back then?"

She nodded and he swept his finger over her lips; they were smooth and red, slightly swollen and glossy from his kiss. "Ever since you told me about the letter, I wondered what happened to it. It finally hit me—I bet Jay took it."

"Jay? How would he have known about it?"

"He was supposed to come over that day, and he never showed. After that he had an attitude and that's when we started drifting. Damn, if I knew you loved me back then, I wouldn't have wasted all these years without you."

Isla ran her finger down his throat. "I think we needed the time to grow. Coming together now makes our love stronger."

"Will you stay in Alina? We can get a place together."

"I want to but what about the band? We have the gig in Sturgis, the tour, and a label interested in signing us. If I leave now, the label will never sign Iris Blue. I can't fuck up this opportunity for them."

"I wouldn't respect you if you did." He cupped her chin. "As much as I want you to stay with me, I know music is in your soul."

She grasped his hand, brought it to her lips, and kissed it. "Long distance relationships are so hard. They really never work," she said softly.

"We'll figure something out. I can meet up with you while you're touring. Stay a couple of days."

"That would be good, but I want to be with you the way we are now."

"I do too, but I can't leave the brotherhood and you can't leave the band. It's the way life plays out sometimes." *I'm gonna miss you too fuckin' much.* "Let's go to Crystal Lake and have a good time. We have a few weeks before Sturgis. And we'll have a kickass time there too. I'll take you for a ride around the Black Hills. You're gonna love it."

She threw her arms around his neck and kissed him hard. "I love you so much."

"Me too, honey." He sat up then bent over her, but she pushed up causing him to fall back onto the mattress.

"Remember your arm?" A sly smile danced on her lips as she straddled him. "I'm going to do all the work, so relax. You're in for a wild ride."

"You sure you're up to this? You went through a lot today."

"Right now, I don't want to think about *him*, me leaving, or anything. I just want to feel and be connected with you. That's all." She slowly undid her short robe and shrugged it off.

Sangre sucked in a deep breath then released it slowly as desire ripped through him. "You're so beautiful," he said in a low voice, his gaze grazing her naked breasts: They were tanned and the nipples were pink and taut, begging him to touch them, taste them. He brushed his fingertips over them, making her arch against his hand. Her skin felt as hot as his desire for her. He began to pull up, but she placed her hands on his shoulders and eased him back, her tits swinging in his face. He grabbed them and drew one nipple into his mouth, nipping and sucking it.

Moaning, she leaned back, her breasts falling out of his grasp. "That'll come later."

"You're quite bossy."

"I'm in control here." A smile played on Isla's lips as she tried to look stern.

He watched her as she unfastened his belt, unzipped his fly, and drew down his pants and boxers. She ran her tongue up his legs then placed her hands on his inner thighs, spreading him wider; his cock sprang upright. Slowly she ran her fingers up his length, teasing him, her eyes locked on his. Then he saw her take the tip of him in her mouth and felt her tongue swirling across it.

He hissed then settled back and watched as she lovingly took him into her warm mouth.

Chapter Twenty-Five

Sturgis, SD

THE BLACK BANNER overhead read "Welcome Harley Riders" and spanned the length of Main Street in downtown Sturgis. Underneath it, the road was thick with motorcycles, tattooed and bearded men, and scantily clad women. For the men, skullcaps, sunglasses, boots, sleeveless shirts, and black leather were the norm while body paint, thongs, and pasties would do for many of the women, but the stars of the rally were the thousands of custom-painted Harley-Davidsons parked four rows deep and lined up for blocks, their chrome sparkling in the sun.

"Fuckin' wicked," Sangre said as he admired Hawk's bike. "I heard you customized it, but you outdid yourself. I'm thinking of buying a new bike. I'll have to ride it to Pinewood Springs to have you do your magic."

"Just give me the heads up before you come." Hawk pointed to his burnt orange bike. "This one took me about six months to do, but I went out of control with it."

"It's a beauty though." Sangre ran his hands over the neon flames and ghoulish skulls. "Are you and Cara staying in a tent or an RV?"

Hawk guffawed. "No way would Cara stay in a tent. We rented a big ass RV. It's like a damn house. What about you?"

"An RV. Eagle, Shotgun, and I went in on it. Who else is here from the Insurgents?"

"Banger, Throttle, Wheelie, Rags, and about twenty more brothers. Did everyone come from the Night Rebels?"

"Pretty much."

"Sangre."

He turned around and grinned when he saw Isla walking toward him.

"Is that your main squeeze in Sturgis?" Rags said. Many of the men had "girlfriends" in Sturgis who they'd hook up with each year at the rally.

Sangre looked at the Insurgent MC member and shook his head. "She's my main squeeze in Alina." *But she's going back to LA.* "She's the lead singer in Iris Blue. The band's playing tonight at Buffalo Chip, and they really know how to rock." He leaned against his bike.

"That's cool. I'll have to check them out," Rags said.

"Hi, sexy," Isla said, lightly punching his arm. "When did you get in?"

"Late last night."

"I've never seen so many motorcycles in my life. I'm sure this is a biker's paradise." The sun bounced off her mirrored sunglasses. She waved her hand at Hawk's Harley. "That is a true work of art. Amazing." Hawk stared at her.

"It's this brother's bike," he said, draping his arm around her shoulders.

Isla cocked her head. "And who is 'this brother'?"

"Hawk. He's the vice president of the Insurgents."

Isla extended her hand. "I'm Isla." Hawk looked down at her hand then at her face.

"She's my woman," Sangre said.

Hawk's features relaxed and he shook her hand. "Nice to meet you." He clasped Sangre's shoulder. "I didn't know you had a woman."

Sangre gave a small nod then bent down and kissed the side of her face. "Do you have some free time?"

"Yes. We aren't playing until tonight. I was checking out the vendor booths before I spotted you. Why didn't you call me this morning?"

"I was planning to, but we came to check out the bikes and I lost track of the time."

"You guys love your Harleys. I never thought I'd have to compete with a motorcycle."

"We love the ride, the freedom, the brotherhood."

"Fuck yeah," Hawk said while Rags raised his fist in the air.

Isla pressed closer to Sangre. "Do you want to grab a bite to eat?"

"Sure. Let's get a beer and some food then go to your hotel and have some fun." He kissed her. "Tomorrow we can go for a ride in the Black Hills. There's nothing like weaving your way through those mountains on winding roads. They're so different from the San Juan Mountains back home. They got meadows and grassland instead of forests. It's so beautiful and relaxing. For me it's damn spiritual."

She ran her hand across the side of his face. "I can't wait for you to share it with me."

Army, Shotgun, Eagle, and Crow came over, laughing and talking with Jerry, Throttle, and Wheelie from the Insurgents MC.

"The fuckin' Satan's Pistons are here," Crow said as he came over to Sangre.

"I saw them earlier. Did they say anything to you?" he asked.

"Nah. If they did, there'd be trouble." Crow cracked his knuckles.

"The Deadly Demons are here as well," Hawk said. "Reaper came over to Banger and me and acted like we were his long lost fuckin' friends. I didn't pick up that they want trouble. They know it would mean war."

Then all the brothers stopped talking and stared at Isla as though they'd just remembered that she was there, privy to their conversation.

"Why don't you and your woman head out?" Hawk said, his eyes fixed on her.

Sangre felt her hand tighten around his arm. "We were just leaving to get a bite to eat. I'll catch up with all of you later. I wanna check out the races later on."

"Just text me, dude, and we can meet up." Eagle said.

As Sangre and Isla wound their way through the people, she chuckled softly.

"What's so funny, honey?"

"That Hawk guy. I thought you and your friends were badass, he takes it to a whole other level. Is he always that hard edged?"

"He doesn't wax too easily to strangers."

"Do any of you? I mean, except to fellow bikers, none of you would win any congeniality contest."

"We're good with that. It's just that club business is kept among members. Even old ladies aren't privy to it. Hawk would've asked his old lady to leave too, but Cara would've beat him to it. She knows the outlaw score."

"He actually has a woman? She must be a doormat."

"No. She's pretty feisty and stubborn as hell as I hear it. I'm sure she doesn't take too much shit from him. Kind of like you with me." He nudged her with his elbow.

"I've never given you a hard time … yet."

He gave her ass a light swat. "Bring it on, baby."

They went into a rustic restaurant a few blocks away from Main Street. Rock music played through the speakers as waitresses in low-cut blouses and Daisy Dukes balanced trays of drinks and food on circular platters.

"Just grab a table," a waitress said to them as she rushed by.

"Let's take that one by the window," Isla said, pointing to a small square table squeezed between larger ones.

Soon two beers were in front of Sangre, and Isla brought a glass of white wine to her lips. The scent of cigarettes mingled with the aroma of charcoal-grilled meats.

"Steak sandwich—medium rare?" Isla pointed to Sangre. The waitress set it down. "Smoked Turkey Cobb," she said, putting the bowl down. "Anything else?"

"Just another bottle of water and glass of wine," Isla replied. The server nodded and dashed away.

"Is a salad gonna be enough food?" Sangre asked as he brought his sandwich to his mouth.

"It's loaded. It has so much stuff in here. I usually don't eat anything super heavy on performance day."

After she finished half of her salad, she opened her purse and took out a prescription bottle. He watched her take out a small white pill and swallow it with a swig of water.

"What're you taking?"

"Just something to take the edge off. I'm nervous about the show tonight and the label."

"How often do you take them?"

Isla popped the bottle back into her purse and took a sip of wine. "Not that much. I used to take them a lot more."

Sangre pushed away his empty plate then took a long pull from his beer. "Are you supposed to be taking those if you're trying to stay clean?"

She jerked her head back. "How did you know about my stint in rehab?"

"I read about it in an article. When your manager called me about the security job, I googled you to see who you were and all these articles came up about your drug problem."

Isla looked out the window. "Oh. I hoped you didn't know about that. You never said anything."

"It isn't my business to question a client about personal shit, but things are different between us now. How're you doing?"

"Sometimes the urge to do some lines is so overpowering that I think I'm going to cave in, but then I remember how hard it was to quit." She took a sip of wine. "That memory keeps me from doing anything stupid. I never want to go back to using coke."

"It must be hard to stay clean in the music industry. I imagine it's all around you."

"It is. The worst is when I'm super stressed or overwhelmed. I didn't use for that long, so I guess that's a plus. Most of the people I know back home have been snorting or smoking the stuff since high school. A few of my friends have been going in and out of rehab for years. I definitely don't want to be like them." She clasped her hands together. "One day at a time, as they say."

Sangre reached over and placed his hand over hers. "I'm here to help you if things get tough. I do think you need to throw away the pills you have in your purse. Addiction is addiction. I don't think you want to replace one for another."

"I know. I guess I just feel like they're my security blanket when things get too hectic and out of control."

"Yeah, sometimes shit hits the fan or life just sucks. I can't say too much because I usually smoke weed when I want to chill. I don't know. I just want you to know I'm here for you."

"Thanks. Are you tense about the Satan's something?"

He chuckled. "*That* asshole MC? No fuckin' way."

"It sounded pretty intense. Are you in danger?"

"Being in an outlaw club, a brother's always in danger. It's the way our world is. I'm used to it."

"Doesn't it scare you?"

"Only if my family is threatened." He brought her hand to his lips and kissed it. "Or you."

"I'd die if anything ever happened to you. Please be safe."

"I'll be fine, babe. When you get back to LA, you watch yourself, okay? If you have a crisis or you're having a real shitty day, call me."

She blinked rapidly. "I will," her voice hitched.

For a long pause, they held each other's gaze then Sangre leaned over and kissed her soft lips. He caught a glimpse of her breasts below the deep scoop neck of her top. Arousal swept through him in a wild rush. "Let's try out the bed in your hotel room," he murmured.

She sat back and placed her purse on the table, a slow smile spreading over her face. "Let's go."

THE CROWD WENT crazy for Iris Blue, and pride swelled in Sangre's chest. *I'm gonna miss you, babe.* A smack on his back tore his focus away from Isla as she bowed on the stage.

"Damn good show, bro. She had the crowd eatin' outta her hand," Army said as he gazed at Sangre with glassy eyes. "Just damn fuckin' good. We need to celebrate." He swayed a bit and grabbed onto Sangre's arm.

"We're all going to The Rifleman's Lounge. You wanna come with Isla?" Eagle said.

"Yeah. I'm sure she'll be down for it."

After Iris Blue finished moving their equipment off the stage, Isla came over to him. She'd given him a VIP pass so he could go behind stage. Her cheeks were red, her face had a sheen, and her hair was wild and tangled from head-banging. He yanked her to him and kissed her, feeling the rapid beat of her heart as his tongue claimed the wine-sweet darkness of her mouth.

"You fuckin' rocked up there, babe. There's no way the record company isn't gonna sign your band," he said against her lips.

"I hope so. The guys *really* want it."

"So do you," Benz said, coming up behind her.

Sangre watched her eyes dart around until they rested on the ground. "Of course I do. I think we have a good chance."

"We fuckin' killed it out there. Damn! Doing this all the time is what I want. It's gonna be awesome touring with national bands all the time. The label said that if they sign us we can get on shows with Megadeth, Suicidal Tendencies, and a whole shit load of other big bands. That would be the life." Benz took out a cigarette and lit it.

For a split second, Sangre saw panic skate across Isla's face but then it was gone. "The brothers are going to party at a bar and asked us to join them."

"We got our own party goin'," Benz said.

Sangre took a step toward the rocker, but Isla tugged him back. "I'm going with Sangre tonight. Arsen's already hooked up with a woman, and Melody and Gage are going to a concert at one of the clubs. I don't know what Jac's doing."

"He's probably got his tongue halfway down a chick's throat." Benz laughed. "Go enjoy yourself. We got a lot of time to party when we're on tour." He flashed a smug look at Sangre then hurried away.

"That sonofabitch is just aching for a beatdown." The muscles in his jaw tightened.

"Don't let him spoil our night," Isla said, running her hand up and down his arm. Her touch was so soft, so soothing, that the tension began to seep out of him.

Soon they were at The Rifleman Lounge drinking beer, eating hot wings, and talking. For the first couple of hours, he talked bikes with his fellow brothers while Isla hung out with Raven, Hailey, Chelsea, and some of the old ladies from the Insurgents—Cara, Kimber, Belle, and Kylie.

As the group got drunker, Sangre led Isla to a booth and slipped in next to her. He snaked his arm around her waist and crushed his mouth on hers while his free hand cupped and squeezed her tits.

Suddenly, Crow's voice, hard and full of hate, cut through Sangre's desire. He jumped away from Isla at the same time a loud crash rose above the din of voices. He slid out of the booth and saw a Satan's Piston punch Crow in the face. It was like a lit match dropped into a box of fireworks: chaos broke out.

"What's happening?" Isla said, climbing out of the booth.

Sangre pushed her under the table. "Stay there. Don't fuckin' move until I get back. Go as close as you can to the wall." He grabbed a couple of bucket chairs and put them in front of the table, locking her in.

"Sangre," her voice quivered.

He bent down low and reached for her hand then kissed it. "Just don't get out. I'll be back. Promise."

"Sangre, don't go. What if you get killed? Please don't go."

"I gotta go. My club's under fire. I'll be back." There was nothing he wanted to do more than take her away from the violence that had erupted, but he couldn't—his brothers needed him.

Sangre rushed into the brawl with fists punching and legs kicking.

Citizens screamed and scurried under tables and behind the bar as the Satan's Piston's, Night Rebels, and Insurgents duked it out. One of the Pistons knocked Sangre down then kicked him hard. He rolled over to avoid another blow and managed to get to his feet in time to deflect the Piston's fist. An animal snarl clawed its way up Sangre's throat. "You fuckin' asshole!" The Piston lunged, swinging and missing and Sangre slammed him into the wall. Then he was burying punches, over and over again.

When a shot rang out, Sangre whipped his head in the direction of it and saw Jigger on the floor bleeding. Before he could react, Crow jumped on the back of the shooter, slamming a bottle over his head. Blood poured down the side of his face, and Sangre saw another Satan's Piston pull out a gun and aim it at Crow's back.

"Fuck!" Sangre screamed out as he rushed over, grabbed a chair, and threw it at the man. He kicked the gun out of the downed man's hand and was ready to stomp him with his boots when a swarm of police officers came into the restaurant.

Isla! I gotta get to her. He tried to make his way back to the booth, but three officers had his arms pulled behind his back as they cuffed him. Outside, a large group of people watched as law enforcement escorted dozens of cuffed men into a large van, carefully separating the rival MCs. As the van pulled away, his heart clenched. *I promised her I'd be back.*

"This fuckin' sucks. The goddamn Pistons started this shit and we're in the back of the fuckin' badges' van." Army's face was red.

"Cara will figure this out for us," Hawk said.

"That's right. Your ol' lady's a defense attorney," Shotgun said.

"Do you think she can get us outta here fast?" Sangre asked.

"She'll do her best, but most probably we're in until morning."

Sangre leaned his head back against the window. *Isla's probably freakin' out. Dammit! I have to talk to her.*

"Anyone know how Jigger is?" Eagle said.

"Paramedics came for him. Fuck. I hope he's okay," Sangre said, staring straight ahead.

Silence descended over them. They stopped talking. As far as they were concerned, the badges probably had the van bugged. None of them would say a word to the cops. Several of them read the name of the Piston who'd shot Jigger. They'd deal with him in their own way; he was a doomed man. Sangre's head bounced lightly against the window as the van headed to the police station.

BY THE TIME Sangre and his fellow bikers were released the following day, Isla's early evening show was over. He glanced at his phone and saw numerous missed calls and unanswered texts from her. He dialed her number as he walked toward his bike.

"Sangre. What happened to you? I was so afraid. I was …." She broke down.

Each sob was a knife wound to his heart. "Honey, I'm fine. The fuckin' badges arrested me and the others. I tried to get to you, but they nabbed me. I'm sorry I didn't come back like I said I would." Isla's staccato breaths and sniffles filled his ears. "Shh … it's all right. I'm good. I'm on my way over to the hotel. Please don't cry."

"I was just so scared. I thought you were dead."

"I know, babe. I'm coming over now." *I wanted to share the Black Hills with her. Fuck!*

When he got off the elevator, Isla was standing in the hallway. Their eyes locked and she ran to him, flinging her arms around his neck and peppering his face with kisses. He picked her up and carried her back to the room, and lowered her to the bed.

"I love you, babe," he said as he hovered over her.

"I love you so much I think I'm going to burst. I want tonight to be special. I don't know when I'll see you again."

"Let's not think about anything but us." He took her mouth in a deep, wet, claiming kiss. "I'm gonna fuck you good and hard, baby, and then I'm gonna make some sweet love to you."

No matter what happened or where they were, Isla would always be his. She captured his heart; she was part of him and always had been.

Sangre pressed his mouth against hers and breathed in each of her tiny moans and whimpers as he slowly slid his hand under her skirt.

Epilogue

One month later

THE BEACHES WENT on for miles as the mini-bus rolled along the highway. Isla stared out at the blue expanse of the Pacific Ocean, wishing she were in it, floating on her back and looking up at the psychedelic sunset. In the front of the bus, Jac listened to rock tunes as his hands gripped the steering wheel, Benz sat behind him, playing a game and cursing under his breath, Gage lay on the seats, sleeping, and Arsen held onto the back of the seats as he walked toward her.

She pretended not to notice him when he plopped down on the seat across from her.

"What the fuck's going on with you?" he said softly.

"What do you mean?" She kept her gaze on the white tips of the waves as they caressed the shore.

"You're not having a good time. You're not feeling the music. We've all noticed it. It's not really fair to the fans."

Ouch. Isla inhaled sharply. "You're right. It's not fair to the fans. I'll sort it out."

"Black Creek expects us to kick ass. You're not doing your part. Tell me what's going on with you."

Sangre's going on with me. I miss him so much it hurts. "I don't know. I guess I thought this is what I really wanted, but I don't think it is."

"It's that dude back in Alina, isn't it?"

"Yes and no. I was having doubts after we came back from our tour last year. That's why I left for a while. I needed the break to think about what I want as a musician."

"What're you guys talking about?" Benz said as he came over.

"We're just shooting the shit, dude. Go back to your game."

"Isla doesn't look like it's nothing. What the fuck's up with you?"

"I don't really like touring." *There. I said it.*

Benz jerked his head back and sank into one of the seats. "What the fuck does that mean? That's what we do. We're a band that's now on a label. We fuckin' record, do shows, and *tour.*"

"I know. I like the recording and doing shows, but not the constant touring, or the stress, or the scrutiny. I guess I'm not cut out to be a mega rockstar. I just like to write songs, sing, and perform in small places."

"Are you fuckin' serious?" Benz glared at her.

"Dude, chill. If this isn't for her then it's not," Arsen said. "It's better we find out now rather than later."

Benz's eyes bulged. "Are you saying you want to quit?" She nodded slowly. "Un-fucking-believable. So where does that leave the band?"

"I'll stay until you get another singer. I should've told you sooner, but I didn't want to blow your chances with Black Creek."

"I appreciate that," Arsen said as he took out a joint and lit it. "Now that we're on a label, we shouldn't have a problem finding a chick who wants to join."

Benz pounded the seat cushion. "It's because of that damn biker, isn't it? Are you really thinking this through? I know you. Music runs through your veins. You're not going to be able to give it up."

"You're right, Benz—music is a part of my life. I can start a band."

"In that shithole town? If you want to blow your life, go ahead and do it. I'm done with you." He slid out of the seat and headed back to the front of the bus. He looked over his shoulder. "I give you four months or less, but don't even think of wanting back in. You're officially out of Iris Blue as soon as we get back to LA." He sat down and went back to his game.

"I know I've really hurt him," Isla said softly. "I didn't mean to."

"He'll live. None of us were in tune to the way you were feeling. We kept thinking you'd get used to the life."

"I tried to, but it's just not me. I like roots. I love to write songs, and I'm pretty damn good at it. I've thought about selling some of the ones I've written that aren't in the style of Iris Blue."

"And you miss the biker dude."

She closed her eyes. "Terribly."

"I'll miss you, but the show must go on. I'll put out feelers when we get back to LA." Arsen stood up.

"I'll be with the band until you find someone. I'd never abandon you guys."

Arsen lifted his chin and walked away.

Three weeks later

WARMTH SPREAD THROUGH Isla when she saw Sangre's Harley in the parking lot of Precision Security. *I'm home.* She'd arrived in Alina the night before, and wanted to surprise him. She was happy and astounded on how fast Iris Blue found another female singer, but a tinge of sadness wove through her at the same time. The band had been her life for the past seven years, and she suspected it would take time for her to get used to not being in it. Jac, Gage, and Arsen had been great when she'd left, but Benz was so angry at her he didn't even tell her goodbye. *That hurt.* She wished they could be friends, but she didn't hold out much hope of that happening.

Isla walked down the hall to Sangre's office and knocked on the door.

"Come in," he said. His familiar gravelly voice made her tingle.

Smoothing her hair down, she took a couple of deep breaths then opened the door. "Hi, sexy." She chuckled at the shock spreading over his face.

Sangre leapt up and rushed over to her, crushing her in his arms, kissing her deeply. Isla ran her hands over his strong arms, breathed in his scent, and leaned into the kiss. *I missed this so much.*

"Why didn't you tell me you were coming?" he said between kisses.

"I wanted to surprise you."

"What a fuckin' great surprise. How long are you staying?" He slid his hands along her body, cupping them around her butt. His kisses and touch sent a carnal tingle down her spine.

"Forever."

He pulled away and shuffled back a couple of steps.

"Is the offer still open to get a place together?"

He nodded, his gaze scanning her face. "What about the band?"

"I quit."

"Won't you regret it?"

"No. I can always start a band here. Music is a part of me and just because I left Iris Blue doesn't mean it stops for me."

"But you're giving up your dream of selling out arenas."

"You're my dream, and there's no fuckin' way I'm leaving you behind again. Anyway, for me, touring and climbing to the top was way better in my dreams than in real life. I'm where I want to be."

He yanked her to him and hugged her so tight she almost couldn't breathe.

"So you're happy that I'm here?"

"Fuck, yeah, honey. I was getting ready to book a trip to LA to see you because I missed you so damn much. I love you babe, and every time I see you, I want to hold you in my arms and never let go. You're the girl that I always wanted to be with. It just took me all these years to realize it. I want you to be my old lady. I gotta get the cut ready. Damn … I didn't know you were coming."

Heat radiated through her chest. "I'd be proud to be your old lady. You've always been in my heart. Fate tore us apart and brought us back together. I love you."

"We need to get a place together. Where're you staying?"

"I'm at a small hotel downtown. We have time to find a place. As long as I'm with you I'm home."

"I feel the same." He kissed her again and led her over to his desk. "I've been burning for you since Sturgis. You're all I thought about. I want inside you real bad."

"I missed our lovemaking. I missed the way you feel inside me."

"I'm all yours. I'll never let you go. You're my passion, my love, and my life. This time, I'm in it for the long haul, baby."

"We both are. *Together*," Isla said softly.

For much of her life there had been so much noise, but with Sangre, she found her signal in all the pandemonium: She'd finally found peace in the midst of life's unpredictable chaos.

Then, ever so slowly, *she* slipped her hands under his shirt, her gaze locked to his, and she glided her fingers over his taut muscles. He sucked in a hissing breath and pushed her down on the desk.

"I'm gonna claim every inch of you, baby."

Isla had never heard sweeter words, and she spread her legs and opened her arms, welcoming him to her.

Notes from Chiah

As always, I have a team behind me making sure I shine and continue on my writing journey. It is their support, encouragement, and dedication that pushes me further in my writing journey. And then, it is my wonderful readers who have supported me, laughed, cried, and understood how these outlaw men live and love in their dark and gritty world. Without you—the readers—an author's words are just letters on a page. The emotions you take away from the words breathe life into the story.

Thank you to my amazing Personal Assistant Natalie Weston. I don't know what I'd do without you. I value your suggestions and opinions, and my world is so much saner with you in it. You make sure my world flows more smoothly, and you're always willing to jump in and help me. I appreciate the time you took in reading and offering suggestions with the book. You were a huge help in making this book ready for publication. Thanks for being there for me during the craziness of me juggling a million things at once. Your support meant so much. And a big thank you for watching out for me when I'm in writer mode and live life with blinders on. I'm thrilled you are on my team!

Thank you to my editor Lisa Cullian, for all your insightful edits, excitement with this book. You made my book shine. A HUGE thank you for your patience and flexibility with accepting my book in pieces. I never could have hit the Publish button without you. You're the best!

Thank you to my wonderful beta readers Natalie Weston. Your rock, girl! Your enthusiasm and suggestions for SANGRE: Night Rebels MC were spot on and helped me to put out a stronger, cleaner novel.

Thank you to the bloggers for your support in reading my book, sharing it, reviewing it, and getting my name out there. I so appreciate all your efforts. You all are so invaluable. I hope you know that. Without you, the indie author would be lost.

Thank you ARC readers you have helped make all my books so much stronger. I appreciate the effort and time you put in to reading, reviewing, and getting the word out about the books. I don't know what I'd do without you. I feel so lucky to have you behind me.

Thank you to my Street Team. Thanks for your input, your support, and your hard work. I appreciate you more than you know. A HUGE hug to all of you!

Thank you to Carrie from Cheeky Covers. You are amazing! I can always count on you. You are the calm to my storm. You totally rock, and I love your artistic vision.

Thank you to my proofreader, Rose, whose last set of eyes before the last once over I do, is invaluable. I appreciate the time and attention to detail you gave to my book. Thanks for putting up for me with this book when things were crazy in my world. Without your support and flexibility, I don't know what I would have done.

Thank you to Ena and Amanda with Enticing Journeys Promotions who have helped garner attention for and visibility to the Night Rebels MC series. Couldn't do it without you!

Thank you to the readers who continue to support me and read my books. Without you, none of this would be possible. I appreciate your comments and reviews on my books, and I'm dedicated to giving you the best story that I can. I'm always thrilled when you enjoy a book as much as I have in writing it. You definitely make the hours of typing on the computer and the frustrations that come with the territory of writing books so worth it.

And a special thanks to every reader who has been with me since "Hawk's Property." Your support, loyalty, and dedication to my stories touch me in so many ways. You enable me to tell my stories, and I am forever grateful to you.

You all make it possible for writers to write because without you reading the books, we wouldn't exist. Thank you, thank you! ♥

SANGRE: Night Rebels Motorcycle Club (Book 6)

Dear Readers,

Thank you for reading my book. I hope you enjoyed the sixth book in my new Night Rebels MC series as much as I enjoyed writing Sangre and Isla's story. This gritty and rough motorcycle club has a lot more to say, so I hope you will look for the upcoming books in the series. Romance makes life so much more colorful, and a rough, sexy bad boy makes life a whole lot more interesting.

If you enjoyed the book, please consider leaving a review on Amazon. I read all of them and appreciate the time taken out of busy schedules to do that.

I love hearing from my fans, so if you have any comments or questions, please email me at chiahwilder@gmail.com or visit my facebook page.

To receive a **free copy of my novella**, *Summer Heat*, and to hear of **new releases**, **special sales**, **free short stories**, and **ARC opportunities**, please sign up for my **Newsletter** at http://eepurl.com/bACCL1.

Happy Reading,

Chiah

Wheelie's Challenge

Coming June 2018

A member of the Insurgents MC, Wheelie is a chick magnate. Having a ripped body, mesmerizing tats, and a boyish grin, he can have any woman he wants. Except for one: Sofia. Ever since he laid eyes on her, he was taken in by her sparkling eyes, her sweet laugh, and her pretty face.

There's just one very big problem: she belongs to another Insurgent.

He knows that means she's off-limits, but he can't get her out of his mind.

The memory of their kiss consumes him.

He now knows how soft and perfect she is.

Pursuing her will get him kicked out of the brotherhood, and the club is his life. He can't betray another brother even if he's a cruel, cocky jerk. He has to be strong, but the more time he spends with Sofia the more tempting it is to cross the line.

Sofia can't get the handsome biker out of her mind. Married to Tigger, she is unhappy and tired of his cruelty and manipulation. She longs to be in the strong arms of Wheelie, but she knows what the consequences are for him if they give in to their desire.

Tigger made Sofia his old lady years ago and she knows he will never let her go. If she ever leaves him, she has no doubt that he will kill her. He's told her that more times than she can count. Is she willing to risk her life and Wheelie's in order to be happy?

Wheelie's fortitude is waning, and he wants nothing more than to claim Sofia and make her his even if that means going against another brother.

Will he be able to turn his back on the Insurgents MC without any regrets? Is he prepared to love and protect Sofia from the demons of her past and present? Will Tigger make sure Sofia and Wheelie never get their happily ever after?

The Insurgents MC series are standalone romance novels. This is Wheelie's story. This book contains violence, abuse, strong language, and steamy/graphic sexual scenes. It describes the life and actions of an outlaw motorcycle club. HEA. No cliffhangers. The book is intended for readers over the age of 18.

Other Books by Chiah Wilder

Insurgent MC Series:

Hawk's Property
Jax's Dilemma
Chas's Fervor
Axe's Fall
Banger's Ride
Jerry's Passion
Throttle's Seduction
Rock's Redemption
An Insurgent's Wedding
Outlaw Xmas
Insurgents MC Romance Series: Insurgents Motorcycle Club Box Set (Books 1 – 4)
Insurgents MC Romance Series: Insurgents Motorcycle Club Box Set (Books 5 – 8)

Night Rebels MC Series:

STEEL
MUERTO
DIABLO
GOLDIE
PACO

Steamy Contemporary Romance:

My Sexy Boss

Find all my books at: amazon.com/author/chiahwilder

I love hearing from my readers. You can email me at chiahwilder@gmail.com.

Sign up for my newsletter to receive a FREE Novella, updates on new books, special sales, free short stories, and ARC opportunities at http://eepurl.com/bACCL1.

Visit me on facebook at facebook.com/AuthorChiahWilder

Printed in Great Britain
by Amazon